D0560753

MERCURY
radio arts

ALSO BY GLENN BECK

FICTION

The Christmas Sweater

The Christmas Sweater: A Picture Book

NONFICTION

Arguing With Idiots: How to Stop Small Minds and Big Government

Glenn Beck's Common Sense: The Case Against an Out-of-Control Government, Inspired by Thomas Paine

An Inconvenient Book: Real Solutions to the World's Biggest Problems

The Real America: Messages from the Heart and Heartland

THE OVERTON WINDOW

GLENN BECK

with contributions from
Kevin Balfe, Emily Bestler, and Jack Henderson

Doubleday Large Print Home Library Edition

THRESHOLD EDITIONS – MERCURY RADIO ARTS

New York London Toronto Sydney

This Large Print Edition, prepared especially for Doubleday Large Print Home Library, contains the complete, unabridged text of the original Publisher's Edition.

THRESHOLD EDITIONS / MERCURY RADIO ARTS
A Division of Simon & Schuster, Inc.
1230 Avenue of the Americas
New York, NY 10020

This book is a work of fiction. Names, characters, places, and incidents either are products of the author's imagination or are used fictitiously. Any resemblance to actual events or locales or persons living or dead is entirely coincidental.

Copyright © 2010 by Mercury Radio Arts, Inc.

All rights reserved, including the right to reproduce this book or portions thereof in any form whatsoever. For information address Threshold Editions Subsidiary Rights Department, 1230 Avenue of the Americas, New York, NY 10020

THRESHOLD EDITIONS and colophon are trademarks of Simon & Schuster, Inc.

Manufactured in the United States of America

ISBN 978-1-61664-374-4

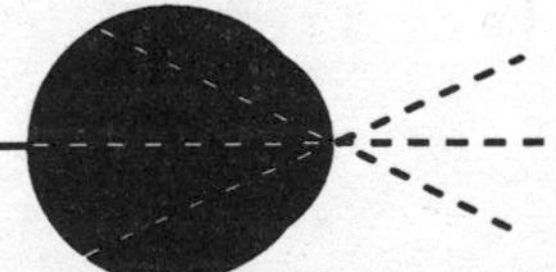

This Large Print Book carries the Seal of Approval of N.A.V.H.

DEDICATION

Faith: To David Barton, a man who knows that the answers were left everywhere in plain sight by our Founders.

Hope: To Marcus Luttrell, a man who has shown us all what it really takes to never quit.

Charity: To Jon Huntsman, Sr., the man I hope to be someday. You are a giant in a world that seems increasingly small.

Never give up, never give in.

ACKNOWLEDGMENTS

Special thanks to . . .

All of the **VIEWERS, LISTENERS, AND READERS,** including the Glenn Beck **INSIDERS.** We're not racist and we're not violent . . . we're just not silent anymore.

All my **PARENTS;** my wife, **TANIA;** and my wonderful **CHILDREN** for their continued love and support, even when I'm up at 3 A.M. working on projects like this one.

CHRIS BALFE, KEVIN BALFE, STU BURGUIERE, JOE KERRY, PAT GRAY, and all of the other remarkable people behind the scenes at **MERCURY RADIO**

ARTS for never laughing at my ideas (at least not to my face).

JACK HENDERSON for pouring his heart and soul into this project. And to Jack's wife, **LORI,** for letting him.

EMILY BESTLER, a world-class editor and, more important, a world-class person. Thanks for getting what this is really all about. And to **LOUISE BURKE, MITCHELL IVERS, CAROLYN REIDY, LIZ PERL, ANTHONY ZICCARDI,** and everyone else at **SIMON & SCHUSTER** for continuing to help turn my dreams into reality.

PATRICIA BALFE, for sharing her love of thrillers and mysteries with all of us. I realize I'm no David Baldacci or Robert Parker, but I still hope this book costs you some precious sleep.

Everyone at **PREMIERE** and **CLEAR CHANNEL,** including **MARK MAYS, JOHN HOGAN, CHARLIE RAHILLY, DAN YUKELSON, JULIE TALBOTT,** and **DAN METTER,** who have helped bring the radio program to more listeners then we've ever had before.

All of my friends at **FOX NEWS,** including **ROGER AILES, BILL SHINE, SUZANNE SCOTT, JOEL CHEATWOOD, TIFFANY**

SIEGEL, BILL O'REILLY, NEIL CAVUTO, along with my extraordinary **STAFF** that has helped me purchase almost every chalkboard in the greater New York City area.

My agent, **GEORGE HILTZIK,** who "doesn't do content" yet still loves to give me his opinion on every piece of content we create.

All of my friends, partners and coworkers who support me both personally and professionally, including **KRAIG KITCHIN, BRIAN GLICKLICH, MATTHEW HILTZIK, JOSH RAFFEL, JON HUNTSMAN SR., DUANE WARD, STEVE SCHEFFER, DOM THEODORE, SCOTT BAKER, RICHARD PAUL EVANS, GEORGE LANGE, RUSSELL M. BALLARD,** along with **ALLEN, CAM, AMY, MARY** and the whole team at **ISDANER.**

EVERYONE ELSE who has fallen victim to my ADD—sorry, I focused on this page for as long as I could.

A NOTE FROM THE AUTHOR

I've been a fan of thrillers for many years. While nonfiction books aim to enlighten, the goal of most thrillers is to entertain. But there is a category of novels that do both: "faction"—completely fictional books with plots rooted in fact, and that is the category I strived for with *The Overton Window*.

As you become immersed in the story, certain scenes and characters will likely feel familiar to you. That is intentional, as this story takes place during a time in American history very much like the one we find ourselves living in now. But while many of the facts embedded in the plot are true (see the afterword for details), the scenarios I create as a result of those facts, along with the way things are tied together and the conclusions that are drawn, are entirely fictional.

Let's hope they stay that way.

I know this book will be controversial; anything that causes people to think usually is. In this case, I hope that you are forced not only to think, but also to research, read history, and ask questions outside of your comfort zone. It will ultimately be up to each of us to search out our own truths.

While this may go without saying even once, I feel the need to say it *again:* This is a work of fiction. As such some of the characters in this book express opinions that I not only disagree with, but vehemently oppose. I included them in the story because these views, like them or not, are part of the current American dialogue. Ignoring them, or pretending that radical ideas don't exist in society, does all of us a great disservice. Silencing voices or opinions only pushes them to the shadows and darkness, where they can fester and grow even stronger.

You may also notice that the words *Re-*

publican or *Democrat* rarely appear in this book, and when they do, it's in an equally unflattering light. We also never meet the president of the United States or learn what party he or she is affiliated with. Those were conscious decisions, and it reflects the fact that what is happening to our country is not about a political party or a particular person, it is about a course of destruction that we have been pursuing at various speeds for the last century. Every day that we scream *"Where were you four years ago?"* or *"It's your party's fault and not mine!"* or *"I didn't vote for him!"* is a day we move closer to the end of America—or at least the America our Founders envisioned.

As I write this introduction, weeks before this book will even go on sale, I already know that my critics will be fierce and unforgiving. They will accuse me of being every kind of conspiracy theorist they can invent—and they will base it all on the plot of a novel that they likely never even read.

Fortunately, none of this is about me. It never has been. I've been called every hateful thing there is to call someone and I can handle it. But when all is said and done and people look back at this time in the history of our great country, there's only one thing I hope that everyone, critics and fans alike, call me . . .

Wrong.

Enjoy the book; I hope that it costs you as much sleep reading it as it cost me creating it.

Freedom had been hunted round the globe;
reason was considered as rebellion;
and the slavery of fear had made men afraid to think.
But such is the irresistible nature of truth,
that all it asks, and all it wants,
is the liberty of appearing.

—THOMAS PAINE,
The Rights of Man, 1791

PROLOGUE

Eli Churchill was a talker. Once he got rolling it was unusual for him to stop and listen, but now a distant noise had him concerned.

"Hold on," he whispered.

He cradled the pay-phone receiver against his shoulder, glanced down the narrow, rutted Mojave dirt road he'd traveled to get here, and then up the long, dark way in the other direction.

In this much quiet your ears could play tricks on you. He could have sworn that there'd been a sound out of place, like the snap of a stalk of dried grass underfoot, even though no other human being had any business being within twenty miles of where he stood, but he couldn't be sure.

The moon was bright and his eyes were well adjusted to the darkness. He didn't see anyone, but with the kind of guys Eli was worried about, you really never do.

When he put the phone back to his ear an automated message was playing; the phone company wanted another payment to allow the call to continue. He worked his last six quarters from their torn paper roll and dropped them one by one into the coin slot.

He had just three minutes left. In a way, it was ironic. After years of planning, he'd brought all the evidence he needed to back up his story, but not nearly enough change to buy the time to tell it.

"Are you still there, Beverly?"

"Yes." The signal in the phone was weak and the woman on the other end sounded tired and impatient. "With all due respect, Mr. Churchill, I need for you to get to the point."

"I will, I will. Now where was I . . ." As he riffled through his pile of photocopies a couple of the loose papers got caught up in a gust and went floating off into the night.

"You were talking about the money."

"Yes, good, okay. Two-point-three trillion dollars is what we're talking about. Do you know how much that is? From sea level that's a stack of thousand-dollar bills that would reach to outer space and back with thirty miles to spare.

"That's how much Don Rumsfeld told the nation was unaccounted for in late summer of 2001. Don't you see? Two-point-three trillion dollars is three times the amount of all the U.S. hard currency in circulation. You can't misplace that much money. That's not an accounting error, that's organized crime."

"Mr. Churchill, you said in your message that you had something to tell me that I hadn't heard before—"

"I know where they spent that money. Or at least some of it."

A brief rush of static came and went on the line. "Go on."

"I've seen the place, one of the places where they're getting ready for something—something big—planning it out, you know? I got a job inside in maintenance, as a cleanup man. They thought I was just a janitor, but I had the run of the place overnights.

"I saw what they're planning to do. They're building a structure." He checked his notes to make sure he was getting it right. "Not like a building, but like a political and economic and social structure. They've been working on it for a long, long time. Decades. When they collapse the current system, this new one they've put together will be all that's left."

"I'd like to meet with you, Mr. Churchill," the woman said. "Where are you right now?"

"I can't tell you on the phone . . ."

"Say that again. You're fading in and out."

The dry desert wind had been steady and cold since he'd arrived, but he noticed now that it had died down to almost nothing.

"They're changing the books so that in a generation from now almost nobody will remember what this country used to be. They've got the economy set up to fall like a house of cards whenever they're ready to tap the first one at the foundation. They've got the controlled media all lined up and ready to carry out their PR campaign. And they've got people so indebted and mind-controlled and unprepared, they'll turn to anybody who says he's got the answer."

"Where can I meet with you, Mr. Churchill?"

"We don't have the time; just listen now. They're going to stage something soon to get it all started. Just like that two-point-three trillion dollars that's missing, there are eleven nuclear weapons unaccounted for in the U.S. arsenal, and I've seen two of them—"

A glint of brilliant red light on the wall of the booth caught his attention. He turned, as the man behind him had known that he would, and let the phone drop from his hand.

Eli Churchill had enough time left to begin a quiet prayer but not enough to end it. His final appeal was interrupted by a silenced gunshot, and a .357 semi-jacketed hollow point was the last thing to go through his mind.

PART ONE

"It is the *power* which dictates, dominates; the materials yield. Men are clay in the hands of the consummate leader."

—Woodrow Wilson in *Leaders of Men*

CHAPTER 1

Most people think about age and experience in terms of years, but it's really only moments that define us. We stay mostly the same and then grow up suddenly, at the turning points.

His life being pretty sweet just as it was, Noah Gardner had devoted a great deal of effort in his first twenty-something years to avoiding such defining moments at all costs.

Not that his time had gone entirely wasted. Far from it. For one thing, he'd spent a full decade building what most guys would call an outstanding record of success with the ladies. Good-looking, great job, fine education, puckishly amusing and even clever when he put his mind to it, reasonably fit and trim for an office jockey, Noah had all the bona fide credentials for a killer eHarmony profile. Since freshman year at NYU he'd rarely spent a weekend night alone; all he'd had to do was keep the bar for an evening's companionship set at only medium-high.

As he'd rounded the corner of age twenty-seven and stared the dreaded number thirty right in the face, Noah had begun to realize something about that medium-high bar: it takes two to tango. While he'd been aiming low with his standards in the game of love, the women he'd been meeting might all have been doing exactly the same thing. Now, on his twenty-eighth birthday, he still wasn't sure what he wanted in a woman but he knew what he didn't want: arm candy. He was sick of it. Maybe, just maybe, it was time to consider thinking about getting serious.

It was in the midst of these deep ruminations on life and love that the woman of his dreams first caught his eye.

There was nothing remotely romantic

about the surroundings or the situation. She was standing on tiptoe, reaching up high to pin a red, white, and blue flier onto a patch of open cork on the company bulletin board. And he was watching, frozen in time between the second and third digits of his afternoon selection at the snack machine.

Top psychologists tell us in *Maxim* magazine that the all-important first impression is set in stone within about ten seconds. That might not sound like much, but when you count it off it's a long damn time for a guy to stare uninvited at a female coworker. By the four-second mark Noah had made three observations.

First, she was hot, but it was an aloof and effortless hotness that almost double-dared you to bring it up. Second, she wasn't permanent staff, probably just working as a seasonal temp in the mailroom or another high-turnover department. And third, even in that lowly position, she wasn't going to survive very long at Doyle & Merchant.

They say you should dress for the job you want, not the job you have. That's especially true in the public relations business, considering that that's where appearance *is* reality. Apparently the job this girl wanted was head greeter at the Grateful Dead Cultural Preservation Society. But that wasn't quite right; she didn't strike him as a wannabe hipster or a retro-sixties flower child. It was more than the clothes, it was the whole picture, the way she carried herself, like a genuine free spirit. An appealing vibe, to be sure, but there was really no place for that sort of thing—neither the outfit nor the attitude—in the buttoned-up world of top-shelf New York City PR.

At about five seconds into his first impression, something else about her struck him, and he completely lost track of time.

What struck him was a word, or, more precisely, the meaning of a word: *line*. More powerful than any other element of design, a *line* is the living soul of a piece of art. It's the reason a simple logo can be worth tens of millions of dollars to a corporation. It's the thing that makes you believe that a certain car, or a pair of sunglasses, or the cut of a jacket can make you into the person you want to be.

The definition he'd received from an artist friend was rendered not in words but in a picture. Just seven light strokes of a felt-tip marker on a blank white page and before his eyes had appeared the purest essence of a woman. There was nothing lewd about it, but it was the sexiest drawing Noah had ever seen in his life.

And that is what struck him. There it was at the bulletin board, that same exquisite line, from the toes of her sandals all the long, lovely way up to her fingertips. Unlikely as it must seem, he knew right then that he was in love.

CHAPTER 2

"Can I help you with that?"

Noah's opener, not one of his smoothest, was punctuated by the *thunk* of his Tootsie Roll into the metal tray of the candy machine.

She paused and glanced across the otherwise deserted break room. It was a cool, dismissive gaze that took him in with a casual down-and-up. Without looking away she hooked a nearby footstool with her toe and dragged it close, stepped up onto it, and then went back to pinning her flier in place high up on the corkboard. The gesture made it clear that if all he could offer was a few extra inches off the floor, she would somehow find a way to live without him.

Fortunately, Noah was blessed with a blind spot for rejection; she'd winged him, sure, but he wasn't nearly shot down. He smiled and, even at a distance, imagined he could see just a hint of dry amusement in her profile as well.

Something about this woman defied a traditional chick-at-a-glance inventory. Without a doubt all the goodies were in all the right places, but no mere scale of one to ten was going to do the job this time. It was an entirely new experience for him. Though he'd been in her presence for less than a minute, her soul had locked itself onto his senses, far more than her substance had.

She hardly wore any makeup, it seemed, nothing needed concealment or embellishment. Simple silver jewelry, tight weathered jeans on the threadbare outer limits of the company's casual-Friday dress code, everything obviously chosen and worn for no one's approval but her own. A lush abundance of dark auburn hair pulled back in a loose French twist and held in place by two crisscrossed number-two pencils. The style was probably the work of only a few seconds but it couldn't have been more becoming if she'd spent hours at a salon.

A number of unruly strands had escaped confinement in the course of the workday. These liberated chestnut curls framed a handsome face made twice as radiant by the mysteries surely waiting just behind those light green eyes.

He walked nearer, reading over her flier as she pressed a final pushpin into its upper corner. It was an amateurish layout job but someone had taken the time to hand-letter the text in a passable calligraphy. The heading was a pasted-on strip of tattered, scorched parchment that looked like it had been ripped from the original draft of the U.S. Constitution.

We the People

If you love your country but fear for its future,

join us for an evening of <u>truth</u> that will open your eyes!

Guest speakers include:
Earl Matthew Thomas—1976 U.S. Presidential candidate (L) and bestselling author of ***Divided We Fall***
Joyce McDevitt—New York regional community liaison, **Liberty Belles**
Maj. Gen. Francis N. Klein—former INSCOM commanding general (ret. 1984), cofounder of **GuardiansOfLiberty.com**
Kurt Bilger—Tri-state coordinator, **Sons of the American Revolution**
Beverly Emerson—Director emeritus, **Founders' Keepers**
Danny Bailey—The man behind the YouTube phenomenon ***Overthrow***, with 35,000,000 views and counting!

Bring a friend, come lift a glass, and raise your voice for liberty!
www.FoundersKeepers.com

The date, time, and location of the meeting were printed underneath.

"This event, it's happening tonight?" Noah asked.

"Congratulations, you can read." She was moving some other bulletins and notices, repinning them elsewhere to give her announcement a bit more prominence.

"Maybe you should have posted that last week. People make plans—"

"Actually," she said, finishing her rearrangement, "this was just an afterthought. I don't really expect anyone here to be all that interested."

"No?"

"No."

"Why not?"

She turned, a little taller than eye level from the summit of her stepstool. Close-up now and face-on, she had a forthrightness that was every bit as intriguing as it was disquieting.

"Do you really want to know?"

"Yes, I really want to know."

"All you PR people do is lie for a living," she said. "The truth is just another story to you."

He felt an automatic impulse to mount a defense, but then swallowed it before he could speak. In a way she was absolutely right. In fact, what she'd just said was an almost perfect layman's translation of the company's mission statement, all weasel words aside.

Seemed like an excellent time to change the subject.

"I'm Noah," he said.

"I know. I sort your mail." The following details were blithely enumerated, thumb to fingertips, summing him up neatly on the digits of a single hand. "Noah Gardner. Twenty-first floor, northwest corner office. Vice president as of last Thursday. And a son of a . . . big shot."

"Wow. For a second I wasn't sure where you were going with that last one."

"Your dad owns the place, doesn't he?"

"He owns a lot of it, I guess. Hey, I have to confess something."

"I'll bet you do."

"You haven't told me your name yet," Noah said, "and I've been trying to read it off your name tag, but I'm worried that you'll get the wrong idea about where I'm looking."

"Go for it. I'm not shy."

On their way down, his eyes wandered only twice, and only briefly. He caught a glimpse of a small tattoo, finely drawn and not quite hidden by the neckline of her top. All that was visible was an edge of the outstretched wing of a bird, or maybe it was an angel. And a necklace lay against her smooth pale skin, a little silver cross threaded on a delicate wheat chain.

Her ID was clipped low along the V of her pullover sweater, which fit as though it had been lovingly crocheted in place that very morning. The badge itself was a temporary worker's tag, only one notch above a guest pass. She was smiling in the photo, but a real smile, the kind that made you want to do something worthy just so you could see it again.

"Molly Ross," he said.

She tipped his chin back up with a knuckle.

"This is fascinating and all, Mr. Gardner, but I need to go and service the postage meter."

"Just wait a second. Will you be at this meeting tonight?"

"Yeah, I sure will."

"Good. Because I'm going to try to make it there myself."

She looked at him evenly. "Why?"

"Why do you think? I'm very patriotic."

"Really."

"Yes, I am. *Very* patriotic."

"That reminds me of a joke," Molly said.

"Noah comes home—Noah from the Bible, you know?"

He nodded.

"So Noah comes home after he finally got all the animals into the ark, and his wife asks him what he's been doing all week. Do you know what he said to her?"

"No, tell me."

Molly patted him on the cheek, pulled his face a little closer.

"He said, 'Honey, now I herd everything.'"

She stepped down to the floor, scooted the stool back to where it had been, and headed for the hallway.

"Don't forget your candy bar," she added, over a shoulder.

Despite his normally ready wit, the door to the break room had hissed closed and clicked behind her long before a single sparkling comeback came to mind.

CHAPTER 3

Classified: TS-CCO//ORCON

"Constitutionalists," Extremism, the Militia Movement, and the Growing Threat of Domestic Terrorism

Executive Summary

As the Administration continues to be tested by economic, social, and political challenges unprecedented in our country's history, the rise of radical/reactionary organizations and the accompanying dangers of "patriotic rebellion," virulent hate-speech, and homegrown terrorism must now be acknowledged as a major threat to national security.

With this clear and present danger in mind, it is our recommendation that contingency plans be developed (using data from previous exploratory actions [e.g., Ops. REX-84] and in accordance with HSPD-20 / NSPD-51) with the following objectives:

1. Identification

Educate law enforcement and enlist the populace in a program designed to profile, identify, and report individuals and groups engaging in suspect behaviors, protests/advocacy, distribution of inciting literature, and/or evidencing support of issues that are known "red flags":*

—Militant anti-abortion or "pro-life" organizers / "Army of God" / home-schoolers

—Anti-immigration / "border defenders" / NAU alarmists / Minutemen / "Tea Parties"

—Militia organizations / military reenactors / disenfranchised veterans / survivalists

—Earth First / Earth Liberation Front /

"green anarchists" / seed-bankers
—Tax resisters / "End the Fed" proponents / IRS/WTO/IMF/World Bank protesters
—Anti-Semitic rhetoric: Bilderberg Group / CFR / Trilateral Comm. / "New World Order"
—Third-party political campaigns / secessionists / state sovereignty proponents
—Libertarian Party / Constitution Party / "patriot movement" / gun rights activists
—"9/11 Truth" / conspiracy theorists / Holocaust deniers / hate radio/TV/Web/print
—Christian Identity / White Nationalists / American Nazi Party / "free speech" umbrella

2. **Classification / isolation / aggressive watchlisting**

Classify identified individuals and groups based on updated DHS threat-level criteria.† Aggressively deploy surveillance, law enforcement tactics (e.g., "knock-and-talk," "sneak & peek," checkpoints, exigent search & seizure), and other available preventive and punitive measures / resources (e.g., No-Fly / No-Buy list) as appropriate to scale.

3. Detention / rendition / interrogation / prosecution

The extralegal practice of indefinite preventive detention / enhanced interrogation / rendition of nonmilitary enemy combatants has been normalized in the public perception, at least to a serviceable extent. The precedent has been established and remains supported by a neutral-to-positive portrayal in the mainstream media. However, with U.S. citizens suddenly in the news in the place of al-Qaeda terrorists, some level of psychological resistance must be anticipated and then defused when it arises. It is the opinion of the committee that such a reflexive populist reaction would prove to be a major obstacle to progress. In fact, absent some catastrophic and catalyzing event (on the order of a Pearl Harbor / 9/11 attack), there is a potential that the government's reasonable actions in this critical area may be met with significant public outrage and even active sympathy and misguided support for these treasonous/seditious elements and their hate-based objectives.

*This list is provided as a representative sample, and is far from comprehensive. See Appendix R, pp. a321.

†See Appendix N, subsection 10.3.

cont'd

"I think I've read quite enough."

Arthur Isaiah Gardner closed his copy of the new client's binder, placed it carefully on the conference room table, and then slid it a precise few inches forward, to a spot just outside his circle of things that mattered.

Noah had grown up with a healthy dread of this gesture but, in more recent years, he'd come to appreciate its versatility. As an all-purpose expression of deep fatherly disappointment it worked just as well for a prep-school report card as it did for a disastrously leaked presidential briefing document set to splash on the front page of Sunday's *Washington Post*.

The old man breathed a shallow, weary sigh and stood at his place, looking every bit as elder-statesmanly as he did in the portrait that loomed over the main lobby downstairs. That oil painting was the closest that most of D&M's four-hundred-odd employees ever got to their company's patriarch. When he wasn't traveling he kept to his office, and his office had an elevator all its own.

"Actually, Mr. Gardner, I think the team would be well served by reviewing—"

"Who spoke?"

Noah's father hardly ever expressed his anger directly anymore. Not like the olden days; his legendary temper had refined with age and in the past ten years it was a rare thing to hear him even raise his voice. The venom was all still there, but it had been distilled and purified to the point that its victims often failed to notice the sting of the lethal injection. "Who spoke?" was uttered with genuine wonder, as though the old man had been addressing a cage full of laboratory rats when suddenly one in the back had raised his little pink paw with a question.

The room fell dead silent.

"I did." It was an older man at the far side of the long table, positioned in the power seat on the client side. Nice suit and a fresh, careful haircut, a touch of a rosy blush now rising in his cheeks.

"Stand up."

The man leaned back a bit in his chair, grinned sheepishly, and then let it fade away. He glanced around, seeking moral support from the others in his party, but no one met his eyes.

"I didn't mean to interrupt," he said feebly.

Arthur Gardner answered only with a slight upward motion of his open hand, reminding the man that he'd been clearly directed to get up onto his feet. A few long seconds crawled by before he complied.

"To put your busy mind at ease," the old man said, "let me assure you that the trifling problem you brought us today is already put safely to bed. The story in the *Post* has been spiked, an eager team of computer sleuths is tracking down the source of your leak, and the memorandum itself is now being thoroughly and plausibly denied by its authors and blamed on an overzealous local bureaucracy somewhere in the barren Midwest. Who will be the culprit again, Noah?"

"Illinois National Guard," Noah said.

"There. Crisis averted. All neatly handled before ten A.M. this morning by my son. Noah is a brilliant boy, if I do say so myself, though I'm sure he would agree that he hasn't yet inherited his father's taste for blood. Even so, he's more than a match for such a minor predicament."

In the midst of a sip of coffee, Noah raised his cup in mock acknowledgment of the faint praise. From the corner of his eye he saw the standing man over on the client side raise a curt index finger for attention.

"With all due respect, Mr. Gardner, that may very well be, but—"

"Enough!"

With surprising vigor for a man of seventy-four, Arthur Gardner suddenly swept the heavy binder from the table and sent it crashing into the wall. The government man stopped talking, his eyes a little wider, the rest of his face suspended in mid-syllable. Before the released papers finished fluttering to the carpet, a set of interns quietly scurried from the shadows like Wimbledon ball boys to spirit the wreckage away.

"A columnist in the *Wall Street Journal* once wrote"—Noah's father straightened his cuffs from the preceding exertion as he spoke—"that I had more money than God. I can't attest to that. I don't believe in God, and like a growing number of the world's other major economies, I no longer believe in the dollar, either. Only two things are sacred to me now. One is my time, and I'll caution all of you not to waste another second of it. The other is my legacy. It had been my wish today to present you with an opportunity to share in that, but these interruptions are making that nearly impossible. Now, if there are no further objections to deviating from your faxed agenda, I would love to continue."

No one said a word, and he nodded.

"Very well, then. In my review of that unfortunate document, along with your wider state of affairs, I was reminded of two significant events in my life. The first occurred in early 1989, when a coalition of businessmen came to me with a challenge.

"Their predecessors had sweated out a tidy little hundred-million-dollar market over the preceding century or so, and these men were happy with the success they'd inherited, but they wanted a tiny bit more. Maybe just three to five percent domestic expansion on an annual basis. So they came to me, hats in hands, and asked if I thought such a heady level of growth might somehow be within their reach. And they brought a binder with them, much like yours, full of their fears and worries and their modest little hopes and dreams."

He turned to directly address the other man still standing across the room. "Mr. Purcell, isn't it? A very slowly rising star, I understand, in our mighty Department of Homeland Security?"

A tight little nod, nothing more.

"You were so eager to guide me along earlier. A virgin whiteboard awaits there along the wall, freshly erased, with a new set of colorful markers all at your disposal. I believe we can even muster a laser pointer to help you direct our rapt attention around your fascinating illustrations. So, would you like to lead this meeting now, or will you indulge me to continue?"

A muscle tensed in Purcell's jaw but he didn't speak. After a moment he moved to return to his chair but was stopped by the slightest tic of the old man's hand. It was the sort of unspoken cue that a dog trainer might give to a spirited bitch on her first session off the choke chain.

"Stay another moment, Mr. Purcell. Help me. Ask me what it was that these men were selling, and I'll show you the path to a whole new world in which everything you want is laid out before you, ripe for the bountiful harvest." The old man walked around to the other side of the table, until the two were nearly toe-to-toe. He nodded, encouraging. "Go ahead, ask me."

When Purcell finally spoke his voice was weak and low. "What was it?"

Arthur Gardner let a smile touch the corners of his eyes.

"Oh, nothing of any value. Only water." The old man put his hand on Purcell's shoulder, gripped it warmly, and then motioned for the bewildered man to resume his seat, which he did. "Forgive me, everyone. Our colleague Mr. Purcell has graciously assisted me in a demonstration, the point of which we will return to shortly."

Projection screens began to hum down from the ceiling, gradually covering the paneled walls of the wide, round room. As the screens clicked to their stops in unison the lights dimmed to half brightness. All that remained was a circle of soft illumination that dutifully followed Arthur Gardner as he made his way back to his place.

"I'll tell you all what I told those bottled-water men, twenty years ago in this very room. If that binder is the limit of your ambitions, then you've come to the wrong place. Both sides of Madison Avenue are lined with hucksters and admen, the most backward of which can deliver such a minor achievement for an insignificant fee. Go in peace if that's all you want. But they stayed, as I hope you will, and I led them to where they stand today, with their goals not only realized, or doubled, or quadrupled, but in fact multiplied a thousandfold. And I can do the same for yours."

A bookish younger woman in the client party hesitantly raised her hand just a bit above the edge of the table, as though volunteering for a solo frontal assault on the guns of Navarone. She spoke, but only after a nod of permission from the man at the podium.

"I'm not sure we understand what you mean, Mr. Gardner," she said. "Our goals?"

"Your goals, yes. Your future. The future

of the government you serve. Which is to say, the future of this country, and the urgency to act on her behalf. And that brings us to my second story, which strangely enough continues our watery theme.

"A while ago I was vacationing abroad in Sri Lanka—what year was it now? Ah yes, 2004, just after Christmas. A servant girl came to me and woke me from the most wonderful dream. She was breathless, the poor young thing, and told me an urgent message had arrived, word of an earthquake near Sumatra, and that we needed to leave as soon as possible. Well, I had my breakfast brought in as my things were packed and an aircraft was chartered, and we all dressed for travel and then went up to the roof to await our departure.

"A wave was coming, you see. This earthquake had released the energy of half a billion atomic bombs under the ocean and a tsunami was spreading out from the epicenter at five hundred miles per hour in all directions."

He took a moment to sample his tea and then set the cup back carefully onto its saucer.

"The helicopter soon arrived and our

party began to board. It was such a beautiful morning, everything seemed as though all was right with the world, and by every appearance all the people down on the beach were completely unaware of what was coming. I wanted to stay, and so we stayed. There were teenagers surfing, families walking their dogs along the sand, or boating, or flying kites; children were searching for shells with their buckets and shovels. I couldn't look away; it was fascinating to me—the people down there either didn't know or didn't understand that something unthinkable was on its way to destroy them.

"From the roof I watched the waters slowly pull back from the beach. They all watched as well. It must have been an illusion but it seemed the sea receded halfway out to the horizon. For every one of those people who turned and ran for higher ground there were hundreds who stayed, mesmerized as their impending doom gathered strength.

"I was later told that there had been some form of warning system in place but it had failed, or that those in charge of the public safety had become so complacent that the red phones and radio alerts went unheard and unanswered. But I'll tell you what I believe.

"I believe those people stayed because they thought the fragile things they'd built would last forever. They looked at the breakwater walls and they trusted them. Nothing could breach those walls, because nothing ever had before. But when the seas came in it wasn't in the form of a wave at all, it was an uprising of Nature herself, steady and swelling and ruthless and patient, completely oblivious to the frail constructions of mankind. And it was all swept away. My holiday was cut short, and two hundred and fifty thousand people in the region lost their lives."

The old man looked to each of the attendees, one by one.

"Bear Stearns, a cornerstone firm of Wall Street founded when my father was a young man, a company whose stock had quite recently been selling at a hundred and sixty dollars a share, was bailed out by the Federal Reserve and J.P. Morgan at two dollars per share. That was the beginning, my friends. That was *your* earthquake under the sea.

"As I reviewed your situation this morning it occurred to me: you're just like those people down on the beach in Kalutara, aren't you? You're watching a world-changing disaster on the rise, and yet for some odd reason you seem to be fretting about how the American people would feel if they were to read of your perfectly justified panic in their morning newspaper. That isn't your problem at all, of course. It's not what they might think of you that should be keeping you up at night; it's what they might very well *do* to you, and to your superiors, in the aftermath of the global catastrophe that's just around the corner.

"Look at you. You're stacking sandbags when your entire coastline is about to change forever. All the while the crimes you're so worried that people will discover are still in progress. We are in the midst of what will become the most devastating financial calamity in the history of Western civilization, and just this week—please do correct me if my figures are wrong—the Congress and the administration have committed to funnel almost eight trillion dollars to the very institutions that engineered the crisis. And in your infinite wisdom you've openly placed their cronies and henchmen in charge of the oversight of this so-called economic stimulus. It's a heist, an inside job. It's been done before, of course. Social Security was the boldest Ponzi scheme in history until now. But all the bills for all those years are finally coming due, and there's not enough money in the world to pay them."

A ring of digital projectors near the ceiling awoke out of standby and the wraparound screens encircling the room came alight with an unbroken panorama of changing, flowing imagery. Charts and graphs, spreadsheets and Venn diagrams, time lines and flowcharts and nomograms, none displayed long enough to absorb, except as a blurry continuum of research and market intelligence behind the old man's words.

"Over the last century you've saddled your hapless citizens with a hundred thousand billion dollars in unsecured debt, money they'll be paying back for fifty generations if there are still any jobs to be had by then. Meanwhile you're up to your necks in misguided, escalating wars on two unforgiving fronts with no sign of the end. That's trillions more in unpayable IOUs.

"Banks are failing across the country. More banks have failed so far this year than in the whole of the last decade. Your debt-fueled economy is entering a spiraling free fall, yet your first reaction was to ignore the needs of the voting public and reward the perpetrators themselves. While foreclosures of your citizens' homes are breaking all records and unemployment is exploding in every state you've been busy dodging audits and nationalizing the mountainous gambling losses of the Wall Street elite. For heaven's sake, you nationalized *General Motors* just to get your union friends off the hook. As you know, those union pensions you just took over are severely underfunded, adding another seventeen billion dollars to your tab. Seventeen billion, I might add, that you don't have."

Arthur Gardner's silvery voice had been gathering strength until it filled the room to the rafters, point upon point with the swelling command and cadence of a tent-revival preacher calling down the Rapture.

"Just to stay afloat the government is borrowing five billion dollars every day at ever-rising interest rates from our fair-weather friends in Asia. But that will all come to an end as they see the waters receding from the beach. Sooner or later the truth will be undeniable, that these massive debts can never be repaid, and there'll be a panic, a worldwide run against the dollar, and through your actions you've ensured that the results will be fatal and irreversible.

"It's not only happening here, it's everywhere. Carroll Quigley laid open the plan in *Tragedy and Hope:* the only hope to avoid the tragedy of war was to bind together the economies of the world to foster global stability and peace. And that was done, but with unintended if predictable consequences. Instead of helping each other, these international bankers have all used their power for short-term gains, running up unimaginable debts on the backs of the public. We're all shackled together at the wrists and ankles as the ship goes down, and, once it begins, this mutually assured destruction will come on us not over months, but overnight. A depression that makes the hell of the 1930s look like heaven on Earth will sweep across this country in a tidal wave of ruin, the scale of which has never been imagined. And when that happens, who do you think the masses will come for? Here's a little hint: The people who will be held responsible are sitting around this table."

The room fell silent. The humming of the projectors was the only discernible sound.

"Yes, they will come for you. All of you. You built this system; you told them everything would be fine. It is your lies they will remember when they realize that their money is as worthless as the promises you made them. It is your deceit they will recall when they realize that the future of their children has vanished. And, trust me when I tell you, it is your faces they will picture when they realize that forty-hour weeks at minimum wage have replaced their retirements.

"How do I know all of this? Simple: When things go wrong, there must always be someone to blame; a villain, if you will. As they say in your neck of the woods, 'If you're not at the table, then you're on the menu.' If you walk out of here today with the same arrogance you came in with, then you, my friends, will all soon be the special of the day."

He paused to take them in again, a half circle of understandably pale, stricken faces lit only by the cold proofs of impending doom projected on the screens around them.

"But all is not lost," the old man said. His features softened with the tiniest hint of a knowing smile.

"Tell us what we need to do." It was the woman who'd spoken up earlier. Judging by the breathy reverence in her voice, she'd already entered the early stages of baptism into the cult of Arthur Gardner.

He stepped to a neat stack of identical folders at the near corner of the table and took the top copy in his hands. "Your answer is in here," he said. "I am a strategist, and a man of some modest renown in that sense, though in this case I'm not ashamed to admit that I'm standing on the shoulders of giants—Woodrow Wilson, Julian Huxley, Walter Lippmann, Cloward and Piven, Bernays and Ivy, Saul Alinsky. The list is long. All I've done here"—he held up the folder—"is to crystallize the vision of those who've come before me, those who dreamed of a new and sustainable progressive nationalism but never saw their dreams fully realized.

"Because we must, we *will* finally complete what they envisioned: a new framework that will survive when the decaying remains of the failed United States have been washed away in the coming storm. Within this framework the nation will reemerge from the rubble, reborn to finally take its rightful, humble place within the world community. And you," he said, looking around the table, "will all be there to lead it."

A hand went up on the far side, a question from the senior member of the party, who'd so far only listened in silence.

"Mr. Gardner," the man said. "What about the public?"

"What about them? The public has lost their courage to believe. They've given up their ability to think. They can no longer even form opinions, they *absorb* their opinions, sitting slack-jawed in front of their televisions. Their thoughts are manufactured by people like me. What about the public? Twenty years ago in this room I showed a small group of shortsighted businessmen how to sell the public the most abundant substance on the face of the earth at ten times the price of premium gasoline, the very same water that flows from their own kitchen faucets for one-tenth of a penny per gallon. That would seem unbelievable; it defies all logic and reason. Your grandparents would have called it larceny, fraud, or wanton thievery . . . and rightly so, I might add. But that experience proved one thing to me: there's a double-edged sword by which the public can be sold anything, from a three-dollar bottle of tap water to a full-scale war."

The screens winked out at once, and left behind were three tall words in black on white, dominating the room from floor to ceiling.

HOPE AND FEAR

"Do you see? If the people are simply swindled there's always a chance they might one day awaken and rebel against the crime. But we don't change their minds; we change the truth. Most people simply want to be left alone; they'll go along with anything as long as we maintain their illusions of freedom and the American way. We leverage their hopes and feed their fears, and once they believe, they're ours forever. After that they can be taken by the scruff of the neck and shown the indisputable scientific proof, with their own eyes they can read the label that says *contents drawn from a municipal water supply*, and they will only nod their sleepy heads and walk past the faucet to the vending machine. That's when you know that anything is possible.

"You!" He pointed to Mr. Purcell at the far end of the table, who flinched as though he'd just been goosed by a cattle prod. "You entered this room thinking of me as a hired hand, believing you were a master of these proceedings, and since you pay my salary, by all rights you should have been correct. Why then did you allow me, your humble employee, to overpower you, to control you, to humiliate you in front of your peers and subordinates? Why?"

When it became clear that not even a stammering answer was forthcoming the old man continued.

"Indoctrination. I made you afraid, Mr. Purcell, and in your fear you accepted *my* truth, *my* power, and you abandoned your own. The public will do the same; leave them to me. The misguided resistance that still exists will be put down in one swift blow. There'll be no revolution, only a brief, if somewhat shocking, leap forward in social evolution. We'll restore the natural order of things, and then there will be only peace and acceptance among the masses." He smiled. "Before we're done they'll be lining up to gladly pay a tax on the very air that they breathe."

Arthur Gardner walked a few steps closer to the group at the other end of the table.

"Each of you was invited here this afternoon at my suggestion. The small but serious problem you brought with you was merely a point of entry, a premise for our introduction today. That leaked document sparked a conversation that I've had with your superiors, and they with theirs and so on, about a wide-ranging plan of action that has long been in development and now awaits its execution.

"I told them that now is the time, and ultimately they concurred, with one condition. You, all of you here, are to be put in charge of enforcement—the boots on the ground, if you will. Before this new order of things can be brought forth, it was decided that you must all, unanimously, agree to protect and defend and rebuild what will remain of this country after its transformation."

On the screen behind him a quotation faded in, finely lettered as though written in the author's original hand. It took a moment but Noah soon recognized the words from *Julius Caesar*.

There is a tide in the affairs of men,
which, taken at the flood, leads
on to fortune;
Omitted, all the voyage of their life
is bound in shallows and in miseries.
On such a full sea are we now afloat,
and we must take the current when
it serves,
or lose our ventures.

The old man watched them as they read, and then he spoke again.

"Shakespeare wrote of a time of great decision, and ladies and gentlemen, that time has come. We stand at a crossroads; the civilized world stands at a crossroads. Down one path all men are created equal: equal in poverty, equal in ignorance, equal in misery. Down the other is the realization of the brightest hopes of mankind.

But not for all men; that was a brief experiment, tried and failed. Abundance, peace, prosperity, survival itself—these coveted things are reserved for the fittest, the deserving, the most courageous of us, the wisest. The visionaries."

The room was still again, and he let it stay that way for a while.

"Now," Arthur Gardner said, his voice just above a whisper, "while the tide is in our favor—come with me. You can still save yourselves, and in so doing, you can help us build a whole new world upon the ashes of the old."

CHAPTER 4

Noah stopped in the middle of the main hallway and stood there for a while, his head full of unfinished thoughts and that troubling fogginess you feel only when you've forgotten where you're going, and why.

That meeting was still going on, but without him. His father had called a break and passed him a note with a list of phone numbers and a few bullet points of instructions—one last errand to perform before he could leave for the weekend. These were apparently VIPs to be invited for the after-hours portion of the presentation, provided the first part had gone as hoped. Evidently it had.

This task he'd been given had started out strange, and then one by one the calls had only gotten stranger.

There were no names, only numbers. Each of the calls was answered before the second ring, not by a service but by a personal assistant. Every one of those phones was professionally attended after business hours on a Friday night, and probably twenty-four hours a day by the sound of it. That seemed oddly extravagant, but maybe it wasn't so unusual considering the circles in which his father was known to travel.

There'd been audible indications of a scrambler during at least four of the brief conversations, and some sort of voice-alteration gizmo on one of them. Everyone had seemed extremely wary of revealing any information about the identity of the person associated with each number, but the last one hadn't been quite careful enough.

Noah had caught a last name spoken in the background during this final call. It was a Manhattan number, a 212 area code, and the name he'd heard was an uncommon one. He'd also seen it in the newspaper earlier in the day. That call had been to the private line of the most likely nominee for the next U.S. Treasury secretary, assuming the election went as forecast.

This man was also the current president of the New York branch of the Federal Reserve. He and twenty or so others of comparable status were apparently now dropping everything and coming here, bound for a conference room where Noah's father was waiting with the previous attendees.

He walked to the southeast corner suite and keyed himself into the private kitchen used to prepare his father's meals on those days he was in town. The room was all tile and polished granite and stainless steel, larger than most of the executive offices and equipped for Arthur Gardner's personal chef.

Noah flipped on the blower over the range, lit the cooktop in back, and followed the final instruction on his list of things to do.

Destroy this paper; be certain to watch it burn.

CHAPTER 5

His errand complete, Noah resumed his drift through the halls. It was hard to say how much time had passed since he'd been ordered out of the remainder of that meeting. No clocks were allowed on the walls or the wrists at Doyle & Merchant.

It was one of the many quirks meant to remind everyone that this wasn't just another workplace. Over the decades this office had morphed into a science-fair diorama of the inside of the old man's brain, furnished with everything he liked and nothing that he didn't. Sometimes these oddities arose from an impulse or an outburst, other times from long deliberation, but once King Arthur had passed final judgment on a thing he never, ever changed his mind. The clock business happened a few years before Noah was born.

In 1978 an account executive had checked her watch during Arthur Gardner's heartwarming remarks at the company Christmas party. She'd looked up when the room got quiet and had seen in Noah's father's eyes what time it really was: time for her to find another job, in another city, in another industry. By the following Monday the unwritten no-timepiece rule was in full and permanent effect. It was only by His grace that windows were still tolerated, though access to any view of the outside world was strictly confined to the executive offices.

Noah resumed his stroll and took a meandering right turn, still without a clear destination. There wasn't a soul in the place, though some would say that in the PR business that phrase always applies.

This particular corridor was the company's walk-through résumé, a gallery of framed and mounted achievements, past to present. Press clippings, puff pieces, planted news items and advertorials, slick, crafted cover stories dating back to the 1950s, digitized video highlights running silently in their flat-screen displays. It was a hall of fame unparalleled in the industry and the envy of all competitors.

No trophy case, though; you'd never see a flashy award show for outstanding PR campaigns, God no, not for the serious stuff. It's the first rule, and one of the only: The best work is never even noticed. If the public ever sees your hand in it, you failed.

Near the beginning of the walk were the relatively small potatoes: crazy Pet Rock–style fads that had inexplicably swept the country, the yearly conjuring of must-have Christmas toys (murders had been committed for a spot in line to buy some of these), a series of manufactured boy bands and teen pop music stars, most of whom could neither carry a tune nor play an instrument. On a dare, Noah's father had once boasted that he could transform some of the century's most brutal killers into fashion statements among the peace-loving American counterculture. And he'd done it; here were pictures of clueless college students, rock stars, and Hollywood icons proudly wearing T-shirts featuring the romanticized images of Chairman Mao and Che Guevara.

Last in this section were a few recently developed pharmaceuticals that had required some imaginative new diseases to match them. Drugs weren't so very different from other products; it was all just a matter of creating the need. If you hear about restless-leg syndrome often enough, one day soon you might start to believe that you've got it. Cha-ching; another job well done.

Farther along, just past Big Tobacco, was a small exhibit devoted to the poster-child client in the world of public relations: the lottery. Fun fact: as a naïve youngster during a rare family chat at the Gardner dinner table, Noah had come up with the tagline displayed in this frame. It had been the first time he'd ever earned a pat on the head from the old man: *You can't win if you don't play.* Sure, kid. And you can't fly if you don't flap your arms.

No other product could demonstrate the essence of their work as perfectly as the lottery. The ads and jingles might remind all the suckers to play, but it was the PR hocus-pocus that kept them believing in the impossible, year after year. A fifth-grade math student could seemingly blow the lid off the whole scam: to reach even a fifty-fifty chance of winning you'd have to buy a hundred million Powerball tickets. Everybody *knows* that, but still they dream on. Take their money and give them nothing but a scrap of paper and disappointment in return, and then—and this is the key—make them line up every week to do it again. If you can pull that much wool over the eyes of the public and still sleep at night, you've got a long and rewarding career ahead of you.

Each of these PR triumphs represented a defeat for someone else, of course. That was simply the nature of the business, of all business really. The whole concept of winning requires that others lose, and sometimes they lose everything. That's just the way it had to be. A person could waste his whole life trying to work out the right and wrong of it all.

Case in point: Noah had a friend in college, not a close friend, but a self-described bleeding-heart lefty tree-hugging do-gooder friend who'd gone to work for an African aid organization after graduation. She'd kept in touch only casually, but her last sad letter had been one for the scrapbook. It turned out that after all the fund-raising and banquets and concerts and phone banks, all the food and clothing and medical supplies they'd shipped over had been instantly hijacked and sold on the black market, either by the corrupt provisional government, the corrupt rebel militias, or both. Most of the proceeds bought a Viking V58 cruiser for the yacht-deprived son of a parliament member. The rest of the money went for weapons and ammunition. That arsenal, in turn, fueled a series of sectarian genocidal massacres targeting the very starving men, women, and children whom the aid was meant for.

Back in his younger days, Noah had been quick to snatch a moral from this story: You can't fix everything, and maybe you can't fix anything at all. It's all too big, and too broken. So don't rock the boat, kid. Just count your blessings, keep your head down, and play the lucky hand that's been dealt to you. This had come as a welcome vindication for a young man who'd given up early on his own high ideals and drifted into the safe though stormy harbor of his father's business. It was a comforting answer, so long as you didn't think too hard about the questions.

And what had that woman said today? *All you PR people do is lie for a living.*

That's right, sweetheart. Well, Miss Holier-than-thou, to paraphrase the artful response of a prominent client of the firm, I guess that all depends on what the definition of *lie* is, now doesn't it? And while you're looking that up in the dictionary under L, run your uppity little finger down the column to the last word of your indictment: *living.* We all have to make one, and unless I'm mistaken, you and I both get paid with the same dirty money. The difference is, one of us isn't kidding himself.

By now he'd arrived at an alcove that showcased the truly world-class events and power players, political and otherwise, that the company had helped to invent.

A number of U.S. presidents were on display here, a nearly unbroken succession from the present and upcoming administrations all the way back to JFK. To hear the old man tell of the only two holdouts, Jimmy Carter had been too high-and-mighty to accept this sort of assistance, and Nixon had been too cheap. Republican or Democrat, it didn't matter; to the realists of modern politics, ideology was just another interchangeable means to an end.

Noah was nearly to the end of the hall when a small, unassuming case study caught his attention. There was no title or description on this one, just a silent running video, the testimony before Congress of a volunteer nurse named Nayirah al-Sabah. She was the fifteen-year-old Kuwaiti girl whose tearful story of infants being thrown from their incubators by Iraqi soldiers became a podium-pounding rallying cry in the final run-up to the 1991 Gulf War.

Undeniably moving, highly effective, and entirely fictional.

The client for this one had been a thinly veiled pro-invasion front group called Citizens for a Free Kuwait. The girl wasn't a nurse at all; she was the photogenic daughter of the Kuwaiti ambassador to the United States. The testimony had been written, produced, and directed by Arthur Isaiah Gardner, the distinguished gentleman sitting just behind her in the video.

A dull headache had begun to pound at

his temple, and Noah abruptly remembered where he'd been meaning to go: the bulletin board in the break room. He had to grab the address of that meeting of flag-waving wackos, and then finish his conversation with an attractive but naïve young woman who might need to be straightened out on a thing or two.

CHAPTER 6

"Aw, come on, man, what are we doing on Park Avenue?"

Over the years Noah had confirmed many times that there truly is such a thing as a bad night. When these doomed evenings arrive you can't avoid them. The jinx comes at you like a freight train, and by the time you're caught in the glare of those oncoming lights it's far too late to avoid the disaster. The best you can do is make your peace with doom and ride out the curse until sunrise.

If there's a bright side to all this, it's that bad nights that don't kill you can sometimes make you a little bit smarter. For instance, he'd learned that when the situation starts to go downhill it's often due to avoidable errors in judgment, always involving things you should have foreseen but didn't, and that those errors usually come in threes. A pilot will tell you the same thing; a plane crash is rarely the result of a single failure. It starts small, an innocent mistake or a bad decision that leads to another one, and then another, and before you know it you're at the bottom of a smoking hole wondering what in the hell just happened.

Take this night, for example: Noah's first mistake had been opting to hail a cab instead of waiting a few minutes for a limo from the company motor pool. Then he'd become immersed in his BlackBerry just after the ride got under way. Minutes later when he looked up, the road ahead was a sea of twinkling red brake lights. The preweekend traffic was stacked bumper to bumper as far as the eye could see. That was his second mistake.

As the windshield wipers slapped in and out of sync with the beat of some atonal Middle Eastern music blaring from the radio, the man at the wheel launched into an animated flurry of colorful epithets in his native tongue. He seemed to be deflecting all blame for the gridlock onto his GPS unit, the dispatcher, the rain, the car ahead, and especially the yellowed ivory statuette of St. Christopher glued cockeyed to the dash.

"Look, forget it, just head west." Noah rapped on the cloudy Plexiglas and caught the driver's eye in the rearview mirror. *"West."* He pointed that way, assuming a serious language barrier, and spoke with exaggerated clarity. "Get us off Park Avenue, shoot crosstown to the West Side Highway, then just take it south all the way down to Chambers Street." To ward off any protest he took a twenty from his money clip and passed it through the flip-door in the bulletproof divider. "I'm late already. Let's go now, okay? *Step on it*."

Those last three magic words were his third mistake.

The shifter slammed into reverse, the steering wheel cranked to its stop, and the engine roared. On instinct Noah turned to look behind, so it was the side of his head instead of his face that thumped into the divider as the cab lurched backward. The Lexus to the rear somehow squeaked out of harm's way with maybe an inch to spare.

They were nearly a full city block from the intersection in a solid traffic jam and there was absolutely nowhere to go, but that couldn't limit a man with this kind of automotive imagination. Apparently at whatever driving school he'd graduated from there was only one rule of the road: Anything goes, as long as you keep at least two tires on the pavement.

Noah braced himself against the roof and the door as the cab mounted the curb and surged forward at a twenty-degree tilt, half on and half off the street, threading the needle between a hot-dog cart and a candied-nut wagon on the sidewalk and the line of incredulous fellow drivers to the left. The right-side mirror clipped a corner bus shelter as the driver pulled a full-throttle, fishtailing turn onto East Twenty-third.

And then he slammed on the brakes and everything screeched to a stop.

A soldier in desert camouflage and a rain slicker was standing right in front of the cab, his left hand thrust out flat in an unambiguous command to halt. His other arm was cradling an assault rifle, which, while not exactly aimed at the cab and its innocent passenger, wasn't exactly pointed elsewhere, either. Other men in uniform came up beside the first and were directed with a muzzle-gesture to positions on either side of the taxi.

It immediately became obvious that this cabdriver had seen a military checkpoint or two in his former homeland. With no hesitation the ignition was killed and both his hands were raised where the armed men outside could see them. Noah had no such prior experience to guide him. All he felt was the Lenny's hot pastrami sandwich he'd enjoyed at lunch suddenly threatening to disembark from the nearest available exit.

Two sharp taps on the window, and through the glass he heard a single stern word.

"Out."

Noah laid his umbrella on the seat, took a deep breath, and got out.

Though the soldier he faced looked to be all of nineteen years old, his bearing was far more mature. He had a command in his eyes that made his rifle and sidearm seem completely redundant. It wasn't just the steely calm, it was readiness, a bedrock certainty that whatever might happen next in this encounter, from a perfectly civil exchange to a full-on gunfight, he and his men would be the ones still standing when all the smoke had cleared.

"Sir, I need to see your ID." The words themselves were courteous but spoken with a flat efficiency that made it clear there would be no discussion of the matter.

"Sure." Despite his earnest desire to cooperate, for several tense seconds Noah's driver's license refused to slide out of its transparent sleeve. Another man in uniform had come near and, after watching the struggle for a while, he stepped up, held open a clear plastic pouch, and gave an impatient nod. Noah dropped the entire wallet into the bag, and after another wordless prompt from the man with the rifle, emptied his remaining pockets as well. The bag was zipped closed and passed to a nearby runner, who trotted off toward an unmarked truck parked up the block.

The rain had been light and sporadic but as if on cue, now that he was outside the shelter of the car, a downpour began.

The young soldier across from him didn't

seem to take any notice of the deteriorating weather. He was watching Noah's face. It wasn't a macho stare-down, nothing of the kind. There really wasn't any engagement at all on a man-to-man level. The soldier kept his cool, stoic attention where he'd been trained to keep it, on the eyes, where the changing intentions of another first tend to show themselves.

A low roll of thunder made itself heard over the city sounds, not close by, just a deep tympani rumble off in the distance. Noah pulled his coat together, one hand clenched at the collar.

"How about this rain, huh?" he said idiotically, as if blowing some small talk was the perfect way to play this out.

No answer. Not a twitch.

He heard a *whump* and a scuffle behind and to his left. When he looked that way he saw his cabdriver being forcibly subdued with his hands held behind him, bent over the hood of the car. He started yelling a plea of some kind over and over, held facedown by one uniformed man as a second went through his pockets and two more set about searching the trunk and interior of his car.

There was a faraway siren somewhere to the south, then more of them, and soon up the street a few blocks away a noisy line of police cruisers sped through the intersection headed uptown, followed by a series of stretch SUVs, all black, late-model, identical.

Of course, that was it—both presidential candidates had flown into town today for a full weekend of campaigning in the run-up to the November election. That meant hundreds of politicians, bigwigs, and assorted hangers-on from both parties were here, too. On top of that, he seemed to recall that some emergency faction of the G-20 was meeting downtown in response to the various calamities boiling over in the financial district. Along with all those high-rollers comes high security; all the cops and evidently some division of the armed forces must be out combing the streets looking for trouble.

Times had certainly changed, seemingly overnight, though Noah hadn't yet seen anything quite as intense as this. Fourth Amendment or not, with all the fears of terrorism in recent years, the definition of probable cause could become pretty blurred around the edges. People were getting used to it by now; a law-abiding citizen could easily get stopped and frisked for taking a cell-phone video of the Brooklyn Bridge or the Empire State Building, never mind riding in a high-speed taxicab that had just jumped the curb to avoid a roadblock.

The soldier on his right touched a free hand to the side of his helmet, squinting as though listening to a weak incoming communication, and then looked up and motioned for Noah to walk with him toward the truck where his pouch of belongings had been taken earlier.

This vehicle was the size and shape of a generic UPS truck but instead of dark brown it was matte black with deep-tinted windows. At a glance the logo on the side looked official, though he didn't immediately recall any government agency to which it might belong.

Inside it was warm and dry, the interior dimly lit only by a desk lamp and the glow of computer screens arrayed around a central workstation. The man who'd escorted him left, the side panel door slid shut with a clank, and Noah was alone with a woman sitting behind a metal desk in front of him.

"Have a seat, Mr. Gardner." She was fortyish, stocky, severe, and clearly wrapped too tight, with prematurely gray hair trimmed like a motel lampshade. Some people just seem like they hatched from a pod at a certain drab midlife age and have never been a single minute younger. Sitting there was a textbook example. Her suit was dark and from the ultraconservative bargain bin, and while it wasn't a uniform, her manner suggested there might be some military discipline in her background. "I just need to ask you a few questions, and then I'm sure you can be on your way."

Noah sat in the straight-back chair across from her. "What's this about? I mean, I understand the traffic stop—"

"One second." She left-clicked the mouse on a pad to her right and a few seconds later Noah's photo appeared within an onscreen form on one of the monitors. There were still some blanks in the form but most of the information fields were already filled in.

"Now hold on a minute," he said.

"Just a few questions, all right? It's just routine, and it's required."

He blinked, and sat back. "Could you show me some identification?"

"Of course." She took out a leather wallet, flipped it open, and held it out under the desk light so he could see. No actual badge, but the gilded crest from the side of the van was there again on her card, along with her embossed name and a title of Senior Field Investigator. And then he remembered where he'd seen that logo before.

Several months earlier Doyle & Merchant had pitched for the international PR business of this company. They'd been in the market for a complete image makeover in the face of some major allegations in the news, the growing list of which ranged from plain-vanilla war profiteering, graft, and smuggling all the way up to serial rape and murder. Noah and his creative team hadn't won the account, but ever since the pitch he'd followed the developments when related stories happened to hit the Internet.

This woman, her hairdo, and her truck were from Talion, the most well-connected private military consulting firm in the foreign and domestic arsenal of the U.S. government.

"Look," Noah said, "I'm aware of who's in town tonight, and I know the whole tristate area's on red alert or whatever, but I was a passenger in a taxi with an overzealous driver, and that's it. I don't know what else I can tell you."

"Are you acquainted with this man who was driving?"

"No."

"Not at all?"

"I don't know anything about him. There are twenty thousand cabs in this city. I hailed one and he pulled over."

The woman was taking her notes on a keyboard beneath the desk with her eyes on one of the monitors. "And where were you coming from tonight?"

"From work."

"And where were you going?"

His heart rate was picking up; adrenaline will do that whether you like it or not. Before he'd been afraid, but now he was getting angry. He didn't answer right away, waiting until she acknowledged the silence and looked over to him. Then he spoke. "Do I need to call an attorney?"

"I don't see why you'd want to do that."

"Am I being detained here?"

"Well . . ."

"Am I being detained."

"No."

"So I'm free to go, then."

"I'm not sure I understand your reluctance to speak with us—"

"Thanks for everything," Noah said, and he got up. "Good night."

"Is this where you're headed this evening?"

She held out the meeting announcement from the break room that he'd folded up and brought along in his pocket.

From some lecture in his first doomed semester of pre-law at NYU, a wise bit of counsel came back very clearly: *The first thing you tell your clients when they call you from custody, innocent or guilty, is don't say a word: never, ever talk to the cops.* But for good advice to work, you've got to take it. And besides, this stiff was no cop.

"I'm just dropping in to meet someone there, and then we're going somewhere else."

"What do you know about this group, Mr. Gardner?"

"Absolutely nothing at all. Like I told you—"

"They have ties to the Aryan Brotherhood," she said, having begun to thumb through a file folder on her desk, "and the Lone Star Militia, the National Labor Committee, the Common Law Coalition, the Earth Liberation Front—"

"Hold it, wait up," Noah said. "The National Labor Committee? The National Labor Committee is a little shoestring nonprofit that busts sweatshops and child-labor operations. You want my advice, lady? You people had better update your watch list if you don't want to get laughed out of this nice truck. And, like I told you, I don't know anything about this group or what they do or who you think you've linked them to. I'm meeting someone there and then we're going somewhere else. Believe me, I wouldn't have many friends in the Aryan Brotherhood." He pointed to her computer screen. "But you've probably checked out my record by now, and you know that already."

"We know who you are, Mr. Gardner."

"By that, I think you mean you know who my father is."

"All right."

"Good. So unless there's anything else, I'm going to leave now."

She nodded, then gestured to the evidence bag of his belongings on the desk. He picked up the bag, plucked the flier from her hand, and left without another word.

As Noah hit the street the rain had subsided again to a chilly drizzle. He walked away, refilling his pockets with his things as he went. Halfway down the block he heard someone calling out behind him. It was the cabbie being manhandled toward the truck by two guys who were each at least twice his size.

Their eyes met, Noah and that driver. What he was yelling now wasn't hard to understand, probably words he'd practiced from a phrase book for some bad night that might come along when he'd need them.

Help me, my friend.

That's what he was saying, over and over in simple variations, as if maybe with the next repetition Noah would understand that this guy was in serious trouble and just needed someone to step up and vouch for him so he could get out of this mess and maybe get back to his family tonight.

But what could Noah do? You can't get involved with every unfortunate situation. It wasn't his place to intercede. For all he knew, the guy was the leader of a major terrorist cell. And besides, he was late for an appointment with a certain young woman who was in dire need of a dose of reality.

Noah turned away and kept on walking, letting the man's pleas fade away and then disappear behind him. It wasn't nearly as hard to do as it should have been.

CHAPTER 7

A lot of empty cabs had passed by on his walk downtown but Noah hadn't been able to bring himself to raise a hand and flag another one down. The gridlock was still a citywide nightmare, and despite the sporadic rainfall it just seemed like a better idea to suck it up and hoof it rather than risk another ill-fated ride. In any case, in keeping with the evening's unbroken run of bad decisions, walking was what he'd decided to do.

Eyes down, shields up, keep a brisk steady pace, and you can get almost anywhere on this island in a reasonable amount of time. Focus is the key. It's not that New Yorkers set out to be rude as they walk along; they simply want to get where they're going. With seventy thousand people coming at you per square mile, the only way to try to keep a schedule is to avoid connecting with random strangers.

But, try as you might, you can't always avoid making contact.

The look on that driver's face earlier, it hadn't really registered until Noah had fully turned his back on the guy, and by then it seemed like it was too late to turn around. It was dark enough and he'd been far enough away that the picture of that hopeful, desperate face should have been too dim to recall, but it was somehow zoomed in close and crystal clear in his memory.

Help me, my friend.

Noah took a deep breath and shook it off as he pressed on. First of all, buddy, I'm not your friend. Second, it wasn't my responsibility. And third, there is no third required. You can't take them all under your wing. Once you start trying to rescue everybody, where would it ever stop?

This sort of glib self-acquittal had worked pretty well in the past but now it left him feeling empty, and worse, guilty. And then as he forced himself to change the mental subject, he found there were some still darker things nagging at the back of his mind.

What had really happened in that meeting back at the office? And what might still be happening there now?

Noah's father had built an empire in the PR industry based almost solely on his reputation as an unrepentant firebrand, a ruthless hired gun for any cause with the cash to buy his time. He went wherever there was a fortune to be made, and those opportunities were everywhere, in good times or bad, provided a person could maintain a certain moral flexibility when scrolling through the client list.

Survey the landscape, identify the players, pick a side, build a battle plan, and execute. That's the game, and old Arthur Gardner had always played it to win. A huckster of the highest order, he could make a do-or-die conflict out of thin air and then cash in selling weapons of mass deception to either side, or, more likely, to both.

And it had long ago gone beyond Coke

versus Pepsi. Pseudoliberal Democrats versus faux-conservative Republicans, union versus management, pure-hearted environmentalists versus the evil corporations, oil versus coal, rich versus poor, engineered problem/reaction/solution schemes to swing elections, manipulate markets, and secure the dominance of the superclass at home and abroad—these were world-spanning issues he exploited, whether real or manufactured, from global cooling in the 1970s to global warming today. Right versus wrong didn't matter to the bottom line, so it didn't matter to him, either. War and peace and politics had always been a part of the business because that's where the real money was.

But money alone wasn't the key motivation. Not money at all, really, not anymore. Arthur Gardner could burn through $30 million a week for the next twenty years before he even came close to clearing out those offshore accounts. The goals and rewards had gotten steadily larger over the years until they'd gone far beyond the merely financial. Today it was only power and the wielding of it that could still fascinate a man like him.

In his distraction Noah had drifted close to the curb on the sidewalk, an error no seasoned pedestrian should ever commit when it's been raining. Right on cue a city bus roared by, *shooshed* through a sink-hole puddle the size of Lake Placid, and a rooster tail of oily gutter water splashed up and soaked him to the waist. As the bus rolled on he could see a bunch of kids in the back pressed to the windows, pointing and hooting, absolutely delighted to have played a part in his drenching.

Perfect.

Noah stopped under an awning and took stock of himself. Now he'd reached a milestone: head to toe, there wasn't a single square inch that didn't feel soaked to the skin. He checked the street signs for a gauge of his progress—just a few more blocks to go.

As he walked he thought back to that meeting with the government reps at the office. Maybe he was overthinking it. Over the years he'd heard his father give a similarly passionate call to action many times, hawking everything from a minor come-from-behind congressional campaign to some spin-off brand of laundry detergent. Whether it was a revolutionary new choice in artificial sweeteners or this afternoon's so-called fundamental transformation of the United States of America, it was all just the same empty carnival-barking the clients loved to hear, and the old man loved to deliver.

That sounded good enough to ease his mind, at least for the time being. Besides, what was that old saying? *Don't ask the question if you don't want to know the answer.* Noah most certainly did not want to know the answer. It was far easier to follow orders and cash the checks if you honestly had no idea what the consequences of those orders were.

According to the flier the location of tonight's all-American shindig was the Stars 'n Stripes Saloon, a charming, rustic little dive down here in Tribeca. Noah had been there a few times before on downtown pub crawls with clients. The Stars 'n Stripes was known as something of a guilty pleasure, a little patch of down-home heartland kitsch complete with friendly, gorgeous waitresses, loud Southern rock on the jukebox, and cheap domestic beer on tap.

In the last remaining block Noah had

been holding out hope that the rally, or whatever it turned out to be, would be sparsely attended and quiet enough to allow him to corner this Ross woman for a quality conversation. The odds of a low turnout seemed pretty good. After all, how many right-wing nutcases could possibly live in this enlightened city, and how many among them would knuckle-drag themselves out of their subbasement bunkers for a club meeting on a chilly, rainy Friday night?

The depressing answer to that question, he saw as he rounded the final turn, was absolutely *all* of them.

CHAPTER 8

From the corner of Hudson and West Broadway, Noah could see the overflow crowd spilling out onto the sidewalk. The place was packed wall to wall; light from inside the tavern was dimmed by the press of a standing-room-only audience lined around the interior windows.

Just keep on walking—this sage advice piped in from his rational side—*write off this whole wretched night, and get home to that nice, hot Jacuzzi*. Maybe a wiser young man would have listened, cut his losses, and punted, but he felt a stubborn commitment that trumped any thoughts of turning back. To stop now would mean the miserable trip had all been for nothing.

Noah checked his look in a darkened shop window, ran a rake of fingertips through his hair until it looked somewhat presentable, straightened his dirty, wet clothing, and crossed the street to wade into the rowdy sea of redneck humanity.

Live music from inside was filtering out through the buzz of the crowd. There were so many people it was impossible to keep to a straight line as he walked. The diversity of the gathering was another surprise; there seemed to be no clear exclusions based on race, or class, or any of the other traditional media-fed American cultural divides. It was a total cross section, a mix of everyone—three-piece suits rubbing elbows with T-shirts and sweat pants, yuppies chatting with hippies, black and white, young and old, a cowboy hat here, a six-hundred-dollar haircut there—all talking together, energetically agreeing and disagreeing as he moved through them. In the press, these sorts of meetings were typically depicted as the exclusive haunts of old white people of limited means and even more limited intelligence. But this was everybody.

As Noah edged his way inside the door he saw the source of the music, a lone guitarist on a makeshift elevated stage. His appearance didn't match up with the power of his voice—on the street you'd never notice him, just another skinny little guy with bad skin and a three-day stubble—but he was owning that stage like a rock star. He was in the middle of a 1960s-era grassroots folk song, singing and playing with a quiet intensity that let every note and phrase say just what it had been written to say.

At the turn of the chorus the musician pointed to the audience, lowered his lips to the harmonica harnessed around his neck, and played on with a rousing, plaintive energy as the people raised their voices and sang along.

This music and the mood it was creating, it was a smart PR move if they could make it work. If their enemies were trying to paint them as a bunch of pasty-white NASCAR-watching, gun-toting, pickup-driving reactionaries with racist and violent tendencies, what better ploy could these people make than to subtly invoke the peace-loving spirits of Martin Luther King and Mahatma Gandhi? If nothing else it would drive their critics on the left right up the wall.

Noah ducked a passing tray of Budweisers and was jostled from behind as he stepped back to let the server squeeze by. He turned to see whom he'd run into, and there, standing before him, was Molly Ross.

The first thing he noticed was that she'd changed her outfit. More stylish jeans and a warm autumn sweater, nails freshly done, a little purple flower in her hair instead of the pencils. But more than just her clothes had changed. The difference was subtle but striking and it probably boiled down to one thing: she gave a damn how she might come across to these people, in contrast to her obvious disdain for those at the office. That's what it was; she seemed like she was right where she belonged, and the effect was very easy on the eyes.

"Well," Molly said, allowing him only a conditional hint of a smile, "look what the cat dragged in." For the first time he noticed a light Southern lilt in her words.

"Yeah, I made it. I said I would."

She pulled aside the lapel of his overcoat, tsked, and shook her head. “What did you do, walk all the way down here in the rain?”

“Don’t ask.”

“Hold still.” With a disapproving sigh she helped him off with his overcoat, then folded it over her arm. “Come on, I’ve got a table over there by the jukebox. I’ll go look around—somebody here’s got to have an extra shirt you can wear.”

“No, really, don’t bother—”

But she’d already turned, offering her hand so he wouldn’t lose her. He took it, following as she worked their way through the thick of the crowd.

Soon they arrived at a little round pub table for two near the stage, with high stools on either side. In a higher-class joint, seats this close would have been reserved for the VIPs.

“I’ll be right back,” she said, and then she disappeared into the noisy multitude.

After one more all-American number the singer finished his set to spirited applause and loud bar-thumping. As the ovation subsided a passing waitress asked Noah what she could get for him.

"For some reason," Noah said, "I've suddenly got a craving for a Samuel Adams." She took the order down on her pad, but his not-so-subtle dig at the goings-on in the bar seemed completely lost on her.

Molly came back with two cups of coffee, a choice of three dry shirts, and an enormous bearded man in jumpsuit coveralls and a Beech-Nut baseball cap. The clothes she'd apparently foraged from the luggage of some out-of-towners in attendance. It wasn't clear where she'd picked up the big guy, but he looked like he might have hiked here straight from a hayride.

The big man ticked his chin in Noah's direction. "Who's your boyfriend?" he asked.

"Not my boyfriend," Molly said, in a tone meant to emphasize what a far-fetched idea that really was. "This is Noah Gardner, from where I work, and Noah, this is my friend Hollis."

A beefy right hand the size of a fielder's mitt came toward him, and Noah put out his own. "Good to know you, Hollis," he said, with a clasp only firm enough to transmit sincerity without throwing down a challenge for that iron-grip competition some men love to engage in upon first meeting.

"The pleasure's all mine," the big man said. Good etiquette had obviously been drilled into him from childhood; by his manner it seemed that shaking hands with a total stranger was an event to be treated with great respect. In contrast to his physical size his voice was unexpectedly high and reedy. The overall effect was something like being introduced to Winnie-the-Pooh, if Winnie-the-Pooh had been a seven-foot, mostly shaven, talking grizzly bear.

Molly had brought back a selection of men's tops, including a faded sweatshirt from Kent State, a dark burglar's hoodie with a torn pocket and a pattern of moth holes, and a two-tone T-shirt that said PRESUMED IGNORANT on the front. He took the sweatshirt.

"Thanks," Noah said, looking around. "Where can I go to put this on?"

"For heaven's sake, it's just your shirt. Go ahead and change right here if you want to." She leaned forward, resting her elbows on the table and her chin in her palms, with a bewitching innocence on her face that was not quite as pure as the driven snow. "I doubt you've got anything under there me and Hollis haven't seen before."

"Aha. So you admit that I'm human."

She seemed to study him deeply, as if the piece to a stubborn blank in a jigsaw puzzle might be hiding somewhere within his gaze. It must have been only a second or two, but it felt so much longer than any other mere moment he could remember.

"We'll see," she said.

CHAPTER 9

Being between tans, Noah had opted to change his clothes in private, though the restroom turned out to be nearly as crowded as the bar itself. There was a definite scent of weed smoke in the air. He'd already seen a few hardcore, single-issue hemp-heads in the crowd. Maybe they were here to attach their cause to the larger group's ambitions.

He slipped out of his damp shirt and into the fresh top he'd borrowed.

His pants he'd have to live with, but they were already starting to dry out. At least without his dress shirt and tie he might blend in a little better with the majority of the yahoos outside.

When he returned to the tavern proper he saw that the big guy was gone, but another man had joined Molly at the small table by the stage.

Noah stopped by a floor column at a point where he was half obscured from their line of sight. It hadn't been his conscious intention to stand there and watch the two of them from a distance, not at all. That would be impolite, not to mention a little creepy if either of them should have glanced over to notice him there. But as the brief pause stretched into a minute or more, his minor worry of what she might think if she saw him watching was pushed aside by a different concern.

They were sitting close together, hand on hand, talking and whispering, intent on one another, each finishing thoughts for the other, laughing easily. It was an intimate relaxation between them, a togetherness without any pretense, the kind of closeness you see only rarely between siblings, and sometimes among old friends, but often between two people in love.

"That Molly, she's a nice girl, don't you think?"

Noah flinched at the sound of the voice near his ear. He turned to see Molly's large friend Hollis towering beside him, watching the distant table just as he had been.

"I was just—"

"Nice girl. Smart one, too. Quick as a whip." Now that he'd said a few more words his regional accent was coming through loud and clear. This guy wasn't just from Appalachia; he looked and sounded like he might've eaten one of the Blue Ridge Mountains.

"Whatever," Noah said, "I just met her, so—"

"That boy with her there, his name's Danny Bailey. Molly tells me they was tight with one another some time ago, but beyond that I didn't pry no further."

Feigning disinterest didn't seem to be of much further use. Either Hollis was an excellent judge of character or it was so obvious that Noah was smitten with this woman that there was no more need to try to hide it.

"Okay, so that's his name," Noah said, "but who is this guy?" His cover was now blown; Molly had just spotted him and was waving him over.

"To be honest I don't know that much about him," Hollis said, and his next words sounded strange coming from a giant of a man who could probably bear-hug the fight out of a silverback at the Bronx Zoo.

"But he scares me some."

When he returned to the table they pulled over another chair and all three sat back down.

"So, you must be Noah," Danny Bailey said. "Molly's told me almost nothing about you."

If the twinkle in his deep voice was any indication, Bailey found himself pretty damned amusing. He had the air of someone who was accustomed to being seen from a stage or on camera and had put his look together accordingly. He was handsome enough, but up close you could see all the things the footlights would obscure: too many crosshatched wrinkles for a man so young, desperately spiky hair with too-careful highlights, face a bit too thin, eyes a little sunken and dry. It was a picture of a guy on the wrong side of thirty trying hard to remember twenty-one.

"I'm not surprised," Noah said. "We hardly know each other, and what she knows so far, I doubt she likes too much."

Bailey nudged Molly with his shoulder. "What do you say about that, sweet thing?" She looked embarrassed, and was rescued from answering by the arrival of the waitress with a round for the table. "Aw, come on, lighten up, everybody. I kid because I love. Here, look." He picked up his shot glass and downed whatever brownish liquor it was filled with, then held up the empty in a toast of sorts. "Here's to new friends, and maybe a new fan."

Noah picked up his glass and sipped it. "I'm sorry, you said a new fan?"

"Yeah, man." He held out his hand in introduction, and Noah shook it. "Danny Bailey." He seemed to wait for a sign of dawning recognition, and got none. "Don't tell me you haven't seen the video."

Noah blinked, and shook his head.

"*Overthrow*, man, the video. It's gonna bring on the total downfall of the whole frickin' evil empire, thirty-five million views on YouTube. That's me. I'm shocked, you really haven't seen it? There's e-mails about me flying around all over the Internet."

"Well," Noah said, "I guess I've got a really good spam filter."

For a long moment the legendary Danny Bailey looked like he'd just been double-smacked across his face with the ceremonial dueling gloves.

"Down, boys," Molly said.

Bailey let the air between them simmer just a little while longer. Then he smiled and shook his head, picked up the shot glass in front of Molly, drank its contents in one gulp, and got up to leave. He leaned down and kissed Molly on the cheek, whispered something elaborate in her ear, and then looked across to Noah.

"Lots of luck," Bailey said.

"Hey, really, you too."

With the other man gone Noah turned to Molly and tapped the lip of her empty glass. "Can I get you another one?"

"No, I don't drink. That's why he did that; he wasn't being rude."

"Oh no, not at all."

"Danny's a good guy, he's just living in the past of this movement, I think. I'm not telling you anything that I haven't said to him. You'll see what I mean when he speaks tonight. He doesn't have much of a BS-filter, and he gets people fired up about the wrong things, when there are plenty of real things to fight against. But, there's no denying he gets a lot of attention."

"Just my opinion," Noah said. "but it's a pretty informed one. You should be careful who you associate yourselves with. In PR we have a saying that the message is irrelevant if you don't choose the right messenger. And it's not always true, you know, that there's no such thing as bad publicity."

"I'll take that under advisement." She looked him over. "I'm glad to see that shirt fits you so well."

"Yeah, I'm an off-the-rack medium-large," Noah said, placing his bundle of wet things on the now-vacant barstool between them. "Thanks again."

She nodded. "I'm happy you came. Now"—she scooted a few inches closer—"tell me something about yourself that I don't already know."

Noah answered instinctively. "I will if you will."

Molly seemed to think about that for a moment. "Okay."

"Okay." He bit his lip as if in deep thought, considering what to choose as a first revelation. "I have an almost supernatural ability to tell when a person is hiding something."

"No, you don't."

"I do. While the other kids went to Cub Scouts I was sitting behind one-way glass eating M&Ms and watching about a million focus groups. I know people." He thumped his temple with an index finger. "Human lie detector."

"Prove it."

Noah looked briefly around the bar and then settled on one man and studied him for a few seconds. "All right. Behind you, over your left shoulder, halfway to the exit sign. Muscle shirt, pirate earring, loose coat, and a blond biker mullet. Be discreet." She turned to look, and then her eyes came back to him. "He's not one of you. If that's not an infiltrator, I've never seen one before."

Molly turned her head again. When she turned back she didn't look impressed; she looked troubled, and then angry.

"Calm down," Noah said. "What do you think, there's not going to be a spy or two from the enemy camp at a thing like this?"

"It's not right."

"Come on, forget about it," he said. "So, I went first, now tell me something about you."

Molly nodded, took a deep breath, and then climbed up to stand on the seat of her stool and shouted across the bar. "Hey, you!" She pointed to the man in question, who had turned to face her along with most of those nearby. "Enjoying the show, are you? Look, everybody! We've got a Benedict Arnold in the house!"

From the malevolent look on the guy's face, getting publicly busted was one of his least favorite things to do on a Friday night. To a rising chorus of jeers from others around him, with a last venomous glance at her over his shoulder he abruptly packed it in and headed for the door.

Molly sat back down, with a sweet, vocal sigh.

"Something about myself . . . let me see." She leaned forward, closer to Noah, as though about to share a secret nobody knew.

"I can sometimes be a little impulsive," she whispered.

CHAPTER 10

The jukebox abruptly faded down to silence and a female speaker took the stage. She was maybe fifty-five years old, with a bright, easy confidence in her eyes. The honest beauty she must have enjoyed in her younger days was still shining through, but mellowed and matured with the years. She waited until some of the noise subsided and then stepped to the microphone.

"As I look out at you all, I remember what James Madison said of his country in those early days: 'The happy union of these states is a wonder; their Constitution a miracle; their example the hope of liberty throughout the world.'"

The applause that followed was loud and enthusiastic. With a gesture she quieted the room and continued.

"The U.S.A. was that example for many years, my friends, and I promise you, we can be again. But today we're facing a threat to our future unlike anything seen since the days of the first revolution.

"There are a hundred conspiracy theories that try to explain what's happened to us over the last century. I've seen many of these theories represented here tonight, in the speeches, in person, and in slogans on signs all around this room. All of us are trying to make sense of the same damning evidence. But I'm afraid that sometimes we see only the symptoms, and not the disease.

"That disease is corruption, plain and simple. Corruption is a virus, always floating in the halls of power, ready to infect and spread among those whose immune systems are compromised by greed and blind ambition. This is the way it's always been, and our system of government was made like it was, with a division of powers among three separate branches of government, all constrained by limited scope and commonsense principles. Our founding documents established this new form of government to protect us from the sickness that has destroyed freedom since the dawn of civilization: the inevitable rise of tyranny from the greed and gluttony of a ruling class.

"The enemy we now face is the same enemy that's always sought to enslave free people. This threat isn't new. Human history is a chronicle of the struggle of the people against oppression by the few. Those few are always among us, in every generation, waiting for an opportunity to step forward and seize power. Thomas Sowell presented our struggle clearly: 'The most basic question is not what is best, but who shall decide what is best.'

"You don't need to create a conspiracy theory to explain what's going on around us today. The ruling class has written and published their plans and their history, as plain as day."

She picked up and held out a massive hardbound book.

"This book is titled *Tragedy and Hope*. It's nearly fourteen hundred pages of the history and the relentless goals of the enemy. We know this book holds the truth because it's not a wild piece of fiction written by one of us; it's a calm and rational book of facts written by an insider and historian sympathetic to the goals of the power elite, and a mentor to presidents, by the way, named Carroll Quigley."

A man behind her reached out and exchanged that large book in her hands for an older, thinner one, and she held it out. "If that's their history, then this is an early, published example of their plan of action. *The Promise of American Life*, by Herbert Croly, first printed in 1909, before the beginning of the great decline. Its author advocated what he called a New Nationalism. Big government, ever-expanding programs and departments, a nanny state with confiscatory powers and jurisdiction over every aspect of our lives. He believed that in the new Industrial Age the people simply weren't fit to rule themselves as the well-meaning but misguided Founders had envisioned.

"Croly renounced his own life's work in the end, when he saw what he'd helped to set in motion. But his writings lived on, and they influenced every fundamental change brought on by what became known as 'the progressive movement' in the first half of the twentieth century, from the Federal Reserve Act and the income tax to the spiral into crushing debt and dependence that began with the New Deal."

She put the book down, and spoke quietly and deliberately when she began again.

"But Herbert Croly was not an evil man." This declaration was met with silence from the crowd, and she let it hang for a while. "He wanted a better life for the people of his country. He wrote about his ideas on achieving that, and he was free to do so. America today is full of opinions and movements and agendas that differ radically from ours; even among us here, we differ, and that's the way it will always be. The danger comes when good intentions are hijacked and perverted by the culture of corruption—when those elected to represent us begin to act not for your own good, but for their own gain.

"It's the same today. People who, for their own gain, would replace equal justice with social justice, trade individual freedom for an all-powerful, all-knowing central government, forsake the glorious creative potential of the American individual, the beating heart of this nation, for a two-class society in which the elites rule and all below them are all the same: homogenized, subordinate, indebted, and powerless. That's what corruption will do, and we've allowed it to run rampant for too long."

Noah looked away from the speaker to take a gauge of the crowd; old habits die hard. Nearly everyone throughout the room was engaged and listening, but there were exceptions. A variety of men and women, about ten or fifteen, were scattered around the bar looking just slightly unlike the others. It wasn't their dress that was out of place, but rather their demeanor. They were far more concerned with one another than with what was happening onstage. And at least half of them were fiddling with small digital videocameras.

"Hey," Noah whispered, tapping the table near Molly's arm. She only shushed him, keeping her attention on the woman in the spotlight. With a last uneasy glance around the room, he turned back to the speaker as well.

"There are thirty-five thousand registered lobbyists in Washington, D.C." the woman said, to a scattering of boos and hisses that arose from the onlookers. "That's nearly seventy lobbyists for each member of Congress. Together they spent almost three and a half billion dollars last year—that's over six and a half million dollars per congressman. With that money they buy influence, not on behalf of you, but to put forward the agendas of their clients. Huge corporations, international banks, the power brokers on Wall Street, foreign governments, media giants, the real, self-appointed ruling class—their lobbyists write the bills, your congressmen work as scripted front men for the tainted legislation, and then they vote as they're told by their handlers.

"Not all of them, mind you. There are still good men and women in Washington, D.C.—but more than enough of them have long gone bad. In return for abandoning their oath of office they're promised fortune, and fame, and reelection if they play along, and if they don't, they know they can kiss their careers in so-called public service good-bye.

"This country was founded as a representative republic, but you're no longer represented here, are you?"

A resounding *No!* was shouted from the back, and that triggered a chorus of more shouts from every quarter of the bar. She let the clamor go on for a while and then motioned for quiet, holding up a thin document in her hand.

"This is the Constitution of the United States of America. It's just about fifteen pages when printed out like this, only four sheets of parchment when it was originally written out by hand. Here it is. That's all of it, the supreme law of the land, the entire framework of our system of government.

"And do you know why it's so small? Because the government itself was meant to be small. Is a federal government vital and important to our country? Yes. Should it exist as the heart and symbol of our unity and a compass to guide our journey as one nation? Yes. But it was meant to be small. And why? Because we, you and I, are the real government in this land of ours. That's the forgotten truth that calls out to us from these few pages here.

"What the Founders knew is that governments go bad. That's why Thomas Jefferson told us that resistance to tyrants is obedience to God. They understood that evil, like gravity, is a force of nature. Corruption always comes. Like weeds in a garden, it infiltrates, gets a foothold, grows, and takes over. Keep watch, we were told, keep the government in check, or this haven of freedom and opportunity could disappear in a single generation. And my friends, we have looked away from our sacred responsibility for too long. We forgot our charge to keep eternal vigilance, and as we slept another framework, corrupt and ever expanding, was being built to replace our founding principles the moment they grew weak enough to fail. And now we look around and find that our future has nearly been stolen away.

"Our representatives in government swear an oath, when they take office, to support and defend the Constitution of the United States. But for many of them these are only empty words. They never even consult the wisdom they've sworn to uphold. Once spoken, that oath is forgotten, and the Constitution of the United States never again enters their mind."

She laid the document in her hand on a nearby table and picked up a dark blue volume the size of the Brooklyn white pages.

"The entire Constitution can be folded and carried in your shirt pocket, and may I recommend that you keep a copy with you like that if you don't already. But this"—she held up the massive book—"is one volume of the federal tax code." She dropped the book flat from waist-high and it *whammed* to the stage floor at her feet. "Fourteen hundred pages, and that's just one volume; there's a bookcase full of these. Sixty-seven thousand pages of rules and penalties and crimes for which you're all guilty until you prove yourselves innocent. There's no due process when the Internal Revenue Service comes to kick in your front door.

"And do you know why they've made it so big, and why it gets bigger every year? It's the same reason the IRS is involved with health-care legislation and the Treasury was in charge of enforcing Prohibition. Because the power to tax involves the power to destroy. That's not my opinion, it's the opinion of the U.S. Supreme Court!

"But you don't need a judge to tell you what is obvious to anyone who's ever tried to fill out a tax form. The tax code is not meant to be read and understood by the people. It's meant as a shelter for those who've taken power from us, and a weapon of selective enforcement to be used against any who would dare to raise an opposing voice. The law is not for them, it's for you: Right now a hundred thousand federal employees together owe almost a billion dollars in back taxes, and the Treasury secretary himself is one of them."

The crowd reacted with loud boos and angry shouting, and it took a while for them to quiet down. When they finally had, she began again, but now her voice was much softer.

"Those of us gathered in this room tonight aren't simply fighting taxes, out-of-control spending, or unsustainable debt, we're fighting for something much larger: equal justice. We're fighting for the end of special exceptions and perks for those who have the right people on their speed-dials. There's no reason why the person who runs the IRS, the congressman who writes our tax code, or the CEO who has friends in the White House should get a free pass when you and I must pay the consequences for our decisions.

"John Adams once said that we are 'a government of laws, not men.' Ask yourself: Is that still true today? Your income, your family name, and your connections matter more than ever. They can help you succeed or they can ensure you fail. How can that reality coexist in a society where all men are created equal?

"The answer is that it can't. That is why we are here. And it's also why our message of equal justice is impossible for any honest person to refute. How do I know that? Because it was the message of Dr. Martin Luther King, Jr."

Noah noticed that the atmosphere in the bar seemed to have changed during the few minutes that the woman had been on the stage. It wasn't just that you could hear a pin drop, it was the whole feel of the place. She had them in the palm of her hand.

"While others throughout our history have resorted to violence to achieve their agendas, it's important to remember that they all failed. But Dr. King was different. He told people to get down on their knees, to be peaceful in their words and actions, to stay together and fight relentlessly for their cause.

"Dr. King understood what all of us gathered here must: that those who fight to correct injustice must be willing to accept suffering, if necessary, but never to inflict it."

All of the normal activity you might expect to see in a bar had stopped. Even the waitresses and bartenders seemed to be completely focused on the words flowing from the stage.

"Dr. King once said that 'no lie can live forever.' He knew that once the American people understood the depth of the injustice being perpetrated on them, they would choose the right side. Today we face that very same challenge, and if we are patient, we can expect the very same result.

"Americans are still a fair and just people. They know the difference between racism and race-baiting, between violence and accusations of violence, between hatred and patriotism. Let them weigh the evidence for as long as they need, because when the verdict comes down, we will once again be on the right side.

"You're angry, I know you are, and you should be," the speaker continued. "but now I need to urge you, to demand of you, that you renounce anyone who suggests violence. Just like Dr. King, we aim to eliminate evil, not those who perpetrate it. To speak of violence in any form is to play right into the hands of those who oppose us. They've already invested countless hours into portraying us as violent, hateful racists, and they are just waiting for the chance to further that story line. Don't give it to them. Instead of Bill Ayers, give them Benjamin Franklin. Instead of Malcolm X, give them Rosa Parks. Instead of bin Laden, give them Gandhi. They are well prepared on how to use violence to their advantage, but they have absolutely no idea how to use peace.

"Besides, everything we need to prevail," the woman on stage held up her printout of the Constitution again, "every shield and weapon against tyranny and oppression, even at the late stages of the cancer of corruption that's sickened us, everything we need is given to us right here. All we must do is find the strength and the wisdom to awaken our friends and neighbors, take back our power under the law, and restore what's been forgotten. *Restore*. Not adapt, not transform . . . *restore*.

"Let me ask you all a question. Many of us in this room are painted as 'anti-government'—but who loves America more, those who want to restore it, or those who want to transform it?"

The hushed silence that had overtaken the room for a while evaporated in an instant. Enthusiastic shouts and chants came from all corners. The misfits at the bar even put their cameras down and turned their backs as if by its nature this material would be of no use to them.

"Don't be fooled, 'transformation' is simply a nice way of saying that you don't like something! If you live in an old house that you adore, do you talk about 'restoring' that home or 'transforming' it into a modern-day McMansion? Same goes for an old car or an old painting—things that have real value aren't changed or transformed, they're preserved."

She paused and looked slowly around

the room as though she were talking to each person individually. "I don't know about you, but I happen to believe that the America our Founders created is still worth preserving. Thank you, all, God bless you, and may God bless the U.S.A."

The woman left the stage on the other side as a Toby Keith song began to play over the sound system, and Molly looked over at Noah as she applauded the end of the speech. Then she leaned toward him, raising her voice over the bar noise.

"So what do you think?"

Noah took a thoughtful sip from his glass, then shrugged as the room quieted down. "Can I get you a club soda, or some juice?"

"No thanks. What did you think of what she said?"

"I don't know. I guess it sounds like she believes what she's saying."

"Wow," Molly said. "That could be the most noncommittal string of words I've ever heard a man put together. You really are a PR executive."

"I'm sorry," he said. "I don't like to talk about politics. I've always thought it was kind of a waste of time."

"So if I'm hearing this correctly, you're willing to grant that the person who was up there speaking—my mother, by the way—probably believed what she was saying, and yet it's not worth a second of your time to even think about?"

"That was your mother?" Noah asked.

"Just answer the question."

"No, I didn't say that. It's complicated."

"No," she said flatly, "it really isn't."

"Could we change the subject, just for a few minutes? I don't want to argue with you—"

"That horse is already out of the barn, Mr. Gardner."

"Okay, then, listen. I see how people of a certain mind-set could start to hate the government—"

"We don't hate government. We're against an out-of-control government that's lost sight of its principles and has been overrun by corruption."

"All right, point well taken. I understand that you're upset about what's being done to the country—"

"I'm so glad you understand that."

"I do. Things are bad, and they're going to get a lot worse before this crash is over, but all this"—he gestured around at the bar full of people—"what do you all think you're accomplishing here?"

"We're getting together and taking a stand."

"Taking a stand? Against what? Against the way things have always been? Because that's not going to change."

Molly shifted in her seat to square off with him, then looked into his eyes. "Why did you really come here tonight?"

He sighed, and sat back. "I guess I just wanted to get to know you."

"Well," she said. "This pointless meeting, that deluded woman onstage, and all these other misguided people? That's me. Now you know me."

With that she gathered her things and left him sitting there alone with his beer.

CHAPTER 11

Noah had lost count of the refills after his first pint, but by then he was averaging around thirty-two ounces of suds per special guest speaker. He'd briefly considered playing a drinking game with himself, wherein he would pound one back each time he heard one of the dirty words *progressive, socialist,* or *globalism*, but by those rules he'd have drunk himself under the table within a few minutes. Their spiels were all different but the highlights were mostly the same, with only minor deviations in two areas: where to place the blame for their country's troubles, and what to do about it.

He was still in his lonely seat by the stage. After he'd struck out with Molly there was no real reason to hang around but he felt too beat to get up and leave. Besides, the angry beer buzz he was stoking seemed like the best medicine for putting this malignant night into remission.

The nearby crowd parted at the end of another onstage musical interlude. He'd been hoping to see the waitress bringing him another tall one, but instead it was a familiar, enormous bearded man who walked up to the table.

Hollis—no last name had been offered for him—gently touched the barstool across from Noah with a finger. The expression on the part of his face not covered with bristly hair asked politely if that seat was taken.

"Please," Noah said, "be my guest." The barstool looked like dollhouse furniture next to this soft-spoken behemoth, but somehow it held up as he sat down. "Though I'll tell you the truth, when you've got your choice of a few hundred people here who I guarantee are better company than me, I wonder why you'd decide to sit here."

The waitress came and put a beer down for Noah and a bottle of Coca-Cola for his new tablemate. Hollis waited until she was gone to answer.

"I don't know," he said. "You looked kinda sad, I guess."

As if to drip gasoline on Noah's already smoldering mood, tonight's headliner, the illustrious Danny Bailey, now took to the stage in a swell of heavy-metal music and an ovation that rattled every shelf of glassware behind the bar.

"Hello, New York!" Bailey shouted, like an aging rock star kicking off his annual farewell tour. He held out the microphone to pump up the roar of the answering crowd and made no move to settle them down. On the contrary, the clamor continued until he produced a piece of paper and took back the mike almost a full deafening minute later.

"Thank you, really. I could listen to that all night long. Let me see if this is my crowd, though. How can we tell if a politician is lying?" He turned the mike briefly to the crowd again for their answer.

"Their lips are moving!" the people shouted.

"That's right," Bailey said. "And watch what they name things, especially those bills they're all voting on without even reading them. If they call something the Patriot Act, you can bet it won't be long before they're using it to hunt down us patriots. If it's called Net Neutrality, it's going to be used to neutralize their enemies. If it's called the Fairness Doctrine, it's meant to *un*fairly put free speech under government control and create a chilling effect on your First Amendment rights. Immigration reform, health-care reform—do me a favor, when you hear them say the word 'reform,' I want you to hear the word '*transform*.' And the next question you've got to ask is, What are they trying to transform us into? A better, stronger, freer country? Or a place filled with more and more people who are easier to control, easier to exploit, easier to keep under their thumb?"

This drew a loud and positive reaction from the crowd, which continued until Bailey produced a piece of paper and made a motion to quiet them down.

"Hey, is anybody out there looking for a job? Unemployment just shot up past twenty percent, *real* unemployment that is, not the bogus numbers we get spoon-fed on the nightly news. And that's nothing; it's almost forty percent if you're a young black man in this free country of ours. Since I thought maybe some of you might be looking for a new career, I brought this job opportunity for you."

He held the printout in his hands at an angle so he could read from it under the lights. "I found this last week on a government website. It's a really good job for what they call an Internment and Resettlement Specialist."

The crowd's reaction was immediate, loud, and angry.

"Now, calm down, give it a chance. Of all the world's prisoners, we've got twenty-five percent of them right here in this country. And hell, the U.S. has only five percent of the planet's population, so there must be a disproportionate number of undesirables in America, don't you think?"

A man just outside the circle of the spotlight handed up a stack of stapled papers.

"Oh, wait," Bailey continued, hamming up an incredulous reaction to the new document on top. "What's this? I don't believe we're supposed to see this. This is Army

Regulation 210-35, dated almost five years ago. And will you look at that? The title is 'Civilian Inmate Labor Program.' Maybe this is what they need all those new internment and resettlement specialists for."

Another burst of outrage from the crowd.

"Now hold your horses. These are dangerous criminals. After all, somebody's got to keep them in line, right? Why not put 'em in a military work camp, where we can get some free labor out of them? As long as we're not the criminals we've got nothing to worry about."

He flipped to another one of the documents in his hands. "But what do we have here? A memo from 1970, written by a man who later became the director of FEMA, advocating the rounding-up and internment of twenty-one million quote—*American Negroes*—unquote, in the event of civil disorder. Now, I left my exact figures at home, but I believe at that time twenty-one million would have been roughly *all* of the black people in America.

"And here"—he squinted as he read briefly from the document on top of his stack—"United States Air Force Civil Disturbance Plan 55-2 will authorize and direct the secretary of defense *to use the U.S. armed forces to restore law and order* in the event of a crisis. Under this umbrella plan they ran an exercise in 1984—so you see they do have a sense of humor—and that exercise was called Rex-84. The purpose was to see how efficiently they could pick up and corral all those disobedient Americans on their lists."

Bailey held up document after document as he continued. "What lists, you ask? All kinds of them. The FBI's ADEX list from the late 1960s—ADEX, that stands for Agitator Index—it was full of dangerous intellectuals, union organizers, and people who spoke out against the Vietnam War. Now there's almost a million and a half people on the DHS Terrorist Watch List, and it's growing by twenty thousand names every month.

"Have you registered a firearm? You're on a list! Have you made a political contribution to a third-party candidate? You're on a list! Have you visited my website? You're on a list! Have you given a speech about government lists to a rowdy group of patriots? You're on a list!

"But who needs a list when they can

monitor you whenever they want? You've all heard of that 'Digital Angel' device that can be implanted under your skin, right? They say it's to store medical information and for the safety of children and Alzheimer's patients."

At that, the crowd began to boo and hiss.

"Now, now . . . maybe for once they are being honest with us, but you know what? It doesn't matter! 'Digital Angel' is a Red Herring. We're all busy worrying about implantable chips as we're standing in line to buy the next iPhone or BlackBerry. Read the fine print, people! They don't need to sell new technologies to track us, we're eagerly signing up for the old ones!

"Oh, and this just in, thanks to our friends on the Internet—a place where, at least for now, we can track them as easily as they can track us."

Noah felt his face getting hot. In Bailey's hand was a printout of the leaked government memorandum from that afternoon meeting at the office, the one he'd spent his entire morning trying to nullify. It was effectively harmless now, it was a nonissue, and he repeated that to himself, but the smug look coming from the guy onstage had already gotten under his skin.

". . . if you speak out against abortion," Bailey continued, reading from the memo, "are a returning veteran, are a defender of the Second Amendment, oppose illegal immigration, are a homeschooler, if you've got a bumper sticker on your car that says 'Chuck Baldwin for President' or, heaven help us, if you're found to be in possession of a copy of the U.S. Constitution, then you good American patriots, you moms and dads and grandmas and grandpas, you guardians of liberty are to be approached with extreme caution and guns at the ready, because you may be a terrorist!"

The overall tone of the crowd's response had been taking a decided turn for the worse. It wasn't everybody who was into this line of rhetoric, maybe only a vocal ten percent or so. And while this minority wasn't quite to the torches-and-pitchforks line yet, they didn't have too much farther to go.

"But wait now, just wait. So they've got us all on a list, but it's not like they're gonna pick us up and send us to a concentration camp out of the blue, right? That could happen only if there's something they can blame on us, some sort of a big emergency. So who decides if and when we're in that kind of a crisis? The Congress, maybe? The same toothless Congress that hasn't actually declared a war on any of the seventy countries where we've sent our young men and women to fight and die since 1945? The same Congress that hasn't even been allowed to read most of the Orwellian continuity-of-government provisions put in place since the 1980s?

"No, the Congress doesn't decide." Bailey held up another document. "It's much worse than that. Since Presidential Decision Directive number fifty-one, it's official. The president decides. The duly selected president takes control of the whole enchilada, what they call in Presidential Decision Directive number sixty-seven 'the Enduring Constitutional Government.' On his command the U.S.A. becomes the ECG, and it stays that way until our new benevolent emperor decides the coast is clear again. The truth is that it could happen anytime they want. In case you don't know it, the powers that be have kept this country in an official, continuous state of national emergency almost every day since 1933.

"Do you realize that if you live within a hundred miles of a coastline or a U.S. border you're in what they call a 'Constitution Free Zone,' where the entire Bill of Rights can disappear in a heartbeat? That's not me talking, that's the ACLU. Two-thirds of us live in that zone; that's two hundred million American citizens. Do you know that tonight, in this very city, our kind leaders have set up what they call a 'Free Speech Zone' where we're allowed to exercise our First Amendment rights, but it's way uptown in a fenced-off parking lot where our rulers and the media don't have to be distracted by what we have to say.

"Well, ladies and gentlemen, I hereby declare this spot where I'm standing now, and every single square inch of this great land from sea to shining sea, according to the unalienable rights and powers endowed to me by my Creator, to be a Free Speech Zone!"

Noah had to catch his beer glass before it tipped over as his table was jostled by the nearby revelers. They were already clapping as loudly as they could and were now on the verge of getting physical in their reactions. From the stage, Danny

Bailey indicated that he wanted to be heard again.

"It looks bad, I know it does," Bailey began. "But do you know why we're going to beat them? We're going to beat them because once the truth gets out there'll be no stopping it. When enough people wake up they'll have no choice but to come out of the shadows and fight, and then we've got them. Remember what a great man once told us: First they ignore you—then they ridicule you—then they fight you—"

"And then they win," Noah said.

It was one of those nightmare moments, like when you dream about showing up to ninth-grade homeroom without your pants. Just as he'd spoken those four words, out loud but only to himself, the entire room had gone dead quiet in anticipation of Bailey's big triumphant finish. And by some cruel trick of acoustics, Noah's sarcastic twist of that Gandhi quote seemed to have carried to every ear in the room.

CHAPTER 12

For an eternal few seconds, Noah held out hope that Danny Bailey would blow right past the interruption, but it just wasn't that kind of a night. Noah stole a glance upward and found himself the sole focus of attention from the man onstage.

"Well, well, well." Bailey moved to the edge of the platform so they were facing each other. "Looks like we've got a junior ambassador from the Ivy League among us."

Noah kept his eyes fixed squarely on his beer glass, but Bailey wasn't going to let it rest.

"Come on up here, Harvard, don't keep us hanging. If you've got so much to say, just dumb it down so all of us hicks can understand it, and then have the guts to say it loud enough so everybody can hear. I doubt if you can tell us much about the Constitution or the Founding Fathers, but maybe you can enlighten us with a little racist, communist wisdom from a real hero . . . like Che Guevara."

Noah looked up at him. "No thanks."

"Oh, but I won't take no for an answer." Bailey turned to the crowd. "You folks won't either, will you?"

Angry applause filled the room along with taunts and chants. It finally became too much to sit and take.

"Fine," Noah said. He finished off what remained of his latest beer, stood, and allowed himself to be fairly manhandled up onto the platform and under the lights. Bailey moved aside from the floor mike with a be-my-guest sweep of the arm.

"I want to start off by saying," Noah began, adjusting his voice to make the most of the sound system, "that because of my job I'm in a unique position to know for certain that most of what's been said here tonight is absolutely true."

The crowd quieted down considerably upon hearing this, as he'd assumed they would.

"Let me see if I can confirm some of the speculation from earlier speakers . . . The Federal Reserve isn't federal at all: you're right, it's basically a privately owned bank, a cartel that loans you your own money at interest, and its creation was the beginning of the end of the free-market system.

"The United States was built to run on individual freedom, that's true, but because you've let these control freaks have their way with it for almost a hundred years, your country now runs on debt. Today Goldman Sachs is the engine, and in case you haven't realized it yet, the American people are nothing but the fuel.

"The Committee of Three Hundred exists. And the Council on Foreign Relations, and the Bilderberg Group, the Trilateral Commission, the Club of Rome—they all exist. And they are globalists; they're wealthy and powerful beyond anything you can imagine. There are predators among them, absolutely ruthless people, but all of them together really do run things in this world, just like you say they do. There's nothing secret about those societies, though. No hidden conspiracies: they do what they do right out in the open.

"See, the place where I work is where all the secrets get told, because they have to tell us their secrets before we can hide them. But here's the interesting thing: Do you know why I'm not worried about sharing any of this with you? Because they're not afraid of the American people anymore, and especially not you people. All they've got to do is keep you bickering among yourselves, overwhelmed with conflicting information, or fretting about conspiracies or hypnotized in front of the TV and the computer, or standing around here thinking you're fighting back, and you'll never even get close to doing them any harm.

"There really is a New World Order on the way, but it isn't new. It's been coming for a long, long time. You let yourselves get distracted with a thousand conspiracy theories, but there's only one truth at the heart of them all. George Carlin said it better than

I can: Up at the very top, it's a big club, and you're not in it. They've got all the power, and you've got none of it."

"Like hell we don't!" shouted a man in back.

"Okay, okay, I think I know what you're trying to say. If you could ever get enough voters together to do anything significant, you might have a shot. But that's easy enough to deal with. Let me show you how."

Noah pointed out a particularly hefty man near the bar.

"Can everybody read what it says on this guy's T-shirt? You know, a shirt that was probably sewn in Bangladesh by a ten-year-old girl who worked sixteen hours that day? Turn around so we can see it, big guy; be proud of it. It says, 'Born in the Jew S A.'

"If he's not already an infiltrator or an agent provocateur, then your enemies should hire him immediately. That guy is exactly why I'm not worried about telling you things that should be secrets: With him standing next to you, who'd ever believe a word you say? At every rally you hold, if you're lucky enough to get the press to cover you at all, he's the one guy who'll get his picture on the front page. If you want to know why you can't get any traction with the other ninety-seven percent of America, it's because you let yourselves be lumped in with people like that.

"Name-calling also works like a charm." He pointed to a different patron with every smear that followed. "There's a Birther, and a Truther, two Paulites, a John Bircher, a Freeper, a white supremacist, a pothead, three tea-partiers, and that guy there is the jackpot: a Holocaust denier. From there it's easy to roll you all up together so that no one in their right mind would want to join you. Why would they? According to the network news, you're all borderline-insane, ignorant, paranoid, uneducated, hate-mongering, tinfoil-hat-wearing, racist conspiracy theorists.

"That's how they keep your eyes off the big picture. All the while the gradual overthrow that you're so passionate about exposing is happening right under your nose. Yet you stand around here preaching to the choir, as if that's going to do anything at all to stop it.

"There's no respect for you in Washington. They laugh at you. You say you want a revolution? That Constitution the lady was holding up a while ago? It gives you the power to revolt at every single election. Do you realize that in a couple of weeks every last seat in the U.S. House of Representatives will be up for grabs? And the presidency? And one-third of the Senate seats?

"The approval rating for Congress is somewhere around fifteen percent. You could turn the tables and put them all out of a job on that one day. But do you know what's going to happen instead? I do. The presidency is going to change hands, but the corruption will accelerate. Over ninety percent of those people in Congress—people who are deeper into the pockets of the lobbyists every day they spend in Washington—over ninety percent of them are going to get reelected."

The crowd was listening intently; it seemed they weren't at all sure if this was just another part of the show.

"That's all I've got," Noah said. "I'll be outside waiting for a car if anyone wants to take a swing at me. To tell you the truth, I think a fistfight might just be the perfect way to end tonight's festivities."

There was a smattering of tentative applause and quite a bit of murmuring from the crowd as he stepped down from the stage, grabbed his bundle of wet clothes, left some cash on his table, and headed for the door. He heard Danny Bailey behind him back at the mike, picking up where he'd left off earlier and doing his best to get the crowd reengaged in his message, whatever the hell it was.

Noah was nearly to the exit when he felt a hand touch his arm. He stopped and turned to see the woman who'd spoken earlier, Molly's mother, standing there.

"That was quite a speech you gave, and on such short notice," she said.

"Yeah," Noah said. "I've got a gift. Look, I didn't mean any disrespect—"

"You don't have to apologize to me." Her face was kind, her eyes intelligent and alight with that same inscrutable glint that had hooked him so hopelessly during his brief time in her daughter's company. "I think we might have more in common than you realize."

Behind him, Bailey was already midway

into a spirited, modern paraphrase of a well-worn Patrick Henry speech. By the sound of it, the audience had fully recovered from Noah's double dose of reality and was working itself into quite a lather again. Maybe it was the late hour, the evening-long buildup of alcohol and anger, or the now-obvious scattering of outsiders around the room who seemed to be acting in concert to fan the flames of the mob mentality—but whatever it was, things were getting ugly.

Noah looked around for Molly but the audience was too thick to penetrate. Two men had stationed themselves in front of the door, in a stance that implied the way to the street was about to be closed.

"Have you seen your daughter?"

"I did a few minutes ago."

"I think we need to get out of here," Noah said, taking the older woman by the arm. "Right now." There was a glowing fire-exit sign on the wall to the rear of the place, and though there were probably other ways out, that seemed to be the easiest.

It was slow going. Bailey's booming speech and the occasional roar of the crowd in response drowned out all of Noah's other thoughts except one: getting outside before whatever bad thing that was surely about to happen did happen.

"Let's stop kidding ourselves," Bailey said. "We've done everything that could be done to avoid the storm that's coming. Our voices have not been heard! The time for simply hoping for change and praying for peace is gone. If our government won't answer our appeals and do what's right, if they've forsaken their oath to defend the Constitution, then an appeal to arms and to the grace of God Almighty is all they've left us!

"I ask you: If not now, when? When will we ever be stronger? Next week? Next year? Will we be stronger when they've taken our guns away, or when a cop or a paid government thug is standing on every corner enforcing the curfew? No! I say, if war is inevitable then let it come on our terms!"

The exit door was almost in reach but Noah stopped short; there was still no sign of Molly. He'd let go of her mother as the two of them had worked their way through the wall-to-wall people, and he'd lost track of her as well.

"There's no longer any peace to be had!" Bailey shouted from the stage. "Whether you know it or not the war has already begun!"

To describe the next few seconds as a blur would make it seem as if the ensuing events were jumbled together or indistinct, and they were far from that. They passed in something like slow motion, like those graceful shots of a drop of milk splashing into a cereal bowl or a rifle bullet cutting edge-to-edge through a playing card at twenty thousand frames per second. But the trade-off for all that visual clarity was a complete inability to act; Noah could see everything, but do nothing.

A slate-gray pistol appeared in a man's hand nearby—a man whom Molly had pointed out earlier as a newer member of her organization. The weapon was drawn down and level toward the stage. There was a flash, and the sonic pressure of a firecracker or the popping of a paper bag too near his ear, and then another, over and over as the crowd surged away from the gunman. The rising sounds of panic, a shower of glass and white sparks as a spotlight shattered in its mount above the stage, the back door banging open, the rush of black-suited officers storming in, a sudden stinging odor like a mist of Tabasco and bug spray, a loud commotion at the far end of the room as another squad in riot gear burst in.

Noah was caught up in the blind retreat of those around him, pushed back toward the center of the room. And there was Molly, maybe twenty feet away, held by her hair and crumpling to her knees, her left arm twisted high behind her by a roughneck the size of a linebacker. Noah heard a stifled cry and a repeating electric sound. He turned to see the big man he'd met earlier, Hollis was his name, stricken and helpless in a seizure on the floor, the barbs of a stun gun buzzing in his chest.

From behind his tinted visor a nearby man-in-black raised his riot club, ready to cave in the skull of the helpless man at his feet.

In this strange, slow procession of vivid snapshots, a random thought made its way back to him from earlier in the day. *We stay mostly the same and then grow up suddenly, at the turning points*. What came next would either go down as one of those dreaded defining moments, or as the final mistake of a bad night that would top any that had ever come before. It didn't matter which; the die was already cast. Just because he spent his days strip-mining the vast gray zone between right and wrong didn't mean he couldn't tell the difference.

Time resumed its proper pace, and he felt his will unfreeze. As the black truncheon swung down Noah reached up and caught the uniformed man by the wrist, stopping him cold with an unexpectedly steely grip toned over years with his personal trainer at the Madison Square Club. It's true what they say: you just never know when all those pull-ups are going to come in handy.

There was no struggle. The other man locked eyes with him, their faces a hand's width apart. Perhaps the man was in the midst of a defining moment of his own. At first he looked surprised, and then incredulous, and then—despite the impressive array of armaments swinging from his belt and the three additional troopers already rushing to his rescue—he looked afraid.

A moment is only a moment, and just like that, it's gone. Noah felt the first savage blow to the back of his head, and maybe another. And then he felt nothing at all.

CHAPTER 13

He opened his eyes, and found her looking down at him.

It was the wide variety of aches and pains that told him for certain she wasn't a figment of his imagination. His head was resting in her lap, and Molly held him steady as the crowded police van bumped and jostled along the patchy downtown streets.

Police van?

"Hey," she said.

"Hi."

The light glaring down was bright blue-white, fluorescent, and harsh. As he turned his head he winced at a sudden stitch in his neck, like a bee sting to the spinal cord. The rear compartment was filled to capacity and beyond, packed with people he vaguely recognized from the bar. Most were sitting up, but some were reclining, as he was, in various states of physical distress.

Noah looked up at her again. "What happened—"

She hushed him with a fingertip to his lips, and he saw that her wrists were bound with nylon ties.

The vehicle lurched and slid to a stop, the double doors in back swung open, and he was pulled away from her and out onto the street. Somehow the news crews had arrived and set up for on-scene reports even before the paddy wagons rolled in. Hot lights flicked on as local and network correspondents began shouting questions and their cameramen pushed in close to capture the scene. Noah's legs would barely stay under him as he was herded into line along with the others.

Once the reporters were left behind, the remaining perp walk through the police station was a gauntlet of pat-downs, prodding, and barked orders, ending with a final, distinctive *clang* as the holding-cell door swung closed.

The pen he was locked in was one of several lining the hall; the total census must have been over three hundred. These were all men, of course; the women were taken elsewhere. Most of the guys nearby him seemed to be from the group at the tavern. Some others around the cell, clearly seasoned veterans of the penal system, appeared to have been brought in for day-to-day offenses ranging from vagrancy to prostitution to drunk-and-disorderliness.

The flood of detainees from the bar had filled the place far beyond its capacity. Most of the people seemed stunned into brooding silence but some inmates were belligerent: shouting, picking fights, taunting the guards, or calling out for their lawyers, their mothers, or any other savior within earshot.

Noah had been among the last to enter and he ended up pressed against the bars at the front of the cell. His head was still swimming and he needed to sit, but the cell felt like the 6 train at rush hour: there was barely enough room to turn around.

After a time he saw something that he couldn't begin to understand; he must have been mistaken. The man from the back of the tavern, the one with the gun, was being escorted from an adjacent cell. He wasn't in handcuffs or restraints of any kind. He was just walking along with the officers toward the exit.

"Gardner!"

Hearing his name shouted out from somewhere down the hall snapped him back to reality. A police sergeant with a clipboard soon appeared with two other officers behind him.

He reached out through the bars. "That's me. I'm Noah Gardner."

The three men gathered around and looked him over, comparing his physical details against whatever description they'd brought with them on the clipboard. It was his gold class ring from Riverdale Country School that seemed to cement the positive ID.

The sergeant double-checked his orders, rattled through his keys until he found the proper match, and unlocked the door. As Noah exited the cell a delirious man behind him made a weak attempt to follow and was firmly encouraged to resume his place among the crowded inmates.

"What's going on?" Noah asked as they walked him out.

"Your attorney's on his way," the sergeant replied, in a tone meant to telegraph a palpable disgust for the entire fickle enterprise of American jurisprudence.

After a short walk through a maze of halls, Noah found himself sitting in a small side office across the desk from a person he presumed to be his arresting officer. The man was in plain clothes, unshaven, and rumpled, as though he was either near the end of a double shift or had been called out of a sound sleep for the beginning of a new one. It wasn't the officer he'd confronted at the bar; that was a face he would have remembered.

The desk was stacked with dog-eared files and clerical debris, the bulletin board an untidy splash of sticky notes, memos, duty rosters, rap sheets, marked-up photographs, and one unfunny faxed cartoon. Overworked, short-staffed, and underpaid: that was the prevailing message in the cramped, stuffy space.

"Mr. Gardner, you have the right to

remain silent," the policeman said, his main attention on a printout of some sort in front of him, "and to refuse to answer questions. Do you understand?"

"Yes."

"Anything you say may be used against you in a court of law. Do you understand?"

"Yes."

"You have the right to consult an attorney before speaking to the police and to have an attorney present during any questioning, now or in the future. If you cannot afford an attorney, one will be provided for you without cost. Do you understand?"

"Yes, I understand."

"Now." The cop looked up at him for the first time. "Before I ask you if you're willing to talk to me, I want you to understand something else. This isn't a parking ticket we're talking about here. Somebody's going to jail tonight.

"You and your friends are going to get on a big bus with some armed guards and take a ride to central booking at the Manhattan Detention Complex—most people call it the Tombs. Over there they'll get your mug shots, your DNA and your fingerprints, and then you'll be formally charged and arraigned in the criminal court and bound over for trial. Though to be honest with you, since it's Friday night and I hear they've got a full house, it might be Sunday or Monday before they get all of you sorted out and ready to appear before the judge.

"If you're not granted bail—and by the nature of these offenses in the prevailing climate, and with Homeland Security getting involved, I seriously doubt you will be—then you'll all get on another bus, and that one'll have shackles on the seats and bars on the windows, because it'll be headed to Rikers Island.

"What you're going to be charged with"—he paused to flip a set of reading glasses down onto his nose—"is inciting a riot, resisting arrest, and aggravated assault on a police officer. That last one carries a minimum sentence of three and a half years in the state penitentiary. And someone among you, I don't know who, is going to be charged with felony assault with a deadly weapon. If that sounds more serious than the others, that's because it is."

He took a sip of coffee and flipped his glasses back up. Noah got the distinct impression that this cop had performed the routine he was witnessing once or twice before.

"Now, unless somebody comes forward and enlightens me on the circumstances—and by that I mean someone like you—well, I'm just as happy to let the officers from the scene separate the innocent bystanders from the perpetrators.

"So we can talk here and now, or you can keep on thinking about it while you're making some new friends with the general population down in the Tombs. And I don't know what you may have heard, but trust me"—he motioned to their gloomy surroundings—"it's not nearly this nice down there."

The policeman leaned forward in his creaky chair and lowered his voice as though a passing colleague in the hall might overhear him going soft on a suspect.

"Listen, you look like a good guy to me. This isn't something you need to be involved in. But my hands are tied here; we've got an eyewitness in the other room who says you hit a cop with a nightstick. I don't want to believe that, but you need to stand up for yourself or I can't help you.

"I'm sure you were just in the wrong

place at the wrong time, and we can figure this out, Noah, but you've got to talk to me right now." He opened his drawer, removed a small voice recorder, checked its display, pressed its thumb switch, and placed it on the blotter between them. "Now that I've advised you of your rights, are you willing to answer questions?"

Before Noah could respond there were three quick raps on the door frame and the Gardner family attorney, Charlie Nelan, walked in without waiting to be asked. He picked up the recorder from the desk, flicked it off, and slipped it into his pocket. An objection from the cop was swallowed before it fully escaped, stifled by a gesture from the counselor that assured him he would get all the attention he could handle in due time.

Charlie turned to Noah. "Have you said anything?"

"No—"

"Nothing at all?"

"I haven't said anything, just that I understand my rights."

"Good boy." Charlie Nelan was one of those old-school, silver-haired überprofessionals who swore by the power of image.

No matter where you happened to see him, he always looked as though he'd just stepped out of the "Awesome Lawyers" issue of *Gentlemen's Quarterly*. Fortunately, he was every bit as sharp as he looked.

Nelan touched Noah's chin and turned his head to get a better view of the damage sustained in the arrest. Then he closed the door and turned back to the other man across the desk.

"Detective . . ."

"Halliday."

"Detective Halliday, I want my client released, and his charges dropped, and I want that arrest report in the shredder."

The policeman released a low snort, but his bravado wasn't totally convincing.

"I put in a call to your captain on my way here," Charlie said. "Right now this is between the four of us, and that is precisely where it will stay."

"Now you listen to me," Halliday said. "I don't care what you want or who you called or how far you want anything to go—" His desk phone had begun to ring, and he did a double take when he read the caller ID.

"You should take that," Charlie said.

"We'll be right across the hall in room G when you need us."

Room G was another interview cube. When the door was closed Charlie sat Noah down, took a bottle of mineral water from his inside coat pocket, and handed it to him.

"How did you even know I was here?" Noah asked.

The look that came back said that young Mr. Gardner was worrying about something far beneath his concern, given the circumstances. Charlie was already punching more numbers on his cell, and as he put the phone to his ear he motioned to the water bottle, as though adequate hydration was the only substantive thing Noah could bring to the party at this stage.

From the sound of it, this new call was either to an assistant district attorney or the DA himself, but before he could pick up the gist of the conversation something grabbed Noah's full attention through the thin window by the door frame.

Out in a common area, a dozen or so men were gathered together having coffee and a collegial chat with some uniformed police. He stood and stepped closer to the glass, trying hard to believe his eyes.

In this surreal gathering was every heckler, every troublemaker who had made himself apparent during the speeches at the bar. Every one of them was dressed similarly, the differences being confined to the inflammatory slogans on their clothing and their selection of cracker-chic accessories. When scattered among a larger group they'd been harder to spot as co-conspirators, but all together like this, with their guard down, their costumes were obvious and their mannerisms out of character. It looked like the after-party of a Larry the Cable Guy stunt-double audition at Central Casting.

One of them matched a picture in Noah's memory to the very last detail. He was sure this time: the man was wearing a loud flannel shirt, a hunter's vest, a do-rag torn from the corner of a Confederate battle flag, and a shoulder holster.

He heard the call end and the phone snap closed behind him.

"Okay," Charlie sighed. "Let's sit down and talk about this, Dillinger."

"Charlie—"

"Correction. You stay quiet and let me talk to you."

They sat, with Noah taking a chair that preserved his view to the hall.

"I don't know what you did or didn't do," Charlie said, "and I don't want to know. What matters is what they could charge you with, which is putting your hands on a cop while he's doing his duty, and that's a first-degree felony in this state. Look at me. If you did that, in the eyes of the law it doesn't matter *why* you did it—self-defense, heat of the moment, temporary insanity, doesn't matter—conviction is a virtual certainty.

"Now, I called in some major favors, and they still wanted to charge you with something less egregious, simple assault, disorderly conduct, whatever. Then I called in some more favors and we worked that out, too. You're going to walk out of here tonight like this never happened."

"Listen to me for a second—"

"This is a big deal, Noah. And I'll tell you something else: this is it. I spent all your get-out-of-jail-free cards tonight. Until further notice if you so much as jaywalk, miss a trash can with a gum wrapper, or play your car stereo too loud, and any of these guys get wind of it? Forget about it. Starting now, if you step out of line below Thirty-fourth Street there won't be much I can do for you."

"I understand, and thank you. Can I say something now?"

Charlie checked his watch. "Go ahead."

"This whole thing was a setup."

"I don't care."

"Those guys, right out there"—Noah pointed through the glass, and Charlie looked briefly in that direction—"they were at this meeting tonight, where all this happened, and they were there specifically to start something. When they got tired of waiting for the people to get violent they did it themselves."

"Let me see if I understand you. You're saying that you think an undercover New York City police officer discharged his weapon in a crowded bar to incite this whole incident?"

"Yes."

"No way. Absolutely not."

"Okay, not a cop, then. I didn't see any badges on the men who burst into that place, maybe they were . . . I don't know, contractors, hired security men who did the dirty work and then turned us all over to the NYPD—"

"Noah," Charlie said. His voice was patient but firm. "Calm down. Whatever really happened, none of this matters to you."

"How can you say that? That guy right there, the one with the visitor's badge and the holster under his vest, that's the guy who fired the shots that started all this! Then the men in riot gear came busting in immediately, there was no call to nine-one-one, no delay, they were right there waiting outside the door. And the press—all those reporters were already here outside the station; how would they have known—"

"Okay, so it was a setup. And what do you think we can do about that, you and I? Who are you now, Nelson Mandela? News flash, son: there's no Santa Claus, no Easter Bunny, and no Legal Fairy who cares about what you think you saw. Injustice exists in this world, and while you're lucky enough to be insulated from the worst of it, most people aren't." He patted Noah on the arm. "Your righteous indignation is noted and filed. Now come on, let's go count our blessings and get a slice of pie, somewhere uptown."

"I'm not leaving."

"I'm sorry . . . what?"

"Not without everybody else who was brought in with me."

Charlie didn't respond right away.

"You're sure about what you saw," he said at last.

"Positive."

"Because if I open this can of worms again and I come up empty-handed? There's a good chance we're going to blow this deal I just made."

"Charlie, I'm sure."

"Okay," the lawyer said quietly. "Let me look into it and I'll see what I can do. But I'll tell you right now, whatever I find out, this is going to take a lot more chips than I've got in my pocket. That means I'll have to call your dad."

That wasn't welcome news, but Noah took a deep breath and nodded his permission.

CHAPTER 14

He'd kept calm as he walked down the last long hallway toward the exit of the First Precinct, but as Noah finally stepped out onto the sidewalk his heart began to work so hard he could nearly see it pounding beneath his borrowed shirt.

Injustice exists, Charlie had said, and for that fact his young client was now profoundly thankful. If it had been an abuse of power that put him in jail for most of the night, then it was surely a second abuse that had coerced the authorities to let him go. But, however it was won, it was still freedom, and maybe for the first time he fully understood the meaning of that word.

According to Charlie, after he'd started digging, a group of cops had eventually come forward to corroborate Noah's version of the evening's events: they'd apparently wanted to play no part in the railroading of this harmless group of like-minded citizens. Just as a minor rebellion was threatening to break out between the actual uniformed officers and the contract security forces who'd been working the scene, a phone call had come in from some high echelon, and right away everything was abruptly and quietly settled.

Noah stopped near the street, suddenly spent and unsteady, and leaned against a lamppost for support. He took in a deep breath of the cold, sobering night air, right through a thin dagger of pain that jabbed hard between his ribs. It hurt, but not as though anything was permanently damaged in there; bent for sure, but not broken.

All the others had begun filtering out behind him, checking their watches, counting and pocketing their returned personal effects, everyone looking thoroughly relieved and happy and hardly any the worse for wear. The out-of-towners were scanning the urban horizon for landmarks as though they'd been airdropped into the darkest corner of Borneo without a compass. But one by one they helped each other, and before long most of them seemed to have gone their separate ways to sleep off the evening's adventure, safe and sound in their own rooms instead of a prison cell.

Noah was surprised by how different things appeared outside. Hours ago it had been stormy, bleak, and miserable, but now the sky was clearing with the soft lights of the predawn metropolis outshining all but the brightest stars.

Something lightly brushed his arm and the contact shook him out of his reflections. As he turned to see who'd touched him he found himself needing to look up to make eye contact.

"Just wanted to say my thank-you," Hollis said. If he'd still had his hat he would have been clutching it shyly in his hands.

"Hey, don't mention it."

"No, no." Hollis shook his head solemnly. "I'm in your debt."

"I'll make a deal with you," Noah said. "Tell me what time it is and we'll call it even."

The big man looked up and seemed to take a bearing on a number of celestial bodies before ciphering a moment. "I'd say she's nigh onto half-past four in the morning, give or take some."

"Four-thirty. Should I assume that's Mountain Time?"

Hollis smiled politely, as though a good friend had made a joke that wasn't very funny. "Good night, now," he said.

"Take care."

Up the street a few blocks Noah saw his car round the corner. He raised a hand to make himself known to the driver and watched the Mercedes blink its brights and signal toward the curb.

Noah took a step toward the car, but stopped when he heard familiar voices behind him. He turned to see Molly and her mother saying good-bye to the last of their departing compatriots. The two of them had apparently stayed back to make sure everyone made it out to the street. When they saw him standing there Molly whispered something in her mom's ear and they walked up to him together.

"We were never properly introduced," the older woman said. "I'm Beverly Emerson."

"Noah Gardner." They shook hands. "It goes without saying, but I wish we could have met without all this trouble."

"I understand we have you to thank for going to bat for all of us tonight."

"That makes me sound a lot more noble than I feel."

"I appreciate what you did, very much." She gave her daughter a small motherly nudge with an elbow.

"So do I," Molly said. There was something hard to place in the way she was looking at him; it wasn't quite an apology in her eyes, but something like it.

For his part, he was feeling more and more uncomfortable with all the misplaced gratitude, as though he'd done any more than throw his father's weight around.

"I'll pass your regards along to my lawyer when I see him again. He's still inside cleaning up after me." The car arrived, eased up to a smooth stop, and its door locks clicked. Given the circumstances he would have preferred less of a showboat, but the dispatcher had sent one of the silver S600 Pullmans from the downtown garage, a vehicle only slightly less ostentatious than a Richie Rich stretch limousine. “Could I offer you two a ride somewhere?”

“Oh, that would be fantastic,” Beverly said.

Molly took the seat across from him, with her mother beside. The interior of this particular car was designed as a four-person conference room and workspace. Even so, its amenities were every bit as over-the-top as any limo devoted to simple luxury. Every point of contact was hand-worked leather and rare polished wood. Each of the four seats, arranged two-facing-two, was bordered by glowing flat panels ready to provide access to a dizzying array of information or entertainment. Touchscreens were embedded seamlessly in the armrests and consoles, poised to order up any conceivable human need. The entire vehicle was a rolling monument to the comforts of First World business royalty; for the cost of the custom work alone within these few cubic feet, you could easily buy a nice house almost anywhere in the world.

“I don’t always get to travel like this,” Noah apologized as the car got under way. “But just for perspective, my dad wouldn’t be caught dead in a Mercedes. He rides in an armored Maybach 62, or he walks."

It turned out that their destinations were all in nearly opposite directions. When the driver asked "Where to?" over the intercom Noah guided him first to the nearest of the three, the Chelsea Hotel. Meanwhile, the two women were looking around at their lavish surroundings, seeming hesitant to touch anything for fear that if they broke it they might have to buy it.

"You'll like this," Noah said, as he opened a center compartment by his side. Behind the sliding door was a neat pyramid of Turkish hand towels, kept constantly warm and moist like fresh dinner rolls. With a set of tongs he passed one to each of them, and then unrolled his own and pressed the steaming cloth to his face, rubbed in the heat, leaned back, and breathed in the faint scents of citrus and therapeutic herbs. His riding companions did the same, and soon there were long sighs from across the compartment, the sounds of unrepentant indulgence, comfort, and relief.

He knew exactly what they were feeling, though he was managing to keep somewhat quieter about it. The physical sensation was nice enough, but a great mental weight had also been lifted, and that was just now sinking in. The bad night had officially run its course and all three of them were still standing.

For the next round of refreshment Noah opened the side bar and passed across a soft drink for each of them. Several blocks whispered past the long windows; despite the occasionally rugged pavement and the never-ending city noises outside, the car's interior was pin-drop quiet and steady enough for major surgery.

"Molly tells me that you're a creative writer."

Noah had been in the midst of a sip, and nearly spit out his ginger ale.

"Oh, is that how she put it?"

"It's such an interesting business you're in," Beverly said. "What's a typical day like, if you don't mind my asking?"

"Typical day," he said, considering. "Looking at Friday, yesterday now, let's see . . . I can't really discuss what I did early in the morning, same with the afternoon, but at midday I wrote some talking points for a man, a U.S. senator from out west who's about to become the subject of an ethics investigation."

"Did he do something wrong?"

"Absolutely yes, he did. He helped set up a former aide as an unregistered lobbyist, and then he sat in some questionable meetings in support of that business, and while he was at it he was also carrying on a hot-and-heavy love affair with the guy's wife for almost a year."

"Oh, my."

"Yeah, it's all connected in some pretty sick ways."

"And what did you give him to say?"

"You've heard it before—there's been no wrongdoing, the charges are baseless, a pledge of full cooperation, faith in the process, a little slam at the motivations of his accusers—short and sweet, because he's so eager to get back to serving the needs of his constituents. Believe me, this sort of thing is routine. It'll be in the papers tomorrow night; that's why I can tell you about it."

Noah had been through this introductory conversation many times and so he knew what the next question would be. He'd answered it often enough, at scores of cocktail parties and on hundreds of first dates, and his answer had become so smooth and automatic that he no longer had to worry much about it. Trouble was, though the words were basically the same, Beverly Emerson asked the question in a manner that no one else ever had.

"But doesn't it bother you sometimes, Noah?"

It wasn't asked in mock amazement, or as a high-handed moral judgment, not even as the (much more common) probe for good advice on how best to sidestep one's conscience in a similarly shady career. Instead she asked the question with genuine compassion, as if she already knew what was in his heart. That gave him no real choice but to answer it honestly.

"Whenever I make the mistake of stopping to actually think about it? Yes, it really does bother me."

The car had pulled up to its first stop, idling there.

"This is me," Beverly said. As the driver opened the side door she hugged her daughter and whispered good night, then leaned forward to pat Noah on his knee.

"My friend, it's been an experience. I hope to see you again real soon."

"Good night." He raised his soda bottle. "Here's to a quieter night next time."

Molly watched her mother's departure until she'd disappeared safely into the hotel lobby. Then the car was moving again; the driver would choose a scenic holding pattern while awaiting further directions. Oftentimes, he'd surely been instructed, his work was as much about the journey as the destination.

"You've been awfully quiet," Noah said.

"I guess I have." There was a display screen on a swing arm that was partially between them, and Molly eased it aside. "Do you have any music in this car?"

"Sure." He tapped a touchscreen near the door, and having no idea what she was into, let the vehicle decide on a playlist.

"It was my twenty-eighth birthday to-day," Noah said. "Yesterday, I mean."

"Happy birthday."

"Thanks. When I blew out the candle on my cupcake, I made a wish that we'd spend some time together tonight."

She smiled a bit. "You probably should have been more specific."

"You're right. I should have said not behind bars."

A song began to play low over the speakers, just a sweet, haunting voice and a quiet guitar.

"Noah?"

"Hmm?"

"I want to apologize."

"For what?"

"I think I misjudged you."

"I don't know if you did or not."

She looked out the window for a while. There was a scuff and a bruise on her cheek from the fight in the bar, but these marks did nothing to diminish the profile that he'd found so enchanting at first sight.

"Where are we going?" she asked.

"Nowhere right now. Do you want to go home?"

She shook her head. "I'm hungry."

"Say no more." Noah touched the intercom. "Eddie, could you take us up to Amy Ruth's, on One-hundred-and-sixteenth? And call ahead, would you? I don't think they're open yet. Tell Robert we need some orange juice and two Al Sharptons at the curb." Through the glass divider, he saw the driver nod his head and engage the Bluetooth phone system.

"What's an Al Sharpton?" Molly asked.

"Fried chicken and waffles. You're a Southern girl, right?"

She nodded. "But I think the South may be a little bigger than you New Yorkers think. I've never heard of chicken and waffles."

"Then I guess you're in for a treat, aren't you?"

On the way to the restaurant he learned a little more about her life. Her family had moved around a great deal when she was young, following her father's job as a journeyman engineer for Pratt & Whitney. They'd ended up living near Arnold Air Force Base outside Manchester, Tennessee. When her dad was killed in an accident at the testing facility there, that's where they stayed. Her mother then reclaimed her maiden name and started the patriot group they were both still a part of, the Founders' Keepers, a few years later.

"How old were you when you lost your father?" Noah asked.

"Nine."

He sighed, and shook his head. "I was ten when my mom died."

"I'm sorry."

"You know what? New topic. Ask me anything."

"Okay. Who's the most fascinating person you've ever met?"

He didn't hesitate. "President Clinton. Hands down."

"Really?"

"All politics aside, you've never seen so much charisma stuffed into one human being. And you brought up the subject of lying earlier—this man could keep twenty elaborate, interlocking whoppers in his head at a time, improvising on the fly, and have you believing every word while you're holding a stack of hard evidence to the contrary. His wife might be even smarter than he is, but she doesn't have any of that skill at prevarication, and Gore was pretty helpless if he ever dropped his script. But Clinton? He's like one of those plate spinners at the circus: he makes everything look completely effortless. And obviously, in a related skill, he's a total Svengali with the chicks."

"I never found him all that attractive."

"Oh, but it's a whole different thing when someone like that is right next to you, as opposed to on your TV. If he was sitting here now, where I'm sitting? I promise, you'd be helpless. He wouldn't even have to try. You'd listen to him recite from the phone book for an hour and swear it was written by Oscar Wilde. Clinton could read you a fairy tale and you'd be down to your panties by the time Rapunzel let down her golden hair."

"I'll have to take your word for it."

"That being said, he's also one of the most ruthless sons of bitches who ever walked the earth, and we won't see another one like him for generations." He briefly checked their progress out the window. "And how about you?"

"Hmm?"

"Who's your most fascinating person?"

"Oh." Molly thought for a moment. "My mother, I guess. I don't travel in the circles you do, but I'm a huge fan of integrity." She took a last sip from her soda, leaned back, and put the bottle down. "Speaking of fascinating parents, your father would be a gripping subject."

"That he would."

"So?"

"Let me think about where to start . . . Rhodes Scholar, that's a little-known fact. He was studying anthropology at Oxford when he met a man named Edward Bernays—Bernays was an admiring nephew of Sigmund Freud, if that explains any part of this messed-up business—and Mr. Bernays needed some new blood, someone with my father's skill set, to give a shot in the arm to the industry he'd invented a few decades before."

"Public relations."

"Right. Bernays got his start in the big leagues helping Woodrow Wilson beat the drums to push the U.S. into World War I. And my father's first project with him was a massive propaganda campaign for Howard Hunt and the CIA, along with the United Fruit Company, when they all got together to overthrow the president of Guatemala in 1954."

"No."

"Yes. And the rest is literally history."

She frowned. "I just imagine armies and tanks in the streets when I think of a coup d'état, not a bunch of posters and leaflets."

"No, no, it's so much more than that—politics and war, it's all social psychology, and maybe it always has been. Look at the PR push that got the American people behind going back to war with Iraq in 2003. That wasn't our company, it was the Rendon Group in Washington, but they do the same work we do. And we don't take sides unless we're paid to do so. If somebody comes to us and wants to drum up support for a war, for example, we don't ask whether it's right or wrong, any more than the ad agency for McDonald's asks whether their client is really better than Burger King. But in our case it's not just words and pictures; that makes it seem too simple. Public relations is the scientific engineering of consent."

"I'm not sure I understand."

"Take a manufactured takeover, like Guatemala. We engineered the overthrow of a democratically elected president, and this guy was popular, he was going to take their land back from United Fruit and return it to the people. So he had to be demonized before he could be taken down. If you just march in one night, the people might rise up and resist, and you don't want that. They have to be pacified, so their minds are the first thing you have to change.

"Use our own country as an example. Eighty million citizens own guns in America, you'd never win if they all started pushing back. You can't take away the freedom of an aware, informed populace; they have to give it up themselves.

"So the soldiers come last, and if the PR job's done right then there's almost no fight left in the public at all. By the time the tanks roll in, the people welcome them. You know, the whole 'hearts and minds' thing. They submit to searches, give up all their rights, and forget about their neighbors that got taken away. Listen, the centerpiece on the bookshelf of Joseph Goebbels was a book by Edward Bernays, and I don't have to tell you how effectively the Nazis used PR. Now, I know that's a hideous example—"

"I'm glad to hear you say that."

"—but from the very beginning, all of the old guys in this business and their friends in the ruling class, they really saw themselves as the new founding fathers. Seriously, they thought of themselves as shepherds, and the great unwashed masses as their helpless flock. Bernays especially, he believed it was the responsibility of the elites in society to manipulate the general public into decisions they weren't smart enough to make on their own, by whatever means necessary.

"His vision for this country, for the world, really, was a huge, benevolent nanny state, a plutocracy, where the people would be spoon-fed in every aspect of their simple, dreary lives. He'd show them how to vote, what to eat, what to love and hate, what to think, and when to think it. And, God help us all, my father took those lessons to heart and built on them. He does what he does better than anybody else ever has."

He realized he'd been going on and on, and noticed only then the bleak expression that had settled into Molly's eyes. She looked like a kid who'd just been told what happens to all the unwanted puppies at the pound.

"That whole subject was kind of a buzzkill, wasn't it?" he said.

"Yeah."

"Okay. No more shop talk."

The car pulled up to the curb outside the

restaurant, the side window glided down, and a broadly smiling man in a white apron approached with a steaming serving tray.

"Young Mr. Gardner."

"Good morning, Robert. Sorry if we got you out of bed."

"No trouble, no trouble at all, I will happily itemize my inconvenience on your tab."

"I'm sure you will. Robert, this is Molly. This is our first meal together, and I wanted to impress her."

The chef passed through his covered plates, carafes, and rolled silverware. "Well, Molly, if nothing else, your new friend at least has some excellent taste in soul food."

There was more eating than conversation as the car made its way south and east again. The chicken and waffles were always amazing, and Molly finished quite a while before he did.

"What was your mom like?" she asked.

"My dad met my mother in 1978, and I'll tell you, I doubt if two people have ever been more different. Oh, this is interesting, my mom is actually in that documentary about Woodstock."

"Which part?"

He waved a hand in front of his eyes. "I don't know exactly, I can't really watch it. She's kind of making out with some hairy guy, and I'm not sure, I think she flashes the cameraman at one point—"

"You're not sure? That's something I'd remember pretty clearly."

"Look, I'm blocking it out, it's my mom, okay? So anyway, years later, late seventies, and she still had her causes that she marched for, but mostly she just loved life, you know? Never wanted much. She had a little apartment in upstate New York, and she was working as a waitress at a resort up there one summer.

"And my father, the man who would become my father, had this huge place down on the lake near there, still owns it, and he saw her in the restaurant, asked her out, and that was it. Kind of a whirlwind romance. I think she was his fourth wife, or maybe his fifth. But he never married again after she was gone."

"So you all lived up there together?"

"Oh, God no. She wouldn't move to the city, and of course he was too big for that little town, so I hardly ever saw him except on holidays. We weren't what you'd call a traditional family unit; hell, I thought he was my grandfather until I was about six. He's quite a bit older than she is. Was." He lost himself for a few moments, and had to take a long look at his hands in order to stop remembering. "Anyway, she died, lung cancer, and I guess Dad didn't know what else to do with me, so he moved me down here."

It was quiet in the car for a minute or so.

"Hey." She tapped him on the knee, and he looked up. "Would you mind if I sat over there with you?"

"No, I don't mind."

The seats were meant for one occupant only but she moved across, put their plates aside, and situated herself easily, side-saddle across his lap, one arm around his back, a hand resting on his chest, her head against his shoulder.

"I think I'm going to like you," Molly said.

"You sound so surprised."

"I guess I am."

He gently put his arm around her, hesitant lest he disturb the moment, but he needn't have worried. She touched his hand, and curled a little closer.

"I think I like you, too," he said. "But I'm warning you right now, if I let down all my defenses, and then you hurt me? Well, you saw what I did to those thugs tonight."

"Oh, no. You'll hit me in the knee with your face?"

"Just as hard as I can."

The ride continued on. Their conversation was easy, just quiet thoughts and topics drifting between the two of them. At Ninetieth Street the driver turned into Central Park and then deftly talked his way past a mounted policeman and a blue barricade at Engineers' Gate. Motor vehicles were strictly forbidden at that time on that day, but it's hard to say no to a car like that, especially when you can't be sure who's riding in the back of it. They took the route slowly, and not just to give the joggers and dog walkers their weekend right of way. For whatever reason the park drive at sunrise on a Saturday had never looked quite so rare, and there was no hurry to leave it behind.

"Noah?"

"Yes."

She stretched dreamily, arched against

him as she did so, and sighed and looked up into his eyes. "Would you take me home now?"

"Sure. Where did you say you lived, down by Tompkins Square Park?"

"No. I mean to your home."

"Oh." He blinked. "Okay."

"I just don't feel safe yet, after last night."

"I can understand that."

"And I'm not talking about anything sexual."

"I'm surprised you even mentioned that. Furthest thing from my mind."

"Really."

"No, not really, but it's okay. So, like a sleepover, nothing sexual. That's cool, I've got an extra room." He touched the intercom and asked the driver to take them to his home at Seventy-ninth and Fifth for their last stop.

"I know it's awkward to talk about it," Molly said, "I just want you to know I wouldn't sleep with someone I just met—"

"Sexually."

"Right. I just wanted to be up front about it. That isn't something I do."

"Got it."

"And I'm not saying I never have. Or that

I might not want to." She straightened his collar, which had apparently been turned under the entire time, and nestled her head against him again. "I've just made some bad mistakes in my life, and I've decided not to repeat them."

"Okay, enough said. You don't know what you're missing in this case, but fine."

CHAPTER 15

They got out at the corner, and as Noah signed off with the driver, he saw Molly standing there on the sidewalk, looking all around as if she'd just stepped off the last bus from Poughkeepsie, taking in the ritzy sights of the Upper East Side.

"Is that where you live?" she asked, pointing.

"No, not there. See those flags? That's the French Embassy." He took her hand and walked her to the intersection. "And down the street there, that's the Metropolitan Museum of Art, which we can walk through sometime if you ever want to get totally blown away. And that's Central Park over there, which you've already seen." He turned her around and pointed up the tower of dark masonry and glass that had been behind her. "And way up there on the twenty-third floor, that's where I live."

They walked inside and made their way across the ornate lobby to the elevator bank. As the double doors were closing a hand reached in to stop them. They reopened to reveal a lanky, fiftyish man in a blue jogging suit. He was flush from a morning run, a rakishly handsome fellow with dark, thinning hair and sharp blue eyes. He thumbed his numbered floor button and those blue eyes gave Molly a leisurely, detailed once-over, which she seemed just barely able to coolly ignore. When the elevator stopped and opened at his floor, the guy glanced to Noah with a subtle nod before he departed, a man-to-man stamp of approval indicating their shared good taste in fine feminine company.

The doors hissed closed again, leaving the two of them alone.

"Was that who I think it was?" Molly asked.

"Eliot Spitzer."

"The governor. Of New York."

"Former governor. And maybe you noticed just then, if you hadn't already read about him in the papers, that he's also a total horndog."

"I did notice."

"Yeah. With great power comes great friskiness. They've all got a lust for something."

"He lives here?"

"That's not all. This five-million-dollar co-op apartment that we're going to stay in tonight? My father owns that. Spitzer's father owns the whole building."

"Gosh."

"Yup."

"He resigned, right?" Molly asked. "What was it that brought him down again?"

"The short answer is, he was caught on a federal wiretap hiring a hooker who makes more in one day than your buddies in the mailroom take home in a year."

"Wow . . . And he fell pretty fast."

"He'll be back in politics before long,

don't worry. The public memory is pretty shallow, and like I said at the bar, up at the top in this world, it's just a big club."

"And we're not in it," she said. "At least, I know I'm not."

The elevator *dinged* and the doors parted, revealing his apartment's elegant entryway.

"Maybe not," Noah said, "but you really shouldn't knock it until you've tried it."

The instant he'd keyed them inside, Molly took off to explore, marveling at the panoramic floor-to-ceiling view, running from room to room like a toy-starved moppet cut loose in FAO Schwarz.

"How big is this place?" he heard her call from somewhere in back.

"It's just half the floor. If you're impressed by this you should see the penthouse sometime."

"And it cost how much again?"

"Five million, plus about sixty thousand a year for maintenance."

She emerged from the guest suite, pointing back behind her. "The shower in that bathroom is bigger than my bedroom back home."

"Speaking of which," Noah said, "I'm going to get cleaned up and turn in. I feel like I've still got jail funk all over me."

"Oh, I do, too."

"Go ahead, then. Everything you need should be in there, and go through the drawers in the dresser, you'll find something to sleep in."

"Okay." She smiled at him then, and it was the one he'd been waiting all these hours to see.

"Okay," he said. "I realize it's seven-thirty in the morning, but good night."

Squeaky-clean at last and dressed for bed, blinds pulled closed, Noah chose a novel from the night table and reclined against a stack of pillows to try to read himself to sleep, within a pale circle of light from his bedside lamp.

In the middle of chapter two he heard a soft knock from the hallway, looked over, then sat up a little straighter when he saw her peeking in.

"Me again," Molly said.

"Hi." He laid his book beside him, holding his page.

"I used your phone. I hope that's okay."

"It's fine, anything you want."

"I was calling about Danny. Remember him? Danny Bailey, from the bar?"

"Yeah. I wish I didn't, but yeah."

"Nobody remembers seeing him after the raid, and he wasn't with the rest of us at the police station. I called around to see if anyone had heard from him."

"And they hadn't, I gather."

She shook her head.

"I'm sure he'll turn up," Noah said. "God knows he's old enough to take care of himself. Go ahead, try to get some rest. We can check again later on."

"Okay," Molly said. But she made no move from the doorway.

"Do you need another blanket or something?"

"Could I come in?"

"Sure," he said, and she did. "Hey, you found my lacrosse shirt. Ten years I've been looking for that thing."

"You played lacrosse in school?" The faded jersey was much too big, of course, and she'd gathered the slack and tied it up, leaving a spellbinding glimpse of a taut, smooth waist above the northern border of a lucky pair of his own navy boxers.

"Rode the bench mostly," he said. Her hair was down, towel-dry and glistening, dark and curly and caressing her shoulders as she walked. "It's funny, that shirt looks a lot better now than I remember it."

When she reached the edge of the bed she crawled up onto the far end of the tall king-size mattress, walked its length on her knees, and then flopped down next to him with an easy sigh, sharing his pillows. "What are you reading?" she asked.

He showed her the title briefly, and then put the book back down. "I thought you were going to sleep in the other room."

"Do you mind?"

"No, not a bit. It's just like that time my aunt Beth took me to the candy store and then wouldn't let me eat anything. I didn't mind that, either."

"I'll go if you want."

"No, stay, stay. I'm kidding. Kind of. Just try not to do anything sexy."

"Thanks." She ran her hands through her hair and stretched again, wriggled herself under the covers, and rolled onto her side with one arm across him, the long, cool silkiness of her bare legs against his skin.

"Now see?" Noah said. "That's what I just asked you not to do."

"I'm only getting comfortable." Her voice was already sleepy, and she shivered a bit. "My feet are cold."

"Suit yourself, lady. I'm telling you right now, you made the rules, but you're playing with fire here. I've got some rules, too, and rule number one is, don't tease the panther."

"Okay, I'll be good." She pulled herself up by the collar of his T-shirt, as if with the last ounce of strength remaining after her long day, and gave him a peck on the cheek.

"Good night," she whispered.

"Good night, Molly."

Noah picked up his paperback and tried his best to rejoin the story there, but when he found he'd read the same paragraph at least twenty times over, he gave it up and put the book aside. In that author's defense no arrangement of ink on a page could possibly hold a candle to the twists his actual day had taken, nor could any fiction likely lure his mind from this strange, beautiful character lying beside him, right there in real life. He was more than satisfied to simply listen to her quiet, steady breathing and watch her settle into a peaceful, deepening slumber. Before too long he'd joined her wherever she was traveling, having begun to dream quite a while before he finally drifted away.

PART TWO

"The argument that the two parties should represent opposed ideals and policies . . . is a foolish idea. Instead, the two parties should be almost identical, so that the American people can throw the rascals out at any election without leading to any profound or extensive shifts in policy. Then it should be possible to replace it, every four years if necessary, by the other party, which will be none of these things but will still pursue, with new vigor, approximately the same basic policies."

—PROFESSOR CARROLL QUIGLEY, AUTHOR OF *Tragedy & Hope*

"The popular will cannot be taken for granted, it must be created."

—HERBERT CROLY, AUTHOR OF *The Promise of American Life*

CHAPTER 16

Stuart Kearns flipped his black ID folder closed when it seemed his credentials had been sufficiently absorbed by the desk sergeant. The man's face was a classic deadpan, but when he looked up a faint glimmer of engagement had finally dawned there.

Kearns passed across a manila envelope that carried authorization forms for the interview and a conditional catch-and-release waiver for the prisoner in question. The papers were curtly received and slid into the queue with all the care and attention of a career man on the assembly line. Then, as he was directed with a wordless tic of the head, Agent Kearns took a short walk to a seat in a small side office to wait his turn, just like everybody else.

It was just another privilege of the badge, he supposed. Civilians have to go all the way to the Department of Motor Vehicles to get this kind of white-glove treatment.

It was a power thing, really, petty but always in-your-face in every bureaucratic exchange. A yardstick of rank and importance gets held up to a person, a pecking order is established with each interaction, and in this case the FBI is taken down a peg or two by a mere drone from the NYPD. To be fair, maybe it wasn't the whole Bureau that had received the brunt of the disrespect, just this one road-worn and burnt-out representative.

The fact that such people and their passive-aggressive infighting were a big part of his professional life bothered him less than it used to. After thirty-one years of beating his head against the wall in law enforcement, a man shouldn't be surprised to find his brains bashed in and the wall still standing. But you can know a thing like that and go on acting like you don't. His first wife had said it best, on her way out the door. *It's not other people, it's not your boss or your enemies or the kid at the supermarket. It's you. You ask for it, Stuart, and all they do is give it to you.*

Thanks again, Sunshine, for all your support. You were the best of your breed; spouse number two didn't even bother to leave a note.

The little space where he'd been seated was broom-clean but musty, windowless and bare, roller-painted a dreary shade of leftover beige, its furniture decades old, stained and mismatched. The scarred wooden desk might well have dated from the days when Herman Melville had written of this jail before the Civil War. Whatever range of guest accommodations might exist in the huge expanse of the Manhattan Detention Complex, this waiting room must have rated somewhere near the bottom of the scale.

A picture frame stood on the desk, still displaying the yellowing promotional family photo inserted at the factory. Overlaid on that warm, staged scene of rural togetherness was the dim reflection of an unexpectedly older man, jowly and gray, looking back at him from the surface of the glass. The years do go by.

The sergeant from the triage desk knocked and entered, then passed him his carbonless copy of the necessary forms, all signed and authorized. "They're getting your man now," he said. "Be out in a minute."

"Fine."

"You should have told me," the sergeant added, suddenly a great deal more civil than he'd been before.

Stuart Kearns straightened his glasses but didn't look up from the papers in his hands.

"Either that," he said, "or you should have asked."

The sergeant correctly sensed he'd been dismissed, and left the room.

The man's sudden snap to attention was no doubt due to the source of Kearns's assignment, which, to be honest, would have become evident only after a look through the sealed paperwork he'd provided. A desk cop with a bad attitude might get a chuckle out of sending the average federal agent to cool his heels for half a morning just because he can, but when the orders come down from the D.C. headquarters of the Joint Terrorism Task Force, well, nobody at that low level wants to be fingered as a bottleneck in the War on Terror.

He checked his watch. Half-past seven on Saturday morning, and by the noise outside, the Tombs were officially awakening.

These places had a sound all their own. Back there among the inmates it would be drowned out by the hue and cry of those right around you, but from a distance those troubled voices all intermingled into a sound something like an ill wind—an airy, echoing howl that drifted up from the cell blocks at certain times of the day and night.

While he was waiting he pulled a hefty folder from his briefcase and opened it flat. This was an abridged version of the FBI file for the young man he was about to see. The guy was a marshmallow, he'd been assured, and by a covert order he'd just spent a long hard night in a cage full of the worst serial offenders this venue had to offer, so he would certainly be softened up even more by this morning. With luck, once a deal was on the table there wouldn't be too much time wasted in negotiation.

It was an unusually thick file for someone who'd never been arrested for anything more serious than fairly minor narcotics offenses. Cocaine mostly, some party drugs, and he'd been busted with a modest grow operation and a trash bag full of premium bud at one point, years ago. He'd plea-bargained his way out of that last one, in exchange for testimony against his accomplices. That fact was worth an underscore.

A halfhearted suicide attempt when he was in his twenties, just a cry for help most likely, but then another one, a real one, during a ninety-day stint in a county lockup in Louisiana—this page was dog-eared, as was his psych evaluation from the time.

There were also some tax problems and other run-ins with the law dating back to his teens, but the latest entries concerned evidence gathered through recent home and business surveillance warrants, highlighted transcripts of a monitored ham-radio show, and a list of some videos he'd produced that were now circulating through the Patriot culture on the Internet. *Hate speech/counterterrorism* was the box that was checked on his first wiretap request, but the latest such authorization had been requisitioned by three cooperating divisions, as abbreviated in the margin: DC-JTTF, NM-DTWG, NM-WMDWG.

The Joint Terrorism Task Force, the Domestic Terrorism Working Group, and the Weapons of Mass Destruction Working Group. The last two offices were based in New Mexico.

Based on this file and, more important, based on Stuart Kearns's own long experience in the field, this little guy didn't seem like he'd ever been much for the government to worry about. It was almost as though they decided years ago that they were going to get him, but they hadn't yet known exactly how. He didn't seem dangerous, only outspoken and troublesome. But, heaven knows, stranger things have happened.

In these times, the tug-of-war between national security and personal freedom was becoming a losing battle for civil libertarians. It had happened bit by bit, with each slight loss of liberty or privacy sounding like a reasonable protection when viewed on its own. The effect was cumulative, however.

Today even the most liberal of politicians were openly floating the idea of preventive detention for terrorism suspects: basically, indefinite incarceration without charges or trial, all for what sometimes amounted to little more than thought crimes.

The presumption of innocence was an admirable doctrine in simpler days, though at best it had always been unevenly applied in practice—more an ideal to strive toward than a true and present cornerstone of American justice. In recent years an increasingly frightened public had approved of that hallowed concept being systematically replaced with another, especially when it came to certain groups and offenses: When in doubt, lock them up.

Clipped to the file was an eight-by-ten photo taken of his man only last night, when he'd appeared at a far-right-wing protest rally of some kind. He'd run afoul of the cops, and that's when Stuart's midnight call had come; a necessary piece of an important puzzle was about to drop into his lap. The hope was that this fellow would be interested in helping his country, but in case he wasn't, the fallback was to make sure he'd be pretty desperate to help himself.

Three corrections officers approached the open door with a heavily shackled prisoner in their charge. He could barely walk on his own, either from the effects of heavy fatigue, the abuse he'd obviously taken from his cellmates overnight, or both.

They brought him in, sat him down across the desk, cuffed him to the chair, dropped a Baggie of belongings on the filing cabinet, and with a nod and a signature from his new custodian, left without a word being spoken.

The guy's head was hanging, chin to his chest. Without the arms of the chair holding him upright he'd probably have slumped right to the floor.

"Daniel Carroll Bailey?"

He flinched at the sound of his name like he'd been roused cold from a nightmare. The chain at his wrist snapped taut; he squinted and hunched down as though expecting another boot to the side of the head. He looked pretty bad, but with some cleaning up maybe not unable to travel, and that was good for the schedule. Beyond the cuts and bruises, if lack of sleep was his main problem then they were in good shape; he could rest on the plane.

"Are you my lawyer?" Bailey asked.

His words were weak and not formed very well. Swollen jaw, eyes trying hard to focus, one ear freshly torn ragged at the lobe from an earring theft, or maybe a bite. Before they'd brought him in someone had done a half-assed job of swabbing the blood that had dried around his nose and mouth, but a bit of real doctoring might be needed before they could get on the road for the airport.

"No, I'm not a lawyer."

"I want my phone call, they won't let me have my phone call—"

"You can make your call now if you want, and line up an attorney. That's your right. But if you decide to go that route I want to warn you. This is from a high authority, the highest; in fact with your past record, your charges from last night, and especially"—he patted the folder in front of him—"the evidence from an ongoing federal investigation, the best any lawyer's going to get you is fifteen to twenty years in a place much worse than this. That's a fact. But it doesn't have to be like that, Danny."

Slowly, the other man seemed to be

recovering his wits, or at least enough of them to understand what he was facing.

"Who are you?"

Stuart Kearns showed his ID, then took out his card and slid it across to the very edge of the desk.

"I've got nine words for you that I'll bet you never thought you'd be so glad to hear," he said. "I'm from the government, and I'm here to help."

CHAPTER 17

Over the intercom came an announcement that they'd just reached cruising altitude at 44,000 feet, and to punctuate that bit of news the NO SMOKING light went off with a quiet *ting*.

It was a nice touch, but on a jet this size the copilot could just as easily have leaned around his seat and shouted down the aisle to update his two lone passengers on the progress of the flight.

Stuart Kearns took a pack of Dunhills from one jacket pocket, his lighter from another, then reclined his seat a notch and lit up. He inhaled deeply, then blew a thin white ring of smoke and watched it drift up toward the rounded cabin ceiling.

"What are you doing?"

Danny Bailey had awakened from his nap and was staring at the lit cigarette across the narrow aisle as though he were watching a bank robbery in progress.

"You can still smoke on a charter. On this one, anyway." Kearns extended the pack to him, shook a filter tip halfway out. "Come on, you know you want to."

"I quit five years ago."

"Last chance. It's not every day you get a free pass to break the rules." Bailey didn't budge, so Kearns returned the cigarettes to his pocket. "Hey, remind me, how old are you?"

"I'm thirty-four."

"In the decade you were born a man could still smoke a cigar on any flight across this country. Can you believe that?"

"Listen," Bailey said, "what's your name again?"

"Kearns. Stuart Kearns."

"That's right—Special Agent Kearns. Well listen, Stuart, I'm glad to be out of jail, but it doesn't exactly feel like I'm free."

He nodded. "That's right."

"Right. So no offense, but there's no reason to strain yourself pretending you're my friend. Let's stick to business. What do you say you just enjoy your smoke and then tell me what the hell I need to do to go home."

It wasn't an elaborate scheme; it couldn't be when success relied on the performance of an informant under duress. In undercover work, if anything can go wrong it generally does. The more straightforward the plan, the better. Keep it simple, and you keep it safe.

The targets for the operation were low-level militia types with a desire to graduate to a full-blown act of domestic terrorism. They were in the market for funding, logistical support, and some serious weapons. If all went well then the only thing they'd be getting at the final handoff was arrested.

Danny Bailey would be brought along to the first in-person meet-up, to lend a crowning bit of credibility to the proceedings; he was currently the closest thing the Patriot underground had to a national spokesperson. In essence, Bailey would play the Oprah to Kearns's Dr. Phil.

The operation itself would be quick, in

and out, but the lead-up to it had required a long and careful preparation.

A few years earlier a website had been set up by the IT guys at the Bureau: www.stuartkearns.com. The backstory on the site went like this: A former federal agent had been run out of his job when he'd tried to blow the whistle on some dangerous truths. After repeated death threats, this ousted agent had gotten angry and gone public on the Web in an effort to protect himself from retribution, and to continue his crusade to expose the dark forces intent on causing a global financial collapse and ushering in a one-world government.

The global villains named on the site were a grab bag pulled from the latest full-color catalog of extremist paranoia: the Zionists, the Royals, the IMF and World Bankers, the Rothschilds and Rockefellers, the Bilderbergers, the Masons, the Grovers, the Vatican, you name it. It was a big tent, and that was the point. Search engines had soon begun to present Stuart's site as a top-twenty destination for all manner of curious like-minded wackos, and traffic became fairly brisk.

It was evident from the home page that

this wasn't a place for the no-guts armchair militiaman. The rants, posts, links, videos, documents, and forums hosted by this fictional ex-fed-turned-Patriot made it pretty clear that he believed a violent uprising, a shooting war, was the only route remaining to set things right again in America.

This site and its inflammatory content formed what's known as a *troll* in the parlance of the Internet culture. Trolling is a fishing term; you toss your lure over the side and forget about it, letting it drag behind the boat in hopes that something you want to catch will eventually take the bait.

With 200 million websites out there no one really expected this obscure destination would make Stuart Kearns a household name among the diverse followers of all the competing hate groups. The FBI and many other agencies maintained thousands of such baited traps; sometimes they paid off, most times they didn't.

But then one day the troll hooked a fish, and from the first tug it felt like a big catch.

A new discussion group had formed in a private chat room on the site, under the heading of "Direct Action." The members began to kick around the logistics of the

Oklahoma City bombing, Tim McVeigh's attack on the Murrah Federal Building in 1995: what had gone right, what had gone wrong, and the various conspiracy theories still swirling around the event and its aftermath. With some encouragement from the forum leader the discussion evolved—some half-baked plans that would've gotten the job done better, other vulnerable targets, men, methods, and materials. Many dropped out of the conversation as things got more serious, but eight stayed on.

This remaining group progressed to tentative voice chats and then to encrypted e-mail exchanges, all the while inching their way from what had started as a mere discussion toward a solid plot that could actually be executed. Three more anonymous participants eventually got cold feet and dropped out, leaving five people ready, willing, and able to commit a grotesque act of domestic terrorism.

And now it was time to reel them in.

"These aren't my people," Bailey said. "You've gotta be kidding me, man, I've never told anybody to do any violence—"

"I've watched your videos, son, and you don't exactly tell them not to, either."

"Aw, come on." Bailey sat back in his seat, shaking his head. "I've got to go over the top just to get people up off the couch. Have any of you guys ever actually read the First Amendment? Tom Clancy wrote two books about how terrorists could use airliners as weapons before 9/11. Did you arrest him for that?"

"No, but I'll tell you what, we sure as hell brought him in for questioning."

"I'm not the right guy for this."

"Well, you're the one I've got. You're a big name to these people. Trust me, they'll believe what you say, and that's all we need. You're just going to come in and stroke them a little bit, tell them you know me and that I'm concerned there might be an agent among them—"

"You're concerned that one of them might be a mole. That's a nice touch."

"Thanks," Kearns said. "And I asked you to come with me and check them out before I'd agree to see them in person. It'll be fine, believe me. Just that first meeting, and maybe a little follow-up afterward. That's all you've got to do."

"And then I'm out of this, and you'll leave me alone?"

"Stay out of trouble, and there's no reason you'll ever have to deal with someone like me again."

"I'm going to need to get that in writing."

"You'll get it." Kearns put out his cigarette in the armrest ashtray. "Have you done any acting, like in high school?"

"Why?"

"Some people get nervous when they have to lie, that's all. This isn't much of a performance, but I want to know you can handle the pressure. You can't flake out on me."

"Oh, you want to know if I can fool a handful of small-time desperadoes role-playing *Red Dawn* in their living room?" Bailey nodded, took off his dark glasses, picked up his surveillance file from Kearns's lap, and went through the stack until he found a series of photos about a third of the way down. "Did you miss these?" he asked.

The photos, time-stamped from earlier in the year, all featured a man dressed and made up in a convincing impersonation of Colonel Sanders, complete with goatee, white suit, and black-string bow tie. In the top picture he was shaking hands with a distinguished-looking gentleman under a huge United Nations seal.

"Is that you?" Kearns asked.

"That's me." Bailey pointed to the man standing next to him in the photo. "And that's Mr. Ali Treki, the president of the UN General Assembly, receiving an official state visit from the founder of Kentucky Fried Chicken, who'd been dead for almost thirty years at the time. Look." He flipped to the next picture. "He even let me sit in his chair and bang the gavel."

"You did this when, last year?"

"Those pictures made the *Daily News* that week. It was a publicity stunt for my DVD on UN corruption, *United AbomiNations.* It's sold out, but I'll see if I can get you a copy."

"I'll add it to my Netflix queue. How did you get past security?"

"What security? Security walked me all the way up to the president's office." Bailey smiled. "Everybody loves the Colonel."

"That's good," Kearns said.

"Oh, Stuart, that's not just good. That's finger-lickin' good."

Despite the circumstances, it was clear

to see what people connected with in Danny Bailey. He had an easy charm about him, a certain smoothness that could draw you in like a great salesman does as he effortlessly talks you right down to the bottom line. When it comes to undercover work that kind of skill is more valuable than it might sound at first. If things start sliding sideways your wits can sometimes get you out of a situation where your gun might just get you killed.

Kearns nodded and took the file back, with a thought to himself that he should find the time to go through it all more thoroughly. There was clearly quite a bit more to this young fellow than initially met the eye.

CHAPTER 18

Bacon.

Scent appeals to the most primitive of the five basic senses. Unlike a sight or sound or even a touch, an aroma can rocket straight to the untamed emotions with no stops required at the smarter parts of the brain. You like it or you hate it; that's the designed-in depth of raw stimulation the nose is built to deliver. So amid all the other deeper thoughts that should have come to Noah's mind upon awakening, it was *bacon* that crowded them out to come in first across the finish line.

Other wonderful smells of a home-cooked breakfast, recalling the finest mornings from his early childhood, were wafting in from a couple of rooms away. Molly was nowhere to be seen, though an alluring girl-shaped indentation was still evident in the gathering of covers beside him.

He pushed back the quilt and squinted to read the clock on the far wall: 4:35 it said, with no clue whether that made it early the following morning or late that same afternoon. It might take all weekend to get his body clock reset to normal again.

He slipped on his robe and pulled open the bedroom curtains. It was cloudy again and the sun was low; still Saturday, then.

"Are you up, finally?" He heard her voice from the doorway.

"Yeah." When he turned he saw she was already dressed for the day. "Looks like you found the laundry room."

"I went out and got some groceries, too. Your refrigerator was freakishly clean and really empty."

"I eat out a lot."

"Well, I made you something." She smiled. "Late birthday breakfast. Come and get it while it's hot."

As they sat together at the sunroom

table he focused on his food while she returned to chipping away at her half-finished crossword puzzle in the next day's Sunday *Times*.

"You like word games?" Noah asked.

"I love word games."

"Well, if you get stumped over there let me know. Not that I'm so brilliant, but I was on the spelling bee circuit when I was a kid."

"Wow. Nerdy."

"Yeah. I was a late bloomer."

"Here's a long one I need to get. Twelve down: One deeply devoted to wine."

He thought for a moment. *"Sommelier."*

She counted down with a fingertip, shook her head. "Not enough letters; you need eleven."

"I wish you would have told me that."

"Sorry."

"Try . . . *connoisseur*."

"Nope. There's a gimmick this week: the answers all start with the first letter of the clue. So 'one deeply devoted to wine,' it has to start with an *o*."

"Again, that would have been really useful information about twenty seconds ago.

You're making it hard for me to help you, Molly."

"Just trying to keep you humble."

He finished his coffee and put down the cup. "It's *oenophilist.*" She gave him a skeptical frown, so he spelled it out. "O-e-n-o-p-h-i-l-i-s-t. Oenophilist. Wine lover. The *o* in the beginning is silent."

She filled in the letters one by one, her lips pronouncing them soundlessly and precisely as she wrote, eyes darting to follow the hints provided by each new entry. It occurred to him that he could have happily watched her do that simple thing all day long.

"I would have gotten that," she said quietly.

"You know, if you like word games so much I might have a better job for you down at the office."

She put down her pencil, but kept her eyes on the paper in front of her.

"I've been meaning to talk to you about something," Molly said. She got up and took his empty plate and silverware to the sink.

"Okay. Let's talk about it."

"I'm not going to be in town very much longer."

"Why?"

"I'm just not. There were some things I wanted to do here, and I've done them now, so I'll be leaving."

He sat back. "When are you thinking of leaving?"

"Soon." Her attitude had changed abruptly, as though she was steeling herself for a discussion she didn't want to prolong.

"Look, I didn't mean anything when I mentioned a job, I know how you feel about that place—"

"You didn't say anything wrong. This is just the way it is, okay?"

"Okay."

She'd busied herself in silence in the kitchen for a little while, rehanging pans and tidying up briefly, but soon she sat down across from him again, reached over, and put her hand on his.

"Cheer up," Molly said. "Go get ready, and loan me a jacket. I think we should take a walk."

When he came back dressed from the bedroom he found her at the table again with a framed sheet of his childhood schoolwork in her hands, reading it over.

"What is this?" she asked.

"That was a penmanship exercise, from the fifth grade." He pulled up a chair and sat beside her. "I don't even think they teach that anymore, do they? Penmanship?" She tilted the frame a bit so they could both see it clearly. "They asked us to write down something we liked, obviously as neatly as we could, and that was my dad's favorite poem, the last bit of it anyway."

In the upper corner was the first gold star he'd received at his new school, near his new home, in the year that everything had changed. One of his nannies had framed the paper to commemorate the occasion. The movers placed it on a vacant desk in the study when he got this place, but he was certain he hadn't looked at it a second time within those years. And it wasn't quite right to say it was his father's *favorite* poem; more like the old man's justification of his life set in verse. He'd directed his young son to study it so he'd always know the way things really worked in this world.

Noah picked it up, let his thumb brush

the dust from the corner of the glass, and read each metered line aloud.

Then the Gods of the Market tumbled,
and their smooth-tongued wizards
withdrew
And the hearts of the meanest
were humbled
and began to believe it was true
That All is not Gold that Glitters, and
Two and Two make Four
And the Gods of the Copybook
Headings limped up
to explain it once more.

As it will be in the future, it was at the
birth of Man
There are only four things certain
since Social Progress began.
That the Dog returns to his Vomit and
the Sow returns to her Mire,
And the burnt Fool's bandaged finger
goes wabbling back to the Fire;

And that after this is accomplished,
and the brave new world begins
When all men are paid for existing and
no man must pay for his sins,

As surely as Water will wet us, as
surely as Fire will burn,
The Gods of the Copybook Headings
with terror
and slaughter return!

When Noah had finished they sat in silence. Seeing these words again seemed to have taken something out of him. Molly must've sensed the change as well. She took the frame from his hands and laid it on the table.

"Who wrote that?" she asked.

"Rudyard Kipling, in 1919. Not one of his better-known pieces. He'd lost his son in the war and his daughter a few years earlier, and I guess he wasn't so happy with the way things were starting to go in the world. This is only the last few stanzas of the poem; that's all I could fit on the page."

"Pretty heavy stuff for a ten-year-old."

"Yeah," he said. "*The Jungle Book*, it's not."

"And what do you think he was telling you with this, your father?"

"He told me the poem meant that history always repeats itself, that the same mistakes are made over and over, only bigger each time. The wise man knows that if you can't change that, you might as well take full advantage of it. But to me it meant something else."

"And what's that?"

"It's a warning, I guess, about what happens when you forget common sense. You have to read the whole thing to get it. I think it means that there really is such a thing as the truth, the real objective truth, and people can see it if they'll just look hard enough, and remember who they really are. But most of the time they choose to give in and believe all the lies instead."

"I'll bet your father was disappointed to hear that coming from his own little boy."

"You know," Noah said, "if I'd ever had the guts to say it to him, I'm sure he would have been."

Getting outside turned out to be a good idea. Noah was still aching from the thumps he'd taken the previous night, like the random pains you feel only in the days after a rear-end collision, but the cold city air and exercise were relieving a good bit of that.

They'd talked some along the way,

though for the most part it had been a quiet walk. But there was nothing tense or self-conscious in those wordless stretches. He found himself at ease in her company, as if a conversation was always in progress, only spoken in other forms. She stayed close to him, at times with an unexpected gesture of casual intimacy: an arm around his waist for half a block, a finger hooked in his belt loop as they crossed a busy street against the light, a palm to his cheek as she spoke close to his ear to be heard over the din of the traffic.

At Forty-second Street and Seventh Avenue she gradually slowed her pace and then stopped just outside the bustling flow of midtown pedestrians.

People say you never forget your first kiss, but that wasn't the case in Noah's life. Superficial things don't carry enough weight to make a lasting memory. For him the first kiss had faded gradually into the hundredth, the faces and names and situations long ago blending together into a vague, pleasant, collective event. A little thrill, a tentative awkwardness, those sweet few seconds of breathless discovery shared with another, and a momentary sense of what the immediate future together could hold, however brief that time would likely be.

This wasn't like that.

Molly looked into his eyes, and what he saw in her was a perfect reflection of a wanting that he also felt, so there was no delay of invitation and acceptance. It was a different sort of desire than he'd known before, an understanding that something now needed to be said that no language but the very oldest could possibly convey. He bent to her, closed his eyes, and her lips touched his, gently, and again more urgently as he responded. He felt her arms around him, her body yearning against his in the embrace, a knot like hunger inside, heart quickening, cool hands at his back under the warmth of his jacket, searching, pressing him closer still.

With everything to see and hear around them there at the very crossroads of the world, soaring billboards, scrolling news crawlers, bright digital Jumbotrons that lined the tall buildings and blotted out the whole evening sky, it all disappeared to its rightful insignificance, flat as a postcard. That place was left outside their small circle, and if asked right then he might have stayed there within it forever. But he felt her smile against his lips as they were brought back to where they stood by the brusque voice of a passing man, who advised in his native Brooklynese that maybe they should go and get a room.

A light drizzle had begun to fall, and down the block they found a coffee shop with two seats by the window where they could wait out the patch of rain. When he returned from the counter with their cups he found her sitting with a folded newspaper, not reading it but lost somewhere in her thoughts. It was a while before she spoke.

"Noah?"

"I was starting to worry you'd forgotten I was here."

Molly took a deep breath and seemed to collect herself for a moment. "I need to ask you something."

"Okay."

"If we hired you, your company, what would you tell us to do?"

He frowned a bit. "You mean if you and your mom hired us?"

"It's more than just the two of us, you know that. A lot more."

"I don't know," he said. "What is it you want to accomplish again?"

"We want to save the country."

"Oh. Okay. Is that all?"

"That's where we start, isn't it? With a clear objective."

"That's right."

"So?"

"Okay. Let me think for a minute."

Molly had become deadly serious; this wasn't party talk. She didn't take her eyes from his as she waited.

"I guess," he said, "I'd begin by sitting down with all these different groups and trying to focus everyone on the things they agree on—the fundamentals. A platform, you know? Make it easy for people to understand what you're about. Propose some real answers."

"Give me an example."

"I don't know—start with the tax code, since your mom is so passionate about that. How about a set of specific spending cuts and a thirteen percent flat tax to start with? Get that ridiculous sixty-seven-thousand-page tax code down to four or five bullet points, and show exactly what effects it'll have on trade, and employment, and the debt, and the future of the country. And I'm winging it here, but how about real immigration reform? The kind of policies that welcome people who want to come here for the right reasons, and succeed.

"Get the fear out of those big questions, and talk about a brighter future, you know? In our business we call it the *elevator pitch:* how you'd explain your whole outlook, features, and benefits if you had only a ten-floor elevator ride during which to get it across to a stranger. So start with a platform. At least that way they can start to speak with one voice occasionally. You have no political power otherwise."

"And what next?"

He held up his hands. "Slow down for a minute."

"No. What next?"

"Do you see that you're maybe putting me on the spot a little here?" Noah tried to take a sip of his coffee, but it burned him. It was still much too hot to drink. "And what did you mean, *save the country,* by the way? Save it from what?"

She looked at him evenly. "You know what."

"Oh, come on now, Molly. Please tell

me you're not really one of those people, I know you're not—"

"I know there was a meeting at the office yesterday afternoon," she said, lowering her voice but not her intensity. "I saw the guest list on the catering order. I know who was there. I know you were in it. And I think I know what it was about."

"Okay, yes, big surprise, there was a meeting, but I wasn't there for all of it. And do you want to know something else? I don't even know what it was all about, so how could you?"

"Then let's both find out."

"What?"

"Prove me wrong. Let's go right now and find out."

"I can't do that."

"Yes, you can. We'll go to the office right now, and you'll show me that I've got nothing to worry about. If that's the case then that'll be the end of it."

"You're not listening to me, I said I can't—"

"You would if you knew how important it was."

"No, I wouldn't. There are a lot of things I'd do for you, but I can't do that."

"When are you going to grow up, Noah? I know you're not who your father is, but then the next question is, Who are you? It sounds to me like you knew the answer to that when you were in the fifth grade, but you've forgotten now that it's time to be a man."

"I *am* a man, Molly, but I'm not going to risk everything for nothing."

"Do you want me to leave?" Her voice was tight and there were sudden tears in her eyes. "Do you never want to see me again? Because that's what this means."

Now they were starting to attract the attention of those nearby.

"That is so incredibly unfair. Did you even hear what you just said? I can't believe you'd put me in a position like that."

But he'd lost her already. She got up as he was speaking, turned from him without a word, and walked straight out the door.

Noah watched her through the glass and let himself hope for a few seconds that she'd have a change of heart and turn back into his waiting arms so all could be forgiven. But, just like falling in love with someone you've known only for a single day, those things really happened only in the movies.

She was going to leave him sitting there. She wasn't coming back. By the time he'd decided what he had to do, Molly had all but disappeared into the river of weekend tourists and theatergoers flowing through the heart of Times Square.

CHAPTER 19

"You must be out of your mind," Noah said, under his breath. He was addressing himself directly.

Molly was right behind him, holding tight to his hand as he led her through the aisles and racks of designer skirts and blouses toward the store's back rooms.

"You're doing the right thing," she whispered.

He'd elected to avoid the main lobby entrance at 500 Fifth Avenue; too many cameras there, not to mention the sign-in desk that would make a record of the weekend visit. A private elevator led to Arthur

Gardner's suite of offices on the twenty-first floor, and that was the way they'd be going in.

The elevator had originally been an auxiliary freight lift, largely unused until its luxury conversion when Doyle & Merchant established their New York offices here in the 1960s. There was only one wrinkle in the layout: the ground-floor entrance to this elevator had to be located on the next-door tenant's property, which was currently a multilevel, tourist-trendy clothing store.

The employees of this shop were aware that well-dressed strangers might occasionally be seen entering and leaving through their employees-only swinging doors in the back. D&M paid the tenant a monthly fee for the easement, and executive assistants occasionally escorted the firm's more reclusive clients into the agency by this odd, private route. The idea of a semisecret entrance added an extra bit of intrigue to the visit for some.

During normal business hours the protocol was simply to raise your company ID above your head and quietly proceed to the rear of the store, as the floor manager knowingly waved you on. Since an encoded swipe card and a restricted key were required to operate the elevator, no further checks were really necessary.

This was Saturday night, however, and the two of them were dressed more like college students than business executives. Consequently they received a good deal of extra scrutiny as they passed through, and the store's rent-a-cop tracked their progress from a discreet distance, all the way down the back hallway and inside the elevator car. So much for keeping a low profile.

Noah swiped his card and the doors closed, then he inserted the stubby cylindrical key and turned the elevator's panel switch to Enable. There was no vertical line of buttons to choose the floor with; this thing went only two places: all the way up and back down again. With the click of relays and a deep ascending hum the car set into motion.

He was silently watching the wall above the doors where the advancing floor numbers should have been when Molly stepped up to him, close.

"Thank you, Noah."

"I'm not really speaking to you right now."

She touched his chest and put a hand on his shoulder; he looked down into her eyes.

"I hope I'm wrong," she said. "I want to be wrong; you should know that. Now please just decide to forgive me, at least until we're out of here again."

He looked away, but after a time he nodded.

"Okay."

There was only one way to warrant a blatant breach of business ethics such as this, and that was to attribute his actions to a higher cause. If Molly was right, then a cute but quirky mailroom temp had identified a grand, unified, liberty-crushing conspiracy that had been hatched in the conference room of a PR agency. The benefits of learning that would easily outweigh the consequences: forsaking his father's trust and violating the ironclad, career-ending nondisclosure clause of his employment contract. After all, with the fate of the free world in the balance, the prospect of getting fired, disowned, and probably sued into debtor's prison should be among the least of his worries.

If Molly was wrong—and no ifs about

it, she *was* wrong—then he'd be vindicated, she'd be deeply apologetic and sworn to secrecy about this whole fiasco, and there might still be a chance to salvage what remained of the weekend.

A flimsy rationale, maybe, but for the moment it helped him avoid the more troubling thought that after all he'd seen in the last twenty-four hours, deep down he needed to know the truth every bit as much as she did.

The elevator eased to a stop and the doors opened.

The old man's office was never dark. Night or day it was always the same: warmly lit and immaculately kept, smelling faintly of pipe smoke, black tea, and silver polish, furnished with all his fine, precious things. From the art on the walls and pedestals to the antiques and small collections of rarities interspersed among the bookshelves, everywhere you turned there was something priceless. For him it was less a place of business than an inner sanctum of quiet meditation and a shrine to the very real forms of happiness that money could actually buy.

Few employees ever had occasion to

set foot in these rooms and see these sights, but Molly paused only at the sight of one thing.

"What is this?" she asked.

She was looking at a marble sculpture on a pedestal in the corner. Noah's father had commissioned it years ago. The figure depicted was a strange amalgamation of two other works of art: the Statue of Liberty and the Colossus of Rhodes. Molly would have known that much by looking; what she'd meant to ask was, *What does this mean*?

"It's the way my father looks at things . . . at people, I mean: societies. The law may serve some superficial purpose, but it only goes so far," Noah said, touching the spear in the statue's left hand. "At some point the law needs to be taken away and replaced with force. That's what really gets things done. People ultimately want it that way; they're like sheep, lost without a threat of force to guide them. That's what it means."

Molly silently took in the statue for a while longer, like she was memorizing it. After a few more seconds she drew in a deep breath, walked to the door, peeked around the corner to make sure the coast was clear, and then turned and motioned for Noah to follow.

"Let's get this over with," she said.

Weekend work was one of the many things his father frowned upon, which led nearly all of the up-and-coming employees to maintain second offices at home. This allowed them to put in the expected seventy-plus hours per week while appearing to comply with company policy. It also meant that, with luck, Noah and Molly would have the place to themselves for the duration of their espionage.

Down the central hall and adjacent to the conference room they keyed themselves into the locked AV booth, where the presentation files were stored. Molly stood by him as he found the coded folders on the computer, entered their passwords, and prepared the show to be launched from a remote controller at the podium inside.

When they entered the conference room the programmed lights had already dimmed and wide white screens were descending around the walls. Digital projectors hummed and glowed as they received their data, and soon the screens lit up with an introductory slide.

In the beginning he clicked through the content fairly rapidly; this was the section he'd already seen. He paused only when Molly asked him to stop while she absorbed the content of some particular display.

Without the benefit of a speaker to explain them, many of the slides and visuals were difficult to understand. Animated graphs illustrated various social and political trends, time lines ticked off progress toward unnamed goals, maps with highlighted regions expanded or contracted to show unidentified changes over months, years, or decades.

"Stop," Molly said. "Go back one."

They were deeper into the presentation now, past the point at which Noah had left the meeting, but nothing had seemed particularly shocking or frightening to him. He'd breezed right past the screen she'd asked to see again. It was an introductory agenda for the group of very important people who'd come to attend the final half of the meeting.

The heading was "Framework and Foundation: Toward a New Constitution." No names accompanied the headings that followed, only the areas of government that each new attendee supposedly represented.

- Finance / Treasury / Fed/Wall Street / Corporate Axis
- Energy / Environment / Social Services
- Labor / Transportation / Commerce / Regulatory Affairs
- Education / Media Management / Clergy / COINTELPRO
- FCC / Internet / Public Media Transition
- Control and Preservation of Critical Infrastructure
- Emergency Management / Rapid Response / Contingencies
- Law Enforcement / Homeland Security / USNORTHCOM / NORAD / STRATCOM / Contract Military / Allied Forces
- Continuity of Government
- *Casus Belli:* Reichstag / Susannah/Unit 131 / Gladio / Northwoods / EXIGENT

"Who was in this meeting, do you know?" Molly asked.

"The people I saw were mostly from some advance-planning division of the DHS; domestic war-gamers, like the international kind at the Pentagon. There's a stack of tent cards here somewhere with their names. I don't know about the ones who came later; I only had their phone numbers."

"Do you still have that list?"

"No, I don't. I was told to burn it, and that's what I did." He walked toward the screen and pointed to the last entry. "What does this term mean? My Latin's a little rusty."

She glanced up from her notes only for a moment. "Casus Belli. It means an incident that's used to justify a war. Come on, let's keep going."

The slides thereafter made continual references to pages in some briefing document that must have been handed out to the meeting's participants. Without those pages it seemed there was little use in continuing further.

"That's it," Noah said. "I don't think there's any more to see."

"It's not over yet. We're not to the end."

He held his thumb down on the advance button and the screens ticked by more and more rapidly. "I'm telling you, look at it, this is nothing but page numbers—"

The walls went black, leaving the room in almost total darkness.

One by one the screens faded in again, encircling the room with new content they hadn't seen before. Each screen contained a linear diagram that was a trademark of the company's strategic plans. These diagrams were used to show the firm's clients a step-by-step layout of what to do, and how and when to do it.

The headings mirrored the disciplines of the attendees shown earlier: Finance, Energy, Labor, Education, Infrastructure, Media, Emergency Management, Law Enforcement, and Continuity of Government.

A security dialog popped up, and with a vocal sigh Noah entered his override password. If anyone ever checked to see who'd accessed these files and when, this would be another nail in his coffin. An hourglass indicator appeared, along with the message: *Please Wait . . . Content Loading from Remote Storage.*

"It'll be a few minutes while this downloads," Noah said. "We keep some of the more sensitive stuff off-site, to guard against the kind of thing we're doing right now."

Molly had left her seat and walked a complete circuit of the round room, looking over the various headings on the screens. She stopped by his side, pointing out a bracketed rectangle that enclosed part of the illustration on the slide in front of them.

"What's that box?" she asked.

"It's called the Overton Window. My father stole the concept from a think tank in the Midwest; it's a way of describing what the public is currently ready to accept on any issue, so you can decide how best to move them toward what you want."

"I don't understand," she said. She was looking at the screen related to national security and law enforcement. Except for the heading and the long thick line with an open box near its center, the slide was mostly blank. "How does it work?"

"The ends of this long line"—Noah walked up to indicate the starting point—"represent the extreme possibilities. At this end of the scale is the unthinkable, and all the way over at the other end is something else you can't imagine ever happening, but in the opposite way. Too much good here, too much evil over there. If we were talking about government, it would be too much liberty at this end—which would be anarchy—and a complete top-down Orwellian tyranny at the other, so no liberty at all. Those in-between points are milestones along the way."

Molly still looked a little lost in the concept, and she motioned for him to go on.

"Use airline security as an example," Noah said. "Forty years ago people could pull up to the airport a few minutes before their flight, be treated with courtesy and respect, present no ID, just a ticket, and then get on the plane with just about anything in their pockets and their bags. There was some security, but it was almost invisible. Today that's unthinkable, right? It seems like we could never go back to those days."

She nodded.

"Now at the other end of the spectrum, let's make the passengers arrive four hours early for the security line, allow no carry-ons, enforce a mandatory strip search, full-body X-ray, a cavity probe for everyone, and you have to stay in your seat the entire flight with a stun bracelet on your wrist in case you try to get up to go to the bathroom—which, of course, no longer exists."

"They're actually talking about doing some of those things," she said.

"That's getting to my point. If you suddenly had to go through everything I just mentioned you'd give up flying, correct? And with no security at all, you'd also never set foot on an airplane. So your Overton Window is somewhere in the middle, within this box. But my goal is to get you to accept more of those radical things over there, one step at a time.

"Let's say tomorrow some idiot makes his way onto a flight with a little tiny homemade explosive of some kind. It'd be all over the news for weeks, whether the guy actually did any damage or not. You get scared, and the TV is telling you that all we have to do is buy some more expensive screening machines, hire some more of the same people who let that nut on the plane in the first place, and give up a little more dignity at the checkpoints, and we'll be safe. That, of course, is a lie, but it has the desired effect."

"It moves the window," she said.

"Right. We put a false extreme at both ends to make the choices in the middle look moderate by comparison. And then, with a little nudge, you can be made to agree to something you would never have swallowed last week."

"Why, though? Why would they want to do that?"

"The airline thing was just a random example, but I can think of a few reasons. If my client sold those X-ray machines, or had a contract for those extra security people, there's quite a bit of money to be made there. It makes the government bigger and more involved in our lives, and that can justify higher taxes and fees, more bureaucracy, bigger budgets; it can build support for an unpopular military action, on and on. And who knows? Some of your friends last night might say that it's all part of a program to condition the American people to put up their hands and submit to anyone in a uniform."

"And this Overton Window, it's used all the time?"

"All the time, everywhere you look. We never let a good crisis go to waste, and if no crisis exists, it's easy enough to make one.

"Saddam's on the verge of getting nuclear weapons, so we have to invade before he wipes out Cleveland. If we don't hand AIG a seventy-billion-dollar bailout there'll be a depression and martial law by Monday. If we don't all get vaccinated one hundred thousand people will die in a super swine-flu pandemic. And how about fuel prices? Once you've paid five dollars for a gallon of gas, three-fifty suddenly sounds like a real bargain. Now they're telling us that if we don't pass this worldwide carbon tax right now the world will soon be underwater.

"And understand, I'm not talking about the right or wrong of those underlying issues. I care about the environment more than most, I want clean energy, I want this country to recover and be great again, people should get their shots if they need them, and Saddam Hussein was a legitimate monster. I'm saying opportunists can attach themselves to our hopes and fears about those things, for profit, and this is one of the tools they use to do that. The question to ask is, if they've got a legitimate case for these things, then why all the lying and fabrication?"

"So even if they can't get us to accept everything at once," Molly said, studying the diagrams, "they're satisfied to move us a little closer toward the end."

"Exactly. In fact, without some big earth-shaking event, like a Pearl Harbor or a 9/11, that's the only way it can work. Just little nudges in the right direction, and before you know it you've progressed yourself right into their agenda. It's evolution they're after, not revolution. And when I say 'they' I don't mean some secret society out there. There's always a prime mover behind these things, and it's easy enough to figure out who it is. Just do a little research to see who stands to benefit; follow the money and power. You know who was one of the biggest lobbyists for this cap-and-trade business, right?"

"Greenpeace?" Molly said.

"Nope. Enron. A lot of powerful people are lining up to cash in on the deal if it happens, but back then it was a huge push at Enron right before the whole company blew up in America's face. Carbon trading was going to be their biggest scam since they shut off the lights in California and held the whole state for ransom. They'd already started trading futures on the weather, if you can believe that, but this heist was going to be a thousand times bolder. Back then everybody thought they were joking."

"Not quite everybody, I guess."

"You're right about that," Noah said. "In fact, Enron was really just a huge diversion, like a Bernie Madoff, a patsy to throw to the wolves. Carbon trading moved forward anyway. The Chicago Climate Exchange is probably the best example, especially since it's basically founded or fronted or funded by a Who's Who list of environmental luminaries, like Al Gore and Goldman Sachs. But I can see why no one really cares—the Exchange's founder thinks it's probably only a ten-trillion-dollar-a-year market."

Molly stared at him in astonishment. "Did you say ten *trillion* a year?"

"Uh-huh. And the backing for it goes right up to the top, internationally. So here's a little pop quiz: What do you get when you combine corporate greed with political corruption and sprinkle a few trillion on top?"

"I don't know . . . fascism?"

Noah shook his head. "You get Doyle & Merchant's newest client."

The hourglass on the screen had disappeared moments before, and was replaced by a dialog box with two buttons, one labeled HALT and the other PROCEED.

"Now I know what I'm looking at," Molly said. "So let's see what's next."

Noah clicked the remote, and the screens all began to change. The slides that had been incomplete filled in with callouts, numbers, names, legends, and dates to illustrate the long-term agendas within each area of American government and society at large. Some of these agendas spanned only a few years, others more than a century.

Pointers along the time lines began to move; text formed and then faded as significant events in recent history were reached and passed by. Milestones appeared, enclosed in the Overton Window of each screen as it moved slowly from left to right.

It was far too much ever-changing information to absorb, like watching all the movies in a multiplex simultaneously. But as they turned and took it all in at the center of the circle of screens, Molly suddenly touched his hand, and gripped it. It seemed the same realization had come over them both, at the same instant: This wasn't eight separate agendas at all. It was only one.

Along the bottom, the steady advance

of time. Through the middle, the slow, sporadic movement of the Overton Window—usually pushing forward, but sometimes pulling back, as though the public might have rebelled briefly against the relentless pressure before giving in to it again.

To the far right of each screen a final goal was listed. As Noah looked to each of them he realized something else that all these endpoints had in common. They weren't written and presented as though they were unthinkable extremes, but rather as achievable goals in some new, unified framework of command and control, ready to come forth on the day the old existing structure failed.

- Consolidate all media assets behind core concepts of a new internationalism
- Gather and centralize powers in the Executive Branch
- Education: Deemphasize the individual, reinforce dependence and collectivism, social justice, and "the common good"
- Set beneficial globalization against isolationism/sovereignty: climate change, debt crises, finance/currency, free trade, immigration, food/water/energy, security/terror-

ism, human rights vs. property rights, UN Agenda 21

- Associate resistance and "constitutional" advocacy with a backward, extremist worldview: gun rights a key
- Quell debate and force consensus: Identify, isolate, surveil opposition leadership/threaten with sedition—criminalize dissent
- Expand malleable voter base and agenda support by granting voting rights to prison inmates, undocumented migrants, and select U.S. territories, e.g., Puerto Rico. Image as a civil rights issue; label dissenters as racist—invoke reliable analogies: slavery, Nazism, segregation, isolationism.
- Thrust national security to the forefront of the public consciousness
- Finalize the decline and abandonment of the dollar: new international reserve currency
- Synchronize and fully integrate local law enforcement with state, federal, and contract military forces, prepare collection/relocation/internment contingencies, systems, and personnel

According to the progress shown, many of these initiatives were already well under way. The slide devoted to Finance showed a time line beginning in 1913, and its Window had moved nearly to the end. The screen for Education began at a point even earlier and was also well along. Advances in one, concerning surveillance, security, and the militarization of law enforcement, had accelerated radically in the years since 9/11.

There's a difference between suspecting a thing and finally knowing it for certain. Noah felt that difference twisting into his stomach. You can hold on to the smallest doubt and take comfort in it, stay in denial and go on with your carefree life, until one day you're finally cornered by a truth that can no longer be ignored.

"Look over there," Molly said.

But he'd already seen it. While every other slide had shown advancement and slow progress over its individual time span, one hadn't moved at all, as though its role in all this was simply to be ready and awaiting activation. Also unlike the others, its time line didn't measure years or decades, but only three final days.

Unlike the others, this slide had no Overton Window. EXIGENT was the legend at the far end of the line, and it seemed there would be no question of public acceptance, no need to rally opinion on this front. Whatever it was, it would bring its own consensus.

"Casus Belli," the heading said, and Molly's translation was still fresh in his mind.

An incident used to justify a war.

CHAPTER 20

Outside the skies were still threatening, and to accompany the frigid light rain a wicked crosstown breeze had begun to blow. In that sort of weather almost everyone on the street is looking for a ride, so it took a few blocks of trying before Noah and Molly were able to hail an empty cab headed downtown.

When they'd closed the door the driver turned and asked where they were going.

"Ninth Street and Avenue B, by Tompkins Square Park," Noah said. "And do us a favor," he added, passing through enough of a tip to make his point. "We're not in a rush, so just take it really, really easy, understand?"

The man in front took the money, gave a nod in the rearview mirror, and then signaled and pulled away from the curb with exaggerated care, hands on the wheel at ten and two o'clock, driving as if an inspector from the Taxi & Limousine Commission were watching from the shotgun seat.

Molly kept to her side of the car, looking out the window in silence as the ride got under way, but after a minute she reached across and found Noah's hand to hold.

"There were no dates on those screens at the end," Noah said. "There's nothing to say that this thing is happening tomorrow, or next week, or next year."

She shook her head. "It's happening now."

"How do you know that?"

"Because I can see it. The economy is crashing, Noah. There's no net underneath it this time. That's why they're rushing through all this stimulus nonsense, both parties. All the cockroaches are coming out of the woodwork to grab what they still can. It's a heist in broad daylight, and they don't care who sees it anymore. That's how I know.

"They've doubled the national debt since 2000, and now with these bailouts, all those trillions of dollars more—that's our future they just stole, right in front of our eyes. They didn't even pretend to use that money to pay for anything real, most of it went offshore. They didn't help any real people; they just paid themselves and covered their gambling debts on Wall Street." She looked at him. "You asked how I know it's happening now? Because the last official act of any government is to loot their own treasury."

He couldn't think of a thing to counter that, at least nothing that either one of them would believe.

"We'll be okay," Noah said.

"Who'll be okay?"

"The two of us. And look, I'm not talking about any commitment you have to make, or a relationship, or whatever, I know we just met so let's take all that out of the picture and not worry about it right now. I'm just telling you that I'll help you, you and your mom, no strings attached."

"I couldn't do that."

"Just give it some thought. I know, it would probably feel like some pact with the devil. I feel the same thing, but it's better than the alternative, isn't it?

"Whatever happens, it isn't going to hit everyone equally. A lot of people I know probably won't feel a thing, and I'm set up to be okay through just about anything. So I'm just saying that we can fix it so you and your mother are okay, too."

"You're wrong—you won't be okay. No one will. If they accomplish half of what we saw on those screens then money won't protect you. Nothing will."

She turned her attention back to the window and the dark, blustery night beyond the glass.

After a time her clasp on his hand tightened for a few seconds, but it didn't really feel like affection. It was more like the grip a person might take on the arm of the dentist's chair, or the gesture of unspoken things an old love might extend at the end of a long good-bye.

CHAPTER 21

When the cab pulled to a stop Molly opened the door and turned back to him as he paid the fare.

"Come on up," she said. "See how the other half lives."

The path to the entrance began with a forbidding metal gate at the sidewalk. The lock took quite a bit of finesse to operate. It looked as though it had been jimmied open more often than unlocked with a key. A dismal courtyard lay beyond the gate, and at the entrance a triple-bolted fire door opened to a sad little front hall lit by a single hanging lightbulb.

He followed as she started up three narrow, creaking flights; he took her occasional cues to avoid a splintery patch on the railing or a weak spot in the stairs. On the second floor the entrance from the landing was secured with a heavy chain and padlock. His first thought was that the door was blocked to discourage squatters, but considering the run-down, gray-market condition of the place, it was probably as much for the safety of the trespassers as a protection for the property itself.

Though the walls and windows showed signs of spotty maintenance the construction was haphazard and incomplete. None of the repair work seemed up to code, but little of the older, existing carpentry did, either. As they continued up the stairs, he saw sheets of plywood over broken windows, and bare studs without plaster here and there. Long, jagged cracks in the remaining walls warned of some structural weakness that might run all the way to the foundation. Random drafts swept up the dim stairwell, accompanied by ominous settling sounds and the distant clank and hiss of old steam heat.

When they arrived at the third floor Molly

had her keys ready, and she set about unlocking several dead bolts on the unnumbered apartment door.

"How long have you lived here?" Noah asked.

"Not that long." She tried the door, and had to put a shoulder to it to bump it free from its swollen frame. "It's a little nicer inside."

And she was right. In fact, across that threshold it seemed like they'd entered a whole different world. As she relocked the door he took a few steps in, stood there, and looked around.

Great effort had obviously been taken to transform this space into a sort of self-contained hideaway, far removed from the city outside. What had probably once been a huge, cold industrial floor had been renovated and brought alive with simple ingenuity and hard work. The result was one large area divided with movable partitions to form an impressively cool, livable loft. From where he was he could see a spacious multipurpose room off the entryway, a kitchen and laundry to the side, and what seemed to be a series of guest rooms toward the back.

Molly hung her keys on a hook by the door. "What do you think?"

"How many people live here?" Noah asked.

"I don't know, eight or ten, so don't be surprised if you see someone. They come and go; none of us lives here permanently. We have places like this all around the country so we can have somewhere safe to stay when we have to travel. That's my room over there for now, but hardly any of this stuff is mine." She stepped into the kitchen, still talking to him. "Have a seat. I'll make us some iced tea. Or would you rather have a beer?"

"The tea sounds good."

"We make it pretty sweet where I come from."

"Bring it on, Ellie Mae. The sweeter the better."

He walked about midway into the front room and found a slightly elevated platform enclosed in Japanese screens of thin dark wood and rice paper panels. There were a lot of bookshelves, a dresser, a rolltop desk, and a vanity. But the space was dominated by a large rope hammock, its webbing covered by a nest of comfy blankets and pillows, suspended waist-high between the red shutoff wheels of two heavy metal pipes that extended up from the floor through the ceiling. This room within a room was lit softly by small lamps and pastel paper lanterns. The total effect of the enclosure was that of a mellow, relaxing Zen paradise.

A glance through the nearest bookcase revealed a strange assortment of reading material. Some old and modern classics were segregated on a shelf by themselves, but the collection consisted mostly of works that leaned toward the eccentric, maybe even the forbidden. There didn't seem to be a clear ideological thread to connect them; Alinsky's *Rules for Radicals* was right next to *None Dare Call It Conspiracy.* Down the way *The Blue Book of the John Birch Society* was sandwiched between Abbie Hoffman's *Steal This Book*, Orson Scott Card's *Empire*, and a translated copy of *The Coming Insurrection*. Below was an entire section devoted to a series of books from a specialty publisher, all by a single author named Ragnar Benson. Noah touched the weathered spines and read the titles of these, one by one:

The Modern Survival Retreat
Guerrilla Gunsmithing
Homemade Grenade Launchers: Constructing the Ultimate Hobby Weapon
Ragnar's Homemade Detonators
Survivalist's Medicine Chest
Live Off the Land in the City and Country

And a last worn hardcover, titled simply *Mantrapping*.

"Those are some pretty good books she's got there, huh?"

It was only the tranquil atmosphere and a slight familiarity to the odd voice from close behind that kept him from jumping right out of his skin. He turned, and there was Molly's large friend from the bar, nearly at eye level because of the elevated platform on which Noah was standing.

"Hollis," Noah said, stepping down to the main floor, "how is it that I never hear you coming?"

The big man gave him a warm guy-hug with an extra pat on the shoulder at the end. "I guess I tend to move about kinda quiet."

"I might need to hang a bell around your neck, just for my nerves."

"Come on," Hollis said. "Let me show you around some."

The loft had more living spaces in back than Noah had first imagined. Some were for sleeping, others for working and meeting. In the room that Hollis identified as his own there was a low army cot, several neatly organized project tables, and a large red cabinet on wheels, presumably full of tools. All these things were arranged as though bed rest wasn't even in the top ten of this man's nighttime priorities.

"What is all this stuff?" Noah asked. One table was covered with parts and test equipment for working on small electronics, another was a mass of disassembled communications equipment, and a third was devoted to cleaning supplies and the neatly disassembled pieces of a scary-looking black rifle and a handgun. More weapons were visible in an open gun safe to the side, but his focus had settled on the nearest of the workbenches. "Are you making bullets there?"

"Making ammunition." Hollis picked up a finished example and pointed to a spot near the grayish tip. "The bullet's just this last little bit on her business end. That right there's a .44 jacketed hollow-cavity; got a lot of stopping power."

Arrayed around this bench were a number of labeled bins and jars, black powders of varying grades and grinds, a pharmacist's scale, a tray of brass casings, and a hand-operated machine that looked something like a precision orange squeezer, attached to the tabletop by a vise.

"Why on earth would you want to make your own ammunition?"

Hollis sat, put on his spectacles, picked up the components of an unfinished cartridge, started working with the pieces, and then spoke. "Noah, do you like cookies?"

"Why yes, Hollis. We were talking about firearms, but yes, I do like cookies."

"And which do you like better?" He'd placed the open powder-filled casing in the lower part of his hand-operated machine, fitted a bullet on top, tweaked an adjustment ring with the deft touch of a safecracker, and then rotated a long feed lever until the two parts mated together into a single, snug assembly. "Do you prefer those dry, dusty little nuggets you get in a box from one of them drive-through restaurants?" He removed the finished cartridge from the mechanism and held it up so Noah could admire its perfection. "Or would you rather have a nice, warm cookie fresh out of the oven, that your sweetheart cooked up just for you?"

"I see what you mean, I guess."

"Oh hell, anything'll do for target shooting, I suppose, but if I know what I'm hunting I can make up something that's just exactly right, and she'll fly straighter and hit harder than anything I could buy in a box from a store."

"I'm not a gun guy, but it's hard to believe it could make that much difference."

"I'd say it makes all the difference." After consulting his calipers Hollis made an infinitesimal adjustment to the press and returned to his work. "Go out sometime and wing a bull moose with a rifle you loaded for a little whitetail deer, and see what happens. Might as well just whack him on the nose with a rolled-up newspaper."

"I see."

"You better see. Nothing quite like a pissed-off wounded moose chasin' you across an open field to teach a man the value of the proper ammunition."

Noah looked over the table again. In a

stack near the other end a number of clear acrylic boxes were already filled with finished ammo. “How many of those things can you do in an hour?”

“With a one-stage press? I’d reckon somewhere between seventy-five and two hundred rounds.” Hollis looked up at him over the rims of his thin safety glasses, and smiled. “It all depends on my motivation.”

“Hey, boys,” Molly said. She’d brought a glass of tea for Hollis. “Catching up?”

“Yeah, we are. Hollis here was just making some helpful suggestions for the next time I need to shoot a moose.”

She patted her seated friend on the back. “I’m going to steal him for a little while, okay?”

“You two kids be good,” Hollis said.

There were other voices nearby, and Molly led him down the line of doorways and partitioned spaces toward the sound. At the end of this hall they came to a large room with a diverse group of men and women sitting around a long conference table. On a second look Noah saw that this furniture consisted of a mismatched set of folding chairs and four card tables butted end to end.

The people inside had been listening to a speaker at the head of the table but the room became quiet when they saw the newcomers.

"Everybody," Molly said, "this is Noah Gardner. And Noah, these are some of the regional leaders of the Founders' Keepers. You said you were good with names, so let's put you to the test."

She started at the near end of the table and proceeded clockwise with introductions around the circle. Molly pointed out each person and gave the historic pseudonym that he or she had taken on when they joined the organization.

"Did you get all that?" she asked.

"Let's see." He began where she'd ended and went around the other way. "That's Patrick, Ethan, George, Thomas, Benjamin, Samuel, John, Alexander, James, Nathaniel, another Benjamin—Franklin or Rush, you didn't say which—Francis, William, and Stephen."

"Very good."

"I owe it all to Dale Carnegie." Each of the attendees had a book open, and from what he could see they all appeared to be similar in every way but their visible contents. "What did we interrupt?" Noah asked. "Is this a strategy session or something?"

"Not tonight," Molly said. She motioned for the speaker at the head of the table to continue from where she'd left off. This woman, maybe ten years Noah's senior, had been introduced as "Thomas."

"Cherish therefore the spirit of our people," the woman said, "and keep alive their attention. Do not be too severe upon their errors, but reclaim them by enlightening them. If once they become inattentive to the public affairs, you and I, and Congress, and assemblies, judges, and governors shall all become wolves."

These words were from the writings of Thomas Jefferson; though Noah hadn't recognized them as such he could see the heading in the open book of the one sitting next to her as she spoke. This man was following along carefully, tracking the memorized text with a moving fingertip. She was delivering the passage with feeling and energy, not as the rote recitation of a centuries-old letter, but as if for the time being, she'd made Jefferson's thoughts her own.

"It seems to be the law of our general nature," she continued, "in spite of individual exceptions; and experience declares that man is the only animal which devours his own kind, for I can apply no milder term to the governments of Europe, and to the general prey of the rich on the poor."

There was an empty chair at the table with one of those little books in front of it. Molly picked up this book and waved a good-bye to the others as they prepared for the next speaker in line. She took Noah's hand and led him from the room and back up the hall again.

"Aren't they going to need that book?" Noah asked.

"No, this one's mine." She handed it to him. "I'm not like they are, though. They've each memorized a whole person, and I've just got little pieces of a lot of them. Mostly Thomas Paine, though."

"So what's the meaning of all this?" The book was clearly hand-bound and not mass-manufactured. It looked old but well cared for, and there was a number on the inside front cover, suggesting that this one and the others were part of a large series.

"It's one of the things the Founders' Keepers do," Molly said. "We remember."

"You remember speeches and letters and things?"

"We remember how the country was founded. You never know, we might have to do it again someday."

"So you keep it in your heads? Why, in case all the history books get burned?"

"It's already happening, Noah, if you haven't noticed. Not burning, but changing. Ask an elementary school kid what they know about George Washington and it's more likely you'll hear the lies about him, like the cherry-tree story or that he had wooden dentures, than about anything that really made him the father of our country. Ask a kid in high school about Ronald Reagan and they'll probably tell you that he was a B-list-actor-turned-politician, or that he was the guy who happened to be in office when Gorbachev ended the Cold War. Ask a college kid about Social Security and they'll probably tell you that it was intended to provide guaranteed retirement income for all Americans. Ask a thirty-year-old about World War II and they'll recite what they remember from *Saving Private Ryan*. Do you see? No one really needs to rewrite history; they just have to make sure that no one remembers it."

He closed the book carefully and gave it back to her. "Molly?"

"Yes?"

"Hit me with a little Thomas Paine."

She took his hand, and spoke quietly as they walked.

" 'These are the times that try men's souls,' " Molly said. " 'The summer soldier and the sunshine patriot will, in this crisis, shrink from the service of their country; but he that stands by it now, deserves the love and thanks of man and woman. Tyranny, like hell, is not easily conquered; yet we have this consolation with us, that the harder the conflict, the more glorious the triumph.

" 'What we obtain too cheap, we esteem too lightly: it is dearness only that gives every thing its value. Heaven knows how to put a proper price upon its goods; and it would be strange indeed if so celestial an article as freedom should not be highly rated.' "

Back in Molly's section of the loft she gave Noah his iced tea and took a seat on the edge of her hammock. He sat on a nearby divan made from crates, a simple frame, and random cushions. The tea turned out to be as sweet as she'd warned it would be, but it was good.

"That looked like a small arsenal Hollis had back there," Noah said. "Are all those guns legal?"

"Two of them are registered. The rest are just passing through. He's on his way to a gun show upstate."

"So the answer's no, they're not legal."

"Do you know what it took to make those two guns legal in this city?"

"I can imagine."

"It took over a year, and the guy who owns them had to get fingerprinted, interviewed, and charged about a thousand dollars to exercise a constitutional right."

"Welcome to New York. There's a lot you've got to live with when you live here."

"Wait, didn't you say you were pre-law in college? I would have thought they'd have spent a few minutes on the Second Amendment."

"Yeah, they did," Noah said. "The experts differ quite a bit on its interpretation."

She spoke the words thoughtfully. "'The right of the people to keep and bear arms shall not be infringed'—that seems pretty clear to me."

"You left out the part that causes all the arguments."

"The word *militia* meant something different back then, Noah. Ben Franklin started the first one here. The militia was every citizen who was ready and able to protect their community, whatever the threat. It was as natural as having a lock on your front door.

"Today the police are there to protect society, but they're not obligated to protect you and me as individuals. The Supreme Court's ruled on that quite a few times. And they certainly won't protect us from the government, God forbid it would ever come to that. So the way I read it, the Second Amendment simply says we have the right to be ready to defend ourselves and our neighbors if we have to."

"Speaking of the way you read it," he

said, "why don't you tell me about your bookshelf there."

She looked over at it briefly. "What about it?"

"I was noticing some of the titles. That's quite a subversive library."

"People use some of those books to smear us, and some of them were written by our enemies. I read everything so I'll know what I'm up against, and how to talk about them. You don't see any harm in that, do you?"

"Who's this Ragnar Benson lunatic?"

She smiled. "He's not a lunatic. That's a pen name, by the way; hardly anyone knows who he really is. He writes about a lot of useful things, though."

"Like how to make a grenade launcher in your rumpus room?"

"That one was from his mercenary days. He's mellowed out some since then. Now he's more about independence, and readiness, and self-sufficiency, you know? The joys of living off the grid."

"It almost sounds like you know this guy."

She considered him for a moment and then leaned a little closer. "Can you keep a secret?"

"This is probably the wrong day to ask me that."

"It's Hollis's uncle," Molly whispered. "And guess who took up the family business and wrote a few of those books himself."

"Hollis?" He pointed over his shoulder with a thumb. "*My* Hollis?"

She nodded, smiling a little. "You shouldn't judge a person by appearances, you know. He's a very smart man."

"Yeah, so was the Unabomber. Top of his class, I hear."

"You make little jokes when you're nervous," Molly said. "That's kinda cute."

"Thanks."

"Now finish your tea or I'll think you don't like it."

He did, in one long drink, and Molly patted a place beside her on the hammock with one hand.

"Oh, no," he said. "I've lived twenty-eight years without trying to get into one of those. You sit over here with me."

"Come on, it's easy, chicken."

"It'll flip over."

"No, it won't." She held out her hands to him, beckoning. "I just want to forget about everything else for a little while, okay? Come here, now. Don't make me ask you again."

It would have been hard to say no to that, and he didn't try. With her guidance he sat next to her on the precarious edge of the hammock.

"Now we just hold on," Molly said. "Let your feet come off the floor and lie down, and try not to roll off the other side."

He followed her lead as she leaned back, and from there it was a touch-and-go fun-house ride for quite a few wobbly seconds. Amid the swinging and shifting and overbalancing and a great deal of welcome laughter, things gradually settled down into a fragile stability. In the end they found themselves pleasantly entwined with one another, held close in the pocket of the hammock in a comfortable, gentle sway.

There was no ceiling to the enclosure of her room, and high overhead among the distant steel beams someone had arrayed several dim strings of white Christmas lights in a pattern reminiscent of a starry evening sky.

"Hey, Molly," he whispered.

"Yes."

"What do you say we just stay here like this, for a really long time."

She held him a little closer. "I wish we could."

He'd noticed her silver bracelet before but now it was close enough to see the marks of its worn engraving. "What does this say?"

She brought her wrist closer to his eyes. "It's been through a lot, and I'm afraid it's getting a little hard to read."

Noah held her hand and found the right distance and the proper angle in the dim light to allow him to make out the faded lettering. When he was sure of what they said he read the words aloud.

"We have it in our power to begin the world over again."

"That's right," Molly said.

"Whose quote is that? I've heard it before."

"Thomas Paine."

He laid his head back down next to hers. "But how do you think you can do that, Molly? I'm not saying you can't, but I don't see how."

"There's more," she said. With her other

hand she carefully twisted the bracelet so the inner face of it turned out, and there was another inscription on that side.

Faith Hope Charity

"That's . . . nice."

"Nice?"

"I guess I don't really understand," Noah said. "I mean, I understand those words, but that's not really a battle plan, is it? Do you know what you're up against?"

"Yes," Molly said. "But I doubt that our enemies do."

"So tell me."

"Okay," Molly said. "Pop quiz: Who fired the first shot in the American Revolution?"

"That's a trick question. Nobody knows who fired the first shot."

"Is that your final answer?"

"Yep."

She worked herself up onto an elbow so she could look at him. "It wasn't fired from a gun. The first shot was a sermon, delivered by Jonathan Mayhew, years before Lexington and Concord. It wasn't a politician who first said 'no taxation without representation.' It was a preacher."

"Ah. So that's the faith part."

"It's more than that. Our rights come from a higher power, Noah. Men can't grant them, and men can't take them away. That's the difference, I think, between what happened in the French Revolution and what we achieved in ours. We believed we had the will of God behind us, and they believed in the words of Godwin. One endures, and the other fell to human weakness."

He touched the second word engraved in her silver bracelet. "And what about hope?"

"That means we believe in the strongest part of the human spirit. Hope and truth are tied together; if everything we know is a lie, we don't have a chance. When a doctor tells you you're sick, you don't blame her for the diagnosis. You have the truth, then, no matter how bad it is, and you can make a plan to get better. That's hope. To know that even when things look darkest, there can be a better day tomorrow."

Molly pointed out the last word of the three. "And charity is simple. We believe that it's up to each of us to help one another get to that better tomorrow. Ben Franklin explained my whole bracelet when the president of Yale asked him to sum up the American religion. He answered: that there is a God, that there is life after this one and He will hold us accountable for our actions in this life, and that the best way to serve Him is to serve our fellow man. That's faith, hope, and charity."

"It sounds good." Noah adjusted a pillow and laid his head back onto it. "I hate to say it, though; I just don't think it's enough."

"Maybe it's not something you get right away," Molly said. "It didn't come to any of us overnight. When you're ready to understand, you'll understand."

A sketch on white paper was attached to the wall at their side, placed so it would be easily visible to someone lying where they were.

"Who drew that, over there?" Noah asked.

She turned her head that way, rolled over slightly, reached out to tug the paper free from its pushpin, and then held it so they both could see. "I did."

It was a drawing of a small log cabin in a valley in wintertime, near a stream within a secluded patch of woods. The details of the place were carefully rendered; a porch swing, a spot for a garden to the side within a low split-rail fence, a path of flat stones to the front steps, puffs of drifted snow on the eaves and windowsills. It was only simple lines and shades from the edge of a pencil, but the scene was fondly captured there in the artist's sensitive hand.

"It's really beautiful," Noah said. "Where is this?"

"Only in my head, I guess." She looked at him. "And do you want to know something?"

"Sure."

"This is all I want, really, this little place. I imagine that makes me sound pretty simple to someone like you."

"No, it doesn't. It sounds good."

"Just a place like this to share with someone, and the freedom to live our lives there. The pursuit of happiness, you know? That means a different thing to everybody, and that's the way it should be. But this is mine; this is what I dream about."

"I hope you get there someday."

"I hope we all do."

He thought for a moment. "Why don't you just go out right now, and find that place?"

"You mean, why don't I just grab mine while I can, and to hell with everybody else?"

"That's not exactly what I meant—"

"There's a cancer in our country, Noah. We've both seen the X-rays now. If we don't stop it, it'll spread wherever we try to hide. And I want you to know something. I *need* for you to know something."

"Okay."

"There's nothing I wouldn't give up to defend my country. No matter how hard it might be, there's nothing that's in my power that I wouldn't do."

"I understand," Noah said. "I admire that a lot."

"But I don't want this on my shoulders. I don't want to be right. I wish things were different. If I could I'd stay here just like this, like you said."

"I just wish I felt that strongly about anything."

Quiet minutes passed, and as he lay there gazing up at those imitation stars, feeling her close to him, he tried without much success to remember exactly what it was he'd been pursuing for all these years, if it wasn't a simple togetherness just like this.

Then he noticed a subtle blur that had crept into his vision. A little shimmer had formed around sources of light, and though he blinked it away the strange haze returned after a moment more, this time accompanied by an odd discomfort, like a passing wave of vertigo.

"Whoa."

"What is it?"

"Nothing. I think I got the whirlies there for a second."

No sooner had the feeling left than it came over him again, but stronger this time, and he stiffened, tried to shake it off. Molly raised herself on an elbow beside him, concern in her eyes.

"Are you okay?"

"Yeah," he breathed out. "I'm fine."

But he wasn't fine. There'd been a time in college after a stupid drinking game when he'd downed far too much of the spiked punch too quickly, and all that alcohol had hit his bloodstream at once. It had been the worst feeling of helplessness, because by the time he realized his mistake there was nothing he could do to stop what was coming.

"I need to get up," he said. His own words were slow to reach his ears, and they didn't sound right. A flutter of panic was beginning to take hold inside, and he felt her cool hand on his forehead, comforting.

"Be still now," she said.

But it had almost all drained away by then, first the strength and then the will to move, all replaced by this building sensation of a slow-motion, backward swoon at the sheer edge of a bottomless ravine.

As the cloudy room began to swim and fade he saw that three strangers were standing nearby, young men dressed in business suits and ties.

"It's time to go, Molly," one of them said, the voice far away and unreal.

"Just give us a minute. Wait for me downstairs."

And they were gone, and another, taller figure appeared.

"You'll stay with him, Hollis, won't you?"

"I'll stay just as long as I can."

He felt her arms around him tight, her tears on his cheek, her lips near his ear as the blackness finally, fully descended.

Almost gone, but the three simple words she'd whispered to him then would stay clear in his mind even after everything else had faded away into the dark.

"I'm so sorry."

CHAPTER 22

Agent Kearns had retired to the kitchenette of his double-wide mobile home to make breakfast. This left Danny Bailey sitting by himself in the parlor in his borrowed pajamas with a wicked sleep hangover, an ugly off-white cat, and a full-scale model of a small atomic bomb.

The Sunday news from some distant city lay folded at the far end of the couch. It would have been nice to see some headlines but the paper was a little too close to the cat to be safely retrieved.

"So you've never been to Winnemucca,

you said?" Kearns called through the narrow doorway.

Again with the frickin' small talk.

"No, can you believe that?" Danny said. He was looking over the elaborate cylindrical device in its heavy wooden cradle on the coffee table. "Never knew what I was missing."

"If you think this burg is dead, wait until you see where we're going to meet these guys tonight. This whole part of Nevada was voted the official armpit of America by the *Washington Post* a couple of years ago."

"Sounds like a hoot. Hey, Stuart?"

"Yeah?"

"I don't want to come off like a puss, but is this bomb-looking thing, like, radioactive?"

"Nah, not too much." Kearns returned with their coffee and sat in a nearby chair. "The core's inert; it's just a big ball of lead. There's some depleted uranium under the lining, so it'll set off a Geiger counter in case anybody checks. Here, look." He flipped a switch on a boxy yellow gadget on the table and brought its wand closer to an open access panel at the fore end of the model.

The meter on the instrument twitched and a rapid clicking from its speaker ramped up to a loud, raspy buzz as the tip of the wand touched an inner metal housing. “Sure sounds hot enough though, doesn’t it?”

“But it’s not dangerous.”

“No, but I wouldn’t keep it under my bed at night.”

“And these dudes we’re going to see, the boys who want to buy this thing, why would they ever believe that a private citizen could get his hands on a working nuclear weapon?”

“Okay, good, we should talk about this. Do you remember about a year ago, there was a story in the news about a live cruise missile that went missing?”

“Of course I do. The Barksdale thing—I did a whole week of shows on that. Somebody screwed up and loaded real warheads instead of dummies onto a B-52 in North Dakota. Six nukes left the base, but only five showed up in Louisiana.”

“Right,” Kearns said. “Now we both know that something like that can’t just happen, not as an accident anyway. It’s like the Secret Service accidentally putting the president into the wrong car and then nobody missing him until noon the next day. It's impossible; there are way too many safeguards in place. Unless, of course, it was an inside job.

"So my online personality is a guy with tons of deep connections from my years with the FBI. About seven years ago I finally got disgusted with the whole crooked government, slipped off the reservation, and disappeared into my own version of the Witness Protection Program. My cover story was that, to get this bomb, I made friends with the right two people on those munitions crews through my website, one at Minot Air Force Base and one at the destination. They fudged the orders and arranged that flight, then helped me get the guts of one of those warheads onto a truck and on its way out of Barksdale half a day before anybody even knew it was missing."

"So you're not trying to claim you built this from scratch, like in your backyard workshop."

"No, hell no, of course not. Just the mount and the housing, and I hooked up some of the electronics; that's all I had to put together here. The warhead itself was intact."

Danny leaned forward and ran a fingertip along one of the smoother welds. "I've gotta hand it to you. It looks pretty bad-ass."

"Yeah, it does," Kearns said, as he stowed the Geiger counter in a gym bag next to the couch, "if I do say so myself."

"And how much of that's actually true?"

"How much of what is actually true?"

"What you just said. That whole Barksdale story."

Kearns didn't answer right away. He zipped up the bag on the floor and then sat back in his chair, frowning. "What is this, *60 Minutes* all of a sudden?"

"No, man, we're just talking—"

"I'm not here to fill in the blanks for your next conspiracy video."

"I'm just trying to get our story straight."

"Okay," Kearns said. "But what's true or not true about what I just said isn't part of the story you've got to get straight."

"Fine, okay, sorry. It just sounded so believable. This is all pretty new to me, you know, and I'm still a little groggy this morning. I haven't slept for twelve hours like that in twenty years."

The other man continued to study him, as if he felt he might have made a slip and was still assessing its severity. But after a few seconds he nodded, seemed to ease down a bit, and pulled the reluctant, rumpled cat a little closer and rubbed its head.

"Yeah, okay," Kearns said. "Sorry, I didn't mean to get my dander up. Maybe I'm getting a little paranoid in my old age. I've been told in the past I've got some issues."

"Hey, pal, who doesn't, right?"

"You said it."

The microwave in the other room beeped at the end of its heating cycle.

"So," Danny said, rubbing his hands together, "what's to eat?"

Agent Kearns brought in some toast and a crusty tub of margarine along with some scrambled eggs and ham from a can. The meat was spongy and slick and the eggs tasted like survival food, but with enough salt and pepper it all became passable enough.

"I only asked what I asked before," Danny said, "because I would have thought you guys had all kinds of labs and engineers back at headquarters that would have built a model like this for an undercover operation. You know, so someone like you wouldn't have to bother with any of it yourself."

"Yeah, they do, but these last few years I've gotten accustomed to working alone. The less contact you make when you're undercover, the safer it is. Hell, I've been out in the cold so long on this one, as far as I know only one guy inside even knows I'm still on the payroll."

"Wow, you must really trust that guy."

Kearns bent and slipped a snubnose revolver from his ankle holster, matter-of-factly, as if it had been just a pebble stuck in his shoe. He swung out the cylinder and spun it with the flat of his hand, flicked it back into place, laid the gun on his side of the table, and then picked up his plate to resume his breakfast. You'd almost think all this had nothing to do with the subject at hand.

"Sure, kid," Kearns said. "I trust everybody."

CHAPTER 23

Sunday afternoon was spent with each of them going over the other's public background. If they were to appear to be old acquaintances, they couldn't hesitate on some obvious detail that might come up in the conversation. Then, before loading up the van, they'd made a telephone call to finalize the evening's meet-up with the targets of the sting operation.

Kearns had used a hacker gizmo called an orange box to fake the caller ID display the recipients would see. It would appear to them as though the call had come directly from Danny Bailey's private number;

his actual cell phone was apparently still stuck in the bowels of some evidence warehouse back in New York.

The man who'd answered had been suitably impressed to be talking to one of his longtime media heroes in the war against tyranny. The time and address of the meeting were confirmed and Stuart Kearns was heartily endorsed as a verified patriot who could absolutely deliver the goods. Before sign-off, the man on the other end had handed the phone around so everyone could have a moment to speak with their celebrity caller.

Under Kearns's watchful eye, Danny had played along with it all quite easily, but something began to nag at him after they'd hung up. The troubling thing was that, though each of those men had laid claim to being his biggest fan, and had seen every video he'd ever produced and read every word he'd ever posted online, they'd all apparently seen and heard and read things that Danny Bailey was pretty sure he'd never actually said:

That the only way left to rally the people was to rip aside the curtain and force the enemy out into the light of day.

That the globalist oligarchs and their puppets in Washington had been spoiling for a fight for sixty years, and now they were going to get the war that was coming to them.

That the souls of the Founders were crying out for true patriots to step up and set things right with the Republic.

And that the time had finally come for a twenty-first-century shot heard 'round the world, the final trumpet to signal the start of the second American Revolution.

But even if not in precisely those words, those sentiments did sound awfully familiar. Maybe he had said those things, and it was only the current context that put them into such a stark new light. After all, things can sound different when echoed back by men who've decided to deliver their message with a fifteen-kiloton city killer instead of with a bullhorn.

CHAPTER 24

They'd been rolling down a desolate, moonless stretch of Interstate 80 for a number of miles. The road was so dark that the world out front seemed to end at the reach of the headlights, and there was nothing to see at all out the window behind.

"Hey, Stuart?"

"Yeah."

"I wouldn't be doing this if I agreed with these hoodlums, even one percent. I'm not a terrorist, and I'm not a turncoat."

"I didn't think you were," Kearns said, his eyes on the road.

"Like I said before, these aren't my people, and what they want to do isn't the way to change things, and I've never said it was."

"I believe you."

For once a little mindless conversation would have been welcome, but since no chitchat was forthcoming from the driver's seat Danny had to occupy himself with his own thoughts, listening to the sound of the road beneath the wheels.

"What kind of a phone is that?" Danny asked. He'd noticed the device before, held in its charger near the center console. It was too big to be a cell phone; it looked more like a smaller, thinner version of a walkie-talkie, but with a standard keypad.

"Satellite phone," Kearns said. "Works anywhere. Cell phone coverage in a place like this is pretty spotty."

"I guess it would be."

After a while Kearns let his foot off the gas, and the van began to coast and slow down as he reached forward and shut off the headlights.

"What are you doing?"

"Roll down your window, stick out your head, and look up," Kearns said.

"Why would I want to do that?"

"Just trust me. I want you to see something. You live in the city, right?"

"Yeah, downtown Chicago," Danny said. "Just about all my life." He cranked the glass down, leaned his head out into the cold wind, and looked up as he'd been directed.

"Well, there's only about three things to see out here in the middle of nowhere," Kearns said, "but this is one of them."

"Oh. My. God."

The air was perfectly clear, it seemed, from the barren ground all the way out to the edge of space. From horizon to horizon there was no man-made light to obscure the view up above. Thousands of stars, maybe tens of thousands of them, were shining up there like backlit jewels in a dark velvet dome. Sprays of tiny pinpoints in subtle colors, blazing white suns in orderly constellations arrayed across the heavens, ageless by the measure of a human lifetime, all light-years away but seeming to be almost near enough to reach out and touch.

Danny pulled his head back in, sat back, and rolled up the window as Kearns flipped the headlights back on and turned up the heater to warm up the van again.

"Thanks, man, really. I was sitting over here in dire need of some perspective."

"Sort of puts a guy in his place, doesn't it?" Kearns said. "That's where we all came from, out there, and someday that's where we're all going back."

"You know? I saw it on your business card, but now I understand why they call you a special agent."

"Well, son, whether you want me to or not, I'm going to take that as a compliment."

A few miles farther on Kearns exited and soon after turned onto a dirt road. The road meandered for a mile or so between barbed-wire fences on either side until they came to an even narrower gravel path. Halfway down that driveway they saw the yellowish lights of a ranch house.

"This is it," Kearns said. "You all set?"

Danny took in a deep breath, and let it relax the tension out of him as he exhaled.

"Yeah. Let's do this thing."

The garage door was up, and from their parking spot Danny could clearly see the men seated around a couple of card tables, surrounded by stacks of stored junk, auto parts, and red tool cases. They'd all turned when the headlights swung across the wide-open doorway and upon recognizing the vehicle they motioned for their guests to come on in.

Kearns stayed in the van as Danny got out and walked up the paved incline toward the house, his hands clearly open at his sides in an effort to let everyone know that he wasn't armed. Evidently these guys had no such concern. They met him halfway up the sidewalk to the garage and greeted him like he was a long-lost friend.

There was only one thing amiss. He and Kearns had come expecting to see all five men at this meeting, and one of them wasn't there.

CHAPTER 25

The gathering got right down to business. It had been all talk up to this point, Danny told them, but now this thing had gotten real. Stuart Kearns had what they wanted, so the only question that remained was whether he'd truly found the right men for the job. There would be only one shot at this, a strike that had been years in the planning, so a lot was riding on the proper makeup of this team.

Danny took a printout from his pocket, a transcript of the most recent chat room conversation, and matched up the four men with their screen names. The fifth, he was told, a guy named Elmer, had taken an unexpected trip to Kingman, Arizona, on a related matter and wouldn't return until well after midnight Monday morning.

At his request they'd each given a bit of background on themselves, sticking to first names only. The one interesting thing about this part was the seamless transition each managed to place between the sane and the insane things they'd said. *I'm Ron, I grew up down near Laughlin and worked out here in the mines since I was a teen-ager. Married at one time, two beautiful kids, and I've been wise to those Zionist bankers and the good-for-nothing queen of England ever since I saw what they did to us on 9/11.*

The four who were present had known one another for years, and they'd first met this man Elmer, the one who was missing tonight, through the chat room on Stuart Kearns's website. All of them agreed, though, that Elmer was a serious player and absolutely a man to be trusted.

One of them had asked about the bruises and other battle damage on Danny's face, and that gave him an opening to explain his own recent part in all this. He'd been picked up by the cops after a patriot meeting in New York City, he told them, and then they'd beaten him within an inch of his life while he was in custody. Everyone has their breaking point, and this had been his. He knew then that there wasn't going to be any peaceful end to this conflict; the enemy had finally made that clear. So he'd called his old friend Stuart Kearns to come and bail him out so he could be a part of this plan. He was here now to help with whatever he could, and then to get the story out to true believers around the world when all of this was over.

When Danny gave him the all-clear sign, Kearns opened his door and motioned for them to come out to the van. As they gathered around he opened up the sliding side panel, hung a work light by a hook in the ceiling, clicked it on, and showed the men the weapon he'd brought for their mission.

As the men looked on with a mix of awe and anticipation, Kearns began to provide a guided tour of the device. The yield would be about on par with the Hiroshima bomb, he explained, though the pattern of destruction would be different with a ground-level explosion. The device was sophisticated but easy to use, employing an idiotproof suicide detonator tied to an off-the-shelf GPS unit mounted on top of the housing. With the bomb hidden in their vehicle and armed, all they'd have to do is drive to the target. No codes to remember, no James Bond BS, no Hollywoodesque countdown timers—just set it and forget it. The instant they reached any point within a hundred yards of the preset destination the detonator would fire, and the blast would level everything for a mile in all directions.

Kearns took two small keys from his pocket, inserted them in the sheet-metal control panel, twisted them both at once a quarter turn, and pressed the square red central button labeled ARM. A line of tiny yellow bulbs illuminated, winking to green one by one as a soft whine from the charging electronics ascended up the scale.

The GPS soon found its satellites and its wide-screen display split into halves, one showing their current position and the other showing the ground-zero objective they'd all decided on: the home-state office of the current U.S. Senate majority leader, the Lloyd D. George Federal Courthouse, 333 Las Vegas Boulevard, Las Vegas, Nevada.

CHAPTER 26

On the face of it the meeting had been civil, even friendly, but it had ended with an uneasy good-bye, and the tension was still lingering.

Neither Bailey nor Kearns spoke until they'd driven almost a mile down the rutted dirt road, away from that house and toward the relative safety of the interstate.

"Tell me what was wrong back there," Danny said.

"A lot of things were wrong." Kearns's attention was split about evenly between the road ahead and the darkness in the rearview mirror.

The plan, plainly agreed upon, had been to leave the dummy bomb with their five co-conspirators in exchange for twenty thousand dollars the men had agreed to pay to cover Kearns's expenses. Tomorrow the men would make the eight-hour drive to Las Vegas and pull up to the target address. Instead of achieving martyrdom they'd be met by a SWAT team and a dragnet of federal agents who'd be waiting there to arrest them. None of these guys seemed the type to allow themselves to be taken alive, so FEMA would be running a local terror drill at the same time. With the area evacuated for blocks around there'd be less chance of any innocent bystanders being caught in the anticipated cross fire.

But tonight's meeting hadn't ended as expected and that could mean a lot of things—none of them ideal.

At best, the problem had been an innocent misunderstanding that would simply lead to a day's delay in getting this over with. At worst, the would-be domestic terrorists had smelled a rat, and were huddling back there now deciding what to do about it. If that was the case—and Danny assumed this to be the source of his companion's fixation on the road behind them—a set of fast-moving headlights might suddenly appear in a surprise hostile pursuit that this old van was in no shape to participate in. If that happened, the odds would be excellent that he and Agent Kearns would end their evening buried together in a shallow, sandy grave.

"Can you handle a gun?" Kearns asked.

"I'm no expert, but yeah."

"If things go bad, there's a pistol in the glove box. The safety's off but there's a long twelve-pound pull on that first round. After the first shot the trigger's really light."

"I'll be okay with the gun. Why don't you tell me what's going on."

Kearns took the ramp onto I-80 and visibly began to relax as the van picked up speed. "First," he said, "we still have their bomb, because they didn't have our money. It might be that they just couldn't get it together until tomorrow, like they said, or it might have been a test of some kind."

"A test of what?"

"Of us. Maybe they wanted to see if we'd leave the goods with them anyway, without the payment. If we are who we say we are they'd know we wouldn't stand for that.

But if we were a couple of feds trying to set them up then we might, just so they'd be in possession of the evidence for a bust tomorrow."

"Okay."

"Second, how would you describe the intellectual level of those four guys we just left?"

"I don't know." Danny thought for a moment. "More like sheep than shepherds."

"Right. And do you know who'd established himself all along as the brains on their side of this operation?"

"Let me guess," Danny sighed. "The one who wasn't there tonight."

"Exactly. I'm not saying those boys we just met are harmless, but they're followers, and this guy Elmer is their leader. If they were lying about his whereabouts then he was probably back there somewhere checking us out, maybe through the scope of a deer rifle. And if he's really up in Arizona like they said then I've gotta wonder what he's doing there."

"So what's next?" Danny asked. "Am I done? Can you cut me loose now?"

"Not yet. I told them to e-mail me when our friend Elmer gets back in town later tonight, and we'll have to arrange another meet-up tomorrow. Meanwhile I'll check in with my contact, and we'll have to play it by ear from there."

They drove on, and as the quiet minutes passed, the glances to the rear became less frequent until finally it seemed the immediate threat of trouble was left behind. Kearns tapped on the radio and worked the dial until he found some golden oldies. He settled back into his seat, just listening to the words and music from his past, as though the particular song that was playing might somehow be a final sign that his worries were over, at least for tonight.

When the chorus arrived Kearns chimed in softly, singing to himself in a private, off-key falsetto.

Danny looked across the seat to him.

"Hey, Stuart?"

"Yeah."

"Can I ask you something personal?"

"Sure. You can ask, but I don't have to answer."

"A career in the FBI is what, twenty or twenty-five years?"

"Usually, yeah. About that."

"So don't take this the wrong way, but shouldn't a man your age be retired by now?"

Kearns glanced over at him, turned down the radio, and then returned his attention to his driving. "You mean, why is a sixty-three-year-old man still doing street duty, instead of running a field office or enjoying his government pension."

"I was just wondering."

"It's a long story."

"Well," Danny said, "it's a long drive."

CHAPTER 27

Stuart Kearns, it turned out, had been in quite a different position a decade before. He'd worked in the top levels of counterterrorism with a man named John O'Neill, the agent who'd been one of the most persistent voices of concern over the grave danger posed by Osama bin Laden and al-Qaeda throughout the 1990s. Rather than being rewarded for his foresight, however, it was thought by many that his warnings, and his way of delivering them, had eventually cost O'Neill his career.

John O'Neill had seen a woeful lack of preparation for the twenty-first-century threat of stateside terrorism, and he hadn't been shy about expressing his opinions. The people upstairs, meanwhile, didn't appreciate all the vocal criticisms of the Bureau specifically and the government in general, especially coming from one of their own.

O'Neill had finally seen the writing on the wall after several missed promotions and a few not-so-subtle smear campaigns directed at him, and he'd left the Bureau in the late summer of his twenty-fifth year on the job. That's when he'd taken his new position as head of security at the World Trade Center in New York City. His first day on the job was about three weeks before the day he died a hero: September 11, 2001.

Stuart Kearns's FBI career had likewise been derailed by his outspokenness and his association with O'Neill, but he'd stubbornly chosen to try to ride out the storm rather than quitting. A bureaucracy never forgets, though, and they'd kept pushing him further and further out toward the pasture until finally, for the last several years, he'd been banished so far undercover that he sometimes wondered if anyone even remembered he was still an agent at all.

. . .

"Slow down, slow down," Danny said.

Kearns let his foot off the gas and looked over. "What is it?"

"Do me a favor and take this exit here, right up ahead."

At the top of the off-ramp there was little indication of anything of interest beyond advertisements for nearby food, gas, and lodging. Oh, and an eye-catching billboard for the Pussycat Ranch.

"You've got to be kidding me," Kearns said.

"We've had a rough night, Stuart, and I'd like to have a beer."

"I've got beer at home."

"A beer in a can in a house trailer with another dude and a beer in a Nevada brothel are two totally different things, and right now I need the second one."

Surprisingly enough, Kearns didn't put up a fight. He followed the signs along the circuitous route to the place without complaining, and pulled up into a parking spot near the end of the lot in front.

Danny got out of the van, straightened his clothes, and looked back. "Aren't you coming in?"

"No, I don't think so. Fake or not, I'm not going to leave an atomic bomb unattended in the parking lot of a roadhouse."

"Okay, your loss. Can you spot me a hundred until payday?"

"I don't have a hundred." Kearns took out his wallet, removed a bill, and handed it to Danny through the open door. "I've got twenty. I'm going to try to make a phone call while I'm waiting out here, but don't take all night. We're getting up early in the morning."

"With twenty dollars I doubt if I'll be ten minutes."

"And I know I don't have to tell you to watch what you say and who you say it to," Kearns said. "Just have your drink and come back out. Don't make me come in there after you."

"I'll be right back."

Inside, he'd barely taken a seat at the bar and placed his order when one of the more fetching young ladies of the evening caught his eye and invited herself over.

"What can I do for you?" she asked.

"That's a loaded question in a place like this, isn't it?"

She frowned a bit and looked at him a little closer. "Do I know you, mister?"

The bartender had returned with his beer, taken his twenty, and left a ten-dollar bill in its place. Danny picked up his glass and his change and took the woman's hand.

"What's your name?" he asked.

"My name's Tiffany." Her eyes lit up suddenly. "You're that guy," she whispered, "on the Internet, in that video."

"I am indeed," Danny said. He leaned in a little closer. "And Tiffany, I need for you to do me a little favor."

In her room in back he gave his new friend an autograph and his last ten dollars, and that bought him five minutes alone with her cell phone.

As he composed the text message to Molly Ross he began to realize how little intelligence he actually had to pass along. He knew the code name of this operation he'd become involved in; he'd seen it on the paperwork they'd made him sign upon his release from jail. He knew when it was going down, and where. And he knew something was going wrong, and that the downward slide might be just beginning.

Outside at the bar the television had been showing the news, and in the crawl along the bottom he'd seen that over the weekend the national terrorism threat level had been raised to orange, the last step before the highest. Maybe that was related to this thing with Kearns, maybe not. All he could do was tell her to try to keep everyone in their movement well clear of the area, and hope for the best.

He checked the message one last time, and hit SEND.

molly -
spread the word --- stay away from las vegas monday
FBI sting op --> * exigent *
be safe
xoxo
db

CHAPTER 28

A small fragment of his awareness saw everything clearly from a mute corner of his mind, but that part had given up trying to rouse the rest of him. Noah still lay where Molly had left him, not exactly asleep but a long way from consciousness.

He heard a faraway pounding and muffled shouts coming from somewhere outside the churning darkness in his head. These sounds didn't raise an alarm; they only blended themselves smoothly into his bad dream.

His nightmares had grown infrequent as he'd gotten older, but they'd always been the same. No slow-motion chases, shambling zombies, or yellow eyes peering from an open closet door; the running theme of his nocturnal terrors was nothing so elaborate. In every one he was simply trapped, always held by something crushing and inescapable as his life slowly drained away. Buried alive in a tight pine coffin, pinned and smothering beneath a pillow pressed to his face by powerful hands, caught under the crush of an avalanche, terrified and helpless and knowing he'd already begun to die.

This time it was deep water. He could see daylight glinting off the waves high above; all the air he needed was there, but it was much too far away. As he tried to swim up every stroke of his arms only sent him farther downward, until at last some primitive instinct took over and demanded that he inhale. Salt water rushed into his straining lungs, heaved out, and poured in again, burning like acid.

This was the part where he knew he had to wake up, because if he didn't he was sure the dream would kill him. But it wouldn't let him go.

There was a *boom*, a clattering much

louder than the earlier sounds, then a grip on his shoulders, someone shaking him. He struggled against the pressure and somehow forced his eyes open.

Black things were crawling across the floor and up the walls, across his arms, and over the face of the man above him. He flailed at them and lost his balance, rolling to the floor and hitting it hard. People ran past, guns drawn and shouting. One older woman knelt next to him and opened the bag she'd set down beside her. She touched his face, said his name as though it was a question, and held open one of his eyes with the pad of her thumb. A hot white light shone in, so bright it stung, and he tried to pull away.

"Easy," the woman said, and she made a motion to someone behind him.

Others came, and Noah felt the buttons of his shirt being undone, hands moving over him as though they were feeling for something, and then a pain and a tearing sound, like a patch of carpet tape had been ripped from his upper chest near the shoulder. One of his sleeves was pulled up and something cold and wet rubbed against the vein at the bend of his elbow.

"You might feel a little pinch," the woman said.

He looked down and watched the gradual pierce of a hypodermic needle, but felt only a distant pressure and then a chill trickling up the vessel as the plunger was pushed to its stop. The room had begun a slow spin with him at its center.

The doctor snapped her fingers in front of his face. "Noah? Can you tell me what year it is?"

"Where am I?"

"You're safe. What's your mother's maiden name, do you know that?" She had a stethoscope to his chest, and her attention was on the face of her wristwatch.

"Wilson. Jaime Wilson." He felt his head beginning to clear. A gradual, unnatural onset of wide-awakeness was taking hold, likely brought on by whatever had been in that injection. A pounding set in at his temple, and he pushed away the hands that were supporting him as he sat up on his own.

"And what day is today?"

"I got here on Saturday night." A few others had gathered around and he noticed them exchanging a look when they heard this answer. "What happened? How long have I been out?"

"It's Monday, about noon," the woman said. She snapped off her gloves and returned her things to the medical kit, then stood and turned to one of the men. "I'll take him now. Three of you come with me and the rest should finish up here, then be sure to call in."

Monday, about noon; he'd been dead to the world for forty hours. Noah tried his best to let that sink in as two of the men helped him to his feet. They stayed close, as though half expecting him to collapse immediately if he tried to walk on his own.

"Where are we going?" he asked.

The woman looked at him, and her demeanor had noticeably chilled. It's a thing with some doctors; the instant you're well they don't see much use in courtesy.

"Your father wants to see you," she said.

CHAPTER 29

"What time zone is Nevada?" Danny called out toward the trailer's kitchenette. His watch was a Rolex knockoff and it wasn't easy to reset, so whenever he was traveling he always put off messing with it for as long as possible. This, however, was shaping up to be a day when he'd need to know the time.

"Pacific Standard, same as L.A.," Agent Kearns shouted back. "It's about twenty-five after eight."

They'd both overslept a bit and now there was a rush to get on the road. To add to the tension Kearns had said he'd been unable to reach his FBI contact the night before, and this morning he'd received a rather cryptic e-mail from their new terrorist brethren.

The message had been from the missing man, the one named Elmer. There was to be another meeting this afternoon, the real meeting this time, at which the weapon would be exchanged for the money, and some final brainstorming would take place on the eve of tomorrow's planned bombing in downtown Las Vegas. The rendezvous was set for 5 P.M., out somewhere in the desert so far from civilization that only a latitude and longitude were provided as a guide to get there.

Between the two of them Danny was more capable on the computer, so it had been entrusted to him to plan the route to this remote location through a visit to MapQuest. While Kearns was in the bathroom Danny had logged on to his favorite anonymous e-mailing site and fired off a quick text update to his staff in Chicago, with a copy to Molly and a short list of other trusted compatriots:

* FYI ONLY DO NOT FORWARD
DELETE AFTER READING *
Big mtg today, Monday PM, southern
Nevada. If you don't hear from me by
Wednesday I'm probably dead*,
and this is
where to hunt for the body:
Lat 37°39′54.35″N
Long 116°56′31.48″W
>S T A Y A W A Y from Nevada TFN<
db

*I wish I was kidding

The message was safely gone, the browser history deleted, and the map to the meeting location printed out and ready by the time Kearns returned to the room.

When the artificial bomb was loaded into the van again Danny sat in the shotgun seat and waited, warming his hands around a cup of instant coffee as the engine idled. An eight-hour drive was ahead, with an unknown outcome waiting at the end of it, but all things considered, he felt unusually calm.

Kearns appeared a minute or so later, but when he was halfway out to the vehicle he stopped and lightly smacked himself on the forehead as though something important had almost slipped his mind. He turned back and hurried to the front door of the trailer, unlocked it and held it open, called inside, and gestured for half a minute until that moth-eaten cat appeared and scampered past him out into the barren yard. Then Agent Kearns knelt and filled an inverted hubcap with water from the hose and set it carefully near the stairs, in a spot where it would stay cool in the shade for most of the day.

This was a thing any person might do if they owned a pet and knew they'd be away on a trip until late tomorrow. But, and it was hard just then to put his finger on precisely why, it certainly seemed to Danny like this man thought he might be going away for an awful lot longer than that.

CHAPTER 30

After they'd delivered him to 500 Fifth Avenue Noah's escorts waited outside his suite as he took a quick shower and then changed into the neatly folded set of fresh clothes his secretary had arranged for him. The entourage then proceeded with him across the twenty-first floor to the far corner office.

Arthur Gardner was there behind his desk, looking thoughtful and sober as a judge, long fingers knit together, slightly reclined and contemplating in his favorite leather chair.

Charlie Nelan was standing by the window. He looked over, then shook his head almost imperceptibly as Noah met his eyes. Charlie seemed worn-out and wired at the same time, his wrinkled shirt undone at the collar, sleeves rolled up to the forearms, no necktie. This was far from the lawyer's polished public face; it was the look of a man who'd been awakened from a sound sleep to help fight a five-alarm fire.

The doctor had given Noah an unlabeled prescription bottle that contained a number of small white pills. It was a low-dose oral variation of the drug in the shot he'd received earlier, meant to counteract the lingering effects of that anesthetic patch she'd peeled off his chest when they found him. He'd taken one of the pills already, and it helped, but even with the aid of the drug he still felt like he'd just stepped off the Tilt-A-Whirl. The bottle rattled in his pocket as he sat in a chair that was pulled up for him, across the wide desk from his father.

The boss of the firm's security service, an ex-mercenary hard guy named Warren Landers, consulted for a few moments with his four employees who'd brought Noah in. There'd been only a few occasions in the past when Noah had come in close contact with this man but it hadn't taken very long to get the intended impression. Landers was the bully in the schoolyard who'd grown up and found himself an executive job where he could dress up and get paid for doing what he still loved to do. There was always an undertone when he spoke, a smirk in his eyes as if something about you was the punch line of a running joke he was telling in his head.

At a slight wave from Arthur Gardner the four underlings left the room and Mr. Landers walked over and stood next to the desk. With everyone facing his chair Noah got the feeling it was his turn to say something, but he was lost as to what it should be.

"Dad—"

"I'm happy to see that you weren't hurt," the old man said. He certainly didn't look happy, but the words seemed sincere enough considering their source.

"How did you find me?"

"The same way I found you last Friday night, at the police station," Charlie said. "We found your cell phone. They'd taken out the battery, but someone put it back in and turned the phone on about an hour ago."

Noah thought about that for a moment. "I'm sorry, I don't understand—you tracked my cell phone? How did you do that?"

Landers finessed right past that question. "The first piece," he said, "was that we figured out who leaked that government document to the press last week."

"Who was it?"

"It was scanned and sent out from right here. About two hours after it came into the mailroom."

"I don't believe it," Noah said.

Landers picked up a manila folder from the desk and put it in Noah's hands. "Take a look for yourself," he said.

The tab on the folder wasn't labeled and the paper inside was still warm from the copier. The top document was the cover page of a dossier, and the bold heading was just a name: Molly Ross.

He flipped the page to find a breadcrumb trail of computer activity sent up from the IT department. There was her log-in and some fairly cagey attempts to hide the suspicious actions through a proxy mask, along with the e-mail message in question, addressed to a list of a few hundred recipients outside the company firewall. And there was the attachment that contained a digitized version of the formerly secret DHS memorandum.

No question that she'd done it; no question that she'd tried to hide what she'd done.

Charlie brought him some water from the pitcher on the sideboard, and he needed it. His hands were unsteady as he retrieved another of the little pills from his pocket. He swallowed it along with the remaining water in the glass.

"Keep going," Landers said. "It gets better."

The next page was a photo of her in some academic environment, and it took Noah a few seconds to recognize all the things that were different. She wore glasses, thin half-rim frames and subtly tinted lenses. Her hair was longer and lighter, almost blond. But the changes went beyond her appearance. There was a sophistication about her in this photo, a style and a seriousness that he'd either overlooked or that she'd somehow hidden in their short time together.

In another shot she appeared to be at a rally of some kind, with her mother on one side and the ubiquitous Danny Bailey on the other, his arm around her waist and hers around his as they all pressed together for the camera.

The next picture seemed more recent. Molly was alone, wearing aviator sunglasses, a backward baseball cap, cut-off Daisy Dukes, and a camouflage tank top. In her hands was what looked like a military-grade automatic rifle with a drum magazine, held as if it were the most natural accessory a pretty young woman could be sporting on a bright summer day at the gunnery range. For whatever reason he was reminded of that famous shot of Lee Harvey Oswald in his backyard, holding his radical newspapers in one hand and his murder weapon in the other, just a few months before his appointment with JFK at Dealey Plaza.

"The way we figure it," Landers said, "these people wanted to get some dirt on the government, our new clients, specifically, and they identified our company as a weak spot in the security chain. So they sent this girl to a temp agency we use, and you can see right there"—he tapped one of the papers in the open folder—"she wrote up a résumé that made her look like a perfect fit for a job here, and talked her way in. This Ross girl, she can be a charmer, I understand."

Noah felt his face getting hot.

"But it wasn't enough just to get into the mailroom," Landers said. "Oh, it gave her some limited access, but to do the kind of damage they wanted to, they needed some inside help."

"Just say what you're trying to say," Noah said. "Do you really think I set out to help these people? I met her on Friday, totally at random, and then I brought her here on Saturday night, and that was a terrible mistake and I know it and I deserve whatever happens to me for that. But don't stand there and insinuate that I was in on this whole thing."

Landers took another folder from the desk, and at a nod from the old man he handed it to Noah. "What I'm saying is, there was nothing random about how you met her, and this all started a long time before Friday."

When he opened the new folder the

picture clipped to the left inside cover was an enlargement of Molly's company ID. It featured the same photo he'd admired so much when it was pinned to that flattering sweater she'd worn—the one that was knit in his favorite shades of blue. She was beautiful, of course, with a look that seemed put together to conform precisely to his personal checklist of attractive feminine qualities. But he'd missed something important the first time he'd seen this picture: she also looked awfully clever.

In the right-hand pocket was a sheaf of printouts, and these pages weren't about Molly, but from their markings they belonged to her. It was everything anyone could ever want to know about Noah Gardner, much of it unwittingly supplied by the subject himself. His Facebook profile, his Twitter history, his full set of responses from a variety of questionnaires at his online dating sites, the rambling, soul-searching posts from his personal blog, even his browser history from a number of recent consecutive weeks—much of this was openly available, but some of it would have required some minor identity theft or targeted hacking skills to obtain.

He had a brief impulse to ask how Landers had managed to gather all of this, presumably from Molly's home computer, but then he remembered where he worked. Noah had seen the same sort of digital thievery performed many, many times in the course of corporate espionage and political dirty-tricks campaigns. The pages were stamped with evidence registers, as though they'd been sent over from Molly's Internet service provider through some shady collusion with law enforcement. As fast and loose as everyone was playing with privacy regulations these days it was probably as simple as knowing the right person to call and paying the standard fee.

Noah turned over another page, and the next item hit him like a blow to the midsection. He'd thought for the first second that it was another picture of Molly, and it seemed that was exactly the point.

It was a photo of Noah's mother that he'd posted on his blog a while back on some anniversary of hers. It might have been her birthday, or the date she'd died, or just one of the many late nights when he was missing her more than usual. She'd been in her mid-twenties in the picture, about Molly's age, a carefree young rebel with a smile that would almost break your heart. She was dressed in faded jeans, sandals, and a powder-blue knit sweater, and she wore a little flower in her dark, curly hair.

"You didn't stand a chance, Noah," Charlie said. "She came here specifically to get close to you and then make the most of it. This Ross girl was so far into your head you never would have seen her coming. Nobody would have." He pulled up a chair and sat down. "Now why don't you tell us what happened with this woman. Start from the beginning. We're in full damage control mode now, so don't leave anything out."

So he told them. In hindsight it was all painfully clear, but Mr. Landers still occasionally chimed in to underscore the more subtle features of the betrayal in case anyone might have missed them.

He'd first met Molly in the break room—this was obviously meant to seem like an accidental encounter but it was nothing of the kind; he visited the snack machine like clockwork practically every day at that time. Her look was subtly put together to hook him in the defenseless depths of his unconscious mind. Then she'd acted completely uninterested, which served only to put him instantly under her spell.

He went downtown after work to see her again at her meeting; Charlie had already supplied the other two men with those details. He took her home to his place, and she'd gone out while he was sleeping—that's when she'd duplicated his keys, Landers said, and she'd also paused to whisper to the doorman that she might be coming back later with some of Noah's friends for a surprise.

Then Noah brought her to the office and showed her that presentation—and in doing so he also showed her how to access those protected files when she returned with her accomplices to try to steal them that same night.

Shortly after this point his recollection ended, of course, so Landers took up the reconstructed story. At her apartment she'd evidently given him some kind of short-acting drug to knock him out, and then they'd applied a fentanyl patch in hopes of keeping him unconscious for the duration of the weekend. The doctor had made it clear that this was quite a dangerous thing to do to a person, and it showed a callous disregard for Noah's safety.

On Saturday night Molly had come back to the office with three men and used her prior experience and Noah's keycard to get access to the floor. They'd tried to copy the electronic files from the conference room, but the network's security system was alerted and the servers locked themselves down before everything had been compromised. What they'd managed to steal was significant, though, and it was still unclear how much of the damage could be contained.

"They cleaned out that squatter's apartment where we found you," Charlie said, "but they left some conspicuous incriminating evidence behind: some radical wing-nut literature, a couple of weapons, and some other assorted contraband. They were probably going to call the police to the place with an anonymous tip."

"Why would they do that?"

"We think they wanted you to be found there with that stuff, so you'd be implicated as an accomplice in this whole thing. That way we'd want to keep it quiet to protect you, and we'd be less likely to make a federal case out of it. We know they went back to your apartment that night. We'll know pretty soon if they planted something there, but it doesn't look like they took anything."

The pounding in his head was worsening, and reliving the weekend's ordeal wasn't helping him feel any better. "So what are you going to do?" Noah asked.

"We won't involve the authorities." It was the first time the old man had spoken in a while. "But there have already been . . . repercussions . . . for the people who've done this. And there are many more to come."

"Yeah, don't worry, kid, we'll make 'em sorry," Landers said, and he clapped Noah on the shoulder a little harder than required for a simple friendly gesture. "Hey, at least somebody got laid out of the deal, am I right?"

At that moment Noah had never felt any more like punching another man in the face, nor any less physically capable of doing so. So he only sat there, eyes down, thinking how good that might feel.

"Gentlemen," the old man said, "could you leave my son and me alone?"

Landers gathered his things and on his way out he paused to whisper for a few seconds at Arthur Gardner's ear. Charlie Nelan stayed where he was, in the chair next to Noah.

"You too, Charlie, if you would."

"I'd like to stay."

The old man had been cleaning his pipe and was now refilling it, and he let his silence provide his answer. Charlie got up, put a hand on Noah's shoulder and squeezed, then left the room and closed the door behind him.

CHAPTER 31

Arthur Gardner's office suite was rumored to be the quietest place on the island of Manhattan. It had been designed that way, as an environment of uninterrupted solitude, completely free of unwanted outside sounds. There was no street or city noise, not a whisper from the heating or cooling vents, no intrusion on the ears from the bustling office floor outside.

The reading rooms of the New York Public Library just across the street were as loud as a bus engine by comparison. This place immersed you in a deep-space quiet you might imagine to exist within the thick steel walls of a bank vault or the inside crypt of a sealed mausoleum. All that echo-dampened stillness made any interior sound seem exaggerated and unnaturally distinct—the *scritch* of the flint in his father's lighter, the hiss of the glowing tobacco in the bowl of his pipe, the steady metal workings of the ancient mantel clock on the corner shelf.

Most people missed the meaning of this peculiarity. It wasn't simply the quiet that was important to Arthur Gardner. His own sounds were probably music to his ears. It was the noise of other human beings—the reminders of their existence—that was what he wanted to avoid. He'd said it more than once: if he stepped out of the house one morning and by some miracle all the people were gone, that would be his fondest wish come true. That's how much he loved to be alone.

The two of them had been sitting for over a minute in that dead, cottony silence when Noah finally mustered the courage to speak.

"I'm sorry, Dad."

"There's no need to apologize to me."

"Really, I'm sorry—"

"No need, I said." His father set his pipe in its rest and leaned back in his chair. "It was more an insult than an injury, the idea that they managed to use you in an attempt to damage our company and our clients. We've known of these people, of course, and we'd thought we were adequately prepared, but they surprised all of us, didn't they? And I must say"—now there was a strange little smile on his face—"this avenue they chose, the seductive infiltration by this girl, it shows a great deal more ingenuity than I would have expected, given the source. It was inspired, really. Ruthless though it was."

"I should have known better."

"Nonsense. Wiser men than you have fallen, and to far less able enemies. Monarchs, captains of industry, senators, sitting presidents, very nearly." He picked up his pipe, tapped it on the desk, and set about the ritual motions of lighting it again. "Let's put it behind us. I'm afraid we have other pressing matters to discuss."

In a quick look back over the years Noah was certain he could have counted the number of actual, heart-to-heart conversations with his father on the digits of a single hand. Now it looked like another one was coming, and frankly, he wasn't in the mood. The shock of it all was fading and now he was angry, and hurt, and sick, and in dire need of a meal and a long rest to try to wash this giant mess away.

"I'm not a hundred percent right now, Dad. What is it that we need to discuss?" His father had made threats of retirement many times in the past, but somehow this didn't feel like one of those.

"Something is going to happen tomorrow morning, Noah. Something that will be the beginning of quite a change in the way things are. This weekend's developments, this theft and the accompanying threat of exposure, have served only to further convince the parties involved that now is the time for this—this course correction."

"What's going to happen?"

For a few seconds the old man seemed uncharacteristically at a loss for words.

"This young woman—this Molly Ross and her people. Do you understand the difference between the world as they see it and the world as it really is?"

"I'm not sure I understand very much right now."

"If they spoke with you at all then I'm sure you received the full picture from their warped point of view. Their proud ethos is generally the first thing to pop out of their mouths, or some variation on the theme." The following words were delivered in a deep tone of mocking reverence. "'We hold these truths to be self-evident, that all men are created equal—that they are endowed by their Creator with certain unalienable rights—life, liberty,' and so on. That is the rallying cry of the modern-day American armchair patriot, and it's a stirring turn of phrase, I must admit.

"But I came to understand at an early age that Thomas Jefferson himself couldn't really have believed what he'd written in his Declaration. No slave owner could. Nor could any man with his intelligence, and his great knowledge of history, believe himself to be equal in any way to the ignorant masses of his time. He was preparing to do battle with an empire, making his case against the divine right of kings, so he brazenly invoked the Creator on his own behalf. He proposed that God was the source of these inborn rights of man, and that, contrary to the popular mythology of the times, the Almighty would not be on the side of the British royalty if the conflict came to war.

"That these rights were granted by God, it wasn't the truth, you see, it was what Jefferson needed to say to give his revolution the moral authority to proceed. But he also must have known he was putting far more faith in the common people than they've ever shown the courage to deserve."

Noah was trying to imagine what possible urgency this subject could have right now, though he didn't see a choice but to sit there and stay with it. "You think Jefferson was wrong, then."

"Oh, I think he was right to try. There's a tale from those days, at the close of the Constitutional Convention, in which someone asked Benjamin Franklin what form of government the people would be given, a republic or a monarchy. Do you remember what Franklin replied?"

"'A republic,'" Noah said, "'if you can keep it.'"

The old man nodded. "If they could keep it, yes. Such a thing had never been attempted before, not on the scale these men proposed. It was a bold experiment whose outcome was far from certain, and it could have worked. But its founding premise was also its great weakness: that these common people of the United States, for the first time among all the people in recorded history, could somehow prove capable of ruling themselves—to hold on to the fragile gift they'd been given. And time and again they've proven they're not equal to the task."

"So what are you telling me, Dad?"

"Let me ask you, Noah. Put their complete incompetence in self-government aside for the moment. Do you believe that people, human beings, are basically good? That—as your loyal friend Molly would no doubt preach to us—all they must do is awaken and embrace liberty and the highest potentials of mankind will be realized?"

"I want to believe that."

"I didn't ask you what you wanted," the old man said, his words carrying a sharp enunciation that made it clear he would accept no such avoidance. "I asked what you believe."

"Then yes. I do believe that people are basically good."

"Easy enough to say, though history sadly proves otherwise. In the face of the worldwide collapse that's soon to be upon us, we'll be lost if we place our faith in wishes and hopes for the best." He picked up a folded newspaper near his hand and passed it across the desk. "This is the essence of human nature, left to its own devices."

Noah took the newspaper, expecting to see a run-of-the-mill story of a faraway genocide or massacre, widespread child abuse by some august religious institution, or maybe a retrospective of Nazi atrocities or the horrors of the killing fields. But it's too easy to indict a powerful regime and its leaders while giving a pass to the followers themselves—they, the people who took the orders without question or stood by, silent, and watched the nightmare come to pass. The example his father had chosen was smaller, and cut deeper, and was a much harder thing to simply chalk up to some vague blanket notion of man's inhumanity to man.

The headline of the story was TURKISH GIRL, 16, BURIED ALIVE FOR TALKING TO BOYS.

The text below went on to explain that a

young girl had been the victim of an honor killing, not an uncommon thing in many cultures, allegedly at the hands of her own father and grandfather. They'd buried her alive under a chicken pen in the backyard behind the house. And this was no crime of passion; it takes a long, thoughtful time to do such a thing. In fact, a family council meeting had determined what her punishment should be for the crime of hanging out with her friends.

Noah put the paper down. "This doesn't mean that all of humanity is evil," he said. "There are always extremists."

"I was a social anthropologist, you'll recall, before I became a pitchman, so with all due respect let me assure you that it's much closer to everyone than you might be willing to believe. People are made of the same stuff around the world. If that girl had been born in South Africa she'd have been as likely to be raped by the time she was sixteen as to learn how to read. Slavery in one form or another is more widespread today than ever before in history. The fact that one in a million of us may have evolved beyond those lower instincts is of no great comfort to me.

"It's getting worse, Noah, not better. There have always been only four kinds of people in the world: the visionaries who choose the course, and we are the fewest; the greedy and corruptible—they're useful, because they'll do anything for a short-term gain; the revolutionaries, a handful of violent, backward thinkers whose only mission is to stand in the way of progress—we'll deal with them in short order; and then there are the masses, the lemmings who can scarcely muster the intelligence to blindly follow along.

"There are far more of them than there are of us, and more are coming every day. When I was born there were two billion people in the world; now that number has more than tripled, all in a single lifetime. And it isn't the Mozarts, or the Einsteins, or the Pascals, or Salks, or Shakespeares, or the George Washingtons who are swelling the population beyond the breaking point. It's the useless eaters on the savage side of the bell curve who are outbreeding the planet's ability to support them.

"A billion people around the world are slowly starving to death right now. Twenty thousand children will die of hunger today.

That's the decaying state of the human condition. And when the real hard times come—and they're coming soon—you can multiply all the horrors by a thousand. In the vacuum created by fear and ignorance and hunger and want, it's evil, not good, that rushes in to fill the void."

It sounded like there was no answer, but he knew his father too well for that to be the case. You didn't have to like it, but the old man always had a solution.

"What we've finally come to understand, Noah, is that the people can't be trusted to control themselves. Even the brightest of them are still barbarians at heart. We've only just bailed out my friends on Wall Street from under the devastation of the last financial bubble they created, and I guarantee they're already hard at work pumping up the next one, even as they know full well that it will be fatal. It's like a death wish of the species: it's in our genes, this appetite for destruction. And if we're to survive, those urges must be brought under control.

"The riddle today is the same one faced by the Founding Fathers when they began their experiment. Societies need government. Governments elevate men into power, and men who seek power are prone to corruption. It spreads like a disease, then, corruption on corruption, and sooner or later the end result is always a slide into tyranny. That's the way it's always been. And so this government of the United States was brilliantly designed to keep that weakness of human nature in check, but it required the people to participate daily, to be vigilant, and they have not. It demanded that they behave as though their government was their servant, but they have not. In their silence the people of the United States have spoken. While they slept the servant has become their master.

"The American experiment has failed, and now it's time for the next one to begin. One world, one government—not of the people this time, but of the *right* people: the competent, the wise, and the strong."

The dope-induced haze was still hanging there before Noah's eyes, and his stomach had begun to churn. Between the remains of the opiates swirling through his brain and the drugs he'd been given to counter those effects, he could feel himself starting to lose the metabolic tug-of-war. All these words his father was saying, all the things he'd seen in that presentation, what he'd learned from Molly in the hours they were together, and what he'd learned of her since—something was trying to come together in his mind but he wasn't fit to think it all the way through.

"You're saying there's no hope for this country," Noah said.

"I'm saying, Noah, that my clients came to me with a problem," the old man said, "and I gave them a solution. We start tomorrow morning. I've stood by and watched the glacial pace of this decline for too many years. Now the remnants of the past will be swept away in a single stroke, and I'll see my vision realized before I die. Order from chaos, control, and pacification of the flawed human spirit. Call that hope if you like, but it's coming regardless. The experiment that begins tomorrow will not fail."

PART THREE

"The conscious and intelligent manipulation of the organized habits and opinions of the masses is an important element in a democratic society. Those who manipulate this unseen mechanism of society constitute an invisible government which is the true ruling power of our country."

—EDWARD BERNAYS, AUTHOR OF *Propaganda*

CHAPTER 32

Noah had excused himself suddenly and then stumbled his way into the elegant stall in the corner of his father's private restroom. You know you're sick when you're still vomiting ten minutes after the last thing was expelled from your stomach. He was still hugging the porcelain bowl, drained and wretched, feeling like he'd just capped off a marathon with four hundred sit-ups.

Once he was fairly sure the nausea had passed, he pushed himself to his feet, walked to the sink, and turned on the water as hot as he could stand. He let the basin fill and then bent and washed his face, let the heat try to revive him until he felt whatever flicker of energy he still possessed begin to gather. He stood then, dried himself with a hanging towel, rebuttoned and tucked in his shirt, and then used his sleeve to clear the steam from the ornate mirror over the lavatory.

His skin was as pale as a Newark Bay oyster, but while he was certainly beat he wasn't quite out of commission yet.

The doctor had said these aftereffects could linger for up to a day, but would ease as the hours went by. He took another of the pills from his pocket and told himself that the worst of it was behind him now. He needed it to be, because in addition to coming to grips with what he'd just heard from his father, there was also a score he needed to settle before a certain young woman's trail became too cold to follow.

As Noah hurried down the stairwell toward the mailroom he lost his shaky footing and nearly tumbled down the last half flight. The people he passed in the hallway stood back and gave him a wide berth; whether they sensed his illness or his anger, they obviously didn't want to catch whatever he was carrying. He was breathing hard as he made the last corner, feeling chilled and damp under his clothes.

It's not that he expected her to be at work that day, innocently sorting the mail as though nothing were wrong. But he was going to find her one way or the other, and this was the closest stop on the tour.

"Frank!" Noah called.

The department manager popped his head out from behind the sorting shelves. "Yes, sir."

"Have you heard from Molly today?"

"No, sir. She was on the schedule but she ain't been in. I called her agency about an hour ago and they haven't got back to me yet."

"Okay, thanks. Does she have, I don't know, some emergency contact numbers down here, from her application?"

Frank looked a little surprised to be asked such a thing. "Maybe that'd be up in Human Resources, Mr. Gardner. All I could give you is the number of the place we hired her from."

"You're talking about that temp girl, Molly?" Another of the mailroom staff had apparently overheard the conversation, and he came nearer. "Somebody called here for her over the weekend. I picked up the voice mail when I opened up this morning."

"Do you have that message?" Noah asked. "It's important."

"I deleted it, and I didn't write anything down, since it was a personal thing. The fellow who called must have just tried all the numbers he had for her. He said her mama was in the hospital."

Noah stood there and let that bit of news sink into his empty stomach. As it gripped him there he remembered what Warren Landers had said, up in his father's office. It had passed in one ear and straight out his other, because, as usual, he was immersed in his own significance, as though the only bad things that existed were the ones that had happened to him.

We'll make them sorry. That's how Mr. Landers had put it.

"Which hospital?"

"Uptown, Lenox Hill," the man said, and then he leaned in and offered a quiet addendum. "None of my business, Mr. Gardner. But it didn't sound so good."

CHAPTER 33

In the cab on the way uptown Noah had made two phone calls, one to the hospital's automated system to find the patient's floor and room, and the other to an old and trusted acquaintance who was now on her way to meet up with him at Lenox Hill.

Over a long-ago summer Ellen Davenport, of the East Hampton Davenports, had become his first real friend who was a girl. It was a new thing for him, because though they'd hit it off immediately, they both also seemed to realize that dating each other was the last thing they should ever do.

They'd actually tried it once just to be sure, and the discomfort of that terrible evening was matched only by its comic potential when the story was retold by the two of them in later years.

Now Ellen was a second-year neurology resident at Mount Sinai Hospital across town. His call had caught her at the end of a twenty-six-hour shift, but, true to form, she'd told him that she'd be right over without even asking why.

As he walked down the hallway of the ward he saw three things: the crowd of people overflowing from the double doorway of the floor's small chapel, a smaller knot of visitors waiting outside a single room down near the end, and Dr. Ellen Davenport, still in her wrinkled scrubs, waving to him from an alcove near the elevators.

Ellen gave him a hug when he reached her, and then held him away at arm's length and frowned. "You look like hell, Gardner."

"Thanks." He was preoccupied, looking over the people milling through the hall, every bit as afraid that he might see Molly as that he might never see her again.

Some of these people were looking back at him, too, and by their manner it seemed they knew who he was.

"Hey." Ellen snapped her fingers in front of his eyes. "I mean it. You look like you need to lie down."

"I need for you to do me a favor," Noah said. There was a slight tremor in his hands as he retrieved the medicine from his pocket, shook out a pill into his palm, and swallowed it dry.

Ellen took the vial from him, rattled it, and held it close to her eyes. She looked at him again with a little more concern than before. "If you're going to ask me to score you some methadone, I left my prescription pad in my other pants."

"That woman in the room down the hall there," he said. "I need for you to help me—I don't know, line up a specialist, make sure everything's being done. I just want her to be taken care of."

"They're pretty good at that sort of thing here, Noah."

"Ellen, listen to me—"

Whatever Noah had been about to confess, he was interrupted by the approach of a stranger. It was an older woman, frail and thin as dry reeds, and from the corner of his eye he'd seen her come from the direction of that room near the end of the hall. The woman nodded her respect to Ellen, turned to him, and then spoke with a gentle gravity in her voice that said more than the words themselves would convey.

"She's awake now. Somebody told her you were here, and she says she wants to talk to you."

CHAPTER 34

He stood just inside the open doorway, watching the remaining visitors say their good-byes before they quietly walked past him, one by one. Flowers were arranged all around the room, in baskets and vases and water pitchers, on extra rolling tables that seemed to have been brought in just to accommodate the overflow of gifts from well-wishers.

The door was closed by the last man who'd left, but still Noah stood where he was until Beverly Emerson looked over and smiled as best she could, inviting him to her bedside with a weak motion of her bandaged hand.

"We meet again," she said. It was barely more than a whisper, spoken as though her lungs might hold the space for only a thimbleful of air.

There were bruises on her face and arms, dark, uneven spots within yellowing patches, and a bandage on her neck with a soak of crusted brown near its center. She was withered, already a shadow of the person he'd last seen on Friday night. The only thing that remained undimmed was that unforgettable spark in her light green eyes.

He had no idea what to say, but he said it anyway.

"You're going to be all right."

That brought a smile again, but she shook her head slowly and touched his hand that was nearest hers.

"We shouldn't deceive ourselves," she said. "I'm afraid there isn't time." She was measuring her breath as she spoke, managing only a few words of each phrase between shallow inhalations. "I don't expect you to understand why Molly did what I asked her to do." The grip on his hand tightened, as though all the strength she had was centering there. "You should blame me, and not her. But I hold the privilege of a dying woman now, and I want you to put everything aside except what I'm about to say."

"Okay."

"My daughter is in danger. I need for you to promise me you'll see her to safety."

There were so many conflicting things hammering at his mind, but despite all that mental noise and everything that had happened, for once in his life he could see it all arranged in its true order of significance, and so he knew for certain there was only one thing to be said.

"I will."

Her grip relaxed somewhat, her head rested back onto the pillow, and she closed her eyes. Soon a private little smile drifted into her features, as though she might have just then put the finish on a silent prayer.

"Thank you," Beverly whispered.

He didn't respond, but only because he didn't want to presume to be the one she was addressing.

"I sent Molly away, but she isn't safe yet," she said. "She's waiting now, near the airport. Look in the top drawer of the nightstand. She called and told one of the nurses where she'd be and they wrote it down for me."

"Okay," he said. "I think I'd better get started, then." He moved to place her hand down on the bed at her side, but she didn't let him go.

"Do you know what we're fighting against, son?"

"Yeah, I think so. Some pretty evil people."

She offered a look that seemed to suggest his naiveté was something she longed for. "Ephesians 6:12—look it up when you get a chance."

"I will," he said.

"There's more to you, Noah. More than you might be ready to believe. I knew of your mother many years ago, and the good she wanted to do. That's what Molly saw in you: she told me. Not your father, but what your mother's given you. And I see it, too."

"I guess I'm glad somebody does."

"Noah . . ."

"Yes."

There was that tiny glint of a smile again. "Noah, from the Bible, you know?"

He nodded, and despite everything, he smiled a bit himself. "Old Testament."

The weak hold on his hand tightened once again.

"He wasn't chosen because he was the best man who ever lived," she said softly. "He was chosen because he was the best man available."

Out in the hallway he hadn't made it five steps before Ellen Davenport caught up to him. She took him firmly by the sleeve, pulled him behind her into a nearby storeroom, and closed the door.

"I need to go, Ellen."

"You need to listen to me first. I learned some things while you were in there just now. Who is that woman to you?"

"She's the mother of a friend of mine."

Ellen nodded. "Sit down."

He could tell by her tone that he shouldn't argue, and he pulled over a nearby stool and sat.

"What is it?"

"She's going to die, you know."

"How can you say that? She just took a bad beating, right? She's not that old. They can fix anything with enough—"

"Shh. Now listen. There are some things we can't fix, Noah. Whoever did this to her did something they knew we couldn't fix."

"What do you mean?"

"You can't tell anyone I'm talking to you about this, understand? And not just because I could lose my ticket."

"Okay."

"They gave her a beating, yeah, probably just for the fun of it. And then they poisoned her."

A chill passed over him.

"What kind of poison was it?"

"Paraquat," she said. She seemed to watch his eyes for signs of recognition but there were none. "Do you see now, the point they were trying to make? The animals who got to this woman? Paraquat is a pesticide. A weed killer."

"A pesticide." He'd heard what she said but he repeated it aloud, just to make sure he understood.

"It starts an irreversible fibrosis in the lungs—a scarring that progresses until you finally can't breathe anymore. If that doesn't kill you first, all the other organ systems begin to shut down, and then it's over. There's nothing we can do about it; we can't even give her oxygen. That just makes it worse. She might have another day, or another week, but it's obvious that they wanted her to suffer."

"How do the doctors here know that's what was used?"

"Well, it's easy enough for the lab to pick it up, but in this case it was even easier than that. The people who did this, they left a veterinary syringe in her neck. It was still there when EMS responded to the call."

Noah stood up, but too quickly, and he could feel the stubborn light-headedness threatening to return. "Where are those pills, the ones you took from me?"

She went to her pocket and handed him the bottle. "I wrote you some instructions for that stuff. Just go easy on it, okay? In fact, whatever you're coming down from I'd recommend you just ride it out and stop self-medicating."

"Good-bye, doctor. Thanks for everything."

"I don't know how you're involved in all

this," Ellen said, "but you'd better know something, Noah. There are a million kinds of murder, but anyone who would do to a person what they did to her? It only means there's nothing at all they *wouldn't* do."

CHAPTER 35

The street address that had been scrawled on the hospital's notepaper didn't lead him to another of the so-called safe houses that Molly had described. When Noah looked up as the cab pulled to a stop he found he was outside what looked like a quaint family-style eatery, the Buccaneer Diner on Astoria Boulevard in Queens, about a mile from La Guardia Airport.

Inside the restaurant the lunchtime rush was winding down, with most of the tables emptying out and the floor staff busy doing cleanup and taking care of departing patrons at the register. But sitting alone in a booth near the back, in the nearest thing to a dark corner that was available in such a place on a sunny Monday afternoon, was the young woman he'd come to see.

When Molly looked over and saw him walking up the aisle she stood and was suddenly overcome by a flood of tears she must have been barely holding at bay. She ran to him and threw herself into his arms.

In the cab on the way he'd given a great deal of thought to what he might say to her if he actually found her waiting at the end of the ride. Now that he was facing her all of the mental dialogue he'd rehearsed had winked right out of his mind. Nothing in his long history of skin-deep relationships provided any clue as to where to begin.

Not only did you break my heart, but you and your friends could have killed me with an overdose, all in the name of a hopeless cause.

I care about you, I was starting to believe in you, and now I don't know if a single thing between us was real.

And of course, there was this one:

I think my father must have ordered

your mother to be murdered, just as easily as he'd ordered his breakfast that morning.

There was too much, so Noah said nothing. Neither forgiving nor forgetting, he put it all aside for the time being and just held her for a while.

She'd asked about her mom in a voice that said his answer should be limited to any hopeful news. Noah told her that her mother was awake and speaking when he'd seen her, and that, despite her concerns for the welfare of her precious daughter, her spirits seemed good.

Molly took that in with a solemn nod, and then she laid out her situation.

Her traveling companions had gone on ahead to test the waters at La Guardia in preparation for their flight west toward less hostile environs. According to the news the DHS had taken the nation to high alert over the weekend, and that put the airports at the very highest level; this was obviously cause for concern. Sure enough, word had reached her that the first of her friends to pass through the TSA checkpoint had been singled out and pulled aside. They weren't just searched and harassed, as had often been the case in recent years; this time they were arrested and detained.

Molly explained that she had to get out of town and make it to a rendezvous across the country as quickly as possible. Driving wouldn't do; she had to fly in order to make it. The problem was how to get her safely onto a flight when her name might very well have made it to the top of the swelling watch lists of Homeland Security by now.

Noah was listening, and he was also studying her face as she spoke. The passing resemblance to that picture of his mother was almost gone now that she'd ceased to maintain it. That likeness had been subliminal at best, just enough to hook into his subconscious. But now, as they sat under the bright fluorescent lights of a Queens diner, he realized that there was absolutely no denying who Molly *did* look like.

And that gave him an absolutely brilliant idea.

CHAPTER 36

Noah returned from the pay phone near the front door, sat down, and scooted half-way around the semicircular padded booth until he was near enough to her for privacy.

"Okay, we're all ready."

"What do you mean, we're all ready? You made one call and shut down security at an international airport?"

"I did better than that." He looked around a bit. "Did I see a carry-on bag?"

"Yeah . . ."

"Let me have it."

Though she appeared to be totally flummoxed she reached to the floor by her feet, brought up her small duffel, and slid it onto the table in front of him.

Noah zipped the bag open and rummaged through, pulling out a baseball cap, a faded university jersey, and her small polka-dot makeup case.

"Do you have a pair of sunglasses? Wait, forget it, I've got mine."

"Okay," Molly said, "this is the part where you tell me what we're going to do."

"Have you ever wondered how celebrities and public figures avoid all the hassle the rest of us have to go through when they need to suck it up and fly commercial?"

"I've never thought about it."

"They make a call like I just made. All the major airlines have a VIP liaison in the big cities, and there's a service company we've used from the office, KTL, that's going to grease the way even more. They'll meet us at the curb and walk us right to the plane—"

"Hold it, hold it," Molly said. "We aren't celebrities, Noah."

"No, you're right. But I'm a rich kid from a powerful family, and it's reasonable enough that they'd believe I could be dating a celebrity."

"What are you talking about?"

He smiled. "I'm now dating Natalie Portman."

She looked at him as though his head had just turned into a pumpkin.

"Wait, what?"

"It's perfect," Noah said. "She's an A-lister but she's done mostly art-house films, so the average Joe probably couldn't pick her out of a lineup. She's about your size—"

"I don't look like Natalie Portman."

"You kind of do, actually, and we've got time to make a few tweaks before the limo arrives." He reached over to smooth one of her eyebrows with the pad of his thumb but she ducked it and swatted his hand away. "Relax," he said. "This is going to work."

"No, it isn't. It's not going to work at all."

He put his hand on hers, and though she still looked completely unconvinced, she didn't pull away.

"Trust me," Noah said.

Molly came back from the bathroom after ten minutes in there with her kit and a few instructions from Noah. She was in her

Vanderbilt sweatshirt, her hair was up in a casual bun at the nape of her neck, and she'd done just enough to her lips and brows and lashes to suggest a layman's conception of a movie star who was wearing no makeup at all. The great advantage of this whole thing was that when celebrities are out in public trying to avoid a mob of fans and paparazzi, the last thing they want to resemble is who they really are.

She sat and looked over, with one of her newly perfected eyebrows slightly upraised in a regal but skeptical arch. Noah gave her the baseball cap and his sunglasses to complete the disguise. She put them on, pulled up her hood, and checked her reflection in the silver side of the napkin holder.

"Perfect," he said. "Absolutely perfect. Oh, wait." He took her makeup kit and searched through its contents until he'd found a small dark pencil with a dull tip. "Lean your face over here." Molly did, and he carefully and gently went to work. "Natalie has got two little tiny beauty marks, one here . . . and one . . . over here." He leaned back, squinted, and studied his masterpiece. "That's it. We can put a bit of powder on those on the way and they'll be fine. Come on now, the car's already outside."

On the short ride to the airport he told her the backstory he'd given to Kyle, the executive service agent from KTL: Noah and young Ms. Portman had spent a wild weekend together painting the town, and things had gotten a little out of hand toward the end. She'd had her purse stolen, she wasn't feeling well at all, and some nasty aggressive photographers had begun to bird-dog them. Now the mission was to spirit her out of the city while keeping her off Page Six of the *New York Post*.

As Noah had anticipated, this wasn't an uncommon thing at all for KTL, and once they'd established who he was they accepted the rest of his story immediately. For a little less than two thousand dollars charged to his expense account—plus the cost of a full row in first class, to be billed separately—the plan was off and rolling with no further questions asked.

With the terminal in sight Noah took in a deep breath and then let it out on a slow count of ten. He looked over at Molly and she seemed to be meditating, or praying, hard to tell which, but any port was welcome in this storm.

"Now remember," he said, "the whole idea is that you don't have to deal with anybody. You don't have to talk to anyone and you don't have to make eye contact with anyone, which is good because your eyes are the wrong color. I told them you've lost your ID so no one's going to expect you to show it. You're in the big club now, you're a hotshot movie star who's had a few rough days of partying, and you're in no mood for any inconvenience. That's what we're paying all this money to avoid. But just keep thinking all that in your head; our guy and I will do all the talking."

True to his word, there ahead at the curb stood Kyle in his dapper suit, waiting with open arms at the appointed meeting place. The limo pulled to a stop, their host opened the door, and with a practiced sweep of his manicured hand he invited them into his care.

"Mr. Gardner, Miss Portman," Kyle said. "Right this way."

And right that way they went.

• • •

Most people know there's a whole hidden part of Disney World the tourists never get to see. Underneath the sidewalks and behind the scenes, in a vast complex every bit as big as the park itself, this insider network of tunnels, workshops, machinery, and control rooms is where the magic really happens. Likewise, a major airport has its own sublevel of secrets, and our man Kyle held all the skeleton keys to this particular enchanted kingdom.

The trip through the public areas had been a breeze. The two men walked purposefully in front with Molly close behind them. For the most part they went unnoticed, though two or three random people did seem to sense that an incognito starlet might be moving in their midst. At every point along the way where the average passenger would have had to stop and deal with some slow, invasive procedure, there was a special someone stationed nearby to give the three of them a knowing wink, lift up the velvet rope, and wave them on through.

Halfway into the terminal Kyle stopped along the wall, looked furtively both ways, and then keyed open a featureless gray door. Like some portal from rural Kansas into the Land of Oz, inside this door was a large VIP room with elegant furnishings and sitting areas, a bar and some bistro tables, and down the center, a privately staffed setup for dignified, one-on-one security screenings.

"And now, my troopers," Kyle chirped, "just a quick run through the metal detector and then we're on to preboarding for a nice, cool glass of champagne. Are we holding up all right?"

"I think we're fine," Noah said. Molly breathed an Oscar-worthy sigh of impatience and leaned her head against his arm.

As they approached the area with the X-ray conveyor a TSA employee got up from his chair, put down his magazine, and sidled up to his security post.

When he saw this man Noah stopped in his tracks so suddenly that Molly bumped into him from behind.

"Is something wrong?" Kyle asked, frowning.

"Excuse us for a minute," Noah said. "I just remembered, we need to make a quick phone call."

He walked Molly over to the telephone

kiosk near the door they'd come in, well out of earshot of Kyle and the others.

"Damn it," he whispered.

"What is it?" Molly asked. "They're all over there looking at us."

"Pretend you're calling someone on the phone. I've got to think for a minute."

Molly picked up the receiver, put it to her ear, punched a few buttons, and pulled him a little closer. "Now tell me what's going on."

"Check out the guy in the TSA outfit."

She did. "So?"

"Are you kidding me? That's a *Star Wars* geek if I ever saw one."

Maybe it was the Luke Skywalker blow-cut, his mismatched socks below the nerdish cut of his high-riding uniform trousers, or the soul patch and horn-rimmed glasses, but everything about this man was screaming *king of the fanboys*, and that was really bad news.

"I don't understand—"

Noah lowered his voice even more. "Natalie Portman is in all three of the *Star Wars* prequels."

"You're remembering this *now*?"

"I guess I hated those movies so much

I'd blocked them out of my mind. But I'd bet my last dollar that dweeb knows Portman's face like the back of his hand. You don't understand these guys; he's probably got a candlelit altar in front of her picture down in his mother's basement."

Molly leaned around him to take another stealthy look, and swallowed hard. "What do we do?"

"I vote we get out of here and think of something else."

"No," she said, and it sounded like the word was final. "We don't have time. This is it. We're here, let's just do it."

After a last few seconds to find his nerve, he nodded, fixed her hood and eased the brim of Molly's baseball cap down a little lower, hung up the phone for her, and then turned around to face the music.

Noah went first, and he passed through the arch of the metal detector without a single blip. Kyle had stationed himself next to the X-ray tech at the luggage conveyor, no doubt ready to smoothly rationalize any oddities that might show up in his clients' carry-on. Their one item, her duffel bag, went into the long machine and came out the other side with no objection raised.

But the TSA man gave Noah a careful, steady look, as if he were toying with the idea of a wand-sweep and a pat-down, just for good measure.

Along with the recent change in alert status, an official DHS directive would have come around to remind all stations, even this special-purpose one, of the key markers for suspicious activity—last-minute ticket purchases for one-way travel, no checked luggage, nervous or flustered behavior, identification papers not in order—and this little party matched every warning sign.

Kyle cleared his throat meaningfully from where he was standing. This subtle, perfectly pitched intervention was sent to remind the room that this trip had already been preapproved from positions much higher than their own, and these two very important people weren't to be unnecessarily troubled by the rigors of the standard inquisition.

With some visible reluctance, the stern young officer nodded and gave a jut of his chin to let the first subject know he'd been provisionally cleared for boarding.

So far, so good.

Noah retrieved his belt and his pocket items from the gray utility tub, and prepared to put on his shoes. He'd just begun to let himself believe that they were soon to be home free when the piercing tweet of the metal detector sounded off behind him.

CHAPTER 37

"Could you remove any metallic items and step back through for me, ma'am."

Polite and professional though it sounded, it was a command and not a request.

Kyle hurried over to escort Molly back to the far side of the electronic gauntlet again, then he looked her up and down in search of whatever offending metal might have set off the alert. In all the rush she'd forgotten about the cell phone in her pocket. Kyle took that and then delicately helped her remove her necklace, bracelet, and the ring on her finger. He placed those items in a tray held out by the officer, and then nodded to her to indicate that all was ready for another try.

Molly walked slowly through the arch again. The vertical line of indicator lights twitched upward from dark green to barely yellow—maybe in reaction to the tiny hinges in her sunglasses—but this time there was no audible alarm.

Noah was the only one in a position to notice a touch of private relief on Molly's face. She was nearly to the end of the exit track of the detector when she was stopped by the officer's voice.

"Miss . . . Portman?"

When Molly turned around she must have seen exactly what Noah was seeing. The TSA man wasn't focused on her at all. He was staring down at her possessions in his plastic tray.

"Yes?" she said softly.

Now he looked up at her, and raised his hand slowly above the tray. Molly's silver necklace with its little silver cross was dangling from the knuckle of his thumb.

"I thought," the officer said, "that you were Jewish."

It felt like the temperature in the room

suddenly dropped by fifty degrees. Noah's mouth went totally dry, his skin tingling as though all the moisture had flash-frozen out of the atmosphere, settling into a thin layer of frost on everything exposed, suspending those six words on the air.

Cops know liars like plumbers know leaks. They encounter them every day, all day; they know all the little signs and symptoms, and they're trained to understand that where there's even a little whiff of smoke, one should always assume there's a fire. As they challenge a person they study their reactions, pick apart the little telltale movements, listen to the timbre of the voice, and more than anything else, they watch the eyes. Most suspects have already made a full confession by the time they begin their denial.

This was one of the topics of light conversation in the wee hours of that first night when he and Molly had met. Noah had been so fascinated by the woman that he hadn't stopped to wonder why she seemed to know so much about the art of deception.

Don't be afraid, she'd said; that's the

key, no matter how bad it gets. If locked in a car that's speeding toward a gap in the bridge and it's clearly too late to stop, most people would still waste their last mortal seconds stepping on the brakes. But what you really want to do is say a little prayer, and then floor it. If you're going down anyway, go all in, go down with courage—because hey, there's always that one slim chance that you'll make it to the other side.

From behind her Noah saw Molly's head tilt slightly, and this movement was accompanied by a subtle hip shift. There was a convex security mirror on a bracket above the metal detector, and in that reflection he saw a patient but serious expression on her face that meant, *You didn't really just say what I think I heard, did you?*

The officer appeared unfazed.

"Would you take off your sunglasses for me, please," he said.

That's all, folks. Curtains, checkmate, game over.

Noah hoped only that his upcoming visit to prison would be more enjoyable than his first. He'd already begun to gauge the running distance to the door when Molly looked back at him. She appeared to be perfectly serene, and she mouthed something to him. He wasn't much of a lip reader and it took his panic-stricken mind a few seconds to recognize her message. It had been the short phrase that's always at the top of any good list of famous last words.

Watch this.

She turned to the officer, pulled back her hood and let it settle onto her shoulders, removed the baseball cap and let it fall to the floor at her feet, and then slow and sure, began to walk toward him.

"The Force is strong with this one," Molly said, as calm and smooth as a Jedi master. Her accent was gone, and her voice was just breathy enough to obscure any other identifying qualities of the real McCoy.

The TSA man's cheeks began to redden slightly. A power shift was under way, and as Noah had learned firsthand, when this girl turned it on you never knew what was about to hit you.

She continued nearer, put a finger to the frames and lowered her sunglasses partway down her nose, tipping her chin so she could look at the officer directly, eye to eye, just over the top of the darkened lenses. As she stopped barely a foot away she subtly passed an open hand between their faces, and spoke again.

"These aren't the droids you're looking for," Molly said. After waiting a moment she gave him a little nod, as though it had come time in their close-up scene for his own line of dialogue.

There was an eternal pause, and then before his eyes Noah saw this big, intimidating young man begin his grinning transformation from the TSA's most vigilant watchdog into Natalie Portman's biggest fan.

"These aren't the droids we're looking for." The officer repeated her words, just as that spellbound storm trooper had said them at the Imperial checkpoint in Episode 4.

After holding his rapt gaze for a few more seconds Molly pulled out the secret weapon more fearsome than any lightsaber—that sweet, wicked smile that made your knees feel like they could bend in all directions. She slipped the pen from his pocket protector, clicked it, took the hand that still held her necklace, and autographed his palm with an artful flourish.

"Bravo!" Kyle said, and his light applause was picked up by all the other employees who had turned their attention that way. That put a button at the end of the crisis; before any further delay could threaten his schedule he bustled around and retrieved her duffel bag, along with her cap, phone, and jewelry. Then with a cheerful, over-the-shoulder "Thank you, everyone," he gathered his clients back under his wing and hurried them to the exit door.

They were to board the plane from the flight crew's side stairway out on the tarmac. When they got outside Noah motioned to Kyle that he needed just a minute with his girl. Their escort nodded and moved off to a discreet distance, pausing only to tap the face of his watch as a reminder to be quick before he turned away to wait.

"How did I do?" Molly asked, obviously fully aware of exactly how she'd done.

"You quoted two different male characters from the wrong trilogy, but other than that, you nailed it."

"I wrote a midterm paper on the first two movies in college. Never saw any of the others."

"Film class?"

"Political science."

He had to wait for a noisy vehicle to pass before he could speak again.

"I need to ask you something," Noah said.

"Sure." It seemed she could see that he'd become more somber.

"When we were there in Times Square, when we kissed that time . . ."

She took off the sunglasses and hooked them on her pocket, moved a little closer to him, brushed a windblown lock of hair from his eyes. "I remember."

"Is that when you pickpocketed my BlackBerry?"

Molly smiled, and pulled him willingly into her embrace. It was no real surprise, but this kiss was every bit as stirring as that first one had been, and as he realized then for certain, as good as every single one would be thereafter.

She stood back a step, her face as innocent as a newborn lamb, and held up his wallet between them.

"I love you," Noah said.

Molly looked up at him with all the courageous resolve of the doomed Han Solo at the end of *The Empire Strikes Back.*

"I know," she replied.

By the time the jet reached its cruising altitude Molly had fallen sound asleep in his arms. They had the entire row to themselves and the crew had taken excellent care of them so far. Now it was quiet, and in the remains of this day a little peace and stillness were more than welcome.

Molly had taken only one thing from her bag to keep with her during the four-hour flight. He recognized the book as the handbound journal she'd shown him back in her apartment downtown.

It would be nice to have something to read, he thought, and after a brief consideration he decided that she wouldn't be likely to object if he took a look through her little book as she slept.

Folded just inside the front cover he found the pencil drawing that had been pinned to her bedroom wall, that idyllic sketch of her someday cabin in the woods.

On the next page was the beginning of

the texts she'd been given by the Founders' Keepers, that portion of the writings from early American history she was meant to preserve and memorize on their behalf.

Thomas Jefferson

> **I have sworn upon the altar of God, eternal hostility against every form of tyranny over the mind of man.**

What followed didn't really seem to comprise the most famous or succinct of Jefferson's writings. Rather, it was as though a great deal of his written legacy, maybe all of it, had been distributed among quite a number of people, and Molly's was only a small, random part placed in her care. Accordingly, the first section consisted of Jefferson's Second Inaugural Address. Noah read through a portion of it.

> **I fear not that any motives of interest may lead me astray; I am sensible of no passion which could seduce me knowingly from the path of justice, but the weaknesses of human nature and**

the limits of my own understanding will produce errors of judgment sometimes injurious to your interests.

I shall need, therefore, all the indulgence which I have heretofore experienced from my constituents; the want of it will certainly not lessen with increasing years.

What struck Noah as he read these words was a fundamental difference in tone from the political discourse of later times. Here was one of the founders of the nation, maybe the greatest thinker among them, and yet he spoke with a quality that was so rare today as to be almost extinct among modern public servants. It was a profound humility, as though nothing were more important to express than the honor he felt in being chosen again as a guardian of the people's precious liberties.

There was a great deal more to read. Noah held his place, looked down at Molly, and found her still sleeping. He adjusted the light above him so it was less likely to disturb her rest.

Then he remembered something else

that he'd been meaning to ask her, if they'd only had a moment to breathe. Nothing important, but he was curious.

Of all the remote destinations Molly could have picked for her flight to safety—anywhere in the world, really—he wondered why she'd chosen Las Vegas.

CHAPTER 38

Danny Bailey and Agent Kearns had been on the road in their bomb-laden van for nearly five hours straight, and they were past due for a fuel stop and a stretch.

After taking his turn in the gas station's cramped restroom Danny picked up a diet soda and a candy bar and brought them to the counter. As the cashier was ringing him up he scanned the visible stories on a bundled stack of newspapers off to the side. Two headlines stood out, and he read them over again.

NATIONWIDE TERROR ALERT STATUS ELEVATED ONCE MORE

DHS CHIEF: INTEL CONFIRMS 'CREDIBLE THREAT' FOR WESTERN U.S.

He looked up into the corner and saw a dusty security camera looking back down at him. Even out here, he thought, on the outskirts of civilization, some backward distant cousin of Big Brother is still watching. From that odd camera angle Danny's fuzzy, jerky image was displayed on a small black-and-white TV on the side shelf, wedged between the cigarettes and a rack of dog-eared porno magazines.

"I'll take one of these, too," he said, holding up the paper.

Stuart Kearns walked past him toward the door, still rubbing his hands dry. "Let's go, kid, we're burning daylight."

Danny nodded an acknowledgment but the words and their urgency had barely intruded on his running thoughts. A few seconds later the cashier had to nudge his hand to snap him out of it, and he picked up his bagged purchases and his change and headed for the van.

• • •

As the trip progressed southward the Nevada roads had gradually become more and more rustic and empty of traffic. From the first wide interstate, to four-lane turnpikes, down to the aging two-lane desert highway they'd now been on for a good while—in a sense it felt as though they were traveling further back in time with every passing mile. At this rate they'd be bumping down a mule trail before sunset.

Danny still had the newspaper he'd bought draped across his lap, though he'd stopped reading it several minutes before.

"Can I run something up the flagpole, Stuart?"

"Sure."

"The terrorism alert is elevated. I take that back—it was already elevated two days ago, and now it's been raised again."

"Right."

"They're talking here"—he tapped the paper—"about what they call a specific credible threat, maybe two, that they're tracking somewhere in the western United States. They're already stopping and searching cars at all the bridges in San Francisco."

Kearns looked over, then put his attention back on the road. "What are you getting at?"

"Put on your tinfoil hat for a minute and I'll tell you."

"Okay, okay, go."

"You remember the 7/7 bombings in 2005?"

"Of course."

"Do you know that a security company, with a former Scotland Yard guy in charge, was running a terrorism drill in London that very morning? And this random drill involving a thousand people was planned out months in advance to simulate the same kind of bombing incidents, on the same targets, on the same day, and at the same times?"

"No, I didn't know that."

"And then it really happened. While they were running the drill, the exact, actual thing they were practicing for actually fricking happened. What are the odds of that being a coincidence?"

"If any of that were true," Kearns said, "I'd know about it. So what does that tell you, Oliver Stone?"

"Well, then," Danny went on, undaunted, "do you know that the guy your old friends in the U.S. government believe was the actual mastermind of those bombings—his name is Haroon Rashid Aswat—was also some sort of protected double agent who was on the payroll of some obscure faction of MI6? The CIA knew all about him but they weren't allowed to touch him; he even lived over here for a few years. Hell, he tried to organize an al-Qaeda training camp in Oregon—"

"You're a real piece of work, you know that?"

"One more thing. The guy that we haven't seen yet, his name is Elmer, right?"

"Right."

"The guy in charge on September eleventh was Mohamed Atta. He had a lot of aliases, and that's the one he started using after 2000 when he got into the United States. He was born Mohamed Elamir awad al-Sayed Atta Karadogan. But the name on his work visa, the one he showed when he enrolled in flight school in Florida, was Mohamed Mohamed el-Amir."

"And *el-Amir* sounds like *Elmer*," Kearns

said. "Do you take a nap during the day? Because you must stay up all night thinking about this crap."

"In English, *el-Amir* translates to 'the general.' It could be a code word. Atta used el-Amir back then in 2001, and this guy's using it now. If this whole thing is part of some false-flag operation—if they're really trying to bring this war back home—they need a new boogeyman right here on U.S. soil, and they need to connect him to past events and to the patriot movement so they can demonize the resistance."

"Mohamed Atta is dead."

"Yeah? So is Osama bin Laden, but that doesn't stop him from putting out a tape every six months. And I'm not even saying it's a real live Islamo-fascist behind any of this, but making it look that way will make the story that much scarier when something happens."

"Look," Kearns said, "I'll tell you one thing I do know. There's an election coming up, and fear has been a swing factor in party politics for as long as I can remember. The timing of this whole thing, the terror alert, and all the rest of it—it wouldn't surprise me one bit to find out after all this is over that we're just playing a bit part in somebody else's political ambitions. Technically, I guess you could call that a conspiracy, if it makes you happy."

It didn't make him happy, but Danny decided to let it lie.

"How much farther now?" he asked.

Kearns checked his watch and then glanced at the screen of the GPS. "About a half hour, maybe less."

As the ride went on in silence Danny looked across occasionally at the older man, hoping that he'd at least planted a seed of warning. In that small way it seemed he'd been successful. You can't see another man's thoughts, but you can sure see him thinking.

CHAPTER 39

The fasten-seatbelt light had just blinked on above Noah's head, accompanied by an intercom announcement that the flight would soon begin its on-time descent into McCarran International.

He rubbed his eyes and they felt as though he hadn't blinked in quite a while. The time had apparently flown by as he'd been occupied reading and rereading the many quoted passages that filled the pages of Molly's book.

In the course of his supposedly top-shelf schooling he must have already been exposed to much of this, and if so, it shouldn't have seemed as new to him as it did. And in a strange, unsettling way—like reading a horoscope so accurate that its author must surely have been watching you for months through the living-room window—it seemed that each of these writings was addressed to this current time, and this very place, for the sole, specific benefit of Noah Gardner. There'd been many examples, but this was one that stood out:

The phrase "too big to fail" had been reborn for propaganda purposes during a brainstorming session at the office last year. This was in the run-up to the country's massive financial meltdown, the multiphase disaster that was only now gathering its full head of steam.

The original purpose of the phrase in business was to describe an entity that was literally too large and successful to possibly go under—think of the *Titanic,* only before the iceberg. But this newly minted meaning, it was decided, would be a threat, rather than a promise.

While the crisis had in truth, of course, been nothing less than a blatant, sweeping consolidation of wealth and power—perpetrated by some of Doyle & Merchant's most prestigious Wall Street clients—it wouldn't do to allow the press and the public to perceive it that way. So the government's bailout of these billionaire speculators and their legion of cronies and accomplices was instead presented as a bold rescue, undertaken for the good of the American people themselves.

We have no choice—that was the sad, helpless tone of both the givers and the receivers of those hundreds of billions of dollars, monies to be deducted directly from the dreams of a brighter future for coming generations. AIG, Lehman Brothers, Merrill Lynch, Citi, Bear Stearns, Bank of America, Morgan Stanley, Fannie and Freddie, and the all-powerful puppetmaster behind it all, Goldman Sachs—these companies are the only underpinnings of our whole way of life, so the breathless story went, and if they go down, we all do.

It was a fresh way of presenting the public with a familiar choice: the lesser among evils. There was talk of a death-spiral drop in the stock market, a wildfire of bank runs and wholesale foreclosures; even martial law was threatened, from the floor of Congress, if the bailout failed to pass. These were the alibis repeated by the PR pundits and the complicit men and women in our supposedly representative government when they were asked, *Why did you do it*?

The choice they made was to reward the corruption, but all of them knew the better answer, or should have. It didn't take a thousand-page bill to get it across.

"Let justice be done, though the heavens fall."

In Molly's book this quote was unattributed but the ideal it conveyed was ancient, and the central pillar of the rule of law. Thomas Paine, quoted on the same page, had put it a different way, in *Common Sense:* "In America, the law is king." Even the most powerful can't place themselves above it, the weakest are never beneath its protection, and no corrupt institution is too big to fail.

So that's what a principle is, Noah thought, as though he were pondering the word for the very first time.

It's not a guideline, or a suggestion, or one of many weighty factors to be parsed in a complex intellectual song-and-dance. It's a cornerstone in the foundation, the bedrock that a great structure is built upon.

Everything else can come crashing down around us—because those fleeting things can always be rebuilt even better than they were before—but if we hold to it, the principle will still be standing, so we can start again.

Next down this page was John Adams's take on something Noah's father had told him only that morning:

> **The desire of dominion, that great principle by which we have attempted to account for so much good and so much evil, is, when properly restrained, a very useful and noble movement in the human mind. But when such restraints are taken off, it becomes an encroaching, grasping, restless, and ungovernable power. Numberless have been the systems of iniquity contrived by the great for the gratification of this passion in themselves . . .**

In short, governments have proven that they always go bad, because they're made up of imperfect people. But unlike Arthur Gardner, Adams believed that that impossible puzzle had been solved by the ingenious separation of powers at the heart of his new country's design. Or rather, it was given to the people to solve it every single day, at every election, in the ever-wary supervision of their dangerous servants.

On the facing page was a quote from another Adams, a cousin of John, and it had been written much larger and bolder than the surrounding text. It was a challenge that Samuel Adams had laid down as the nascent revolution was nearing its point of no return, a gut check for all those who would call themselves Americans:

> **If you love wealth greater than liberty, the tranquility of servitude greater than the animating contest for freedom, go home from us in peace. We seek not your counsel, nor your arms. Crouch down and lick the hand that feeds you; May your chains set lightly upon you, and may posterity forget that you were our countrymen.**

Put up or shut up, in other words; go hard or go home. Freedom is the rare exception, he was saying, not the rule, and if you want it you've got to do your part to keep it.

The plane touched down on the runway with barely a jolt and soon began to slow for its turn toward the arrival gate. Something touched Noah's leg and he looked up from his reading. Molly was finally awakening from her nap; as she finished a languid stretch he passed her a bottle of water.

"Thanks," she said. "I didn't mean to sleep this whole time."

"You must have needed it."

Molly noticed the book in his hands. He closed it and handed it to her. "I hope you don't mind that I was reading this."

"No, not at all." She pulled her bag from under the seat, zipped it open, and returned the book to a sleeve inside.

"Hey, Molly?"

"Yes?"

He touched her hand. "I think I get it now," Noah said.

"You get what?"

"I really didn't before, but I understand what you're doing now, you and your people."

"Oh." She nodded, and continued to check over her things.

"I mean it."

"I know you do," she said, in the way you might address an overly needy child in recognition of some minor accomplishment. "Good. I'm glad."

He didn't know what response he'd expected when he told her of his newfound understanding, but it wasn't this. There'd hardly been enough of a reaction to qualify as one.

Before long the plane had reached the gate, and the door nearest them was the first to be opened. She was walking ahead of him in the exit tunnel, as though with some purpose that she hadn't paused to share. He caught up to her as she stopped to scan an informational display with a backlit map of airport services.

"I say we grab a meal," Noah said, "spend the night, and then try to figure something out tomorrow."

His suggestion was overlooked as if he hadn't spoken it at all.

"I need for you to help me rent a car," Molly said.

CHAPTER 40

"This must be the place," Danny said. He folded the printout of directions and slipped them into a side pocket of the door.

According to the map and the van's odometer, the rendezvous location for the final exchange was right here, somewhere off to the side of the faded gravel road. Out his passenger window there was nothing much to see but a flat expanse of desert and some faraway mountains at the horizon.

Kearns tapped him on the leg. "Over here."

The stark landscape had begun to take

on warmer hues as the sun got low, but there was still enough daylight to see things clearly, provided you were shown where to look. Way off to the driver's side, maybe three hundred yards distant, Danny saw what looked like the only man-made thing for miles around. Whatever it was, it wasn't much.

No trail led out there and this vehicle wasn't made to go off-road. Kearns seemed to know what he was doing, though. He made a careful turn toward their final destination, nursing the van over the lip of the road and out across the hard-packed ground.

As they got close the scene became clearer. Danny saw the rear ends of two vehicles, a car and a midsize, unmarked yellow cargo truck, both of which were parked behind a square, gray, one-story building.

"Building" was an overstatement, actually; the simple ten-foot-high enclosure appeared to be made of nothing but cinder blocks and dark mortar. There was an open arched doorway but no roof overhead. About a stone's throw away from the main structure, in a perfectly spaced circle surrounding the building on all sides, were a number of bizarre, freestanding walls and angled edifices jutting up out of the sand. Some looked like backstops from a playground handball court, one like the black alien monolith from *2001: A Space Odyssey.* The layout reminded him a little of Stonehenge, but only if Stonehenge had been built over one hurried weekend by an amateur bricklayer on acid.

"What the hell is this place?" Danny asked.

"Out here you never know. This part of Nevada's full of surprises." Agent Kearns stopped the van well away from the other vehicles and put the shifter into park. "It could be something the military threw together for part of a nuclear test, could be a target for a bombing range that used to run through here." He clapped Danny lightly on the shoulder. "What do you think: Are you ready for this?"

"I already told you what I think."

"Don't worry so much," Kearns said, "or you're going to look nervous. Listen, this is a milk run. We'll be in and out of here in five minutes, and then we'll go get us a hot dog and a cold beer before I drop you off at the airport—"

He'd stopped talking because something had caught his attention out the front windshield. One of the men they were meeting had appeared by the corner of the main cinder-block building, and with a broad gesture he beckoned them to come on over. Another of the men was behind the first, standing there with an assault rifle slung over his shoulder.

"Okay, then," Danny sighed, "let's rock." He opened the door, stepped out, and waved back to the guy who'd greeted them, then put on the light jacket Kearns had loaned him. It was a size too large, but that was fine for his purposes. He reached in and slipped Kearns's satellite phone from its charger on the console and put it in the left-hand pocket, then flipped open the glove box and removed the pistol. "Do you have an extra clip for this?"

"No, I don't. What are you doing?"

The pistol went snugly into Danny's belt in back, not in the middle but closer to the right side; the long jacket hid it completely. "I'm getting ready for this whole thing to go to hell in a handbasket. If everything's fine you can say I told you so. But in the meantime, if I can make a suggestion, why don't you take that .38 out of your ankle holster and put it where you can get it if you need it."

Thankfully, the older man was listening, and even if he wasn't quite convinced that there was going to be trouble he was at least open-minded enough to move his small revolver to the right-hand pocket of his bomber jacket.

"I thought you said you didn't know much about guns," Kearns said.

"That's not what I said. I said I wasn't an expert."

Expert wasn't a term to be bandied about among Danny's gun-savvy friends. An expert might be someone who could call their shot from ten yards and then, from a cold start, draw their pistol from concealment and put a bullet right where they said it would go, all in seven-tenths of a second or less. Molly Ross was one of those, and a few years back over one hot and memorable Tennessee summer, she'd taught him everything he knew. He'd been getting even more death threats than usual that year, and she'd wanted him to be safe. So, while he wasn't an expert, his draw was pretty fast—it was the part about hitting what he shot at that still left a lot to be desired.

"Okay," Kearns said. His demeanor was a bit more grim than it had been a few minutes before. "Let's do it."

CHAPTER 41

Their model bomb wasn't that heavy, maybe eighty or one hundred pounds, but it was unwieldy to carry between them. When they came within sight of the men they were here to meet—and like last time, there were only four of them, not the expected five—one of them motioned to a spot on the ground to show where they should leave their burden. When they got to that spot, they put it down.

One of the other men had a brand-new-looking satchel at his feet, a bag of the sort that might be holding their twenty thousand dollars for the exchange. The last two men were the ones with the automatic rifles.

The weapons these guys were sporting appeared to be some knocked-together variant of an AR-15, but with a very short barrel, stock target sights, custom noise suppression, and a nonstandard magazine. Good luck trying to buy something like that off the shelf. Not the most versatile choice for all-purpose combat, obviously laughable for hunting or target practice, but flip it to full auto and it would do every bit as well as a sawed-off shotgun for antipersonnel work at close quarters.

Situations like this one, for example.

The armed man to the left held his gun like he'd been born with it in his hands. The other one didn't seem at all at ease, either with his weapon or his assigned enforcer's role. His hands were deep in his pockets and his rifle hung haphazardly by its sling over his shoulder, as though it had been put there against his will and he had no desire to deal with it.

Upon their arrival Kearns had made a bit of small talk with each member of the group, and soon all agreed it was time to do the deal they'd come to do.

"Here's your money," said the man on the end. He'd introduced himself as Randy at their meeting the previous night. As Kearns walked over to retrieve the satchel Randy motioned to his men to pick up their merchandise and stow it in the back of the cargo truck.

The rear door was opened and two of them carefully carried the bomb up the mover's ramp, set it down, and flipped on a hanging work light in the compartment to check over their purchase. Meanwhile, Kearns had come back with the satchel to stand at Danny's side.

"Ain't you gonna count it?"

This deadpan question came from one of the guys with the guns, the one doing his level best to come off like a natural-born bad-ass.

Kearns shrugged. "If we're short, at least I know where to find you guys tomorrow morning, am I right?"

That brought a little chuckle from everyone—everyone except the man who'd spoken up.

Danny's attention was on the other contents that were now visible in the truck's rear compartment.

Down the center, on a welded-together, waist-high metal rack, was what appeared to be a long, silvery torpedo. Not really, though; the nose was too blunt and flat and its far end was tapered and ringed by large aerodynamic fins. It looked like something from a war museum, an overbuilt piece of heavy-duty air-dropped ordnance from a bygone era of the Cold War.

That wasn't all. Tucked back in the corner, away from the light, something was wrapped up and bound in a black plastic tarp on the floor. It could have been a lot of things, but to Danny's current frame of mind, what it looked like most was an occupied body bag.

He glanced at Kearns, and by all appearances he was seeing the same thing.

A loud ringtone from the phone on the belt of the man named Randy broke the silence. He held up a polite index finger, as if to say, *Sorry, I've got to take this*, turned, took a half step away, and answered.

And that, Danny thought, would be a call from el-Amir.

Kearns bent and put the satchel down between them, shivered a bit, breathed some warm air through his hands, and then put them into his jacket pockets. When he looked at Danny, just for a second or two, there was such a crystal-clear communication between them that he almost heard the words form in his head.

You were right. Now we're going to let these guys give us just one more bad sign, the tiniest sign, and then we put their lights out. No "freeze, FBI!," no warning shots; we shoot to kill until they're all down, or we are. And you and I both know who gets it first.

Danny took his right hand from his pocket, casually scratched the side of his nose, feigned a leisurely yawn, and then let his arm hang back down by his side.

Randy, the one still on the phone, looked back over his shoulder.

He was listening intently, not talking; his eyes went first to Stuart Kearns, and then over to Danny, and then he turned back around, with his back to them, as he'd been before. A few more seconds passed, and still facing away, Randy's free hand came up slowly and touched the shoulder of the man to his right, the mouthy guy who looked like he just couldn't wait for the lead to start flying.

And that was it.

When you've practiced enough it gets to look like one fluid motion, but there are four distinct parts to a quick draw, at least to the one that Molly had taught him. In the beginning the count is slow and you stop between the steps so your teacher can make sure you've got them right. After a few months and several thousand repeats, though, it starts to go so fast that if you blink, you might miss it.

Danny's right hand swept back to clear his clothing and found the pistol grip just where he'd left it; he pulled the weapon free and brought it forward, the barrel coming parallel to the ground and his left hand joining the solid grasp; he extended toward center-mass of his target with the iron sight rising level to his eye; and at the end of the forward movement, as it all came together at his ideal firing position, without a pause he squeezed the trigger to its stop.

The *boom* of their first two shots was almost simultaneous, though Kearns had a much easier draw from his pocket. They'd chosen the same primary target, the man to whom Randy had given his too-obvious go-ahead, the guy who would have cut them in half with a hail of bullets if they'd given him half a chance to shoot first. As Kearns took off to his left, still firing, their designated executioner was crumpling backward, likely dead on his feet, but surely out of commission.

Danny broke right, aiming by the seat of his pants and squeezing off another shot as soon as any one of the scattering men appeared in his line of fire. He was a below-average marksman on a static range, but now he and his targets were moving and they were starting to return fire, so he was shooting a lot but not hitting much of anything.

But at least he'd gotten their full attention. In the next moment he ran out of ammo and good ideas at the very same time as the second man with the heavy artillery had finally found his wits and started shooting. A jagged line of bullet impacts stitched across the sand toward him, and as Danny dropped to the ground in a shallow gully he heard a tire explode and the windows shatter in their van just behind him. He saw Stuart Kearns step from behind the cover of one of the random concrete walls, and the

FBI man made his next four rounds count. As the last gunshots echoed back from the mountains, three of the men were lying motionless on the ground, and one was unaccounted for, but only for the moment.

The silence was broken by the sound of a diesel engine turning over and starting. Danny watched Kearns limping toward the back of the truck, then grabbing on and hoisting himself up into the open compartment.

As the truck dropped into gear and started to roll Danny got to his feet and ran for it. The faster he ran the faster it went, and it had nearly accelerated to the point of no return when he caught up to the tailgate, stumbled forward to get a grasp on to Stuart Kearns' extended hand, and felt himself pulled up and in.

CHAPTER 42

Noah had shaken his one remaining pill out of the prescription bottle halfway through the flight, and now as the last of the medicine was wearing off, a nasty withdrawal was setting in with a vengeance. By the time they reached the car rental counter he could feel himself starting to fade. Headache, chills, dizziness, a general sickening malaise—it was already bad, and he could tell it was going to get much worse over the next few hours.

Molly was driving, since he clearly wasn't fit to sit behind the wheel, and to put it delicately, she drove with a purpose.

If he'd been feeling good and in the right sort of daredevil mood her driving might have been easier to take in stride. As it was, though, between his worsening physical condition and being jostled around the front seat by all the surging and braking and swerving through traffic, he wasn't having any fun at all.

Plus, she wasn't talking. Since they'd started out in the car all he was getting were one-word answers, along with clear unspoken signals that there was nothing so important that it needed to be discussed at the moment.

They'd left the city limits of Las Vegas over half an hour ago, so his hope of a good night's recovery in a five-star bed was more than thirty miles behind them and fading fast. According to the speedometer, wherever she was taking them she was trying to get there in way too much of a hurry.

"We're going to get stopped," Noah said.

She didn't answer, and she didn't slow down.

"Where are we going, Molly?"

"To help a friend," she said curtly. "Now would you please just let me drive?"

"Fine."

"Thank you."

Before long they'd left the main highway and were barreling down some narrow desert road that was only a thin single line on the GPS screen. Before they'd gotten started she'd spent quite a bit of time and frustration entering their destination into the device. It was hard, she'd said, because it wasn't a street address that she'd been given, only a latitude and longitude.

The sheet of paper from which she'd read those coordinates was still tucked into one of the cup holders.

Okay, then.

If she didn't want to take a few seconds to tell him what was going on, he could damn well figure it out for himself. Before she could stop him Noah picked up the sheet and opened it up, tapped on the overhead map light, and held the paper near his eyes.

What was printed there appeared to be two cut-and-pasted text messages or e-mails, he couldn't tell which. Maybe it was because his mind was working only at half capacity, but he had to read it all over twice.

The first time through he couldn't accept what he was seeing.

molly -
spread the word --- stay away from las
vegas monday
FBI sting op --> * exigent *
be safe
xoxo
db

* FYI ONLY DO NOT FORWARD
DELETE AFTER READING *
Big mtg today, Monday PM, southern
Nevada. If you don't hear from me by
Wednesday I'm probably dead*,
and this is
where to hunt for the body:
Lat 37°39′54.35″N
Long 116°56′31.48″W
>S T A Y A W A Y from Nevada TFN <
db

*I wish I was kidding

"Unbelievable."

She glanced over at him, but only for a

second before she got her eyes back on the road. When he looked down he found he'd crumpled the paper in his hand so hard that it might never come unfolded.

"I can't believe it," Noah said. "You people got me again."

CHAPTER 43

"Nine-one-one, this call is recorded, what's your emergency?"

Wherever they were going, the ride was awfully rough. Danny was holding on tight to a cargo strap near the open door at the rear of the moving truck, the only place in the metal compartment with a signal solid enough to make a call on Kearns's satellite phone.

"My name is Danny Bailey, I'm out in the desert somewhere northwest of Las Vegas, and I'm with FBI Special Agent Stuart Kearns. I'm in the back of a truck that's on the move, and this truck belongs to a terrorist organization that might have their hands on a nuclear weapon."

"What's your location, sir?"

"Listen, I know what you people can do. You already know where I am better than I do, you know whose phone I'm calling from, you know the route I'm on, and in about ten seconds you'll be sure who I am because you'll have verified my voiceprint, so stop wasting my time."

Some odd noise broke onto the line for a time; not interference, but a series of electronic clicks, tones, and dropouts.

"Okay, good deal, is everybody on now? Everybody listening? This is about an operation code-named Exigent. Did you get that? *Exigent.* So now you know who I am, who I'm with, why I'm here, and where to send the cavalry, and you'd by-God better know this is real. Just follow this signal down and get here, understand?"

He left the phone switched on and placed it in a niche on the bed of the cargo compartment.

Kearns was near the front wall, kneeling next to the tarp-wrapped bundle they'd both seen earlier, before the shooting had started.

It was a body, of course, and the face of the dead man had been uncovered. When Kearns turned to look at him, Danny didn't have to ask who it was that was lying there. He'd already known who it would be.

Agent Kearns had said that after these last few years of working this operation undercover—all the while doing his best to appear to be a raving militant agitator who'd turned against his government and was openly calling for a violent revolution—he really had only one remaining contact in the FBI. His frightening online persona was well-known to tens of thousands of fringe-group wackos and law enforcement personnel alike, but only one person alive could have credibly testified that Stuart Kearns was actually a loyal American doing his duty to protect and defend the United States. And here was that person, dead.

"Did you call 911?" Kearns asked.

"Yeah, I did. And now they'll either come or they won't."

"What do you mean by that?"

Danny touched the metal gantry next to him, the frame that held the thing that at first glance he'd thought might be a torpedo.

"Take a look at this thing with me, and tell me what you think."

As Kearns moved to stand, he winced and leaned his head back against the corrugated wall of the compartment. Below the knee his right pants leg was stained with blood.

"Are you okay?"

"I'll be fine. Just help me up."

They stood on either side of the framework, bracing themselves on its crossbars as the truck moved over the rough road they were traveling.

"This looks like an old Mark 8 atomic bomb," Kearns said, "from the early 1950s." He pulled the light down closer and ran his hands over the surface, stopping at a series of seals and stickers that carried dates and the initials of inspectors. "It's been maintained all these years."

"So this is a live one, then?"

"Sure looks that way to me." A line of heavy metal conduit ran from the rear of the thing and Kearns followed it with a finger, pointing. The tubing went across the floor and through the wall to the driver's compartment. "And it looks like they've jury-rigged it to be set off from the front seat."

"So your guy over there on the floor: he brought them this one, and you brought yours. You both got managed so you didn't know what the other was doing, and we all got set up at once."

"But why," Kearns said. He wasn't really asking; he was thinking it through.

"It's like I told you before. Whoever's behind this needed a patsy for a false-flag domestic attack, Stuart, and that's you. And they needed to make my people the enemy, and that's why I'm here."

"Based on your file, they could have had you picked up anytime they wanted, but they picked you up Friday night, to make you a part of this. And me, they've just kept me in cold storage—"

"Waiting for the right time, when they needed a couple of fall guys," Danny said. "The crazy Internet conspiracy theorist who incited these thugs into violence, and the lone nut ex–FBI man who helped them pull it off."

"Well, whoever's behind this, we've screwed up their plans for now."

"But not for too much longer. This guy's driving somewhere like he means to get where he's going, but if he calms down long enough to stop and come back here to check his load, we're toast. We're unarmed, and he'll just stand back and shoot us like fish in a barrel. Then he'll go on to Vegas tonight and do what he's going to do. We can't wait for him to do that."

Kearns looked up at him. "So what do we do?"

The truck slowed briefly, made a turn onto what felt like a much smoother roadway, and then began to pick up speed again.

"I've got an idea," Danny said, "but I don't know if you'll like it."

He walked toward the tailgate, where the package they'd brought was strapped against the side of the compartment, and motioned for his partner to follow. When Kearns had sat and situated his injured leg, Danny crouched down and pulled off the tarp that was covering the device. He peeled off the keys that were taped near the arming panel and handed them to Kearns.

If one of these bombs was real, then it stood to reason that they both were real. And there was really only one way to find out.

• • •

"Here we go," Kearns said.

He inserted the two keys into the control panel, twisted them a quarter-turn, and pressed the button labeled ARM. The line of yellow bulbs illuminated, winked to green one by one as the soft whine from the charging electronics ascended up the scale.

Once the device had gotten its bearings, it was simple enough to reset the final destination on the touchscreen of the GPS detonator. It wasn't an address they selected, of course, just an empty point on the deserted road they were traveling, a little less than three miles ahead and counting down.

The older man lit up a cigarette, and he shook another one up from the pack and offered it across.

"Nah, I told you," Danny said. "I quit five years ago."

"Aw, come on. Special occasion."

"I took an oath to an old friend, Stuart, and if you met this woman, you'd know why I can't break it."

"When you put it that way, I guess I see what you mean." Kearns winced and straightened his leg, leaned his head back against the corrugated wall of the compartment, eyes closed.

"Hey," Danny said, and he waited until his partner looked over. "The other night when you were telling me about your career with the FBI, you said that after all they'd put you through, you wondered sometimes why you stuck it out."

"Yeah."

"This is why, man. Tonight is why you stayed on. What was it they had you say, when you put your hand on the Bible and they swore you in?"

"It's been so long, let's see if I even remember . . . 'I do solemnly swear,'" Kearns said quietly, "'that I will support and defend the Constitution of the United States against all enemies, foreign and domestic, and that I will bear true faith and allegiance to the same.'"

"Damn right."

"And how about you?"

"Me? Oh, this is the perfect way for me to go out, really. The more I think about it, the more I realize I must have outstayed my welcome in my own movement. I take that back; it's not even mine anymore. If guys like these can agree with anything I say, then I've been saying something wrong. And you know what, Stuart? A long time ago I pledged my life, my fortune, and my sacred honor to this country, and now I get to give all three of them at once."

Kearns took a last drag and stubbed out his smoke on the metal floor. "Does it matter that nobody will ever know what we did out here?"

"Oh, somebody'll figure it out. Somebody like me. Not that anybody else will ever believe them."

The device next to them issued a loud tone. A bright red light illuminated on the panel, under the word *Proximity*.

"Nice working with you, kid," Kearns said.

He reached out a hand and Danny Bailey took it in a firm clasp of solidarity, and just a moment later, they were gone.

CHAPTER 44

"We got you?" Molly shouted. "We got *you*? Are you really self-centered enough to believe that any of this is about you?"

"It's only about me because you keep putting me in the middle of it," Noah said. "You people could have killed me, for God's sake, so maybe you can forgive me for taking this personally."

"Hollis stayed with you every minute until they came for you; he made sure you were okay. I'm so sorry you've got a headache now, but nobody tried to kill you."

"That's just great to hear. You know, you people are really incredible. My father told me this morning that something is going to happen that's going to change everything, and I'm thinking, okay, a big stock market correction, or another war going hot in South Asia or the Middle East, or a couple of planes crashing into buildings like the last time everything changed forever. And your mother asked me to help you get away to somewhere safe"—he held up the paper in his hand—"and idiot that I am, I let you lead me right to the last place on earth we should go."

"I'm here to stop this thing if I can."

"Well, you can't!" he shouted over her. "Open your eyes, for God's sake. They've got everything, and you've got nothing. All you're going to do is get us both arrested or killed or put into an unmarked hole in the middle of the desert."

"I have to try."

"*You don't have to try.* I told you, we can both ride this thing out. I can't believe I'm hearing myself say this, but I still want to help you, Molly. That cabin in the woods that you talked about, wherever you want to go until this blows over, I can still make that happen."

"How *dare* you dangle that in front of

me again! What do you think, that I don't want it? That I don't want you? Don't you think I'm scared, and I dream some nights about getting away and never having another worry about the people like your father and what they're trying to turn this world into?"

"As bad as it would be to let me take care of you, it's better than dying for nothing, isn't it?"

Molly's expression changed. She took a deep breath and then spoke in a much more measured tone. "Before we got off the plane you told me that you got it; you said you finally understood what I was about."

"I do."

"No, you don't, Noah. You have no idea. You think knowing the truth is enough? A lot of people know the truth, and nothing changes. So today, after twenty-eight years of drifting through life and taking everything from this country and never giving anything back, today you tell me you've finally seen the light and that's supposed to mean something to me?"

"Doesn't it?"

"Once you know the truth," Molly said,

"then you've got to live it. That's all I'm trying to do."

He saw her look up at the rearview mirror, and something froze in her.

Noah turned to look through the back window. The visibility must have stretched for miles and miles, and way back at the edge of what the eye could see, a tiny line of strobing police lights had appeared.

She was driving as hard and fast as she had before, but there was something in her face, in her eyes, that he hadn't seen before. Molly was afraid. And he knew then that she wasn't afraid of the police, or of going to prison; she wasn't afraid of getting killed in her cause; she wasn't even afraid of Arthur Gardner. She was afraid only that her fight was over.

There'd been turning points in his life that he'd seen coming months away, but this one appeared in an instant. He was safely on one side of it a second before, just being who he'd always thought he was, and then he blinked and he was on the other, waking up to realize who he was going to be.

Up ahead he could see that the road narrowed onto a short bridge over a shallow chasm, which ran across the terrain for several hundred yards.

You see the truth, and then you have to live it, she'd said. It was too late, maybe, and too little, but he knew what he needed to do.

"Slow down," Noah said. "I'm getting out."

"What?"

"Don't stop, just let me out." He cracked the door and the wind whipped inside, and she let her foot off the gas and braked until the car had slowed to the point where he might just survive if he stepped out onto the road whizzing by under them. There was no way to be sure if she understood what he was doing; no time to explain. Maybe he'd never know, but like she'd said, none of this was really about Noah Gardner.

He took a last look at Molly. There were tears in her eyes but she kept them firmly fixed on the way ahead.

"Good-bye," Noah said.

She answered, but so quietly and privately that the words clearly weren't intended to reach him. If they were never to see each other again, it seemed, this was just something that she must have wanted read into the record. Wishful thinking, maybe, but he felt he knew in his heart exactly what she'd said.

I love you, too.

He opened the door and dropped to the pavement, rolling and bouncing and banging along for what seemed like the length of a soccer field. At last he stopped, and he watched for a few seconds as the car he'd left picked up speed again and began to recede toward the horizon.

He tried to stand but the pain prevented it, so he crawled to the center line and knelt there in the middle of the narrow bridge, hands up and out so he'd be more visible, watching the line of cars with flashing lights fast approaching.

Maybe they'll stop in time, and maybe they won't, Noah thought, but either way he'd slow them down. Other than that, he knew only two things: Molly Ross was still fighting, and that despite what was bearing down on him ahead, he wasn't afraid.

By the time the lead car had skidded to a stop he could feel the heat on his face from its headlights. Some of the vehicles behind were backing up and their drivers were trying to find a way around the bottleneck, but off the road the sand was too soft for traction and those who'd gone into the gully were stuck, their tires spinning uselessly.

He looked up and saw five uniformed men approaching, their guns drawn. They were all shouting orders he couldn't really understand.

And then they disappeared, as did the rest of the world, in a silent split-second flash of bright white light from behind him. It was so bright that it crossed the senses. He could feel it on his back, he could hear the light and smell it. When his vision returned Noah saw the officers standing in the road where they'd been, some covering their eyes, but most looking past him, blank-faced, their hands hanging down at their sides.

He turned to look back over his shoulder, in the direction Molly had gone, and miles away he saw the rising mushroom cloud, a massive, roiling ball of fire ascending slowly into the evening sky. The expanding circle of a shock wave was tearing across the desert toward them, toward everything in all directions, and a few seconds later it arrived with a crack of thunder and the sudden gust of a hot summer wind.

CHAPTER 45

It could have been most of the night that they worked him over. It could have been days for all he knew. All sense of time had left him while he was still out there on the road.

The questioning had started in one place, and at some point they'd satisfied themselves that the worst they could do wasn't going to be good enough. There'd been a dark ride in a car, and then a flight somewhere. At the new place they'd started in on him again.

They knew a lot already. They knew that calls had been made from Noah's apartment to a long list of accomplices of a known agitator who'd conspired to destroy an American city or two. They knew that Noah helped one of the central figures in this conspiracy gain access to classified files and information. They knew that he'd helped her evade security and fly across the country to play her part in the failed attack. They knew that two nuclear weapons had fallen into the hands of these terrorists, and that one of them had detonated but the other was still unaccounted for.

This second group of interrogators was more organized and clinical in their methods, and far more creative. It wasn't only pain they inflicted, but terror; the most effective torture happens in the mind. After many hours and methods they'd eventually settled on using a reliable old standby that seemed to have the most immediate and positive effect for their purposes.

Strapped flat to a cold metal table, head immobilized and inclined to be lower than the feet, a wet cloth over the face to restrict his breathing—and then just a slight dripping of water, maybe half a glass, just enough to begin to run down the nostrils and into the throat. Some primitive part of the mind simply comes unhinged when it knows it's drowning and knows it can't get away. Try to be as strong as you want; it doesn't matter. If he'd actually known anything at all that they wanted to learn, before ten seconds had passed he would have told them, and they would have known he was telling the truth.

In the course of their work they told him a lot of things to encourage him to break his silence. They told him that Molly's mother, under similar questioning, had revealed the entire plot, including the depth of Noah's involvement. They said that Molly herself had been apprehended and they described in excruciating detail the particular techniques they had employed on her. She'd given him up almost immediately, they'd claimed, along with all of her co-conspirators.

After all they'd put him through, Noah would have gladly believed almost anything they'd said, but even to his clouded, brutalized mind these last two assertions didn't ring true—those two would never betray their cause. If Molly was going down, she would go down swinging and silent. Knowing that gave Noah the first bit of hope that he'd had in a long time.

It went on that way, though, again and again, as if they had nothing but time and nothing to lose by confirming over and over that he didn't know anything that could help them. They seemed to take his complete lack of useful knowledge as a sign of stubborn resistance to their questioning. And, after all, you never know when a valuable little nugget of intel might surface.

And then they stopped.

They spent a few minutes cleaning him up as well as they could, unstrapped one of his hands, adjusted the table to a more natural recline, and even slipped a couple of flat pillows beneath his head. They never addressed him directly, but Noah was able to gather from what they said that a special visitor was coming, someone special enough to put a hold on the most critical interrogation since they'd captured Khalid Sheikh Mohammed two years after 9/11.

As they prepared to leave, they put their things in order, like a team of seasoned mechanics might tend to the tools of their trade. These actions made it clear that they'd be back if necessary after this brief interlude, to take up their work right where they'd left it off.

A number of dark plastic surveillance domes were distributed across the ceiling. The chief interrogator looked up at one of the cameras and made a gesture to those watching to indicate that the subject was now ready to receive his guest. On that cue, the tiny red lights of the surveillance cameras winked out in sequence.

A few seconds later, a figure appeared in the open doorway.

CHAPTER 46

Noah had been savaged for many hours, of course, brought to the brink mentally and physically in his interrogation. No one would blame him if he didn't immediately recognize his visitor—the man was so rarely seen outside of his natural, elegant habitat. Yet despite all of these mitigating factors, Noah knew instantly whom he was staring at because it was his own flesh and blood: the legendary Arthur Gardner.

The old man came in and walked to the middle of the room, discharged his bodyguard and the others with a slight dismissive wave, and he and Noah were left alone.

His father pulled over a high stool instead of the rolling office chair that had been arranged for him. He was taking the high ground, as usual; seated in this way the old man towered above his son, who was still bound securely to the metal bed.

For a time they only regarded each other in silence. It might have been a bit of his father's mano a mano gamesmanship, often employed in business interactions: in hostile negotiations it's often the first one to speak who loses. After a while, though, the quiet must have outlasted his patience.

"This woman you became involved with," Arthur Gardner began, "do you have any idea what she has cost us?"

"I don't know," Noah said. His voice was hoarse from lack of moisture, and from the suffering they'd already put him through. "Billions?"

The old man's fist came down on edge of the table, hard enough to break a bone.

"She cost us *impact!"* he shouted. "It was to be a clean and spectacular event, a thing to be leveraged into a leap forward toward our new beginning. Instead it's become a complete debacle. We were left with an almost unnoticed explosion out in the empty desert that barely rattled a teacup in the nearest town. There aren't even any pictures—we've had to resort to artists' conceptions and special effects. We'll be up all night trying to make a credible story of it all, to salvage the greatest effect we can. After all the years of preparation it was rushed forward, against my advice, due to the actions of this meaningless resistance. Which *my son* was somehow a part of."

By all appearances his father must have been thinking that some form of apology would be appropriate at this point. Noah chose his words carefully.

"I didn't set out to be, Dad."

The old man muttered something poisonous under his breath and then seemed to make an effort to gather his dignity again. He straightened the already-perfect knot of his Persian silk tie, and when he spoke again his voice was under somewhat tighter control.

"Not that it's been a total failure. Your friends lost before the fight even began. We've spent years painting them as a fringe group of dangerous heirs to the likes of Timothy McVeigh, and of course they'll be revealed as the villains behind this failed attack." He stared off into the distance as if he were talking to no one in particular. "It's too bad that these friends of yours have been so transparent in their desire for violence. They wave signs with slogans about 'reloading' and watering the tree of liberty with the blood of tyrants. They wear shirts that endorse the 'targeting' of politicians, and, Noah, let's not forget about that unfortunate incident you got yourself caught up in at that downtown bar. These people never wanted to give peace a chance—and now they've shown just how far they are willing to go to send their message." He was actually smiling, clearly enjoying a sadistic satisfaction with it all.

"Thankfully, there's already talk of suspending the presidential election. Though either candidate would have been equally useful in the aftermath, it will be a powerful bit of symbolism nevertheless. Many sweeping pieces of helpful legislation will be rushed through in the coming days with little or no debate, and those will be used to clamp down further on what remains of this Ross woman's pitiful movement. And naturally, a wholesale roundup is under way to ferret out all those connected with these backward revolutionaries, with full support of the media and the cowering public.

"Saul Alinsky was right, Noah—the ends do justify the means. I can't imagine how any thinking person could believe otherwise. Which do you really think the huddled masses would prefer if they knew what I know—that they have only two choices: a quick if somewhat painful transformation, or yet another century of slow progress and suffering toward the same inevitable end, only this time with all of the country's wealth and potential stolen away from them before the decay even begins.

"And yet these selfish and ignorant meddlers—*patriots,* they have the gall to call themselves—they would stand in the path of destiny. What do they think they've accomplished? The lives of how many were saved tonight? Thirty thousand? Five times that many people die around the globe every day. They die in obscurity at the end of an aimless existence, and they disappear to dust as though they'd never been. But those thirty thousand, they would have died for a cause greater than any other, their names would have been etched in monuments in the new world, on the granite markers heralding mankind's new beginning. One world, ruled by the wise and the fittest and the strong, with no naïve illusions of equality or the squandered promises of freedom for all.

"How many times must we learn the same lessons? Leave the useless eaters to their pursuit of happiness, and the result is always slaughter and chaos and poverty and despair. What your new friends fail to see is that this country was nothing more than a brief anomaly, a mere passing second in the march of time. People often ask how slavery could've happened, but that just shows their ignorance. Slavery and tyranny have been the rule for thousands of years; freedom is the short-lived exception.

"The United States should never have survived as long as it has, but all good things must come to an end. The system is broken beyond repair. It costs a billion dollars to run for president these days; Abraham Lincoln would never have lasted past the Iowa caucuses. And if the occasional visionaries actually make it into office, their corruption begins immediately. They're overcome by the problems they inherit. But the majority of politicians are only prostitutes and puppets, and they always will be. Their simple-minded lusts for money, and sex, and power make them controllable, but they disgust me. When they've served their purpose, they'll learn what real power is, along with everyone else.

"Whatever chance we have to take control of this world is in controlling who pulls the strings. Presidents, senators, governors—all of these come and go, but I and my peers have been here all along, raising them up and tearing them down. The real enduring powers in this world are older than any modern government, and it's past time that we put an end to these empty dreams of liberty. Now, we openly take the reins. Now, we'll give the people the government they've shown themselves to deserve. No one knows the people better than I do, and I know what they need. We'll give them a purpose: a simple, regimented, peaceful life with all the reasonable comforts, in service of something greater than any single, selfish nation."

The old man stood, walked to the door, rapped on the frame three times, and then came back and took his seat again. After a moment, others entered the room, a different group of professionals than Noah had seen before.

"Your mother," Noah's father began, "meant a great deal to me. I saw in her my last hopes for humanity. She had her weaknesses, but in thinking back on it now, those weaknesses may have been what drew me to her. She believed in people, for one, that the good in them could outweigh the bad. For the brief time I was with her, a touch of those weaknesses even spread to me. We had a child together, though I'd sworn I'd never bring another human being into this world. But she poured all of her innocent dreams into her son.

"And as she lay dying, your mother told me that I should expect to see wonderful things from you, Noah. I've held on to that hope. But as I stood out there just now, watching outside this room for the preceding hour, I had to wonder if this was to be the end of my ambitions for you."

"Your ambitions . . . for me?"

"Believe it or not, my boy, I won't live

forever. There's much to do before I die; the outcome of my life's work is still very much in doubt, and I need help to see it through. I need *your* help.

"My wish has been that you would someday stand beside me as we bring forth this new world together. You have great gifts, Noah, but those gifts have been kept dormant by a trick of heredity. I know you've felt this conflict, and it must have been quite painful at times. You have your father's mind, but your mother's heart. Neither will permit the other to come to the fore.

"But it seems you may have been exposed to a disease in your thinking over the last few days. I'm familiar with this infection, and once it takes hold in a person I'm afraid it's shown itself to be quite incurable. It will be with you until you die, in other words. And so, before you can help me, Noah, before I can trust you to do so, we must be certain that this woman and her friends haven't passed you a sickness that cannot be permitted to spread."

The technicians had already begun their preparations. Now some brought heavy copper cables and electrodes and fastened these to various points on Noah's body with wraps of white tape. A cold dab of conductive gel was applied to his temple on one side, and then on the other.

"'I'm here to save you, Noah," his father said, "one way or the other, and to preserve my legacy. One of two young men will leave this room with me. The first was taken hostage by this Ross woman and her terrorist militia, but he managed to escape and then bravely risked his life by standing in the road to prevent a group of policemen and federal agents from being killed in that terrible explosion in the desert. This man is a hero, and will carry on my work and be my eyes and ears in the field as our plans proceed.

"The other man played a part in a similar story, with one sad exception: This other man is dead."

Arthur Gardner nodded to one of the seated technicians.

"And now," he said, "let's find out together, once and for all, if Noah Gardner is really his father's son."

CHAPTER 47

They'd refashioned his bonds in a manner that would still restrain him, but with less likelihood of causing him to injure himself in the course of the coming ordeal. He was instructed to bite down on a length of hard rubber hose they'd placed between his teeth.

What they did, they'd learned from decades of trial-and-error and thousands of prisoners who'd been down this last road before him. Even in a clinical setting, electroconvulsive therapy was far more an art than a science; the results were never fully known until the procedure was finished.

The goals were different here, but their main purpose was plain: to destroy any remaining will to resist or evade, so the truth would be the only thing he'd be left capable of speaking.

For a long while his father sat silently next to the metal table as the technicians administered the voltage with a jeweler's precision. Noah could hear the screams, and he knew they were his, but a small part of him was detached enough to simply observe the suffering.

His mind, once his greatest, if least used, asset, was no longer under his control. He couldn't focus on the technicians or the pain and he'd long ago stopped wondering how much longer it would go on. All that was left were random snapshots of the past that flashed uninvited into his head.

All his defenses had left him hours before. In this state if he'd had any information to reveal he would have gladly offered it, but they were now probing for something much deeper than mere intelligence. Each time he thought there was nothing left, they found another fragile layer of his soul to peel away. In the end, when all he could see was darkness, whatever was left of him finally gave in and tried its best to surrender.

As if sensing it was finished, the old man stood from the rickety wooden stool and stood over his son. "Now, now, Noah, I think we are both finding out what kind of man you are, and I have to tell you, it's quite disappointing." He referred briefly to a sheet of notes he'd been handed. *"Inconclusive.* I'm sure you know, that's a word I hate more than any other. And doesn't it place a sad little period at the end of the story of a rather aimless and forgettable young life?

"While you've given us nothing that implicates you in the treachery of the preceding days, you've also said nothing to exonerate yourself to my side of the conflict. A true believer or a traitor to the cause, either one of those I could at least respect. But you're weak, aren't you? And fatally so."

Neither of Noah's eyes would open fully, and what vision he had was dim and watery. His father looked like a giant silhouette, a featureless shadow. Fragments of memories intruded, a flash from the office break room when he'd first seen Molly, but her image was replaced in his mind with the outline of seven light strokes from a felt-tip pen.

"Continue," his father said to the technicians.

The lines that had once represented Molly's exquisite form dissolved into a pool of blackness and pain.

"Noah, I last told you this when you were only a boy, so I doubt you'll remember." His father had retaken his position at the side of the table. "It's a rhyme I made up for you, in answer to some childish question you'd posed. I think it fitting in our present situation."

When he spoke again the old man's voice had taken on a softer, more fatherly tone.

" 'There are men who are weak and few who are strong / There are men who are right and more who are wrong / But of all the men huddled in all the world's hives / There's but one thing that's true: It's the fit who'll survive.'

"Noah, the meek will not inherit the earth. A faint heart is as great a weakness as a feeble mind. It pains me to say it, but

I'm afraid we've reached a parting of the ways."

It was then that Noah felt something beneath him, and behind him, all around him—something outside himself that he couldn't quite identify.

His father's mind, his mother's heart. What the old man had given him was all that these men could tear away, but it was her heart that they couldn't quite reach. His mother had passed it on to him, and even after her strength had lain unused and scarcely remembered for all these wasted years, it seemed that Molly Ross had somehow awakened it again.

The idea of dying wasn't nearly as frightening as he would have thought it would be. But somewhere he also knew that this wasn't how it was supposed to end. Molly had taught him the importance of living to fight another day. She hadn't been captured, she hadn't been killed. A spirit like that doesn't die so easily. He had no facts whatsoever to assure him of this, but he knew it. Maybe it was a bit of that faith that she'd spoken of.

The old man pulled away with a stoic

finality and picked up his suit jacket, which had been folded neatly over the back of the office chair. As he put it on, he turned to the man who was clearly in charge of things. "Finish the job and then craft a story to ensure my son is remembered in a way that will bring dignity and honor to our family."

There was a way out of this, but Noah didn't know what it was until he heard the answer whispered at his ear, as though Molly were there right beside him. The fight would go on, she'd said, with her on the outside and him on the inside, where she'd already shown him that the deepest kind of damage could be done. And then she added one thing more:

Don't be afraid.

As the old man turned away, Noah tried to speak the words she'd given him, but his mouth and lips were so dry that the words were barely audible. "As it will be in the future," he whispered, "it was at the birth of Man."

He didn't even know if he was saying the words aloud or reciting them only in his mind. "There are only four things certain since Social Progress began." His father's hand was on the doorknob when he suddenly froze and looked back.

"What did you say?" the old man asked.

Noah continued, his voice becoming stronger. "That the Dog returns to his Vomit and the Sow returns to her Mire." His father had taken a few steps closer to him now. "And the burnt Fool's bandaged finger goes wabbling back to the Fire."

Arthur Gardner's usually dispassionate face, so long accustomed to the denial of emotion, could not contain his surprise. He resumed his seat next to the table and motioned the others from the room.

The old man leaned close and squeezed his son's hand. Noah smiled as best he could and let his father believe what he surely thought he was seeing. "I knew it was in there somewhere," Arthur Gardner said. "We had to strip all of the other nonsense away, but there it is, from the root of your being; the essence of what I've taught you. I knew you couldn't forget, though I must admit that you had me concerned."

Noah looked directly into his father's keen, discerning eyes and nodded.

"Those people you were with," the old man continued, "they somehow believe that we can have a brighter future by resurrecting the failed ideas of the past. They're wrong, and their ideas would lead to untold misery for millions. The answer is a new vision, *my* vision, and together we can make it a reality."

Noah realized something else then, another thing that Molly had taught him: When you lie for a living, you sometimes can't see the truth even when it's staring you right in the face. That's a weakness that could clearly be exploited.

It was a matter of pride with Arthur Gardner that his heir should be involved in the transformation that was coming. His son, then, would do his best to prove the adage that pride comes before the fall.

The old man smiled. The ordeal was finished, and though he clearly felt he'd won the day, what Arthur Gardner couldn't know was that the battle lines had only just been drawn.

Noah felt himself fading, and he spoke again, but scarcely at a whisper. These words were meant for different ears, and wherever Molly was, he knew for certain she would hear them.

"We have it in our power," Noah said, "to begin the world over again."

EPILOGUE

A month to the day had passed since Noah had arrived in his new quarters.

The days in this place had started to meld into one another, so he'd resorted to noting each sunrise with a mark on one of the painted bricks in the wall near his bed. While actual calendars were available for residents of his moderate status, these private etchings seemed to be a more fitting method to keep a tally of his time inside.

With the stub of a pencil from the nightstand he inscribed another X at the end of the last line, and then he began another empty grid beside the first in anticipation of the new month to come.

Noah was familiar with the atmosphere of a dormitory, though he'd never actually had to live in one while in college. That was the style of accommodations this place most resembled. Just a simple bedroom with a pressed-wood desk and a shared bath, more than a cell but considerably less than a real apartment. Some no-nonsense designer had tacked on a veneer of generic warmth just sufficient to allow the space to be thought of as a modest home by its resident, rather than as a place of confinement.

Two floors down it was more like a barracks, and the levels below those floors weren't on the tour.

A man walked by out in the hall, glancing briefly through the window in the door as he passed. Not a guard, Noah had been reminded at his orientation, but more of a floor monitor; just a benign, overseeing administrator, there for security and safety.

And this wasn't a prison, not at all, the welcoming committee had gone on to emphasize. This complex and its surrounding buildings might have been originally *constructed* as a prison, but funding cuts and changes in policy had orphaned the place in recent years. Local officials in the small Montana town nearby had been delighted to learn that their costly investment might finally be put to profitable use, providing local employment and helping the country deal with its recently declared emergency.

The old man had arranged his son's reservation here, and his job. As soon as he'd healed, Noah was to become a key asset in the all-important public-relations push behind the nation's unfolding, brave new direction. He wouldn't return to New York right away—he'd be a sort of field correspondent, helping to manage the flow of information from the ongoing fight against the dangerous homegrown forces who'd recently declared open war on American progress.

Noah's original accommodations had actually been much nicer; a private suite on one of the upper floors—but his unsatisfactory performance in his first real work assignment had resulted in his lodgings being downgraded a notch.

This failed assignment had been pretty

straightforward: He was to write up an in-depth piece for the news, outlining the inner workings of the recent homegrown conspiracy that had nearly led to the destruction of Las Vegas and San Francisco. The story was to be told from his own point of view as a courageous hostage and unwilling insider.

His first draft was rejected immediately; there'd been a consistent undertone in the text that seemed to paint the ringleaders, the Founders' Keepers, in a subtly but unacceptably positive light. His second try wasn't an improvement, it was even worse. The strange thing was, if only out of self-preservation, Noah had been trying hard to write what they wanted, but the stubborn truths just kept elbowing their way in.

After an informal inquiry, this first glitch was chalked up to the lingering effects of the Stockholm syndrome, that passing mental condition through which hostages sometimes develop an odd sympathy for the cause of their captors. For the time being it was determined that, until he was better, Noah would be given less-demanding duties and an additional editor to watch over his work.

There was no shortage of things to do, large and small. A lot of PR spin needed to be applied to the changes that were already well under way across the country. Noah was given a stack of small writing tasks, mostly one-liners and fillers that required far less of a commitment to the web of new truths being woven for consumption by the press and the public. For one of these jobs, he was to simply come up with a suitably harmless-sounding name for a new Treasury bureau that would be put in charge of the next wave of government bailouts for various failing corporations and industries.

This was the work of only a few seconds; Noah called it the *Federal Resource Allocation & Underwriting Division.* Nearly a truckload of boxes of letterhead and business cards had been printed before someone in production noticed the problem: The five-letter acronym for this new government bureau would be *FRAUD.*

They'd said they believed him when he told them it was an accident, but they'd also moved Noah to this more secure, probationary floor of the residence building just as a temporary precaution.

Once you know the truth, Molly had said, then you've got to live it. What she'd apparently neglected to add was that you'll also tend to randomly *tell* it, whether it gets you into trouble or not.

Noah rearranged his pillows and lay down on his cot, not with an intention to sleep, but just to rest his eyes for a while and try to clear his head.

A thousand things were flying through his mind. It was a condition that his father referred to as a *topical storm,* a state in which so many conflicting thoughts are doing battle in your brain that you lose your ability to discern and to act on any of them. This state was regularly induced by PR experts to cloud and control issues in the public discourse, to keep thinking people depressed and apathetic on election days, and to discourage those who might be tempted to actually take a stand on a complex issue.

They'd given Noah a radio and a small TV, but he knew those wouldn't help to clarify anything for him. On the contrary; the Emergency Alert System had kicked in shortly after the thwarted attack, and though some individual stations and networks were active again, the news still had the distinctive sameness of single-source coverage. While no real disaster had actually happened, the selected newspeople were breathlessly working 24/7 to puff up the disasters that *might* have happened, and what might still be looming ahead tomorrow. Fear, uncertainty, and doubt—the three most effective weapons in the arsenal of Arthur Gardner—were keeping the country in an uneasy state of tension and helplessness, much like his own.

"What can one person do?" That was the passive, rhetorical question that kept people silent and powerless in the face of things that seem too large and frightening to overcome. It was the question in Noah's mind, as well. *Now I see the truth, and yes, I want to live it, but what can I do?*

He decided to sleep on that, because so far he'd been unable to come up with a good answer.

Noah brushed his teeth and washed as soon as the bathroom was free, left the sink and the shower and the commode a lot cleaner than he'd found them, dressed for bed, and turned in. He rolled over onto his side and saw his first filled calendar grid, with the second empty one beside it on the wall.

Where would he be a month from now?

That answer seemed depressingly certain. But then, where might Molly be? Asking that question had become a nightly ritual at the end of these dreary days, and it was still on his mind as he fell asleep a while later on.

There was no hard transition between consciousness and the beginning of his now-familiar dream.

Noah opened his eyes and looked around. He was in the small, warm family room of a rustic little cabin. Surrounding him were simple furnishings, hand-made quilts, and corner shelves of keepsakes and photographs. Unlike the mass-produced, impersonal flash of the world he'd left behind, the things here had been built and woven and carved and finished by skilled, loving hands, things made or given by friends and family, made to mean something, to be passed on, and to last through generations.

Snow fluttered down outside the wide windows, big flakes sticking and blowing past the frosted panes, an idyllic woodland scene framed in pleated curtains and knotty pine. He was sitting in front of a stone hearth. A pair of boots were drying there, with space for another, smaller pair beside. A fire was burning low, a black dutch oven suspended above the coals, the smell of some wonderful meal cooking inside. Two plates and silver settings were arranged on a nearby dining table.

A simple evening lay ahead. Though it might seem nearly identical to a hundred other nights he'd spent with her, he also knew it would be unlike any other, before or after. It always was; being with Molly, talking with her, listening to her, enjoying the quiet with her, feeling her close to him, thinking of the future with her. Every night was like a perfect first date, and every morning like the first exciting day of a whole new life together.

Like Molly had said, such a simple existence certainly wasn't for everyone. But the freedom to choose one's own pursuit of happiness—that's what her country was founded on, and that's what she was fighting for.

Noah heard a sound at the entrance, and he turned to welcome her home again.

But when he looked, it was a different room he saw around him. He blinked repeatedly, but the reality he'd woken up to wouldn't disappear so easily. The man from the hall was looking through the window in the frame, beckoning Noah to the door.

He sighed, got up, walked over, and turned the lock. It was only a formality, of course; it wasn't as though the guy outside didn't have a key of his own.

After the usual pleasantries the man in the hall offered Noah a tray from the rolling cart beside him.

"Looks like I woke you up. Sorry about that."

"That's okay," Noah said. "What's for dinner?"

The man lifted the round stainless steel cover from the plate on the tray. "Sure looks like Thursday to me," he replied.

"Ah, my favorite."

The man had nearly returned to his cart, but he stopped and came nearer again. "Say, I see you here every day, and it occurred to me tonight, we've never been properly introduced."

Noah put down his tray on the side table inside his door. "I'm Noah Gardner."

The man nodded, and casually glanced left and then right down the hallway before he answered, quietly, "My friends call me Nathan. I've got a message for you," he said. "Would you mind if I came in for just a moment?"

"Of course, come on in."

He stepped aside and closed the door as the other man walked past him into the room. Noah watched as he unplugged the TV, ran his fingers along the edges of the desk as though feeling for something hidden, and then clicked on the radio and turned it up loud enough to establish some covering background noise.

"What is this—?" Noah began, and before he could finish that question he found himself pushed hard against the wall with a forearm pressed against his neck and the other man's face close to his.

"You want to know what this is?" Nathan hissed. "It's a wake-up call. You're in a valuable position, my friend, and we need for you to snap out of it and start doing the work we need done." He adjusted his grip on Noah's collar, and continued. "Now listen closely. Tomorrow, at your job, you sign into your computer right before you leave for the day, but you don't sign out. Here's a key." Noah felt something shoved roughly into his pocket. "You're going to leave it under the mouse pad on the desk two places down from yours, to your left. Got all that?"

Noah nodded, as best he could.

"I hope you do," Nathan said. He took a step back, smiled and straightened his clothing as if the two of them had just been engaging in some mutual, spirited rough-housing. "To quote a good friend of mine," he added, on his way to the door. "If they're gonna call this treason anyway, we might as well make the most of it."

"Wait," Noah said.

"Enjoy your dinner," Nathan said. "The meat loaf ain't much, but I think you'll like the dessert." With that, he left the room and resumed his walk down the hall, pushing his meal cart.

Noah closed the door and stared at the tray of covered plates on the table in front of him. He went right to the smallest of them, lifted the lid and found exactly what he was looking for inside: a lukewarm square of runny peach cobbler. He took the knife, cut down the center, and, just as he'd hoped, felt it hit something solid.

He extracted the object from the gooey syrup, took it to the sink in the bathroom, locked the door to the adjoining room, and held it under the cold running water until it was washed clean.

It was Molly's silver bracelet.

He held it close to his eyes; maybe the words engraved there were a little more worn than they'd been before, but he would have remembered them even if they'd been gone completely.

She was alive. Whatever other message he'd been hoping for, whatever guidance he'd been seeking, this was better. Not just a plan, because a plan can be defeated. This was a foundation.

As he returned to the bedroom he remembered the key he'd been given and he pulled it from his pocket. It was wrapped in paper, and, as he unfolded it, Noah saw the simple words written there, in Molly's familiar handwriting.

"We're everywhere. Stay with us; I'll see you soon. The fight starts tomorrow."

AFTERWORD

"Believe those who are seeking the truth. Doubt those who find it."

—André Gide

There's a very good reason we called this book *The Overton Window,* and it's not just because it's one of the techniques that Arthur Gardner uses to push his objectives. We chose this title because it's also a technique that, to one extent or another, we just used on you. (The key difference is, I'm openly telling you that's what I'm doing; I don't have a hidden agenda here.) In the course of reading and thinking about this story, it's simply my hope that you've spent a little bit of time entertaining ideas that you might not have considered before.

Remember, the Overton Window concept is that only the few scenarios that currently sit inside an established window of acceptable debate will be taken seriously by the public. To move the Window toward their ultimate goal, those pushing an agenda have to introduce radical ideas that fall outside of the current comfort zone. While those fringe ideas will normally be dismissed, the Window will also be subtly nudged in their direction. This allows ideas that would've previously seemed unthinkable to be introduced and, eventually, even seriously considered as solutions.

Applying this concept to our story, it should be obvious that we set out to create a plot based in reality, and then we pushed it to an absolute extreme. It's one of the intriguing potentials of this sort of fiction: When your mind suspends disbelief, it may also become more willing to consider a broader spectrum of possible outcomes to the events and agendas that are playing out around us every day.

For example, fighter pilots often use flight simulators to train for real combat. In a safe environment, these simulators force pilots to consider a confluence of events that would otherwise seem ridiculous, like dual engine failure while being shot at and simultaneously having to land on an aircraft carrier in thirty-foot seas. It's extreme, but it works. Many pilots who've been through a hair-raising mission in a live war zone come out saying that it wasn't nearly as bad as what they'd faced in the simulator.

This book is your simulator. It's unlikely that we'll face anything close to the challenges that Noah and Molly are up against. But, after experiencing their scenario in its fictional setting, maybe it will become a little easier to have deeper conversations about the important forces that are actually at work in the real world.

As I told you at the outset, while I certainly used a lot of dramatic license, this story is loaded with truth. But facts can easily be manipulated, and that's why we are including this section. I want you to decide for yourself exactly what is fact, what is *based* on fact, what is a common belief possibly based on a *distorted* fact, and what is complete fiction. Don't stop at my sources; find your own. That way, you can determine where your own Overton Window should be located as we continue to debate what kind of America we want to live in.

And remember, this list is only a starting point. If a passage or a statement in the book intrigued you but isn't specifically mentioned here, take a minute and type some key words into your favorite search engine. (Try "KFC UN Security" from Chapter 17, for example . . .) You might be surprised at where your search will lead you.

—gb

In the Prologue, Eli Churchill mentions to Molly's mother (did you pick up on whom he was speaking to?) that, in the late summer of 2001, Donald Rumsfeld announced that the U.S. government could not account for $2.3 trillion dollars. That actually happened. The date was September 10, 2001. A day later, some missing money (even trillions of it) didn't seem quite so important anymore.

Rumsfeld announces $2.3 trillion unaccounted for on September 10, 2001: "Defense Department Cannot Account For 25% Of Funds—$2.3 Trillion," *CBS News*, January 29, 2002, http://www.cbsnews.com/stories/2002/01/29/eveningnews/main325985.shtml

See also: A video of the *CBS News* segment, http://www.youtube.com/watch?v=3kpWqdPMjmo

A small side note: As you read this scene, if you were wondering what a phone booth was doing out in the desert in the middle of nowhere, this is an interesting location that actually existed until fairly recently. Google "Mojave phone booth" to learn more.

In Chapter 3 we are presented with a government memo outlining the "Growing Threat of Domestic Terrorism." This memo was, of course, was modeled after the real-life memo issued by the Missouri Information Analysis Center (MIAC) that caused an uproar because of its overgeneralizations on who might be a dangerous militia member.

Government Memo: "The Modern Militia Movement," Missouri Information Analysis Center (MIAC), issued in February 2009: http://www.scribd.com/doc/13290698/The-Modern-Militia-MovementMissouri-MIAC-Strategic-Report-20Feb09-

Inside our fictional memo is a reference to a government program called "REX-84." According to published reports at the time, this program involved emergency actions that would be implemented in the event of a national crisis. In 1986, the Associated Press reported on a FEMA directive that described a REX-84 exercise preparing for the detention of more than 400,000 Central American refugees in ten military detention centers located across the country.

A *Miami Herald* story from 1987 again addressed REX-84, this time reporting that Oliver North had worked closely with FEMA to develop a contingency plan should America face a major crisis, like nuclear war or insurrection. That plan called for actions such as the "suspension of the Constitution, turning control of the United States over to FEMA, appointment of military commanders to run state and local governments and declaration of martial law."

In a "heavily censored FEMA memorandum" that was obtained by *The Herald,* the REX-84 exercise was described as calling for the "activation of 'emergency legislation, assumption of emergency powers . . . etc.' "A source familiar with the exercises said North was aware of the simulations and collaborated with FEMA and the Pentagon in producing them. While the simulations were in progress, the Pentagon staged the first of several annual large-scale military exercises in Honduras, deploying thousands of troops near contra supply bases.

"A Pentagon spokeswoman, Capt. Nancy LaLuntas, declined to discuss contingency plans or details of the FEMA-Pentagon exercises, citing 'security reasons.' Yet she confirmed that the exercises, code-named Rex 84 Alpha and Night Train 84, took place April 5–13, 1984. FEMA spokesman Bill McAda also confirmed the simulations and, like LaLuntas, declined to give details."

These days, REX-84 is part of the everyday language of conspiracy theorists, and for good reason: There is not a shred of evidence to suggest that any of these exercises resulted in anything other than embarrassment for the government. On the other hand, given our government's reaction to catastrophe in the past (i.e., the forced internment of more than 100,000 Japanese Americans in 1942), it doesn't take a conspiracy theorist to understand that all of us need to be vigilant and ensure that the only document we look toward in the next crisis is the Constitution.

REX-84:
Associated Press, "Administration Denies Existence of Detention Camps for Illegal Aliens," December 16, 1986, http://news.google.com/newspapers?id=ueAIAAAAIBAJ&sjid=UPwFAAAAIBAJ&dq=rex-84&pg=6740%2C4955414

See also: Alfonso Chardy, "Reagan Advisers Ran 'Secret' Government" *Miami Herald,* July 5, 1987.

See also: Alfonso Chardy, "North Helped Revise Wartime Plans" *Miami Herald,* July 19, 1987.

To illustrate how public perception and behavior can be shaped over time, we used the story of bottled water, a product which seemed to come upon us out of nowhere to become a huge industry that's nearly ubiquitous. How did it happen? Read *Bottlemania* for a great primer.

The marketing of bottled water: For the spirit of this scene, see Elizabeth Royte, *Bottlemania: The Marketing of Bottled Water and Why We Bought It* (Bloomsbury, 2008), http://books.google.com/books?id=LwUUAQAAIAAJ

More from Chapter 3:

Tsunami warning system inadequate: Laura Smith-Spark, "Indonesia Tsunami System 'Not Ready,'" *BBC News,* July 19, 2006, http://news.bbc.co.uk/2/hi/asia-pacific/5191190.stm

Virtually the entire speech that Arthur Gardner gives in the boardroom is based on fact; of course, in keeping with his character, he presents his own version of those facts. Here are a few specific examples:

Committed $8 trillion to those that engineered the financial crisis: David Goldman, "The $8 Trillion Bailout," CNN Money.com, January 6, 2009, http://money.cnn.com/2009/01/06/news/economy/where_stimulus_fits_in/index.htm

Social Security is a Ponzi scheme: Jeff Poor, "Cramer: Social Security a Bigger Ponzi Scheme than Madoff's," *Business & Media Institute,* December 18, 2008, http://www.businessandmedia.org/articles/2008/20081218091211.aspx

A hundred thousand billion dollars: Also known as "$100 trillion," this is a chilling estimate of our unfunded Social Security and Medicare liabilities. Pamela Villarreal, "Social Security and Medicare Projections: 2009," *National Center for Policy Analysis,* June 11, 2009, http://www.ncpa.org/pub/ba662

Nationalizing General Motors: Kimberly S. Johnson, "GM to reorganize in government-led bankruptcy," *AP Foreign,* June 1, 2009, http://www.guardian.co.uk/world/feedarticle/8535026

$17 billion in underfunded union pensions: Nick Bunkley, "Automaker Pensions Underfunded by $17 Billion," *New York Times,* April 6, 2010, http://www.nytimes.com/2010/04/07/business/07cars.html

We're borrowing $5 billion a day from Asia: Statement of C. Fred Bergsten, Director, Institute for International Economics, February 2–4, 2005, http://www.uscc.gov/hearings/2005hearings/transcripts/05_02_3_4.pdf

In Chapter 10 we meet Molly's mother for the first time as she gives a speech at the bar. Much of what she references is accurate, including:

"The happy union of these states . . .": James Madison, edited by Gaillard Hunt, *The Writings of James Madison* (New York, NY: G. P. Putnam's Sons, 1910): 357, http://books.google.com/books?id=V7jGAAAAMAAJ

"The most basic question is not . . .": Thomas Sowell, *Knowledge and Decisions*

(New York, NY: Basic Books, 1980): 79, http://books.google.com/books?id=4kqTMrEKWXoC

Carroll Quigley's book *Tragedy & Hope* makes a few appearances in this novel, and for good reason: the premise that he outlined, Mutually Assured Destruction, is now a reality. But it's not just military destruction that we've got to worry about, it's economic destruction as well. Economies have become so intentionally intertwined that a collapse anywhere else in the world has major ramifications for us. Quigley's book is a must-read if you want to really understand the theories of a man who was inspirational to many leaders, including President Bill Clinton.

Carroll Quigley: Carroll Quigley, *Tragedy & Hope: A History of the World in Our Time* (G.S.G. & Associates, 1975), http://books.google.com/books?id=KQZxAAAAIAAJ

Herbert Croly: Herbert Croly, *The Promise of American Life* (New York, NY: The

MacMillan Company, 1909), http://books.google.com/books?id=EoxIAAAAYAAJ

Thomas Jefferson: "Resistance to tyrants is obedience to God": Willard Sterne Randall, *Thomas Jefferson: A Life* (New York, NY: Harper Collins, 1993): 275, http://books.google.com/books?id=jxh4rGiz7GgC

35,000 registered lobbyists: Jerry Kammer, "A Steady Flow of Financial Influence," *Copley News Service,* August 25, 2006, http://www.pbs.org/now/shows/234/money-politics.html

Spent almost $3.5 billion last year: Oxford Analytica, "Lobbyists' Sway in Washington," April 13, 2010, http://www.forbes.com/2010/04/12/lobby-politics-elections-washington-business-oxford.html

The incredible 67,000 page tax code: "67,204-Page Code Confounds Taxpayers, yet Congress Sits By," USAToday.com, April 4, 2007, http://blogs.usatoday.com/oped/2007/04/post_7.html

IRS involved in the health care legislation: Kim Dixon, "U.S. budget office: 4 million likely to pay health fine," *Washington Post,* April 22, 2010, http://www.washingtonpost.com/wp-dyn/content/article/2010/04/22/AR2010042204286.html

Treasury enforced Prohibition laws: "Narcotic Bill Now Law: Hoover Signs Measure Creating a Bureau in the Treasury," *The New York Times,* June 15, 1930, http://select.nytimes.com/gst/abstract.html?res=F30910F73D5C14738DDDAC0994DE405B808FF1D3

"The power to tax involves the power to destroy": "The Supreme Court: The Power to Tax," Time, March 17, 1958, http://www.time.com/time/magazine/article/0,9171,863135,00.html

100,000 federal employees owe back taxes: Devin Dwyer, "Tax Scam Uncle Sam? You Oughta Be Fired! Says Utah Rep. Chaffetz," *ABC News,* March 18, 2010, http://abcnews.go.com/Politics/Tax/100000-federal-employees-owe-irs-back-taxes/story?id=10125860

Treasury Secretary owes back taxes: Jonathan Weisman, "Geithner's Tax History Muddles Confirmation," *The Wall Street Journal,* January 14, 2009, http://online.wsj.com/article/SB123187503629378119.html

John Adams: "A government of laws . . .": David McCullough, *John Adams* (New York, NY: Simon & Schuster, 2001): 378, http://books.google.com/books?id=GHMnz8G0GTcC

"No lie can live forever": Dr. Martin Luther King, Jr., edited by James Washington, *A Testament of Hope: The Essential Writings and Speeches of Martin Luther King, Jr.,* (New York, NY: HarperCollins, 1986): 230, http://books.google.com/books?id=k8uPHtrU8BsC

In Chapter 11 we hear from spirited conspiracy theorist Danny Bailey for the first time. Danny is the kind of guy who likes to string together a variety of facts in an attempt to make something crazy sound plausible. His speech is important because it shows how selected facts and truths can be used as the foundation for an overall thesis that is entirely fictional.

Bailey starts by citing some unemployment data that differs significantly from the official government estimates. Those statistics, and a lot more, can be found at a website called **Shadow Statistics** that is run by economist John Williams.

> **Real unemployment past 20%:** John Williams' Shadow Government Statistics, *Shadowstats.com,* http://www.shadowstats.com/alternate_data/unemployment-charts

The job ad that Danny cites is a great example of how fact can fuel conspiracy thinking. Is there really a job ad posting for an "Internment and Resettlement Specialist"? Yes—and it's right there on the public goarmy.com website. Why would they list such an incriminating job publicly? Simple . . . because it's not incriminating at all. The Army has detention facilities all over the world that need to be staffed. If they posted a job opening for an "Experienced Sniper" would people jump to the conclusion that they want to assassinate Americans on U.S. soil? Of course not, yet that's what some people immediately think when they read "Internment Specialist."

Internment and Resettlement Specialist: Job listing posted at goarmy.com, http://www.goarmy.com/JobDetail.do?id=292

25% of world's prisoners in U.S.: Jim Webb, "Why We Must Fix Our Prisons," *Parade,* March 29, 2009, http://www.parade.com/news/2009/03/why-we-must-fix-our-prisons.html

Army Regulation 210-35: Civilian Inmate Labor Program, http://www.army.mil/usapa/epubs/pdf/r210_35.pdf

In 1987, as Oliver North was testifying before a Congressional Committee on the Iran-Contra affair, the *Miami Herald* ran a series of articles detailing North's participation in emergency-response contingency planning. In a piece published July 5, 1987, the *Herald* wrote about a memo outlining emergency plans that apparently bore a resemblance to a college paper written by the then-FEMA director:

"The scenario outlined in the Brinkerhoff memo resembled somewhat a paper Guiffrida had written in 1970 at the Army War College in Carlisle, Pa., in which he advocated martial law in case of a national uprising by black militants. The paper also advocated the roundup and transfer to 'assembly centers or relocation camps' of at least 21 million 'American Negroes.'"

"A memo from 1970 . . .": Alfonso Chardy, "Reagan Advisers Ran Secret Government," *Miami Herald,* July 5, 1987.

Agitator Index (ADEX): Earl Ofari Hutchinson, "The Dangerous New FBI," June 4, 2002, http://www.salon.com/news/feature/2002/06/04/cointelpro/print.html

You may be a terrorist: "Missouri Report on Militias Draws Fire," *The Associated Press,* March 14, 2009, http://www.fox4kc.com/wdaf-story-militia-report-031409,0,5591136.story

Last declared war in 1945: "The Declaration of War: One for the History Books?" National War College, 1998, http://www.dtic.mil/cgi-bin/GetTRDoc?AD=ADA441475&Location=U2&doc=GetTRDoc.pdf

The same *Miami Herald* article that uncovered the FEMA director's college paper also detailed the drastic continuity-of-government proposals that FEMA was formulating:

"FEMA's clash with (Attorney General) Smith occurred over a secret contingency plan that called for suspension of the Constitution, turning control of the United States over to FEMA, appointment of military commanders to run state and local governments and declaration of martial law during a national crisis.

"The plan did not define national crisis, but it was understood to be nuclear war, violent and widespread internal dissent or national opposition against a military invasion abroad."

Orwellian continuity-of-government provisions put in place: Alfonso Chardy,

"Reagan Advisers Ran Secret Government," *Miami Herald,* July 5, 1987.

Presidential Decision Directive 51: National Security and Homeland Security Presidential Directive, *whitehouse.gov,* http://georgewbush-whitehouse.archives.gov/news/releases/2007/05/20070509-12.html

See also: Charlie Savage, "White House Revises Post-Disaster Protocol," *Boston Globe,* June 2, 2007, http://www.boston.com/news/nation/washington/articles/2007/06/02/white_house_revises_post_disaster_protocol/

Presidential Decision Directive 67: Enduring Constitutional Government and Continuity of Government Operation, October 21, 1998, http://www.fas.org/irp/offdocs/pdd/pdd-67.htm

See also: Francie Grace, "'Shadow Government' News to Congress," *CBSNews.com,* March 2, 2002, http://www.cbsnews.com/stories/2002/03/01/attack/main502530.shtml

Constitution Free Zone: Ellen Nakashima, "Citizens' U.S. Border Crossings Tracked: Data from Checkpoints to Be Kept for 15 Years," *Washington Post,* August 20, 2008, http://www.washingtonpost.com/wp-dyn/content/article/2008/08/19/AR2008081902811.html

See also: Ellen Nakashima, "Expanded Powers to Search Travelers at Border Detailed," *Washington Post,* September 23, 2008, http://www.washingtonpost.com/wp-dyn/content/article/2008/09/22/AR2008092202843.html

See also: Fact Sheet on U.S. "Constitution Free Zone," The American Civil Liberties Union, http://www.aclu.org/technology-and-liberty/fact-sheet-us-constitution-free-zone

Free Speech Zone: Marcella Bombardier, "Boycott Is Planned in Free-Speech Zone," *Boston Globe,* July 25, 2004, http://www.boston.com/news/local/massachusetts/articles/2004/07/25/boycott_is_planned_in_free_speech_zone/

In Chapter 12 the meeting at the bar is disrupted by someone referred to as a newer member of the organization. This, of course, is inspired by those who have publicly stated their goal to infiltrate the Tea Party, the 9/12 Project and other like-minded organizations and stage violent acts or hate speech. According to one anti–Tea Party group, their mission is to "act on behalf of the Tea Party in ways which exaggerate their least appealing qualities."

One other important note on this scene: While Noah initially thinks that the instigators were New York City policemen, he is quickly proven wrong. If there is one thing that virtually every group fighting for our rights and freedoms agrees on, it's that those entrusted with the public safety, from local cops to federal agents, are on the side of the good guys.

Agents provocateurs inside Tea Party events: Valerie Bauman, "Foes of tea party movement to infiltrate rallies," *The Associated Press,* April 10, 2010, http://www.washingtonpost.com/wp-dyn/content/article/2010/04/12/AR2010041203358.html

See also: Brian Montopoli, "Tea Party Foes Target Movement 'Morons,'" *CBSNews.com,* April 13, 2010, http://www.cbsnews.com/8301-503544_162-20002377-503544.html

These next two statistics are related in a pretty amazing way: While Congress's approval rating continues to be abysmal, historically *more than 90 percent of incumbents are still reelected.* People always want to know how they can help change the course of America. This is it! While the answers are undoubtedly more complicated than they used to be, the easiest solution is still the best: Turn your back on those who've turned their backs on you by voting them out. Actions speak louder than words, and right now our actions are showing that we tacitly approve of the lies and corruption.

Congress's Approval Rating: Gallup.com, http://www.gallup.com/poll/127343/Congress-Job-Approval-Rating-Improves-Low.aspx

Congressional reelection rates: "Reelection Rates Over the Years," http://

www.opensecrets.org/bigpicture/reelect.php

In Chapter 14 Noah and Molly have a conversation in the limousine. Several things cited during this talk are factual, or based on real events.

U.S. Senator out west about to be involved in an ethics scandal: Eric Lichtblau and Eric Lipton, "Senator's Aid After Affair Raises Flags Over Ethics," *The New York Times,* October 1, 2009, http://www.nytimes.com/2009/10/02/us/politics/02ensign.html

The Rev. Al Sharpton (fried chicken and waffles) **at Amy Ruth's:** Amy Ruth's Menu, http://www.amyruthsharlem.com/dinnermenu/waffles/wafflemenu01.html

Edward Bernays served as one of the inspirations for Arthur Gardner. Several sources below reference Bernays, but if you really want to understand the reach and power of public relations (and why Joseph Goebbels found Bernays to be so instructive) then be sure to read Bernays' own book *Propaganda,* which includes this assertion right on the cover:

> "As civilization has become more complex, and as the need for invisible government has been increasingly demonstrated, the technical means have been invented and developed by which opinion may be regimented. Democracy is administered by the intelligent minority who know how to regiment and guide the masses."

Edward Bernays, Woodrow Wilson and United Fruit: Larry Tye, *The father of spin: Edward L. Bernays & The Birth of Public Relations* (New York, NY: Crown Publishers, 1998), http://books.google.com/books?id=Dk0SPKpYCsQC

If you're interested in reading more about a real-life example of a modern force in public relations, take a look at John Rendon. His company is a leader in "perception management" and, according to *Rolling Stone,* "fills a need that few people even know exists."

PR push behind the Iraq War/Rendon Group: James Bamford, "The Man Who Sold the War," *Rolling Stone,* November 17, 2005, http://www.rollingstone.com/politics/story/8798997/the_man_who_sold_the_war

Guatemalan Coup: Central Intelligence Agency Freedom of Information Act document archive, http://www.foia.cia.gov/guatemala.asp

80 million gun owners: Wayne LaPierre, "Sotomayor's Bias," *CBSNews.com,* July 15, 2009, http://www.cbsnews.com/stories/2009/07/15/opinion/main5162054.shtml

Bernays' book: Edward Bernays, *Propaganda,* (New York, NY: Ig Publishing, 1928), http://books.google.com/books?id=JlcPgPt17KcC

Bernays' book on Goebbels' shelf: Larry Tye, "The Father of Spin: Edward L. Bernays & The Birth of PR," *PR Watch,* Second Quarter 1999, Volume 6, No. 2, http://www.prwatch.org/prwissues/1999Q2/bernays.html

In Chapter 15: This may not exactly be the most critical fact in the book, but Eliot Spitzer's father really is a real estate mogul, and at one time Spitzer really could have run into Noah and Molly in that elevator car on the Upper East Side of Manhattan.

Eliot Spitzer lives in his father's building: Douglas Feiden, "Empire of the Son. How Dad's Real Estate Fortune Pays Spitzer Benefits," *NY Daily News,* October 29, 2006, http://www.nydailynews.com/archives/news/2006/10/29/2006-10-29_empire_of_the_son__how_dad_s.html

In Chapter 17: Tom Clancy's book *Debt of Honor* included a sequence where a plane loaded with fuel is hijacked and flown into the U.S. Capitol. Some conspiracy theorists might say that this means Clancy was involved in planning 9/11, but the rest of us realize that this shows just how outside-of-the-box thriller writers think. Clancy himself has talked about meeting with an Air Force officer during the writing of that book and asking the officer about the planes-as-weapons scenario he was spinning.

The officer replied, "Mr. Clancy, if we had a plan to deal with this, it would be secret, I wouldn't be able to talk to you about it. But to the best of my knowledge we've never looked at this possibility before."

Clancy writes about crashing planes into buildings: Steve Bradshaw, "A Warning from Hollywood," *BBC,* March 24, 2002, http://news.bbc.co.uk/hi/english/static/audio_video/programmes/panorama/transcripts/transcript_24_03_02.txt

In Chapter 18: Rudyard Kipling was fifty-three when he wrote the poem I excerpted in the book. As Noah explains, Kipling had lost his son in World War I and his daughter prior to that, and he was in a dark place in his life. The "Copybook Headings" he refers to are the headings from the handwriting-practice notebooks that used to be distributed. In these, a famous quotation or commonsense adage would be printed at the top and the student would practice their penmanship by rewriting that sentence over and over, all the way down the page. This would accomplish two things: handwriting practice (obviously), and a subtler reinforcement of practical knowledge and life lessons from history. As Noah says, the entire poem is well worth a read.

Rudyard Kipling's poem: Rudyard Kipling, "The Gods of the Copybook Headings," See the full text here: http://www.kipling.org.uk/poems_copybook.htm

Kipling's biography: Harry Ricketts, Rudyard Kipling: *A Life* (New York: Carroll & Graf, 2001), http://books.google.com/books?id=x4sTAiRqhKMC

In Chapter 19, we see the term "COINTELPRO" included in the agenda that Noah and Molly discover. This term seems to have now been adopted by conspiracy theorists, but before you write it off it's worth looking at what this real government program was originally intended to accomplish.

COINTELPRO: Ed Gordon, "COINTELPRO and the History of Domestic Spying," *National Public Radio,* January 18, 2006, http://www.npr.org/templates/story/story.php?storyId=5161811

See also: Michelle Goldberg, "Outlawing Dissent: Spying on Peace Meetings, Cracking Down on Protesters, Keeping Secret Files on Innocent People—How Bush's War on Terror Has Become a War on Freedom," Salon.com, February 11, 2004, http://www.salon.com/news/feature/2004/02/11/cointelpro/print.html

See also: David Horowitz, "COINTELPRO's Overdue Return: The New FBI Will Be Able to Investigate Americans Who Pose a Threat to National Security—and That's a Good Thing," Salon.com, June 4, 2002, http://dir.salon.com/story/news/col/horo/2002/06/04/cointelpro/index.html

More from Chapter 19:

Casus Belli: Daniel Schorr, "In Search of a Casus Belli," *Christian Science Monitor,* August 9, 2002, http://www.csmonitor.com/2002/0809/p11s02-cods.html

The Overton Window: Nathan J. Russell, "An Introduction to the Overton Window of Different Possibilities," *The Mackinac*

Center, January 4, 2006, http://www.mack inac.org/7504

Airline security reacting to failed threats: Alan Gathright, "No Small Feat, Tightening Up Shoe Inspections," *San Francisco Chronicle,* July 12, 2003, http://www.seat tlepi.com/national/130541_shoes12.html

If you want to understand what programs like "cap and trade" are really all about (money) then start doing some homework on the intersection of corporations, politicians, and special interests. The links below on Enron, the Chicago Climate Exchange (CCX) and Fannie Mae are a great place to start:

Carbon trading and Enron: Lawrence Solomon, "Enron's Other Secret," *Financial Post,* May 30, 2009, http://network.nationalpost.com/np/blogs/fpcomment/archive/2009/05/29/lawrence-solomon-enron-s-other-secret.aspx

See also a video of Rep. Scalise (R-LA) questioning Al Gore along these lines: http://

www.youtube.com/watch?v=cpEcPFSEIwQ

U.N. Agenda 21: See the U.N. Department of Economic and Social Affairs publication: http://www.un.org/esa/dsd/agenda21/index.shtml

The Chicago Climate Exchange: "The $10 Trillion Climate Fraud," *Investor's Business Daily,* April 28, 2010, http://www.investors.com/NewsAndAnalysis/Article.aspx?id=531731

See also: Ed Barnes, "Obama Years Ago Helped Fund Carbon Program He Is Now Pushing Through Congress," *FoxNews.com,* March 25, 2009, http://www.foxnews.com/politics/2009/03/25/obama-years-ago-helped-fund-carbon-program-pushing-congress/

See also: Barbara Hollingsworth, "Barbara Hollingsworth: Fannie Mae Owns Patent on Residential 'Cap and Trade' Exchange," *The Washington Examiner,* April 20, 2010, http://www.washingtonexaminer

.com/opinion/columns/Fannie-Mae-owns-patent-on-residential-_cap-and-trade_-exchange-91532109.html

In Chapter 20 we get a chance to hear Molly begin to state her case, and she focuses on the economy. If you were still doubting that both political parties are driving us toward the same place at different speeds, the first statistic she cites is pretty eye-opening:

National debt has doubled since 2000: Mark Knoller, "National Debt Up $2 Trillion on Obama's Watch," *CBSNews.com,* March 16, 2010, http://www.cbsnews.com/8301-503544_162-20000576-503544.html

Bailout money going overseas: Eamon Javers, "AIG Ships Billions in Bailout Abroad," *Politico,* March 15, 2009, http://www.politico.com/news/stories/0309/20039.html

See also: **Sharyl Attkisson,** "Following Bailout Money to Tax Havens," *CBSNews.com,* February 23, 2009, http://www.cb

snews.com/stories/2009/02/23/evening news/main4822689.shtml

In Chapter 21: Ragnar Benson, whose books we hear about here, is the pen name of a survivalist author who has written some pretty edgy books over the years. (The story goes that the pseudonym *Ragnar Benson* was originally borrowed from the name of a construction company outside Chicago.) Benson's book *Mantrapping* (which is actually available on Amazon.com) opens with the line: "Without question, man can be the most difficult animal on earth to trap . . ." But, as Molly tells Noah, "he's mellowed out since then" and his more recent books deal with survival and self-sufficiency techniques.

Ragnar Benson: Mary Roach, "The Survivalist's Guide to Do-it-Yourself Medicine," December 17, 1999, http://www.salon.com/health/col/roac/1999/12/17/survivalists

See also: Paladin Press's list of books by Benson: http://www.paladin-press.com/category/Ragnar_Benson

More from Chapter 21:

"Cherish, therefore, the spirit . . .": Thomas Jefferson, Merrill D. Peterson, The Political Writings of Thomas Jefferson (Jefferson Foundation, 1996), http://books.google.com/books?id—lhB2iCTq60C

Washington, wooden dentures and the cherry tree: "Facts and Falsehoods about George Washington," http://www.mountvernon.org/visit/plan/index.cfm/pid/808/

"These are the times that try men's souls." Thomas Paine, *The American Crisis,* http://books.google.com/books?id=vDq6AAAAIAAJ

Many in Washington want us to start looking at regulation as a good thing, but here's an example of what can happen when government gets to regulate existing law. Sure, the Second Amendment says that you are allowed to own a gun, but it doesn't say that it has to be easy! In New York City they've taken that to the extreme by crafting an application process that can take well over six months and cost hundreds, if not thousands, of dollars.

Obtaining a gun permit in New York City: NYPD Handgun Licensing Information, http://www.nyc.gov/html/nypd/html/permits/handgun_licensing_information.shtml

See also: NYPD Licensing FAQ, http://www.nyc.gov/html/nypd/html/permits/gun_licensing_faq.shtml

See also: A first-person account of the licensing process: Glenn Beck, *Arguing with Idiots* (New York, NY: Simon & Schuster, 2009): 49.

See also: An internet account of the licensing process: http://angrynyer.com/?p=422

The militia was every citizen: Jonathan Elliott, *The Debates in the Several State Conventions of the Adoption of the Federal Constitution 425* (2nd ed., J. B. Lippincott 1836).

See also: James Madison, "The Federalist Number 46," in *The Federalist Papers,* eds. George W. Carey and James McClellan (Indianapolis, IN: Liberty Fund, 2001): 244.

"We have it in our power to begin the world over again": Thomas Paine, *Common Sense,* http://books.google.com/books?id=e0oqAAAAYAAJ

Jonathan Mayhew "No taxation without representation": Raja Mishra and LeMont Calloway, "Vandals Tear a Bible in Half, Ransack Old West Church," *Boston Globe,* August 12, 2006, http://www.boston.com/news/local/massachusetts/articles/2006/08/12/vandals_tear_a_bible_in_half_ransack_old_west_church/

In Chapter 22:

Nuclear materials flown from Minot to Barksdale Air Force Base: Michael Hoffman, "Commander Disciplined for Nuclear Mistake," *Military Times,* September 5, 2007, http://www.usatoday.com/news/military/2007-09-05-b<->52_N.htm

In Chapter 23:

For entertainment purposes only we present the **Orange-box hacker tool:** http://www.artofhacking.com/files/ob-faq.htm

In Chapter 27 we reference John O'Neill, the former FBI antiterrorism expert who had been sounding alarm bells on al Qaeda. O'Neill began his new job at the World Trade Center in New York City on August 23, 2001.

John O'Neill and al Qaeda: "The Man Who Knew," *Frontline,* http://www.pbs.org/wgbh/pages/frontline/shows/knew/

In Chapter 31:

"A Republic, if you can keep it": Michael Richards, *A Republic If You Can Keep It: The Foundation of the American Presidency* (Westport, CT: Greenport Press, 1987), http://books.google.com/books?id=ItOARcaN54sC

"Turkish girl, 16, buried alive for talking to boys": Robert Tait, "Turkish Girl, 16, Buried Alive for 'Talking to Boys,'" *The*

Guardian, February 4, 2010, http://www.guardian.co.uk/world/2010/feb/04/girl-buried-alive-turkey

". . . the useless eaters on the savage side of the bell curve": This quote is modeled after many of the real life arguments in favor of eugenics, in all of its many faces and forms.

George Bernard Shaw: "I think it would be a good thing to make everybody come before a properly appointed board just as he might come before the income tax commissioner. . . . Just put them there and say 'sir,' or madam, 'now will you be kind enough to justify your existence. If you can't justify your existence, if you're not pulling your weight in the social group, if you're not producing what you consume, or perhaps a little more, then clearly we cannot use the big organization of our society for the purpose of keeping you alive, because your life does not benefit us and it can't be of very much use to yourself.'"

—*From Shaw's speech as shown in Glenn Beck's "The Revolutionary Holocaust: Live Free or Die,"* http://www.foxnews.com/story/0,2933,583732,00.html

Theodore Roosevelt: "Society has no business to permit degenerates to reproduce their kind. . . . Some day we will realize that the prime duty, the inescapable duty, of the good citizen of the right type is to leave his or her blood behind him in the world; and that we have no business to permit the perpetuation of citizens of the wrong type."

—From a letter to Charles Benedict Davenport on January 3, 1913

Margaret Sanger: "The mating of the moron with a person of sound stock may . . . gradually disseminate this trait far and wide until it undermines the vigor and efficiency of an entire nation and an entire race. This is no idle fancy. We must take it into account if we wish to escape the fate that has befallen so many civilizations in the past."

—From Sanger's book "The Pivot of Civilization," page 176

In Chapter 34:

Paraquat: "Facts about Paraquat," U.S. Centers for Disease Control, http://www.bt.cdc.gov/agent/paraquat/basics/facts.asp

In Chapter 36 we use some dramatic license to show how the other half flies when they're forced to travel commercially. And who knows, Natalie Portman might even be able to actually fly without an ID if she found the right TSA agent:

Airline VIP liaisons: Gabe Weisert, "How the celebrities fly," *Forbes Traveler,* October 11, 2006, http://www.msnbc.msn.com/id/15133601

In Chapter 37:

"I have sworn upon the altar of God . . .": Thomas Jefferson, John P. Foley, *The Jeffersonian Cyclopedia: A Comprehensive Collection of the Views Of* (Funk & Wagnalls, 1900), http://books.google.com/books?id=ZTIoAAAAYAAJ

"I shall now enter on the duties to which my fellow-citizens . . .": Thomas Jefferson, John P. Foley, *The Jeffersonian Cyclopedia: a comprehensive collection of the views of* (Funk & Wagnalls, 1900), http://books.google.com/books?id=ZTIoAAAAYAAJ

In Chapter 38, we again see Danny Bailey's conspiratorial side come out. He mentions, for example, that there was a training exercise going on in London on the morning of the 7/7 bombings. That is completely true, but this is a good example of the difference between something being a fact and an assumption that is *based* on fact.

The facts of this incident in London on 7/7 are hardly in doubt: A crisis management company, run by a man with Scotland Yard ties, held a terror-drill exercise on the morning of July 7 involving multiple subway bombings. Later that day, the drill played out in real life in almost exactly the same way and in almost exactly the same locations.

No one disagrees on those events, yet those facts are interpreted in widely varying ways. For example, Danny Bailey recounts those events to FBI Agent Kearns as though the corporate drill might've been some kind of "cover story" for the British government's own role in the real bombings. But slightly more research into the exercises held that morning reveals why the mainstream media didn't find that to be such a plausible scenario.

In a Channel 4 News article titled "Coincidence of bomb exercises?" (see: http://www.channel4.com/news/article.jsp?id=109010), Nicholas Glass points out that the bombing scenario that morning was one of three that the company was working on. More important, there were no physical resources deployed anywhere in the city, and the drill involved a few people sitting around a conference table talking about how they would respond. In other words, if this drill was supposed to be the government's alibi, the perpetrators would probably be serving life in prison right now.

In response to the 7/7 conspiracies, Peter Power, the crisis management executive who ran the drills, issued a fairly clear-cut statement in which he responded to what he called the "inaccurate/naïve/ignorant/hostile" accusations being made. Of course, no matter how persuasive his statement was, conspiracy theories always have the same convenient response to fall back on: *Of course he said that, he's probably a government agent.*

My point is that there is great danger in the way facts can be spun or strung together to give credibility to what is otherwise a wild-eyed conspiracy theory. It is our responsibility to look at everything with a skeptical eye, and also to be aware that many will try to twist reality to serve their own agenda or reinforce their worldview.

Terrorism drills run in London on morning of 7/7 bombings: Judi McLeod, "Business Exec Confirms Same-Time-as-Attack Underground Bombing Exercise," *Canada Free Press,* July 14, 2005, http://www.canadafreepress.com/2005/cover071405.htm

See also: Peter Power interview on *ITV News* July 7, 2005: http://www.youtube.com/watch?v=JKvkhe3rqtc

Haroon Rashid Aswat tried to set up terrorist training camp in Oregon: Alan Cowell, "Briton Sought on U.S. Terror Charges Appears in London Court," *New York Times,* August 9, 2005, http://www.nytimes.com/2005/08/09/international/europe/09london.html

Mohamed Mohamed el-Amir Awad el-Sayed Atta: Terry McDermott, "Seeing

What We Want to See; How Could It Be That, Despite the Facts, People—and Computers—Place One of the Sept. 11 Hijackers in Places He Probably Wasn't?" *Los Angeles Times,* August 26, 2005.

In Chapter 39:

"We have no choice" on the financial bailouts: There are many great examples of panicked reaction from our leaders as the financial crisis unfolded and wore on. For example, Fed Chairman Ben Bernanke said: "If we don't do this, we may not have an economy on Monday."

See also: Joe Nocera, "36 Hours of Alarm and Action as Crisis Spiraled," *New York Times,* October 2, 2008, http://www.newsweek.com/id/197810/page/1

Bailout recipients: "Tracking the $700 Billion Bailout," *The New York Times,* http://projects.nytimes.com/creditcrisis/recipients/table

"Let justice be done, though the heavens fall": "The States: Though the Heavens

Fall," October 12, 1962, http://www.time.com/time/magazine/article/0,9171,829233,00.html

"In America, the law is king": Thomas Paine, *Common Sense,* http://books.google.com/books?id=e0oqAAAAYAAJ

"The desire of dominion . . ." Thomas Jefferson, "A Dissertation on the Canon and Feudal Law," *Boston Gazette,* 1765.

"If you love wealth greater than liberty . . .": William Vincent Wells, The life and public services of *Samuel Adams,* (Boston: Little, Brown, and Company, 1865).

In Chapter 46:

Freedom is the exception: Thomas Sowell, *Applied Economics: Thinking Beyond Stage One,* (New York, NY: Basic Books, 2004): 31, http://books.google.com/books?id=0AShGTKZzWgC

As I said before, this list is far from complete, so I hope you'll continue exploring on your own. We've also started a website, the address of which is listed somewhere in this book, that will link to many of the sources we used and will also serve as a repository for new information as it develops. Happy hunting!